Jack Marlowe sat on his horse, surveying the distant enemy lines. "I don't mean to alarm you, Your Highness, but we appear to be significantly outnumbered."

Prince Alric smiled. "Don't worry. Fitz has it all in hand."

The cavalier turned to look at his master. "We are outnumbered two to one. Granted, the fellow has some experience, but I think this time he might have bitten off more than he can chew."

"The baron knows what he's doing."

"Then why is he being advised by a smith?"

Alric chuckled. "You mean Aldwin? He's a lord now, remember?"

"Yes, but hardly a military advisor."

"I doubt the baron's seeking advice. More than likely he's taking the opportunity to teach his new son-in-law a thing or two about battle." The prince shifted his gaze to the cavalier. "Why so glum, Jack? I thought you lived for combat?"

"I do, but I'd feel much better knowing we had our own cavalry here instead of these…"

"Mercerians?"

"I have nothing against them as a people, but I can't accept that a bunch of commoners could make effective horsemen. And even then, we have very few of them. Why couldn't we have the Queen's Guard?"

"You mean the Guard Cavalry?" corrected the prince. "That's simple; they were needed elsewhere. There's still a frontier to guard, and they can't send everything they have here to Eastwood."

"But the Norlanders have had all winter to rest, and we've had to march through rain and mud."

Alric chuckled. "We'll win. Just you wait and see."

"I admire your faith," said Jack, "but I'd prefer to trust in the power of a good blade."

Also by Paul J Bennett

HEIR TO THE CROWN SERIES

BATTLE AT THE RIVER - PREQUEL

SERVANT OF THE CROWN

SWORD OF THE CROWN

MERCERIAN TALES: STORIES OF THE PAST

HEART OF THE CROWN

SHADOW OF THE CROWN

MERCERIAN TALES: THE CALL OF MAGIC

FATE OF THE CROWN

BURDEN OF THE CROWN

MERCERIAN TALES: THE MAKING OF A MAN

DEFENDER OF THE CROWN

FURY OF THE CROWN

WAR OF THE CROWN

THE FROZEN FLAME SERIES

THE AWAKENING/INTO THE FIRE - PREQUELS

ASHES

EMBERS

FLAMES

INFERNO

POWER ASCENDING SERIES

TEMPERED STEEL - PREQUEL

TEMPLE KNIGHT

WARRIOR KNIGHT

THE CHRONICLES OF CYRIC

INTO THE MAELSTROM

MIDWINTER MURDER

THE BEAST OF BRUNHAUSEN

FURY OF THE CROWN

Heir to the Crown: Book Eight

PAUL J BENNETT

First Edition: December 2020

ePub ISBN: 978-1-989315-53-8
Mobi ISBN: 978-1-989315-54-5
Apple Books ISBN: 978-1-989315-55-2
Smashwords ISBN: 978-1-989315-56-9
Print ISBN: 978-1-989315-557-6

This book is a work of fiction. Any similarity to any person, living or dead is entirely
coincidental.

Dedication

To gamers everywhere.
All your base are belong to us.

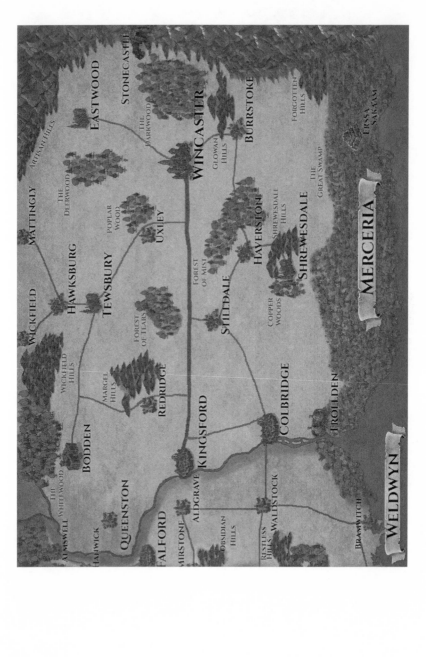

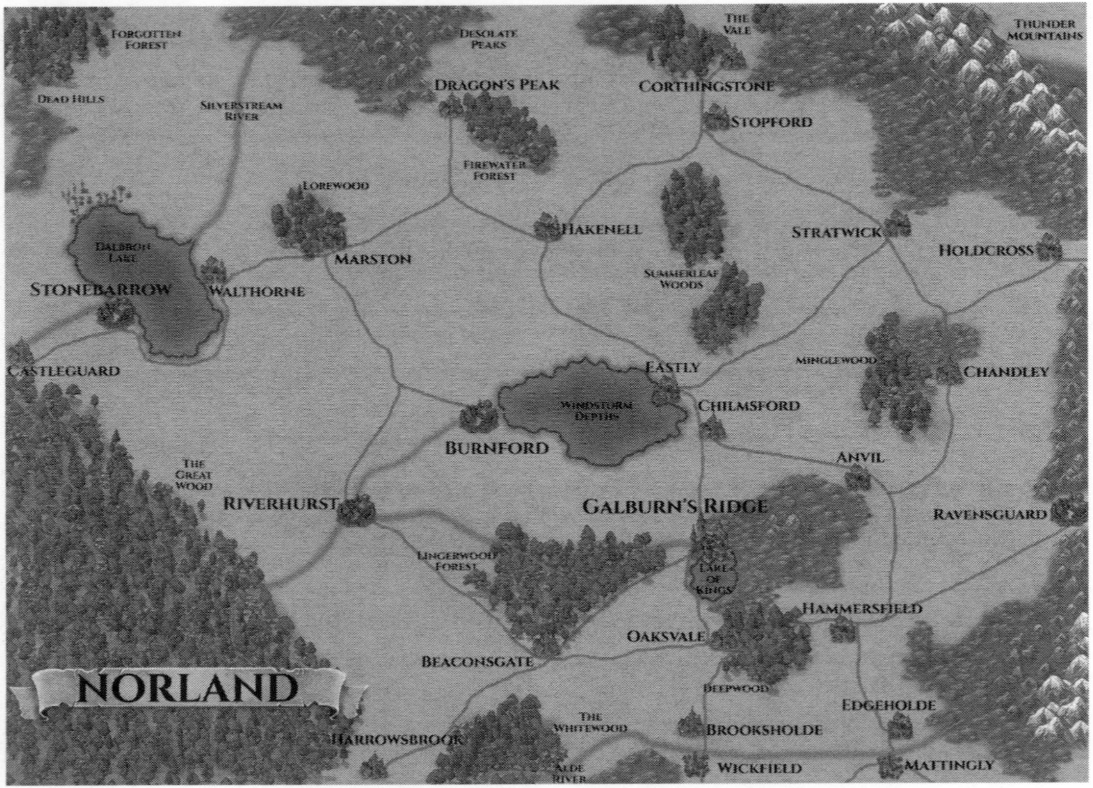
NORLAND
Forgotten Forest
Dead Hills
Silverstream River
Desolate Peaks
Dragon's Peak
Corthingstone
The Vale
Thunder Mountains
Stopford
Firewater Forest
Lorewood
Dalbron Lake
Stonebarrow
Walthorne
Marston
Hakenell
Stratwick
Holdcross
Summerleaf Woods
Castleguard
Minglewood
Eastly
Chandley
Windstorm Depths
Chilmsford
Burnford
Anvil
The Great Wood
Riverhurst
Galburn's Ridge
Ravensguard
Lingerwood Forest
Lake of Kings
Hammersfield
Oaksvale
Beaconsgate
Deepwood
Edgeholde
The Whitewood
Brooksholde
Harrowsbrook
Alde River
Wickfield
Mattingly

ONE

Battle

Spring 965 MC*
(*Mercerian Calendar)

Jack Marlowe sat on his horse, surveying the distant enemy lines. "I don't mean to alarm you, Your Highness, but we appear to be significantly outnumbered."

Prince Alric smiled. "Don't worry. Fitz has it all in hand."

The cavalier turned to look at his master. "We are outnumbered two to one. Granted, the fellow has some experience, but I think this time he might have bitten off more than he can chew."

"The baron knows what he's doing."

"Then why is he being advised by a smith?"

Alric chuckled. "You mean Aldwin? He's a lord now, remember?"

"Yes, but hardly a military advisor."

"I doubt the baron's seeking advice. More than likely he's taking the opportunity to teach his new son-in-law a thing or two about battle." The prince shifted his gaze to the cavalier. "Why so glum, Jack? I thought you lived for combat?"

"I do, but I'd feel much better knowing we had our own cavalry here instead of these..."

"Mercerians?"

"I have nothing against them as a people, but I can't accept that a bunch of commoners could make effective horsemen. And even then, we have very few of them. Why couldn't we have the Queen's Guard?"

"You mean the Guard Cavalry?" corrected the prince. "That's simple; they were needed elsewhere. There's still a frontier to guard, and they can't send everything they have here to Eastwood."

"But the Norlanders have had all winter to rest, and we've had to march through rain and mud."

Alric chuckled. "We'll win. Just you wait and see."

"I admire your faith," said Jack, "but I'd prefer to trust in the power of a good blade."

Lord Richard Fitzwilliam, Baron of Bodden, turned in the saddle. "Well? What do you make of them?"

"Their footmen look solid enough," answered Aldwin, "but the real threat is their horse. Is that horse bowmen I see? I thought we'd destroyed most of them at Uxley last fall?"

"Yes, so did I, but we must remember, this is a completely different army. Now, how do you think they'll attack?"

"Their horsemen are massed to our left. They'll try to outflank us."

"Yes, convenient, isn't it?"

"Convenient?"

"Of course. Had they been on our right, it would have ruined our plans."

"Saxnor must favour us."

Fitz laughed. "It was a lot of hard work, not Saxnor that arranged such a thing."

Aldwin looked at his father-in-law in surprise. "Hard work?"

"Yes, the queen sent in agents to spread rumours. They're of the belief our left is our weakest flank, manned only by inexperienced troops who have been rushed into battle."

"But all of that is true, surely?"

"It is," the baron agreed. "We had few enough troops left after the Battle of Uxley. Even now, we have to rely on the Dwarves to hold the centre."

"Some Elves wouldn't have gone amiss."

"Yes, but with the death of Telethial, their future employment is in doubt. Still, we have plenty of stalwart fellows here. They'll hold. You can count on that."

"How can you be so sure?" Aldwin asked.

"It's simple, really. Our men know what's at stake. They also know they can count on their fellow countrymen to do their part, just as we must. In the end, it will be their discipline that wins the day, not numbers."

"And the Norlanders? Are they not disciplined?"

"Certainly, to a point, but they do not have the warrior culture that we do."

Aldwin frowned. "But aren't they descendants of Mercerians?"

A look of surprise appeared on the baron's face. "I suppose they are. I'd completely forgotten about that."

"Does that change your assessment?"

"Not in the least. Now, where is Sir Preston?"

"Over there," said Aldwin, "in the rear with our heavy cavalry."

"And why are they there?"

"To act as a reserve so we can deploy them as needed to trouble spots."

"Excellent, Aldwin. You're learning."

The enemy troops slowly began their advance, moving across the field like a large, undulating snake. The sun, finally breaking through the clouds, reflected off the enemy's weapons.

"There," said Aldwin, pointing. "More troops, on the right, coming from around those trees. It looks like horsemen."

"By Saxnor's beard," swore Fitz. "It appears our plans weren't as successful as we thought. You've got sharp eyes. Can you see what type they are?"

Aldwin stared, using his hand to shade his eyes from the sun. "They're wearing heavier armour by the look of it."

"Any sign of horse archers?"

"No, not that I can see."

"Thank the Gods for small miracles," said Fitz.

"Do they pose a problem?"

"Naturally, but it's nothing we can't handle. Still, we'd better let Sir Preston know. He'll need to bring in the right flank a little sooner than expected."

"I'll go and tell him, shall I?"

"I'd be obliged," said Fitz.

The Norland line marched inexorably closer, maintaining their solid line of steel. On either flank, the cavalry kept a similar pace, conserving their strength for the final charge. On the northern end of the line, their light cavalry would race down along the Deerwood's edge, forcing the Mercerians into a defensive position and shrinking their frontage. On the southern end, the heavier cavalry kept their distance from the queen's archers, manoeuvring to get in behind the defenders. It would be numbers that would tell this day, overwhelming the defenders and forcing them to break.

The Norland light cavalry broke into a gallop as they drew nearer the woods. Their horse archers began loosing off arrows, more to intimidate than to do any actual damage. It had the desired effect. Faced with the threat of horsemen, the northern end of the Mercerian line began to fall back. The Norland commander smiled. The plan was working splendidly. The enemy would soon be completely surrounded, their utter destruction only a matter of time.

~

Sir Preston swore, a most uncharacteristic expression for the newest Knight of the Hound.

"Sorry to be the bearer of bad news," said Aldwin.

"Not your fault, my lord," replied the knight, "but it does accelerate my plans. Please excuse me while I see to my men."

"Of course," the smith replied, riding back towards Baron Fitzwilliam.

Sir Preston's attention returned once more to his own command. "Send word to the footmen to begin their manoeuvres," he said to his aide. The man repeated the orders, then rode off as fast as his horse could carry him.

The knight turned his attention to the heavy cavalry. He recognized their look of apprehension. Most of them were recently recruited from the countryside and equipped at the Crown's expense. They were a new type of warrior, dedicated professionals in the mould of the Guard Cavalry, but they had yet to be tested in battle.

"Keep your eyes on the enemy," he ordered. "They'll try to surround us. Your job is to make sure our infantry can complete the defensive formation."

"And how do we do that?" asked Sergeant Hampton.

"By executing a series of sudden strikes on the enemy horsemen."

The sergeant stared back with a look of shock. "Those are armoured riders," the man said, "and they significantly outnumber us."

"All true," said Sir Preston, "and yet we have the discipline and skill to best them. Remember your training, and for Saxnor's sake, keep an ear out for the horns. If you don't withdraw when called, you'll be massacred. The whole point is to hit them and then withdraw before they can react, understood? Do that enough times, and they'll think twice about getting closer to our footmen."

"Aye, sir," said Hampton.

The knight returned his attention to the footmen of Merceria. They were beginning to fall backwards on the flank, taking up their positions to the south as the entire army began forming into a sizeable defensive circle.

∼

The first sign of trouble was when arrows flew from the Deerwood. They did little damage to the Norland cavalry, but the mere presence of the archers took them entirely by surprise.

The Norland commander tried to ignore them. After all, what could a smattering of bowmen do against the hundreds of horsemen under his command?

His confidence soon shattered as more archers stepped out from the woods. These were no skirmishers but massed bowmen of the Mercerian army. Where were they coming from?

He watched in fascination as a woman appeared. She began waving her hands about, and then a small dot of light flew from her fingers to land in amongst the horsemen. Obviously, she was a spell caster, but he thought she had failed when he saw the spark sink into the ground.

His belief was soon shattered as the ground began to tremble, and then small rocks broke the surface, sending the Norland advance into disarray. Horses fell, their riders thrown while others swerved to avoid the panic. All sense of order was abandoned in an instant.

The Norland horse archers, more disciplined, wheeled their mounts, heading straight for the Mercerian archers. Closer they drew, and then more enemy soldiers exited the woods. This was no militia. Rather, it was trained Orcs in tight formations, long spears reaching out like the spines of a porcupine.

The commander swore, pulling up his men to loose off a volley of arrows. Just as he did, what he saw made him turn pale. Massive creatures, close to eight feet tall, stepped from the woods, their grey skin making them look like they were carved from rock. Each carried a large stone, and even as he watched, they were tossed through the air to crash into the massed cavalry. The first struck a horse archer, tearing him in half at the waist and continuing into the man beside him. His horse ran off in fright, still bearing the man's lower abdomen and legs.

Another stone sailed past, narrowly missing his own head. The commander was about to call back his men, but then an arrow took him in the eye, toppling him from the saddle to leave his men leaderless.

∼

"Good shot," said Gorath as he placed another arrow onto his warbow.

"What can I say?" said Hayley. "I wasn't given the position of High Ranger for my looks." She glanced around. Her rangers were picking their targets, working in pairs, and calling out as they shot. The men and women of the Queen's Rangers were said to be the best shots in the Three Kingdoms, something she had worked hard to train into them. The addition of Orcs to their ranks had been a difficult choice, for not every Human was comfortable in their company. In the end, it turned out they had worried for naught, for a large portion of the rangers had been recruited in Hawksburg, a city the green folk had helped rebuild. Their familiarity with the Orcs had soon settled any objections.

"This is like target practice," Gorath complained. "They're packed so close I can't miss."

"Even so, keep your wits about you. They can close in an instant."

As she spoke, a dozen Norland horsemen broke off from the main group, heading directly towards the rangers. Gorath switched targets, letting loose another arrow, taking a horse in the chest. The beast went down, then tumbled, crushing its rider.

As more arrows flew forth, wolves appeared from nowhere, their howls echoing across the fields. Hayley had a brief glimpse of Albreda urging on her pack, and then the enemy horses began to panic. The riders broke off their attack, fleeing to the safety of the central formation once more.

∽

Gerald Matheson, Duke of Wincaster and Marshal of the Army of Merceria, looked at his queen. "I still think you should have stayed in the capital."

Anna removed her helmet, wiping the sweat from her brow, and then tried to tuck an errant blonde strand back in place. "Nonsense. I need to be here with my people. Besides, you know the army is more successful when we're together."

He smiled. "So we are. Would you care to give the signal for the attack?"

"And steal the glory? No, that honour should fall to you. You're the one in command here."

"You're the queen."

She replaced her helmet. "Yes, and wise enough to let the professional lead the army. Now, I shouldn't wait too long if I were you. Timing is everything."

Gerald rose in his stirrups, raising his sword high in the air and then sweeping it downward. The men around him gave a cheer as they began their advance, their boots crunching on the dead leaves and branches of the forest floor. It had taken the Orcs of the Black Arrow to guide them here. The marshal had worried they might be too late, but Chief Urgon had, true to his word, known the Deerwood like the back of his hand and delivered them at precisely the right moment.

He gazed off at the chief's banner. Unlike the Mercerians, who employed flags, the Orcs preferred banners hung from a horizontal pole affixed to a spear. The banner that signified the Black Arrow tribe was a simple black cloth that stood in sharp contrast to the red-and-green flags of the Mercerian troops.

The Orcs were heavy into the enemy horsemen now, their spears wreaking frightful damage. Off in the distance, Gerald could see Sir Heward and his heavy cavalry hitting the front of the Norland cavalry column. Past them, Beverly should have been commanding the Guard Cavalry, but he could only assume she had become aware of a greater threat, for nothing else could explain her absence.

Gerald's footmen, now formed up in a solid line, began their advance, keeping their ranks closed as protection against the enemy horsemen. He had insisted on arming those in the second rank with spears, and should the enemy threaten, their job would be to lower them, presenting a solid wall of iron-tipped death.

~

Dame Beverly Fitzwilliam, Knight of the Hound, guided the Guard Cavalry out of the woods. From her vantage point atop her massive Mercerian Charger, Lightning, she spotted the beleaguered forces of her father, Baron Fitzwilliam, raising a blue flag, signalling they were in distress. Beneath it was a small red flag, indicating the threat lay to the south. She thanked Saxnor the marshal had come up with the idea of a General Staff. These people were trained to send commands across the battlefield. At first, they had thought to use horns, but those were difficult to hear at long range, so a system of flags was introduced. Beverly had adjusted to them quite quickly, but the older warriors had found the concept difficult to grasp. A winter's worth of practice with the technique had led to its adoption army-wide, leading to their present circumstances.

She turned south, leaving the enemy horsemen to Sir Heward, and led the Guard Cavalry in a wide arc around a small group of nearby trees. As soon as they cleared the woods, she saw a group of armoured horsemen threatening her father's flank. The infantry had managed to get into some semblance of a circle, but their defensive formation was being put to the test as the Norlanders engulfed them.

She looked around, making sure her men had kept up, but she needn't have bothered. With their Mercerian Chargers, they were more than capable of maintaining their tight ranks at the gallop.

∿

Sir Heward's men drove deep into the enemy cavalry. With their light armour, the Norlanders were little match for the heavily armoured horsemen of the Mercerian army. The strength of light horsemen was their ability to outmanoeuvre their foes, but here, packed in tightly as they were, there was no way for them to take advantage of their mobility.

The knight swung his axe, taking off a man's arm just below the shoulder. He urged on his mount, concentrating on his next target. A slender blade scraped along his arm, but his metal armour easily deflected the blow.

He kept advancing, pushing aside the lighter mounts of the enemy. A flicker of movement to his left captured his attention, and he raised his shield just in time to catch another sword. Heward twisted in his saddle, bringing his axe down in an overhead strike. It snapped the blade and dug into the man's saddle, narrowly missing a leg.

The enemy horseman grinned, thinking he had avoided his fate, but the axe had penetrated the saddle, and his horse reared up in pain. For a moment, the man struggled to maintain his balance, but then he was tossed from his seat, landing in amongst the hooves of the general melee.

Sir Heward felt his horse drive a shoe into the man's chest, a cry of pain cut off short as his rib cage collapsed. The knight moved his charger farther into the melee, ignoring the scene of destruction beneath his mount's hooves.

∿

Sir Preston spotted the danger to the south and immediately reacted, taking his horsemen out into the swirling mass of Norland cavalry. They cut deeply into the enemy force, driving them back with the unexpected counterattack.

Swords rose and fell, wreaking havoc amongst them, and then the notes called out, sounding the retreat. The knight watched with pride as the Mercerians withdrew to the safety of the circle, and then the footmen resumed their positions, closing the gap.

He removed his helmet, the better to take in his surroundings. Norland horsemen were swirling around the defenders now, struggling to make any progress against the tight formation. Only to the east was there any problem. There, the Norland footmen had closed to engage in a fierce hand-to-hand action. The fighting was intense, but the Dwarves had held, refusing to take even a single step from their opening position. To his right, he could see the southern portion of the circle coming under heavy attack. Enemy spearmen were advancing, threatening to create an opening through which the heavier horsemen could charge.

Sir Preston thought to take his men there to reinforce the line, but then he spotted Aldwin. The smith was standing with the Mercerian foot, urging them to hold their position, a mace held tightly in his fist. The knight surveyed the rest of the battlefield, secure in the knowledge at least one part of the circle was safe.

~

Tog took another step, swinging his club with the strength that only a Troll could bring to bear. It struck a rider, collapsing his chest and sending the man flying from the saddle. The horse reared up in a panic, then galloped off, eager to be free of the carnage.

All around him, his Troll comrades advanced as he struck again, knocking aside a desperate attempt to parry. He prepared for another swing, but before him stood a bewildered warrior wearing the red-and-green livery of Merceria. Tog swivelled his gaze left and right, finally realizing they had reached the beleaguered defenders. Baron Fitzwilliam was nearby, beneath the banner of Merceria, and the great Troll walked up to him, his head towering over the mounted general.

"We have come," he said.

"So I see," said Fitz, "and welcome it is too. You've arrived in the proverbial nick of time."

"Where do you want us?"

The baron pointed. "Over there. We're in danger of the line breaking, and if that happens, they'll be all over us."

Tog nodded, then turned westward, lumbering back into the fray.

~

Turning her force eastward, Beverly could make out the battle, but her view of the Mercerian defenders was completely blocked by a swirling mass of armoured cavalry. She slowed, waiting for her men to form line, then gave the signal. With a sweep of her hammer, they began the advance, slowly at first and then picking up speed as they drew closer.

The enemy, intent on the defenders' destruction, didn't see them approach until it was too late. Only a few turned shouting out in alarm, but the sound of battle drowned out their voices.

The Guard Cavalry struck the line like a giant wave, pushing aside the enemy to leave a bloody smear in its wake. Norland horses galloped off, their riders no longer mounted, as all opposition began melting away.

Beverly swung Nature's Fury left and right, clearing a path towards her father's forces. Lightning, who towered over Norland's smaller horses, gave her the advantage of height, which she used to the best of her ability.

After she struck down yet another warrior, caving in his helmet, she spotted Sir Preston off in the distance, leading his own men out from the defensive circle. Closer they drew until no Norlanders were left between them. Beverly nodded in greeting.

Sir Preston lifted his visor, the better to be heard above the din of battle. "It is a victory," he proclaimed.

Beverly cast her eyes around, watching as the fighting began to die down. The Guard Cavalry, disciplined as they were, resisted the urge to pursue, looking instead to their leader. Removing her helmet, she took a deep breath of fresh air. There would be no pursuit today, not from her men, at least; that was the job of the Kurathians.

Sir Preston, noticing her eyes searching the battlefield, smiled.

"He's over there," he said, pointing. "Don't worry, he's fine." He saw the look of relief flood her face.

"How was he?" she asked.

"He did quite well for himself. He steadied the line when it looked like they might crumble."

Beverly wore a surprised look. "He did?"

"Yes. Why? Does that surprise you?"

"My husband is a master smith. I never thought him to be a warrior."

Sir Preston laughed. "I expect he's following in the family's footsteps. After all, he's a Fitzwilliam now."

She grinned. "So he is, and full of surprises, apparently."

"Have you orders for me, Commander?"

Beverly looked around at the battlefield. The Mercerians still held their ground, but the enemy was fleeing in every imaginable direction. "We'll let Commander Lanaka and his Kurathian horse take care of those who are fleeing. In the meantime, take your men, and see what horses you can round up. There's no use in letting them go to waste."

Sir Preston followed her gaze. "I daresay if we manage to gather even half of them, we'll have doubled our mounts. It'll be a good day for our new troops."

"It will," she agreed. "And tell your men they've done exceptionally well today, Sir Preston. Their hard work has paid off."

"I could say the same for you."

"I'll let you get on with it, then. I must find the marshal and give my report."

Sir Preston turned south, ready to ride off when an arrow sailed out of nowhere and struck his visor, narrowly missing his face. He instinctively leaned back, but the sound caused him to flinch.

Beverly turned, seeking out the archer responsible. A Norland rider, bow in hand, was notching another arrow. She turned Lightning, urging him into a gallop, but before she could go more than a horse's length, an arrow took the man beneath the armpit, and he fell, his bow dropping to the ground beside him. She soon saw the source of the arrow.

"Good shot, Hayley."

"Thank you, Bev," the ranger replied. "I would have let you have him, but I didn't think you'd make it in time."

"I shan't take offence," replied the knight. She looked at Sir Preston. "Are you all right?"

"Yes," he replied, "merely startled. That was a mighty close call."

"So it was," said Beverly. "You might want to keep your visor down next time."

"This coming from the woman who removed her helmet?"

She grinned. "Good point. I suppose we'd best chalk it up to happenstance."

Hayley nocked her bow, keeping it at the ready as Gorath searched through the dead and wounded. Survivors would be disarmed, and then the Life Mages could begin the arduous task of healing.

"I'll be reporting to Gerald," said Beverly. "Anything you need to pass on?"

The High Ranger thought a moment. "No, I don't think so. Things went pretty much as expected, though I imagine we weren't anticipating these additional horsemen."

Beverly looked at one of the fallen riders. "No, we weren't," she agreed. "They must have received reinforcements over the winter. You're senior to Sir Preston, so you take over command of this section of the line, and let him sort out the situation with all these loose horses."

"Will do," said Hayley. "Anything else?"

"Yes, I expect the queen will want you at dinner tonight."

"In Eastwood?"

"No, there's a Royal Estate nearby. I'll send you directions when I get a chance."

"I'll be there," Hayley promised.

Halting his horse, Gerald dismounted and then passed the reins to an aide. He stretched his back, letting out a grunt as he straightened. "I'm getting too old for this."

Anna laughed. "No you're not."

"All right, I'm not," he hastily added, "but it's been a long day." Hearing a heavy footfall, he turned to see Tempus bounding towards him. The great hound halted, wagging his tail enthusiastically.

"Someone's happy to see you," said the queen. "Come, sit for a moment. There are plenty of others to see to things."

"I wish I could, but there's still the matter of the city to take care of."

"Already done." She smiled. "I just sent Sir Heward to talk to them."

"And if they put up a fight?"

"I doubt they will. The Norlanders look like they threw everything they had at us. I imagine there aren't any soldiers left in Eastwood."

"They might have left a garrison," Gerald warned.

"True, but the city has no walls. If there was a garrison, I'd expect it to be halfway to the border by now."

"I doubt the Orcs will let them go in peace."

"Yes. Between them and Lanaka's forces, I doubt many will get through."

"Still," said Gerald, "we should let a few make it. They can take back word of their defeat."

"A splendid idea."

"What about us? Are we to pursue?"

"No," said Anna. "Not immediately, at any rate. We still haven't finalized our plans to invade Norland, and I might remind you we have to coordinate things with Weldwyn. They are our allies after all."

"True enough. I suppose that means we'll be returning to Wincaster?"

She smiled. "It does. I want to send the bulk of the army to the border to keep an eye on things. Who do you want to command it?"

"I'd say Fitz, but I have a feeling we'll need him when we meet with King Leofric."

"Who's your second pick?"

"I know we can't send Beverly, so I'll send Heward. He has experience on the frontier. You know it really would be easier if we had more Knights of the Hound."

"Agreed," said Anna. "Do you have any suggestions of who we might induct into the order?"

"No, I've been too busy to consider it. In any event, it's your order of knighthood, not mine."

She laughed, bringing a smile to his lips. "So that's how it's going to be, is it? Very well, I promise to give it some thought."

Tempus barked, his tail wagging again, this time at an approaching rider.

"Beverly," called out Anna as she watched her approach. "Glad to see you made it through unscathed. I hear your new heavy cavalry acquitted themselves well today."

"They did, Your Majesty," replied the red-headed knight. "Particularly those under Sir Preston's command."

"It seems we no longer have need of knights," said Gerald.

"Not for cavalry," said Anna, "but they make good leaders, particularly the well-trained ones. How were the casualties?"

"Heavy amongst the enemy."

"And our own troops?"

"I'm afraid my father's men took quite a beating. Revi and Aubrey are looking after them now, with help from Kraloch."

"I don't envy them the job," said Gerald. "They'll be at it for most of the afternoon and well into the evening."

"Keep an eye on them, Beverly. I don't want our Life Mages exhausting themselves."

"The problem is the weather," replied the knight. "It looks like rain is moving in, and we can't have the wounded lying around outside. They'll get soaked."

"All the more reason to get into Eastwood," said Gerald.

Anna placed her hand under her chin, unconsciously mimicking one of his expressions. "We'll move them into the Royal Estate. It's nearby."

"I thought you were hosting a victory celebration?" said Beverly.

"It can wait," said the queen. "Their recovery is more important. Oh, and see if you can find Arnim. He should be back with the baggage train."

"What's he doing there?" asked the knight.

"Fuming, probably," suggested Gerald.

"He and Nikki were in Eastwood," Anna explained, "spreading false information. I'm afraid they didn't get out fast enough to include them in the battle plan, so they've been guarding the supplies."

"I can't imagine he liked that," said Beverly.

"You'd be surprised," said Anna. "Now that he's a father, he's a lot more amenable to such things."

Gerald looked at her in surprise. "Are you trying to tell me Arnim's gone soft?"

"If, by going soft, you mean he's concerned about the welfare of the twins, then yes, I suppose I am."

"Never thought I'd see the day," he muttered.

"What was that?"

"I said that's quite the display... of loyalty, I mean."

Beverly noted the smirk on Gerald's face. "No meal, then?"

"We'll sort something out," said Anna, "so make sure that husband of yours is presentable. I trust he is well?"

"He is," said Beverly, "as is your own husband. I saw him on the way over here."

"Good, then dinner is still on, though what we'll be eating and where, I have no idea."

TWO

Dinner

Spring 965 MC

Gerald leaned his back against the wall. They were out the front of the Royal Estate beneath the covered archway that served as its entrance. Gazing towards the edge of the woods, he noted the downpour. "It's cold," he said, "and wet."

"That's pretty obvious, isn't it?" said Anna. She took a seat on the flagstones, setting down her goblet. Beside her loomed Tempus, stretched out and acting as the back of a chair while around her sat most of her friends, each seeking what comfort they could while Sophie passed out drinks.

"The food will be along shortly," the maid added.

"There's no hurry," said Gerald. "It's not like we're going anywhere."

She passed a tankard to Sir Preston, and as he took it, their hands brushed each other. Anna noted the looks on their faces and turned to Gerald, smiling. The marshal grinned back.

"You know," the queen said, "I think it's time we gave our gallant knight a more permanent command, don't you?"

"I should think so," he replied. "What did you have in mind?"

"How about captain of the heavy cavalry?"

"Surely Sir Heward is more deserving," offered Sir Preston.

"Perhaps, but we have other things in mind for him," said Anna.

"Oh?" said Beverly. "Care to share that information?"

"I'll leave that to the marshal. After all, it's army business. Gerald?"

Gerald straightened himself. "Yes, I've decided to promote him to commander. His experience in the north has proven him more than capable of operating in that capacity."

"And well he deserves it," added Beverly.

"Indeed he does," said Anna. "And we'll be needing more commanders when we push into Norland."

"So we're finally going to strike back?"

"We have little choice. We can't just sit back and relax after their invasion of Merceria."

Everyone went quiet, their concentration on their young queen. They had all known it was coming, but the details had been scant. Doubtless she had discussed it with Gerald, but not a word had leaked out.

"Well?" prompted Beverly. "Are you going to tell us or not?"

Anna wore a grin. "Not just yet, no. The plan is to return to Wincaster, then recall to Summersgate to discuss strategy with King Leofric."

"Yes," agreed Gerald, "he may have other ideas on how to proceed. In any event, we'll come to some sort of agreement to coordinate our actions. Once that's done, we'll return and start putting things into place."

The door opened, and Baron Fitzwilliam came outside, Albreda clutching his arm.

"Sorry," he said as everyone looked at him. "Did I interrupt something?"

"We were just discussing plans," said Gerald.

"Oh? What did I miss?"

"The queen is going to Weldwyn to confer with King Leofric," offered Beverly.

"Is she now," said the baron. "Good for her."

"I was hoping you'd accompany us," said Anna. "And we'll need Albreda to help take us there, of course."

"I should be delighted," said Fitz.

"Yes," Albreda agreed. "How many are going?"

"Aside from you two, I'll take Gerald and Beverly."

A bark erupted from behind her, causing her to laugh. "And Tempus, of course."

"A small enough party," said Albreda, "but shouldn't you take some guards as well?"

"I hadn't thought of that."

"That means we'll need more mages," said Gerald. "No offence to Albreda, but even she can't take everyone."

"How about Aubrey and Kraloch?" said Beverly. "That would give you two extra casters."

"I wonder what King Leofric will make of an Orc?" mused Gerald.

"I think he'll take it in stride," said Anna. "Of course, I'll want to take Alric. It's his home after all."

"Speaking of Prince Alric," said Gerald, "where is he?"

"Looking after the troops," noted Anna. "He's taking his position as your aide very seriously."

"Oh?"

"Yes, though I think he's a little miffed you didn't let him in on the full battle plan."

"It couldn't be helped. Secrecy was important to its success. Only Fitz and I knew the full details, aside from you, of course."

"Aha!" said the baron. "You finally called me Fitz!"

"Merely a slip of the tongue, my lord," said Gerald, adding a deep bow.

"Perhaps, but I shall remember it."

A servant appeared, edging past Fitz and Albreda.

"Ah," said Gerald, "the food."

"Just some cold meat," said Anna. "We must make do with what we have."

"Fine by me." He selected a piece of ham, taking a bite.

"So," said Fitz, "I suppose they'll call this the Second Battle of Eastwood."

"I propose a different name," said Anna.

"Oh? And what might that be?"

"The Battle of the Deerwood. After all, it was Gerald's use of the forest that made all the difference."

"So it was," said Fitz.

"We're lucky to have you as our marshal," added Beverly.

"Let's not forget the Orcs," said Gerald, blushing profusely. "If it wasn't for Chief Urgon, we'd have become lost in the trees."

Anna held up her cup. "To our noble allies," she toasted.

"Hear! Hear!" they all echoed.

An exhausted-looking Revi Bloom came out of the estate, interrupting their conversation.

Anna looked at him in sympathy. "I trust all is in order, Master Bloom?"

"It is, Your Majesty, though there's more work to be done, but I must rest and recover my strength."

"How is everyone?" asked Gerald.

"We dealt with the most seriously wounded first. Now that they're recovering, we can look after the others. On the whole, our casualties have been light, but I'm afraid I can't say the same of the enemy."

"Still," said Anna, "we must treat them as we do our own."

"It's strange," interjected Sir Preston, "that we should even be having this discussion."

"Oh?" said the queen. "Why would you say that?"

"It wasn't so long ago that the wounded would've had to fend for themselves. Under your father's rule, the Royal Life Mage only worked for the Royal Family."

Anna turned frosty. "King Andred was NOT my father!"

The knight turned crimson with embarrassment. "I'm sorry if I caused offence, Your Majesty. I merely meant—"

"I know what you meant, Sir Preston." She took a breath. "I'm sorry. I shouldn't have snapped, and in actuality, you are quite right. Under my rule, however, the wounded will be given every consideration. I only wish we had more Life Mages to help."

"We need to train more," insisted Gerald.

"Yes, but how?"

"Actually," said Revi, "Aubrey's been working on that very idea."

"Oh?" said Anna. "Do tell."

"She has been consulting with Kraloch and Roxanne Fortuna."

"The Weldwyn Life Mage?" said Gerald.

"Yes, that's the one. In any event, Aubrey's been able to identify people's magic aura while in spirit form."

"Meaning?"

"Meaning," continued Revi, "she can now discover others who have the potential to learn magic."

"Then she'll finally be able to get that school up and running in Hawksburg."

"It's an academy, Your Majesty, not a school."

"What's the difference?" said Gerald.

"A school is for teaching children," explained Revi, "while an academy takes a more mature approach to learning."

"But surely children could learn magic?"

The Life Mage laughed, cutting it off when he saw no one understood. "No, Gerald, that's not possible."

"Why ever not?"

"Well, for a start, they don't manifest until they get older."

"Manifest?"

"Yes, develop their magical power. Magic, you see, is in the bloodline but lies dormant until the child reaches maturity. It's only at that point they can learn to harness the power that lies within them."

"Not always," objected Albreda. "I seem to recall being quite young when I first found my power."

"There are exceptions, of course," said Revi, "but, by and large, we have found these things generally activate at puberty. I believe thirteen is the usual age."

"Oh," said Albreda, "I suppose I'm much like the rest, then. I was that age when I first entered the Whitewood."

"In any event," continued Revi, "we usually don't discover their potential until many years later, if at all."

"And just how common is this potential you speak of?" asked Anna.

"No one truly knows, though some have speculated it might be as common as one in a hundred."

"One in a hundred?" said Gerald. "That would mean the realm is crawling with them."

"As I said, that's mere speculation. As for myself, I think the odds are much lower, perhaps only one in a thousand. Mind you, there's nothing concerning which schools of magic are more common. We have no information on how many would be Earth Mages versus Life Mages, for example."

"It would be nice to have a Fire Mage," said Gerald. "At least then, the campfires would be easy to set up."

Anna laughed. "Trust you to think of that."

"It does raise an interesting point," said Revi. "If we did find a potential Fire Mage, we'd have no way to train him."

"Or her," added Albreda. "You can't assume they're all men."

"I stand corrected, but the point still remains."

"What about Weldwyn?" asked Gerald. "Have they no Fire Mages?"

"They do," said Albreda. "A fellow by the name of Osbourne Megantis. A fairly difficult man to get along with if his reputation is anything to go on. They have a Water Mage too."

"That's good news," said Revi. "It allows us to cover off all the disciplines, assuming they agree to help, of course."

"I see no reason why they wouldn't," said the queen. "They stand to benefit as much as we would. I shall be sure to bring it up when we go to Weldwyn."

"That still leaves the matter of air," said Revi.

"Having trouble breathing?" said Gerald.

"No, I mean Air Magic. I don't suppose they have an Aeromancer, perchance?"

"I don't believe they do," said Albreda. "Still, at least we have the other disciplines covered."

"What of the Orcs?" suggested Sir Preston. "Do they have any Air Mages?"

"That's a good point," said the queen. "Though I believe they would use the term 'Master of Air'. I shall have to talk to Kraloch. He would know."

"Personally, I doubt it," said Gerald. "If they did, they would have sent them to fight, wouldn't they?"

"Possibly, but you must remember, the Orcs can communicate over long distances. If the Orcs of the Black Arrow cannot use Air Magic, perhaps another tribe can?"

"A fascinating idea," said Gerald. He turned to Master Bloom. "Tell me, Revi, when can we expect our own mages to be able to communicate over long distances? It would certainly benefit the army."

The mage's face showed a look of disgust. "There's more to magic than simply battles, you know. In any event, we must consider how to pay for all of this training. Learning magic takes time, and we can't have the students working on farms while they learn how to harness their power."

"The Crown will assume the cost," said Anna.

"That's most generous of you, Your Majesty."

"It is not without a price," she added. "In exchange, your students will be required to render services to the Crown."

"I should have expected that I suppose," said Revi, a trace of gloom entering his voice.

"When would you start?"

"That depends on Aubrey. She's the one with the expertise. Of course, there's also the matter of where the school would be located."

"We already know that," said Anna.

"We do?"

"Yes, at the old Royal Estate on the outskirts of Hawksburg. I gave it to Aubrey for that very purpose."

"You did? Why wasn't I notified?"

"You were unavailable," said the queen, "due to your infirmity."

"Still, she could have told me about it afterwards."

"A great deal has occurred in your absence, Master Bloom, and we cannot spend all day catching you up on things. Your presence is most welcome, of course, but you must make an effort to find out what you missed on your own. We are far too busy."

"I humbly apologize, Your Majesty."

"As well you should," rebuked the queen. "Now, let us get on to other things, shall we?"

"Shouldn't we wait until the Nobles Council can be convened?" asked Fitz.

"That can wait," said Anna. "And in any event, all the important people are here. Well, most of them, anyway."

"And what news is there?" said Fitz. "Other than the war, I mean?"

"I hear the Trolls have finished building their town," said Gerald.

"Yes," said the queen. "They're calling it Trollden. I understand it's quite breathtaking."

"It's in the swamp, isn't it?" said Revi. "I'd hardly call that breathtaking."

"I think you'd be surprised. Most people think of them as brutes, but according to Tog, the Trolls are quite adept at construction. Some say they even rival the Dwarves though naturally, the scale of their buildings is larger due to their physique."

"Do they use stone?" asked Beverly.

"No," answered Anna, "they prefer wood, and they use timbers that are much larger than we would be used to."

"I suppose that has to do with their strength."

"In any event, they've also cleared out the mouth of the river. By now, the first Weldwyn traders have likely sailed up to Colbridge, maybe even as far as Kingsford."

"That should help our economy," said Fitz.

"And how is Bodden?" asked Gerald. "I haven't been there since my return from Norland."

"It's doing quite nicely, thank you. We've seen an increase in trade since Queenston was founded, and it'll only get better as the roads are cleared."

"That's excellent news," said Gerald, "but is it enough to get us out of debt?"

"Eventually," said Anna, "but the war has set us back significantly. After the Battle of Uxley, we had to rebuild our forces, and that didn't come cheaply."

"And the war itself?" said Revi. "I know we won this battle, but where does that leave us?"

"I'll let Gerald answer that."

Gerald tucked another morsel of meat into his mouth, chewing as he thought. He swallowed, then took a sip of ale. "There are no longer any Norland warriors on Mercerian soil," he began, "aside from the wounded and a few stragglers. The bulk of our army will move north to reinforce the garrisons on the border and prepare to carry the war to the enemy once we decide on a strategy. The remainder will return to Wincaster to rest and recuperate."

"Shouldn't we just invade?" asked Revi.

"It's a difficult task, made all the more so by our lack of maps of the area. We'd be stumbling around in the dark, so to speak, and that's no way to run a campaign."

"We have sent scouts north of the river," added Anna, "with the purpose of gathering more information."

"What about allies?" asked Beverly. "Some of the Norland nobles seemed to be amenable."

"We are making plans to contact them, but repelling the invasion of Merceria takes priority." The queen looked over at Gerald, who was staring off into the distance. "Gerald? Is anything wrong?"

"You just reminded me of something," he replied, patting down his tunic. "Now, where did I put it?"

"Put what?"

"It was a letter. You remember, Beverly, we were given it by Lord Creighton."

"Yes," added the knight. "I remember now."

"What did this letter say?" asked Anna.

"I don't know," admitted Gerald. "It was sealed. I was supposed to give it to you when we got back, but I completely forgot about it."

"You were badly wounded," Beverly reminded him.

"Yes, but that's no excuse. I must have put it in my trunk."

"Shall I fetch it for you?" offered Sophie.

Gerald glanced over at the queen's maid. "Would you? I'd be ever so thankful. It should be easy enough to spot. It has a red seal on it."

"I'll be back in a moment." She disappeared indoors.

"What do you think it says?" asked Fitz.

Gerald shrugged. "It was Beverly who was given it." He looked at his Commander of Horse.

"Lord Creighton mentioned Hollis had enemies," said the red-headed knight. "He saw the king's death as the start of a civil war."

"If that's true," said Anna, "then we may have allies in Norland after all. This may change our strategy."

"How so?" asked Beverly.

"Well, for one thing, we would need to support our allies. Until we know who they are, we really can't start anything."

"So we're back to waiting," said Fitz.

"It's still early in the campaign season," said Gerald, "and we've got the whole summer ahead of us for marching. Don't worry. One way or the other, we'll have Mercerian troops across the border eventually. The only question is where they'll be marching."

The conversation died down as trays of food were brought out. It was odd, sitting outside and watching people sip soup from bowls, but it still somehow felt like home.

Sophie's reappearance brought them all to their feet, their food all but forgotten.

"Is this it?" she asked.

"It is," said Gerald. "You can give it to the queen if you like. It's for her anyway."

She placed the letter in Anna's hand, then stood back as it was examined.

"The seal is intact," mused the queen. "I wonder what secrets it holds?"

"You'll never find out if you don't open it," said Gerald.

"No, I suppose I won't." She broke the seal, then unfolded the letter, scanning its contents. All eyes were on her as she finished. Anna looked up to see everyone staring at her. "It seems we have an opportunity."

"Oh?" said Gerald, trying to sound only mildly interested.

"It appears the late King Halfan's son died some years ago, but not before his wife gave birth to a Royal Granddaughter."

"So there's a child out there who can claim the throne of Norland?" asked Revi.

"Not quite," the queen said, "at least not as I understand it. A woman can't rule in Norland, but her husband could."

"She's married?"

"No, but Lord Hollis has her at his estate. Or rather, he did as far as Lord Creighton knows."

"How old is she now?" asked Gerald.

"She'll soon be old enough to wed, according to this. I suspect that's why Lord Hollis has her."

"But Lord Hollis is already married, isn't he?"

"I believe he is," Anna confirmed.

"Even so," offered Fitz, "I wouldn't put it past him to get rid of his current wife. Men like that will do anything for power."

"How much time do we have?" asked Gerald.

"I have no idea," said Anna. "But we should act on this as quickly as possible."

"Act on it, how?"

"That's easy," said Beverly. "We send in a force and rescue her."

"What if she doesn't want to be rescued?" said Fitz.

They all looked at him in shock.

"It's a reasonable assumption," he continued. "We know nothing of this girl. Perhaps she desires power of her own?"

"By marrying Hollis?" Beverly asked.

"Stranger things have happened."

"Richard makes a good point," said Albreda.

"Then what are we to do?" pressed Beverly.

"I propose," said the baron, "that we send a small group to try and get in contact with her. They can determine what her own wishes are in this regard. Then, if she wants to, they can bring her back to Wincaster."

"I think that an excellent idea," said Anna, "and there are directions in the letter. The estate is just north of Beaconsgate. That's close to the White-wood, isn't it, Albreda?"

"It is," the Druid agreed. "That being the case, I think it only reasonable I should accompany whoever goes."

"Certainly, but it will have to wait until we return from Weldwyn as we need you for that."

"I'm sure Aubrey and Kraloch are capable of helping you to their capital. You can also use Aldus. He's more than powerful enough."

"Can he use the spell of recall?" asked Gerald.

"He can," said Albreda. "I taught him myself."

"Then it's settled," said Anna. "Albreda shall accompany the rescue party."

"Hold on," said Beverly, "we still haven't discussed who else is going."

"That's easy," offered Sir Preston. "Lady Hayley. She is the High Ranger, after all, and she can take some of her rangers with her."

Anna nodded. "That's an excellent suggestion, Sir Preston."

"Speaking of which," said Gerald, "where is Hayley?"

"Setting up pickets," said Revi, "but she sends her regards."

"When do we leave?" asked Albreda.

"We'll return to Wincaster first," said the queen. "There's a few things that need seeing to before you go. Then you can use your magic to travel to the Whitewood from there. How long would you need, do you think?"

"To get to the estate?" said the Druid. "I don't know. No more than a week, I should think. The real question is, what will we find when we arrive? In any event, returning should be no problem. I'll bring her straight to the capital."

"Assuming she's willing," added Anna.

"Even if she's not." Everybody looked at Albreda in shock. "What?" she asked. "We can't let her be controlled by Hollis. Better she be a prisoner here in Merceria than aid our enemy, surely?"

"She does have a point," said Fitz.

The queen nodded her head. "Very well, but let's hope it doesn't come to that." Anna looked around at the small gathering. "Is there anything else we need to discuss?"

"Not at the moment," said Gerald.

"Good, then you'd all better get some sleep"—she stared at Gerald—"especially you."

"Me? Why would you single me out?"

"Because I know how involved you get planning out battles."

"Very well, I'll head off to bed as soon as I've seen to the guards."

"I'll do that," offered Beverly. "You need your rest."

He was about to object, but her smile disarmed him. "Very well, I know when to admit defeat."

"Good," said Anna, "because tomorrow we're starting early. I want to be back in Wincaster by noon, assuming our mages have enough power left."

THREE

The Mages

Spring 965 MC

L ady Aubrey Brandon, Baroness of Hawksburg, took her seat. To her right sat Revi Bloom, the head of this council, while to her left was Albreda. Aldus Hearn was also present, along with Kiren-Jool, the Kurathian Enchanter. Kraloch sat at the end of the table to give his Orcish frame more elbow room, while across from her sat two visitors. The first was Roxanne Fortuna, the Weldwyn Life Mage who had been helping her and Kraloch with their research. The other visitor, Lord Arandil Greycloak, was a far more forbidding prospect. As Lord of the Darkwood, he had come to claim the body of his daughter, Telethial, who had died some months previously. She had long since been buried, but the brooding Elf had remained, determined to have his say in matters as an ally of Merceria.

Revi looked around the room. "It's been some time since we last met," he began, "though I hear you did manage to get in a session or two while I was indisposed."

"It's good to have you back," said Aubrey.

"Thank you, but let us dispense with such frivolities, shall we? We have important matters to discuss."

"Where would you like to start?" asked Albreda.

"I'd like to talk of the Saurian gates for a moment." He held up his hands to halt any argument. "Don't worry, it's not what you think."

"Then what is it?" asked Aldus Hearn.

"We now know we cannot use them without some risk of developing a strange malady," Revi continued, "except for the Orcs, of course. Aubrey, you and Kraloch developed a cure for that. How's that been going?"

"We have been systematically identifying everyone who went through the gates and using the new technique to cure them. Only a few people remain, and none of them are in any immediate danger."

"That's a relief," said Hearn. "I feared we might have an outbreak of madness."

"I wasn't mad," insisted Revi. "I was just... extremely distracted."

"Well, in any event, we can do without that distraction."

"Agreed," said Revi. "Though I would like to point out there are other possible uses for these gates, even if the Orcs are the only ones who can use them safely."

"Such as?" asked Albreda.

"They tap into the ley lines, and I have managed to unlock the secret of unlimited travel."

"Meaning?" said Hearn.

"Meaning we can use gates to travel to any intersection of ley lines, regardless of whether they hold a physical structure or not."

"And how would we return?" asked Kiren-Jool. "Or haven't you thought of that yet?"

"By use of the recall spell," said Revi. "I've actually learned it myself. Quite a useful bit of magic, that."

"You're welcome, by the way," said Albreda.

"I'm sorry?" said Revi.

"You're welcome for being able to learn the spell of recall."

"I don't understand. Aubrey taught me."

"And who do you think she learned it from?"

Revi blushed. "Ah, I hadn't realized. My apologies."

"You know," said Hearn, "I think I liked it better when Revi was short with everyone."

"When was I ever short?"

"When you were mad... or distracted, as you like to call it."

"Ah, well, I apologize for that too. Now I realize we have a war to think about, so I'll leave the matter of the gates for now. What else have we on our plates?"

"There's the matter of the academy," said Aubrey.

"Yes, how is that going? Have you found us any students yet?"

"Not yet. We're not quite ready for them at this point in time."

"Why not?" asked Revi.

"We have to develop a system of training. After all, we've never had an academy before."

"We simply teach them what we know, don't we? How much harder can it be?"

"We can't just start teaching," insisted Aubrey.

"Why not? It worked when I took you on as an apprentice, didn't it?"

"Yes, but I already knew a lot of the theory of magic. We can't expect the same from every student."

"Then what do you have in mind?"

"I suggest we start with the theory of magic, and leave the spell casting for later."

Kraloch raised his hand, garnering the attention of all.

"Yes?" said Revi. "You have a suggestion?"

"I do," said the Orc. "I am led to understand my people use a different method than Humans to train those gifted with magic."

"Different, how?"

"Humans always tend to teach the student everything about the theory of magic before they even learn to cast a spell."

"Of course," said Hearn. "It's the most effective method of training. How else would you do it?"

"We teach one spell at a time, starting with the simplest. As the student learns to master each spell, they are presented with a greater level of knowledge."

"It would never work with Humans," said Hearn.

"Agreed," added Kiren-Jool. "Without proper understanding, they would never be able to master magic."

"But it has already succeeded with Humans," said Kraloch. "And the man who was taught became a very powerful master of flame."

"You never told me this," said Aubrey.

"It is something I only recently became aware of. Our cousins far to the east rescued a man from certain death, and they taught him to harness the spark within."

"Remarkable," said Kiren-Jool.

"Astounding," agreed Hearn. "But likely the exception rather than the rule."

Albreda slammed a fist onto the table. "Must you two be so obstinate? If one of us can learn using that technique, then others can too. What have we got to lose?"

"But none of us know how to do that," said Hearn.

"No, but neither do we know how to run an academy. We shall do what the non-magical world does when they come across something they don't understand."

"Argue?" suggested Kiren-Jool.

"No, you fool, we shall learn. Kraloch will be our teacher, providing he's willing to undertake that responsibility."

"I shall be pleased to," said the Orc, "though I should consult with the Ancestors to gather their thoughts on the matter first."

"Good, then it's settled." She turned her attention once more to Revi. "Please continue, Master Bloom."

"Yes. Now, where was I?"

"We were talking about the academy," Aubrey reminded him.

"Yes, that's right. I suppose we need to develop a structure of some sort. One of the problems with using the master-apprentice system is that things frequently get overlooked. Look at my own situation. If Andronicus had been more organized, I'd be much further ahead in my studies."

"I'll work with Kraloch and see what I can come up with," offered Aubrey. "If the council here approves it, we'll take the next step and start searching for students."

"Excellent," said Revi. "Then we'll put further discussion of the topic on hold until you've completed your research. The only other thing I'd like to address is the war."

"What about the war?" asked Hearn.

"I thought we might consider how we can be of assistance once the army marches into Norland. I know my familiar has been of use in the past. I was hoping Albreda and Master Hearn might be able to use similar means to keep track of our enemies."

"I see no problem," said Hearn.

"Nor do I," added Albreda. "Is there anything else?"

"Not at the moment, but if anyone comes up with anything, let me know. I'll be at my house."

Lord Greycloak interrupted. "May I speak?"

"Certainly," said Revi.

"I have been giving the matter careful consideration, and I have come to the conclusion that the Elves of the Darkwood can no longer send troops to aid Merceria in its time of need."

"That's a matter best brought to the attention of the queen," said Revi, "but may I ask why?"

"We are a diminished people," said the Elf, "and recent losses at Uxley have taken their toll. We shall, of course, continue to provide financial aid in return for a seat at the Nobles Council, but I'm afraid our fighting days are over."

Those at the table sat in stunned silence. It was Aubrey who finally spoke. "I shall bring this to the attention of Her Majesty," she said.

Greycloak rose, bowing respectfully. "I will now take my leave of you." The Elf turned, departing the room quickly.

"Well, that's a shock," said Hearn.

"I'll say," said Revi. "I wonder what brought that on?"

"It's his daughter, Telethial," offered Aubrey. "She was killed at Uxley."

"Many people died at Uxley," said Kiren-Jool, "but you don't see others pulling out."

"You don't understand," said Aubrey. "The Elves have been barren for some time."

"Barren?" said Revi. "Are you saying they can't have children?"

"So it would seem. It was the queen who first noticed it, but I've come to realize she might have a point. I have a solution if I can ever get around to it, but I'm afraid I'm stretched too thin at the moment."

"A solution?"

"Yes, the magic Kraloch and I discovered might be able to solve their problem, but it would take cooperation on their part, something I doubt will happen anytime soon."

"They are a stubborn race," said the Orc, "even more so than the Dwarves, but at least the mountain people can be made to see reason."

"Well," said Revi, "there's little we can do about it if they refuse to talk to us. We'll simply have to put it aside for now and hope the future brings an opportunity. I think we've had more than enough for one meeting, don't you?" He cast his eyes around the room, noting the nods.

"Very well, then, I'll let you get about your business. Good evening, everyone."

They all rose and began making their way out the door.

Albreda hung back. "Aubrey, if I might have a word? You too, Kraloch."

They waited as the room cleared. "I wonder if you two might accompany me back to the Fitzwilliam house. There's something I'd like to talk to you about."

"Certainly," said Aubrey, "but wouldn't it be easier to talk here?"

"I think the house is more private, and I know Richard would let us use his office."

"It's that important?"

"I think so."

"Then lead on," said Kraloch, "and let us be quick about it. You have intrigued me."

"That's his way of saying he's excited," said Aubrey.

They set off from the Palace at a brisk pace.

. . .

Before long, they were at the baron's Wincaster townhouse. Albreda pushed open the door, ignoring the servants attempting to take her cloak.

"Is the baron in?" she asked.

"He's in the library," said Lucas, the head servant, "along with Lady Beverly and Lord Aldwin."

"We'd best pop in and say hello," said the Druid. "Then we can get down to business."

They stepped through the doorway, interrupting a discussion.

Baron Fitzwilliam rose. "Good to see you, my dear. I trust everything is going well?"

"It is," replied Albreda, "but before we sit down to chat, I wonder if I might borrow your office for a while? I need to discuss a few things with Aubrey and Kraloch."

"Of course. I hope it's nothing serious?"

"Only mage things, nothing that would interest you."

"I'll have the staff fetch you something to eat, shall I?"

"That would be marvellous, but have them bring it in here, will you? I don't wish to be interrupted."

The baron looked at Lucas, who simply nodded in return, then disappeared off to the kitchen.

Albreda led her associates to a cozy room where a solid wooden desk took up a good portion of space, but she chose to sit in front of it, indicating that they should do likewise.

"What is it?" said Aubrey.

"Yes," said Kraloch. "What is so important we couldn't talk about it at the Palace?"

Albreda dove right in. "Tell me more about this ability to detect magical potential."

"It's pretty straightforward, actually," said Aubrey. "We go into the spirit realm and look at people's auras."

"And you can both do this?"

"Yes," said Aubrey, "though it's harder for Kraloch to detect the colours. Apparently, Orcs' eyes see things a little differently in the spirit realm."

"It seems a clumsy way of doing things. Is there a way to detect this aura without going into the spirit realm?"

"That's something I'm still working on. Why?"

"The ability to detect this type of thing could prove quite dangerous in the wrong hands," said Albreda.

"Are you suggesting we give up?"

"No, but you might consider restricting who has knowledge of this. I also suggest that once you succeed, you limit who has access to cast it."

"Surely not?" said Aubrey.

"The Magic Council is growing," continued Albreda, "and the larger it gets, the more difficult it will be to contain such knowledge."

"Are you suggesting someone has a hidden agenda?"

"Possibly, but the mere mention of such things could be disastrous. Think of what the Dark Queen could do with such knowledge."

"But she's a Necromancer," declared Aubrey. "Surely such a spell would only be usable by a Life Mage."

"You forget, Life and Death Magic are mere reflections of each other."

"Do you suspect someone," asked Kraloch, "or is this merely a general warning?"

"I do not trust Lord Greycloak."

"But he helped us," said Aubrey.

"True, but the Elves always look to long-term advantage, and his statement today shows how fickle they can be as an ally."

"I shall heed your words," said Aubrey. She turned to Kraloch.

"Don't look at me," said the Orc. "I do not socialize with Elves, let alone talk to them."

"Good," said Albreda, "then it'll be our little secret for now."

Revi wandered down the street so deep in thought he almost missed his own house. He shook his head, astounded by the depths of his distraction, then turned up the walkway, looking forward to a little rest. The smell of food drifted to his nose as he opened the door.

"Hello?" he called out. "Is someone here?"

"Just a moment," came back Hayley's voice.

"What in Saxnor's name are you doing?"

"Making you dinner," she replied, coming out of the kitchen.

"I must say that's a surprise. I didn't know you'd be here."

She placed her hands on her hips. "That's the whole point of this. It wouldn't be a surprise otherwise, would it? Now, come along, it's almost ready."

He followed her back into the kitchen. As a mage dedicated to a life of study, Revi Bloom had never thought of using his dining room to eat; it was far too cluttered with books. Instead, he had a small table in the kitchen, and it was here she led him to where a plate of food waited. He sat, staring down at the feast before him, trying to identify what type of meat it was. At least he assumed it was meat.

"Well?" she said. "What do you think?"

He leaned over the plate, taking a deep breath and almost choking on the smell. "It's very... what's the word I'm looking for?"

"Strong?" she asked, hope written on her face.

"Is this beef?"

"No, it's pork. Can't you tell?"

"It's rather dark. Are you sure that's what it is?"

She sat down opposite him. "Oh, I don't know. I'm terrible at this sort of thing."

"I thought you were a ranger?"

"I am," she replied.

"Aren't you an expert at hunting?"

"Hunting, yes. Cooking? Not so much."

He poked the food, then took a morsel, lifting it to his mouth. One whiff was all it took to convince him to abandon the attempt.

"I'm sorry, Revi. I tried, I really did."

He reached across the table, taking Hayley's hand. "It's all right. It's your company I wish to keep, not your cooking. If need be, we can hire someone to prepare food."

"What do you mean, 'we'?"

"I mean, I'd like you to stay here, in this house, with me."

"Is this a marriage proposal?" she asked.

He fumbled for the right words, suddenly finding his mouth dry. "I suppose it is," he finally managed to get out. "I do hope you agree. I need my lucky charm."

She leaned forward, kissing him on the forehead. "I should be delighted to accept your proposal, Revi Bloom."

He smiled. "You've made my day. Now, what do you say we head down to the Queen's Arms and find something a little more palatable to eat?"

"I'd love to, but I must be off."

"Off? But I just got here."

"True," said Hayley, "and I'd like to stay, but I have to leave."

"Why?"

"I have to tell Bev the good news!"

FOUR

The Rangers

Spring 965 MC

Gorath stood in the centre of the magic circle examining the gold and silver inlaid into the floor. "It is quite remarkable work, this."

"It is," agreed Hayley. "I understand Lord Aldwin was the artisan who crafted those runes."

"Lord Aldwin? Beverly's bondmate?"

"Bondmate? Oh, you mean husband? Yes, that's him."

"I had no idea he could craft magic."

"He can't. He's a smith. It was Lady Aubrey who empowered the circle."

"But didn't Aldwin forge Dame Beverly's hammer?"

"Yes, he made Nature's Fury from sky metal, but it was Albreda who gave it the power of the earth."

"This all sounds so complicated," said the Orc.

"I don't see why it should. Your own chief, Urgon, has an enchanted sword, doesn't he?"

"He does, though that was handed down by his forebearers."

"As Nature's Fury will be, I would imagine."

"So they're expecting younglings?"

Hayley laughed. "I suppose they will eventually, but I don't think they're in any hurry. There's a war on after all."

"And what of you?"

The laugh died, the High Ranger's face growing serious. "What about me?"

"Nothing," said Gorath.

"You can't get my attention like that, then ignore me," she warned. "Go on, say what you mean."

"I merely assumed, now you and Master Bloom are to be wed, your thoughts might turn to the raising of your own younglings."

Hayley blushed. "Children are the furthest thing from my mind at present. And you should at least give me a chance to get married first. Why is this so important to you?"

The Orc grinned, displaying his ivory teeth. "It is always a joy to welcome newcomers to the tribe."

"But I'm not a member of your tribe."

"And yet you are seen as such by the Orcs who serve as rangers."

"Am I? I had no idea."

"Perhaps, when we return, I shall suggest to Urgon he induct you into the Black Arrows."

"I would be honoured," said Hayley.

"It's very fitting."

"How so?"

"Well, you are a ranger, and the symbol of our tribe is an arrow. It must be fate."

"I don't believe in fate," said Hayley. "I think we make our way in the world by our actions, not some predetermined destiny."

"As do the Orcs," said Gorath, "but it doesn't hurt to have a little mysticism in your life every now and again."

"Spoken like a true Orc."

He bowed. "Thank you."

"Now, where are the others? You did tell them to meet us here, didn't you?"

"I did. They should arrive shortly. In any case, Albreda has yet to put in an appearance."

"Yes, but once she gets here, she'll be eager to leave. I shouldn't like to keep her waiting."

Outside, they could hear the guards challenging an arrival. A moment later, the doors opened, revealing four rangers: two Orcs and two Humans.

"Samantha," said Hayley, "I didn't know you'd finished your training?" She turned to Gorath. "She came from Bodden, you know."

The Orc gave her a puzzled look. "Do Humans lose their memory when they become engaged?"

"No, why?"

"I am the one who oversees the training of the rangers. I know all of them by name. Did you forget that?"

"Sorry, I suppose I did. Would you care to make the introductions?"

"Certainly. This, as you pointed out, is Samantha, though she commonly goes by Sam. Is this a common tradition amongst Humans? Shortening names?"

"I suppose it is."

"Then I will have to make more use of it. Shall I call you Hay?"

"I'd rather you didn't."

He frowned. "I'm still not sure what I should call you."

"Would you please get on with the introductions?"

"Certainly. This is Bertram Ayles; he comes to us from Stilldale. He is also a recent addition, having been trained in the same group as Samantha."

"Good to have you with us," said Hayley.

"Next in line is Urzath. She has been with us ever since we became allies. She is also one of the best hunters in the Black Arrows."

"Excellent," said Hayley. "I'm glad you'll be going with us." She looked at the last Orc, noting his small size. "And this is?"

"Skulnug," said Gorath. "An Orc renowned for his stealth. It is said he could steal an egg from a dragon without waking it."

"Have we any dragons in the area?" asked Hayley.

"No," said Skulnug, "but if we did, I would be tempted to steal its egg."

"Well, there's a lot to be said for confidence."

"There certainly is," came Albreda's voice.

They all turned to see her enter.

"I didn't hear the guards challenge you," said Hayley.

"Why would they? I use the circle often enough that they all know me by sight." She looked at the gathering. "Is this everyone?"

"It is."

"Good. Then let's get to work, shall we? Let me stand in the centre, and the rest of you gather around me." Albreda watched as they took up their positions, then grabbed Samantha by the shoulders, moving her slightly. "There, that should do nicely. Is everyone ready?"

They all nodded. Albreda closed her eyes, taking a calming breath. The rangers stood silently as words of power began tumbling out of the Druid's mouth. They were indistinct, but their very sound filled the room with energy. One by one, the runes began to glow, and then a solid wall of white light erupted from the outer edge of the circle, encasing those inside in a cylinder of energy. After pulsing twice, the light dropped to reveal a group of stones forming a circle in a forested clearing filled with the scent of fresh pine. They had arrived. A low growl erupted on one side, and Bertram Ayles hastily nocked an arrow.

"Stay your hand," ordered Albreda. "There shall be no hunting in this wood."

"It's a dangerous creature," insisted Ayles. "Surely we can protect ourselves?"

"That is no danger," said Sam, "that's Snarl."

"Yes," added Albreda, "and he's a dear friend. Harm him, and you'll never set foot outside the Whitewood again."

Ayles turned to Samantha. "How do you know him?"

"He would often accompany Albreda to Bodden."

"That thing? But he's a wolf!"

"Is he?" she said, her eyes going wide in mock fear. "I hadn't noticed!"

"Now you're pulling my leg."

"Are you two quite done?" said Albreda. "We do have a reason for being here, you know."

"Would you care to show us the way?" asked Hayley.

"Certainly. Come along, Snarl. Let's show them the quickest route, shall we?"

The great wolf let out a howl that echoed off the trees, then padded over to her side. The Druid gave one last look at the group, then started heading north, setting a brisk pace.

"Quite spry for someone her age," said Bertram Ayles.

"Don't let her hear you say that," warned Sam, "or she's likely to take a dislike to you."

"And what would that lead to?"

"Well, when Baron Fitzwilliam needed rescuing, she used her magic to tear down the portcullis. I'd hate to think what that spell could do to flesh and bone."

Ayles paled. "In that case, I shall keep my thoughts to myself."

Samantha smiled. "A good decision."

That evening, they camped under the watchful eyes of the Whitewood. Hayley marvelled at the way in which the animals were drawn to Albreda. The rest of the group looked decidedly more ill at ease.

After gathering sticks from the forest floor, they built a fire to keep the cold night air at bay. When they finally settled down for the night, Hayley insisted on setting up a system of watches despite Albreda's insistence they weren't in any danger.

This was how Samantha found herself staring into the shadows beneath the trees in the middle of the night. Hearing someone approach from behind, she turned to see Albreda, who had shifted closer to the fire while Snarl had chosen to lie nearby, his tail twitching while he slept.

"So," said the Druid, "what do you think of being a ranger? It's a far cry from being a simple archer."

"True, and this is much different than Bodden."

"In a good way, or bad?"

"I quite like it here, actually," Sam admitted. "There's a certain feeling of peace to the place." She looked over at Snarl. "Though I must admit it's a little odd having a giant wolf amongst us."

"Snarl's no giant, just well-fed."

"You mean there are bigger wolves in these parts?"

"Not in the Whitewood, but go north, and you'll see wolves the size of ponies."

"Like the queen's hound?"

Albreda chuckled. "Not quite that large. You know the Orcs of the Black Arrow sometimes have their younger hunters ride wolves, but as they grow to maturity, they weigh too much for the poor animals to carry."

"Do they have a lot of wolves?"

"They do, and they accompany them on the hunt from time to time much as dogs do for Humans. You should talk to Urzath. She could probably tell you more."

"How did you learn so much about animals?"

"It's this place," said Albreda. "It speaks to me."

"You mean with actual voices?"

"No, but over the years, I've felt a strange sort of connection here. It's as if I'm part of the land. When I stretch out my senses, I feel as though the forest is part of me. That's how I call on the animals, you know."

"Like Snarl?"

Albreda stroked the wolf's head. "He's easy to find. I've known his pack for years, ever since I entered the Whitewood. He's a descendant of my first friend here, Fang."

"Fang?"

"Yes, not the most original of names, I'll grant you, but I was only thirteen when I named him. He was such a devoted soul."

"Soul? You make him sound Human."

"Do you not think animals have souls?"

"I never really gave it much thought," said Sam, "but I suppose it makes sense."

"Of course it makes sense. All mammals have souls."

"What about fish or insects?"

"I never had much interest in them," said Albreda. "Although Snarl does like a nice salmon every now and again. They swim up from the coast, you know, but they're very seasonal."

"Is he good at hunting?"

"Fish? No, but he can follow the scent of a deer for days. I took him to Hawksburg once, but he refused to enter."

"But he's been in Bodden?"

"He has, but I think that's about as far into Human lands as he cares to go."

"Can you actually talk to him?"

"Of course! I can also share images, a gift I first discovered with Fang, as a matter of fact."

"How do you do that?"

"I place my forehead against his and then concentrate. The communication is very deep."

"So you read his thoughts?"

"More or less. I see images and feel emotions. I've become quite adept at learning to interpret them."

"And is this a two-way process?"

"It is. Of course, he also understands when I speak to him, though he had to learn that over time. He was a much more stubborn student than his sire."

"I suppose that means he has a personality?" said Sam.

"Of course," said Albreda. "The whole pack does."

"How many wolves are in this pack of yours?"

"The pack Snarl belongs to numbered twenty-three the last time I counted, although I rather suspect they've had some fresh pups by now."

"The pack he belongs to? You mean he's not in charge?"

"No, he's more of a lone wolf. He still visits them from time to time, but he spends most of his days wandering the Whitewood. He also visits the other packs."

"How many packs are there?"

"Three. One of them hunts just north of the river. We'll be passing through their territory over the next day. Perhaps I'll introduce you."

"So you get along with them, then?"

Albreda frowned. "Get along with them? What a strange thing to ask. Why wouldn't I get along with them?"

"Don't they compete for prey?"

"Not at all. In fact, they get along better than most Humans do. They all used to be one pack, you see, so they're truly one big family. When Snarl crosses the river, he's visiting his cousins."

Sam glanced at the sleeping wolf. "He seems so peaceful. Is he always this calm?"

"Usually, but sometimes things will set him off. I remember when a wildcat made its way into the Whitewood some years ago. He was quite incensed his home had been invaded."

"I hope it didn't lead to trouble?"

"Thankfully, I managed to intervene in time. His ancestor was badly mauled by a wildcat, you know."

"I take it you mean Fang?"

Albreda nodded. "I do. The cat had killed one of the pack's pups, you see. It also attacked me. Fang came to my rescue, but he bore the scars from it for the rest of his life." She fell silent, and Sam could see a sadness come over the Druid's face.

"Well," said Albreda at last, "I should get some rest. It's likely to be a long day tomorrow."

They were up at the crack of dawn, continuing their trek northward. By noon they had reached the banks of the River Alde, its swift current swelled by melting snow from its source.

"This is it," announced Albreda. "The border of Merceria. Everything north is technically part of Norland."

"Should we be alarmed?" asked Ayles.

"Of course not. We're still in the Whitewood."

"How much longer will we be in the cover of the forest?" asked Hayley.

"We shall turn northeast while we are still within the woods, allowing us to remain concealed until we are much closer to Beaconsgate. Another day or two, and you'll be able to see the city itself."

"What's it like?" asked the High Ranger.

"Dirty," answered the Druid. "The city grew haphazardly, and little has been done to improve its appearance. It's a strange sight actually—a grey smear against a rather pristine countryside."

"Will there be patrols, do you think?"

"Possibly. It has been some time since I was in that part of the woods." She held up her hands to stall any comments. "Of course, there won't be any patrols in the Whitewood itself. The Norlanders fear it."

"Why is that?"

"I have been the guardian of this area for some time. No Norlander has ever set foot in these woods and lived to tell of it."

"That's a bit harsh, isn't it?" offered Ayles.

Albreda gave him a stern look. "It's the law of nature," she said. "And besides, how else would I protect my domain? Send them a letter nicely asking them to leave us alone?"

"I suppose that's reasonable enough," the ranger grumbled.

"The water is quite deep," noted Hayley. "Is there a ford nearby?"

"There is. It's just up there." Albreda pointed. "Snarl will show us the way, as long as he doesn't get distracted."

"By what?"

"Knowing him, anything. Sometimes all it takes is a hawk or a gryphon, and then he loses track of what he's doing."

"You have gryphons in the Whitewood?"

"On occasion. They nest in the Wickfield Hills."

"I didn't know that," said Hayley. "You have me intrigued."

"I had no idea you were so interested in them. I'll have to introduce you sometime."

"You can do that?"

"Of course I can do that. I offered, didn't I?"

"So you did," said Hayley. "I'll hold you to that promise."

"And I should be delighted to keep it, but for now, we have more important matters to consider, don't you think?"

"Yes, certainly."

They proceeded eastward, following the southern riverbank until they came upon a series of small rapids.

"Here it is," said Albreda.

The small group halted, looking across the swift water.

"I don't see anything," said Ayles.

"That's because you don't know where to look," said Albreda. "Now, wait just a moment." The Druid closed her eyes, calling on arcane powers. The air began to tingle, and then a massive tree on the far side stretched out its branches, bending to reach the nearby bank. "I hope you don't mind walking along a branch or two."

Snarl leaped onto the tree's limb, crossing quickly. Hayley laughed in delight at the sight of the wolf up a tree. "Does he do that often?"

"No, just ignore him; he's showing off. Usually, he swims across."

They followed one at a time, with Gorath bringing up the rear. Once they were all safely across, Albreda released her magic, and the tree returned to its natural state.

"A handy spell, that," remarked Ayles. He was about to say more, but Snarl halted, his hackles rising.

Albreda knelt, searching the ground. She waved Hayley over. "What do you make of this?"

The High Ranger drew closer, her eyes looking down. "Footprints," she said.

"Yes, but they're not mine."

"No, they belong to soldiers. Note the nails."

"I'm not sure I understand," said Ayles.

Hayley turned to the new ranger. "The soles of soldiers' boots are nailed on rather than sewn."

"Why is that?"

"They march a lot. It makes it easier to replace the bottoms when they wear out."

"But surely there aren't soldiers here?"

"This footprint would seem to indicate otherwise. Spread out, all of you, and look for more."

They all began searching the ground.

"Over here," called out Urzath. She waited until Hayley was beside her, then knelt, feeling the ground. "These plants are freshly crushed. I would say they're nearby."

"How many?"

The Orc moved around on all fours, taking a closer look. "Close to a dozen, at least."

"What in Saxnor's name are Norland troops doing in the Whitewood?" asked Hayley.

"Something I'd very much like to know," said Albreda. "And more importantly, why wasn't I notified?"

"Notified?"

"Yes, the pack here should have given ample warning, yet I've heard nothing."

"I don't know," said Hayley, "but I suggest we tread carefully."

FIVE

Wickfield

Spring 965 MC

Sir Heward, better known as 'The Axe', exited the tavern, stretching his back while looking up at the clear sky. With the new garrison in place and construction started on a wooden palisade, the village of Wickfield was a busy place. He strolled across the street, ignoring the sounds of axes and hammers at work. It was still weeks away from being complete, but the locals were pleased their safety was being taken seriously.

Pausing mid-street, he gazed north to where the Wincaster Light Horse was lending a hand by using their horses to drag logs into place. The task required stamina, and the company had bent to the task with enthusiasm. The knight reminded himself to mention his pleasure to Carlson, their captain.

Someone called his name, and he heard approaching footsteps. Sergeant Hugh Gardner was making for his location at full speed, so the knight turned, waiting to see what new problem had developed.

"Sergeant," he called out, "is something wrong?"

"We have reports of activity across the river, sir."

"What, exactly?"

"Captain Caluman reports his riders have spotted movement around Brooksholde. He's waiting to give you a full report."

Sir Heward looked at the sergeant, his mind whirling. It was not uncommon to spot movement amongst the enemy, but Brooksholde was very close to the border, far closer than was comfortable. "Take me to him," he finally said, "and we'll see if we can't get to the bottom of this."

Sergeant Gardner led him to the new headquarters, part of the marshal's effort to establish a more permanent garrison at the border. Inside, he quickly spotted the Kurathian, wearing one of the dull green cloaks his scouts had recently adopted. "Captain Caluman, you have news?"

"I do, sir. We spotted a large group of soldiers near Brooksholde."

"How many?"

"Difficult to say with any accuracy, but I would place an estimate at two hundred, maybe two-fifty."

"Any idea as to their type?"

"They looked to be poorly outfitted," offered the captain, "perhaps even militia."

"I doubt it's anything we need to worry about, then."

"There's more, sir."

"Oh?" said Heward. "Go on."

"I've had reports of more troops moving in from the north. Mostly footmen, but with a small contingent of horse."

"That doesn't sound like one of their typical detachments."

"That's what I thought, Sir Heward, so I sent extra riders to gather more information, but we have yet to hear anything back."

"Something must have upset them."

"They may be trying to counter our garrison here, sir," offered Gardner.

"That's an excellent observation, Sergeant," the knight acknowledged.

"Should we take precautions?" asked Gardner.

Heward turned his attention back to Captain Caluman. "How far away did you say they were?"

"Miles yet," replied the Kurathian. "And I have men out to send word if they should move any closer."

"Good. You may return to your men, Captain, but send word if anything changes."

"Aye, sir."

Heward watched the captain depart.

"Sounds like trouble, sir."

"So it does," the knight agreed. "You'd better double the guards on the workers. I'd hate to get caught by surprise."

"Yes, sir."

Heward made his way to his desk and pulled out his logbook. As descendants of highly organized mercenaries, his people had prided themselves on centuries of professionalism, an ethic that had saved their kingdom on numerous occasions. Now he sat, quill in hand, recording all he'd heard. Once he was complete, his assistant would copy the ledger, sending the note by rider to the regional command in Hawksburg. All of that would, quite naturally, take time, and there was the very likelihood that if something were going to happen, it would be long done by the time word arrived. He had no doubt his decisions over the next few days might have far-reaching consequences.

Looking across the room, he spotted his fellow Knight of the Hound, Sir Preston. The marshal had sent him, along with his heavy cavalry, to Wickfield to handle just this type of situation, and Heward, for one, was quite relieved to be able to share the burden of command.

"Preston?" he called out.

"Yes?"

"Can I have a word?"

"Certainly." Sir Preston rose, walking over to Sir Heward, wearing a serious expression. "Something wrong, sir?"

"We're both knights. You can call me Heward."

"If you insist... Heward."

"There. That wasn't so bad, now, was it?"

"Not at all. Still, it begs repeating the question. Is something wrong?"

"You might say that. I've received reports of Norland movement. We don't know what it means at this point, but I think we should be prepared for any eventuality."

"You want me to ready the heavy cavalry?"

"Yes, I think that's for the best, don't you? They don't need to be mounted quite yet. We've plenty of time for that, but I'll need them in fighting shape by this afternoon."

Sir Preston smiled. "I'll make sure they stay clear of the tavern, then. Will this be an extended trip, do you think?"

"I can't really say. It depends entirely on our foes."

"Then I'll have the men sleep in shifts."

"An excellent idea. You're a good man, Preston."

"Thank you—"

"Heward," interjected the Axe, "not sir."

"Yes, of course, Heward."

"You know, you and I are very similar."

"We are?"

"Yes, we were both Knights of the Sword before becoming Hounds."

"I suppose we were, now that you mention it."

"Anyway," said Heward, "you should probably get some rest yourself. This could be a long day."

"If you insist."

"I do, and good work, Sir Preston. I'm glad you're here."

"Thank you. Is there anything else?"

"No, that's all for now."

Heward watched Sir Preston as he exited the building. Next, his eyes fell on Captain Wainwright. "Harold?"

The archer looked up. "Yes, Sir Heward?"

"The Norlanders seem to be up to something."

Wainwright stood. "Oh? Anything I should know about?"

"Not yet, but make sure your men are stocked up on arrows, would you?"

"Of course, sir."

"Are any of those towers complete yet?"

The captain thought for a moment. Along with the palisade, the Crown had authorized the construction of six towers. Although they were to be made of wood, they would still provide an ideal place to observe any approaching enemies.

"Not yet, but there's enough scaffolding for me to put a few men up there if you like."

"Then do so," said Heward, "and let me know if anyone sees anything out of the ordinary."

"Yes, sir."

Heward finished his entries, then turned the book over to an aide. It was strange to have so many people dedicated to assisting him, but he had to admit it freed him up to do so much more. Of course, the downside to having all the help was that it gave him much more time to worry.

The afternoon wore on. A Kurathian rider rode into Wickfield a little before dark. It seemed the Norlanders were moving, but the reports made little sense. The men from Brooksholde were moving east, marching parallel to the river while those from the north were approaching the newly vacated village. He wondered if this might be some sort of raid about to get underway, but then he remembered the rumours of civil war north of the river. Were they about to witness a clash of rivals?

Heward was jolted awake by Sergeant Gardner. The knight sat up at his desk, his back complaining.

"You should have gone to bed, sir. Did you manage to get any sleep at all?"

"A little. Have you news?"

The sergeant handed him a note. "This just came in."

The knight unfolded it, reading over its contents.

"Something happen?" the sergeant asked.

"Yes," said Heward, rising to his feet. "Please inform Sir Preston I'd like his men mounted as soon as possible."

"Trouble?"

"You might say that. The troops that came south to Brooksholde are heading eastward."

"Isn't that where the other lot marched?"

"It is," said Heward.

"What do you think that means?"

"I think there's going to be a battle."

"You mean they're going to kill each other? Surely that's good for us?"

"Not if they're fighting one of our allies."

"And how will we tell that," asked Gardner, "if you don't mind me asking?"

"We shall take some men north and see what we can learn."

"To fight?"

"Yes, why? Does that worry you?"

"No, sir, but crossing the border might create problems."

"I might remind you we're already at war, Sergeant, and in any event, we won't be going far."

"Yes, sir, only close enough to see who's fighting. And if one of them is an ally?"

"Then we help them, of course."

"Very well, sir."

Sergeant Gardner left the building, not so much running as moving at a quick pace, something Heward would have found quite comical had the situation not been so dire.

He called for some help, then began donning his armour in preparation for battle.

It was halfway through the morning by the time they crossed the river. Commander Lanaka led the three companies of Kurathian horse while Sir Preston and Sir Heward each brought a company of heavy cavalry. The Wincaster Light Horse brought up the rear under the command of Captain Carlson. Wickfield had ceased all work, instead erecting temporary barricades to help defend the village where the palisade was still under construction. Heward felt comfortable leaving the town's defence to the Wincaster bowmen but had sent riders to take word to both Hawksburg and Mattingly in case the situation should deteriorate.

They rode north, led by Lanaka's scouts. By noon, the Norlanders were in sight, but it wasn't quite what any of them were expecting. They topped a rise, halting to take stock of the view before them.

A group of people had formed into a rough line, armed with a variety of weapons. Heward stared for some time before realizing they held pitchforks and spears while wearing little armour, save for the occasional helmet. To their west, however, was arrayed a much more professionally equipped army. Heward pointed at the solid ranks. "Their flag, can you make it out?"

Lanaka strained. "It looks like a boar's head."

"That's the flag of Lord Hollis," said Sir Preston. "This part of the country belongs to him."

"Isn't he the fellow who invaded Merceria?" asked Captain Carlson.

"He is," said Heward. He looked around at his companions. "What do you say? Shall we teach him a lesson?"

He didn't need to ask twice. They all nodded, then rode off back to their respective companies. Heward sent the light cavalry off first, with the heavier horse waiting behind the ridge, keeping them hidden. His hope was that Hollis's troops would make straight for this other group, whoever it was, bringing them within striking distance.

The Kurathians went north, maintaining their distance, their intent to observe until the attack began. The Wincaster Light went south, keeping well out of sight until they could effectively cut off the enemy's retreat. They had talked of using this strategy for some time, occupying the nights of boredom with such, but now, having the chance to actually employ their plans, it was anything but dull.

Heward remained at the top of the rise, watching events unfold below. Lord Hollis's foot troops began moving forward, the sun glinting off their armour while his horsemen were deployed to either flank, though in relatively small numbers. The knight grinned, for Norland had lost a good portion of its cavalry trying to invade Merceria.

The enemy cavalry advanced at a sedate pace, holding back to remain beside the foot troops and look threatening. The defenders, for lack of a better term, stood their ground, brandishing weapons that identified them as mere villagers.

Heward raised his hand, signalling to those behind him who were hidden from the Norlander's view. When his hand sliced down, the Mercerian heavy cavalry started moving. Sir Preston called out the command, and the horns sounded, announcing to the world that battle was about to commence.

The Norland horsemen, hearing the horns, halted, and then the Wincaster Light appeared to the south, while to the north, the Kurathian cavalry were just coming into view.

Sir Heward could well imagine the enemy's panic as he rode to rejoin his men. He trotted his heavies around the edge of the ridge, conserving their strength for the final charge. He had a brief glimpse of his own light cavalry, both groups moving farther west to cut off the enemy's retreat, and then his attention was drawn back to the Norland footmen. Much to the poor villagers' relief, Hollis's men had halted and were now desperately trying to get into some sort of defensive formation.

Sir Heward urged his men into a gallop, closing the distance with all haste. They struck the line with a thunderous clap, the sound of steel on steel echoing through the air as weapons clashed. He was soon amongst them, slicing out with his axe. A man's head fell beneath his blade, then Heward's horse reared up, smashing another foe in the chest with its hooves. Beside him, his cavalry struck out, their practiced strokes felling the enemy left and right.

It was over almost as soon as it had begun. One moment the knight was swinging his axe into someone's arm, the next, there was no one left, for the enemy had broken, fleeing westward with no semblance of order. The Mercerian light horsemen would soon be picking them off in small groups as they sought safety.

Heward gave the order, and they began rounding up prisoners. Those who threw down their weapons were taken into custody, while those who didn't were promptly killed. It didn't take long for the Norlanders to realize the best chance for survival lay in surrender.

Dismounting, Heward passed the reins of his Mercerian Charger to one of his men, then looked over at the defenders. The villagers stood watching them warily, and he decided to remove his helmet to talk to them.

"Who speaks for you?" he called out.

"I do," replied an elderly man.

"My name is Sir Heward, Knight of the Hound. I represent the Amy of Queen Anna of Merceria."

"And what is that to us?"

"As you can see, we have defeated a common enemy."

"And now you will turn your troops to our destruction?"

"I promise you we mean you no harm. Tell me, what will you do now? Return to your homes?"

"We cannot," admitted the elderly villager. "The earl has seen to that."

"Then I invite you to come back with us to Merceria."

"To what end?"

"We will keep you safe until you can return home without fear of reprisal."

"Why should we trust you?"

Sir Heward shrugged. "If we'd wanted you dead, there's little you could have done to stop us."

Mutterings erupted from the villagers.

"Tell me, is it Lord Hollis who persecutes you?"

"It is," the man answered. "He has taken everything from us. Now he demands our very lives in sacrifice."

"I'm not sure I follow," said Heward.

"He is forcing us to fight for him, but we've had enough."

"And so you would fight against him?"

"We would," the man admitted, "or die trying, at any rate."

"What if you could fight on even terms?"

"What are you suggesting?"

"We could train and equip you, for a start."

"Why would you do such a thing?"

"Because your cause is just," Heward said. "Merceria has no designs on your kingdom. We wish only to live in peace."

"And yet you prepare to invade, or so we're told."

"That's true, I won't deny it, but do so only to defeat the lords who stand against us. Our conflict is with them, not you, the people of Norland."

"I wish I could believe you."

Sir Heward tossed his axe aside, then removed his gauntlets, throwing them to the ground as he stepped closer. "Then come, let me offer you the hand of friendship."

The villagers parted, allowing the old man to squeeze through. A battered old helm sat upon his head, while in his hand, he carried a rusty knife. As he walked closer, he tucked it into his belt and then halted right before the Knight of the Hound, who towered over him. The man gazed up into Sir Heward's eyes, trying to read his expression.

"I am Ardith," the man said, "a smith from Brooksholde."

"Greetings, Ardith of Brooksholde," said Heward, extending his hand. "Will you now accept my friendship in the spirit in which it's offered?"

The old man grasped Heward's hand in a firm grip. "On behalf of my people, I do so accept."

The knight nodded. "My men are from the village of Wickfield. Do you know of it?"

"Of course, though I have never set foot there."

"Then I invite you to do so now. I shall use my men to protect you while we march south. I can guarantee you, once across the river, your people will be safe from the hand of Lord Hollis."

"What will your queen make of such an offer?"

"She is a just and fair ruler," insisted Heward. "She will see the right of it, I am sure."

"Then lead on, Sir Knight, and take us to safety."

"I shall need time to see to my men, then we will be on our way." Taking note of the approach of Sir Preston, Heward paused. "You must excuse me a moment," he said. "There are things I must attend to."

"Very well," said Ardith. "I shall wait with my people."

Heward moved away from the villagers, plotting an intercept course with his fellow knight.

"Everything well?" called out Sir Preston.

"It is. I've convinced these poor people to accompany us back across the river."

"To what end?"

"They wish to fight Lord Hollis."

"They are untrained and ill-equipped, Heward."

"That they are, but both can be rectified."

Preston looked around the battlefield, a smile cracking his face.

"Something amusing?" Heward asked.

The younger knight swept his hand over the field of conflict. "It seems Lord Hollis has provided them with arms and armour."

Heward couldn't help but laugh. "So he has. We'll collect what we can and sort it all out, back in Wickfield."

SIX

Trouble in the Wood

Spring 965 MC

U rzath peered through the underbrush, then looked behind her, signalling with her hands.

Hayley interpreted the ranger's signs for Albreda's sake. "It looks like about two dozen, and they've set up a camp."

"I still can't imagine how they made it this far," said the Druid. "We're deep into the forest. I should have received warning."

"I can't explain that," said Hayley, "but the question still remains—what we can do about those intruders?"

"Do? We must eliminate them, what else?"

"We are outnumbered," cautioned the High Ranger.

Albreda gave her a look that would brook no argument. "I might remind you I am the Mistress of the Whitewood. I shall deal with them myself if necessary."

Hayley held up her hands. "We'll work together, but let's not just stumble in there with arrows flying. We don't want anyone getting away."

"You have a point, I suppose. What do you suggest?"

"It's getting dark. Once they've settled in for the night, we'll send in Skulnug to take out those on watch. When they've been eliminated, we'll move in and finish off the rest of them."

"And what am I to be doing during all of this?"

"I would prefer you to stay back here and watch."

"I will not sit back and do nothing!" insisted Albreda.

"Nor would I ask you to, but from here, you'll be better able to oversee the entire camp. That will allow you to use your magic however you see fit."

"A remarkably keen observation," said Albreda, a hint of reluctance to her voice. "I suppose there is hope for you after all."

"I shall take that as a compliment."

"If you must."

Hayley fell back, well out of earshot of the camp. There, she gathered the rest around her to explain what she had in mind.

"Bert, you and Sam make your way over to the south side of the clearing. Once Urzath and Skulnug begin their part, there's a good chance someone might awaken. If they do, you'll take them down with arrows, understood?"

"If Sam is going south, shouldn't I go north?" asked Ayles.

"No," said Hayley. "You might get in each other's way. The last thing we need you to be doing is shooting each other in the dark. Skulnug, you'll work your way around to the far side. When Urzath moves in from this side, you'll take out the sentry on the opposite side."

"What of the horses?" asked Gorath. "We don't want anyone using them to escape."

"That's where you and I come in."

"Might I suggest that I take care of that?" offered Albreda.

"What are you going to do?" said Ayles, a smirk on his face. "Talk to them?"

Albreda gave him a withering glare. "That is precisely what I'm going to do. Horses can be quite reasonable animals if one treats them with a little respect. Now off you go, all of you. We haven't a moment to waste."

Ayles was dumbstruck. It took Sam giving him a shove to get him moving into position. Hayley moved up to the edge of the camp, Gorath beside her. They watched, waiting for everyone else to get into position.

A bird chirped, the signal to begin, and Urzath moved forward, a long knife in hand. The sentry didn't stand a chance. One moment he was warming his hands by the fire, the next, he was lying in a pool of his own blood. Skulnug's target never saw the attack coming either. He was pacing, his feet obscured by the brambles and weeds, then he just fell to the ground, his cries stifled.

～

Albreda quietly approached the horses, then reached out a soothing hand, pausing when her eyes caught sight of a pile of saddles sitting nearby. But it was not the saddles that stopped her in her tracks and turned her curiosity into rage, it was the collection of wolf pelts. She felt her blood boil, and without even thinking, turned from the horses, heading directly towards the sleeping Norlanders.

Into the camp she strode as bold as brass. When words of power thundered from her mouth, the entire forest came alive. Skulnug dove to the side when the trees began to move, whipping their branches across the clearing, plucking men from their blankets. A distant howl echoed through the woods as Albreda turned and pointed at the fire. A tiny dot of light flew from her finger to sink into the ash, and then something began to sprout from its depths.

The Norlanders, those not already thrown into the woods, began shouting in alarm. One stood, only to be brought down by Urzath's knife. Another rolled over, grabbing a crossbow, but an arrow took him in the chest, with Sam yelling, "Got him!"

Small green vines stretched out from the fire, growing thicker as they searched for victims. Some caught fire, creating a macabre scene as the burning vines began sprouting razor-sharp thorns.

One of the Norlanders, leaping to his feet with a hatchet in hand, rushed at the Druid with a primal scream. A grey blur sprinted across the clearing, grabbing the man's leg before he could reach her and bore him to the ground. Snarl growled as he attacked, rending flesh from bone.

The remaining Norlanders were now up, having seized whatever weapons were at hand. Hayley kept up a constant barrage of arrows while Gorath moved in closer, drawing his axe.

A yelp issued from the great wolf as a sword scraped across his side. His attacker pulled back his blade for another strike, but an arrow took him in the shoulder. He fell to the ground in agony, only to be smothered by the ever-growing flaming vines.

Albreda's voice grew in intensity as the very forest began to loom over them. With the sound of a tremendous crash, a mighty root broke the surface, reaching out to grasp a Norlander by the ankle. He screamed as it twisted around his leg, then pulled him into the ground, driving the air from his lungs. Moments later, all that remained was his head and shoulders protruding from the ground, all sign of life extinguished.

Hayley, calling the rangers back, stared in awe at the devastation unleashed by the Druid. Then the ground began to tremble, small gaps appearing and growing in size to form an ever-widening chasm that seemed to have no bottom.

Albreda fell to her knees, tears streaming down her face. There she remained for just a moment before her eyes rolled up into her head, and she keeled over. As suddenly as the rumbling began, it ceased, and the forest grew quiet once more.

"Wait here," ordered Hayley as she made her way towards the fallen Druid. Pausing at the ravine, she looked down into its depths, but it was not as deep as she had feared. She jumped across the gap, careful not to lose her footing as she landed on the other side. Snarl limped towards the motionless Druid, crouching by her head to lick her cheek.

"Albreda?" called out the ranger. "Can you hear me?"

The Mistress of the Whitewood sat up rather unexpectedly and wiped her nose with her sleeve, noting the blood. "What happened?"

"You destroyed the Norlanders," said Hayley.

"Oh, yes. I remember now."

"What happened to the plan?"

"I couldn't help myself. I saw the pelts, you see."

"Pelts?"

"Yes, over by the horses. Wolf pelts."

"You mean?"

"Yes," Albreda said, "they must have slaughtered the pack. They were my family, Hayley. Would you have done any less for yours?"

"I understand, but you very nearly got us all caught up in it. A little warning would have been nice."

"I do apologize, but I was upset."

"So we saw," said Hayley. "I had no idea you could do something like that."

"Nor did I. I'm afraid I lost control. One of the hazards of being a wild mage, I suppose."

"Has this ever happened before?"

"Not to this scale." Albreda spat out some blood. "My throat feels absolutely parched."

"You must rest," insisted Hayley.

"But we have to get to the Hollis estate."

"We have plenty of time for that. And in any event, now that we have horses, we'll be able to make up for lost time."

"Yes, I suppose we will," muttered the Druid. "Help me to my feet, will you? I feel a little weak."

With Gorath's help, they steered her over to an overturned stump. Urzath and Skulnug began searching the bodies, looking for anything that might give a clue as to why the Norlanders were here in the Whitewood.

Hayley examined Snarl's wounds, then used a damp cloth to clean them as best she could. Throughout the ordeal, the great beast simply sat there, his eyes locked on his mistress.

"There, that should do, though I wish Aubrey were here."

"You need a paste of kingsleaf," suggested Albreda.

"Kingsleaf?" said Sam. "That has to be brewed, doesn't it?"

"Usually, yes, but it's rather difficult to get a wolf to drink it. I've found a paste works rather well, especially when you combine it with warriors moss."

"A great idea, but where in the world do we find such luxuries?"

"Right behind you, dear," said Albreda. "You're almost sitting on it."

Samantha turned in surprise. "So it is!"

"Come," said Hayley, "you look after our Druid friend while I see to that."

The young ranger replaced Hayley. Albreda reached out, holding the woman's arm to steady herself. "I feel quite faint."

"You're not going to pass out on me, are you?"

The Druid's voice grew frosty. "I'm not THAT faint."

"She's back to normal," announced Sam.

Hayley smiled. "So I see. Keep an eye on her anyway. She's too stubborn to admit she needs rest."

"I do not need rest!" insisted Albreda.

"See what I mean?"

The High Ranger got to work collecting some warriors moss.

By the next morning, the Druid looked much recovered. They buried the wolf pelts by dropping them into the fissure, then Albreda used her magic to seal it, returning the woods to its original state. Snarl let out a mournful howl that felt like it lasted an eternity.

"What do we do now?" asked Ayles.

"We continue on," said Hayley. "Are you up to it, Albreda?"

"Of course," said the Druid, but her face still looked drawn and pale. "Snarl can lead the way."

They rose to continue, but Albreda stumbled. Sam moved up beside her. "Here, lean on me," she said.

Hayley wore a worried look but hid it quickly. "Put her on one of the captured horses," she said.

"What do we do with all the extras?" asked Urzath.

"Let them go," said Albreda. "They will be safe within these woods."

Halfway through the morning, they stopped to rest. Hayley crouched by a small stream, scooping up handfuls of water while Snarl drank thirstily. The great wolf's ears pricked up, and then he went rigid, an action that was not missed by the ranger. She acted quickly, stringing her bow and nocking an arrow. The rest of the group was some distance off, resting amongst a small clearing and chatting amiably, but the wolf was focused in the opposite direction.

Snarl let out a howl that echoed through the woods, then waited, his eyes facing eastward. Hayley heard the reply—a higher-pitched sound, far off in the distance. She glanced back at the camp, but there was no sign anyone had caught wind of it. She thought of informing Albreda, but the Druid had yet to fully recover from her ordeal.

"Looks like it's up to us," she said. Snarl's head pivoted to look at her. "Go on," she urged, "I'll be right behind you."

The great wolf ran off into the forest, leaving Hayley struggling to keep up. She leaped over a fallen trunk, then passed by a low-hanging bough, feeling the branches sting her face as she ploughed on. Ahead of her, she could barely make out Snarl, hurtling into the distance.

In a moment of distraction, Hayley's foot snagged on a twig, and she tumbled to the forest floor, the wind driven from her lungs. Cursing her bad luck, she rose, shaking loose the leaves that clung to her. Looking around, she realized the wolf was out of view, leaving her in the middle of an unknown forest with no sight of friend or foe. Others might have panicked, but Hayley was raised by a poacher; such terrain held little fear for her.

"Snarl?" she called out. "Where are you?"

The answer came as another howl, allowing her to determine the general direction. She took a deep breath. "All right, let's see if you can do this without tripping," she said to herself as she exploded into a run, eager to close the distance.

The wolf howled again and again, a mournful cry that tore into Hayley's heart. Was he injured? She finally stumbled into a glade, almost tripping over the wolf in her rush. Fighting to catch her breath, she looked around. Snarl was standing over something and howling. It took a moment for the ranger to realize what it was. Moving closer, she spotted fur, then it moved, revealing blue eyes and a pale-grey muzzle.

"You found a wolf pup," she said, leaning closer.

The poor little thing looked lost and forlorn, its coat matted and covered in burrs. Hayley dug through her pack, fishing out a piece of dried meat. The animal stumbled forward, limping slightly. Snarl moved closer to the ranger, sniffing her hand, then took the meat, dropping it before the pup. The tiny wolf picked it up hesitantly, then began chewing.

"Well, aren't you the cutest little thing," said Hayley, "and out here all alone? We can't have that, now, can we?"

She reached out, touching the rough fur gently. The pup shrank back, the meat still held firmly in its mouth.

All her life, the High Ranger had found nature fascinating. She was under no misconceptions, of course, for animals could be dangerous creatures, but here, in this glade, this little one tugged at her heartstrings.

Snarl lay down on the forest floor, and the pup began to relax. Hayley, seeing the effect, sat, determined to wait out this encounter. Her hand sought her pack, pulling forth more meat. At this rate, she'd run out of food before they reached Beaconsgate, but she thought the situation worth it.

The ranger wasn't sure how long she sat there, but she must have dozed off. She awoke to find the wolf pup snuggled into her leg, fast asleep. Carefully, lest she wake the poor thing, she began plucking the burrs from its fur.

"Well now," she said in a soothing tone, "what are we going to do with you?"

Snarl looked up at her, and she could sense a smile behind his eyes. "Don't worry, we'll look after him."

The snap of a twig brought her senses alive. At first, she thought a predator had found them, but Snarl appeared unconcerned.

"Hayley?" came a familiar voice. "Where are you?"

"Over here," she called back. The pup stirred but overcome with its exertions, it soon fell back asleep.

The sound drew closer, and then Albreda appeared from behind some trees. "What have you there?"

"A wolf pup," said Hayley. "Snarl found him."

The Druid looked down at the little creature. "He must belong to the pack the Norlanders killed."

"What do we do with him?" Hayley asked, fearing the answer.

"We must take him with us, of course."

Relief flooded the ranger. "Thank Saxnor for that. I thought you'd want us to leave him."

"Why would I do that?"

"It's the law of nature, isn't it? The strong survive, the weak perish?"

"What a load of rubbish," said Albreda. "The strong look after the weak. It's the whole basis of the pack."

"But he's so young."

"Old enough to eat meat, at least. Any younger, and we'd have had no choice but to let him perish."

"How old do you think he is?" asked Hayley.

"No more than a month, I should think. I'm surprised to see him here. His den must have been relatively close by."

"He looks to be having difficulty chewing."

"He's still young. At his age, his mother would have pre-chewed the meat. You'll have to do the same for him."

"You mean I have to vomit?"

"No," said Albreda, "though that's what his mother would do. Just take a bite and chew it, then spit it out. He'll carry on from there."

"Can't you do that?"

"You're the one he's chosen as his new mother."

"Me?" said Hayley. "I can't be his mother. I'm the High Ranger."

"And?"

"I'm too busy!"

Albreda looked down at the small pup and smiled. "It seems you have little choice."

The ranger's hand instinctively stroked the little creature. Hayley could feel tears welling up inside of her. "Oh, very well."

"You should give him a name, you know. Something to call him other than 'pup.'"

"How about Gryph?"

"A fine name, and one that reflects your fascination with nature." Albreda knelt, reaching out to touch the pup. "Well, Gryph, what do you think of your new name?"

In answer, the tiny wolf opened his eyes, letting out a big yawn. Hayley moved slowly, rising to her feet. Reaching down, she plucked her new friend from the ground and held him against her chest. He responded by licking her face. "He likes me."

"I'm sure he does," said Albreda, "but he's actually telling you he's hungry."

"He is?"

"Yes. A wolf pup will lick its mother's mouth, and that's what causes her to regurgitate food."

"I wish you hadn't told me that."

"Why?"

"It makes my stomach feel queasy."

"It's a perfectly natural behaviour."

"Not to me," said Hayley. "In any event, he's had enough to eat for now. Hadn't we best get moving?"

"Yes, of course. The others are right behind me."

Albreda retraced her steps, leading them back to the rest of the group. The sight of Gryph soon took their attention, resulting in all sorts of questions that threatened to delay their mission even further. Hayley finally put an end to the discussion by insisting they leave the subject alone until they camped for the night.

That evening they sat around the fire, discussing their plans.

"We shall soon be reaching the edge of the Whitewood," said Albreda. "From there, we'll be crossing relatively open ground."

"And where is the estate of Lord Hollis?" asked Sam.

"North of the city," said Hayley. "Close to another great forest."

"The Lingerwood," added Albreda.

"Funny name, that," observed Bertram Ayles. "Why do they call it that?"

"Because people who travel there often remain."

"So they live in the forest?"

"No," said the Druid. "They die there, and their souls linger."

The man's face turned ashen. "And we're going there?"

Hayley chuckled. "Not directly, no. The estate is just outside of its borders."

"Thank the Gods for that."

"Ouch," said Hayley, turning her attention to Gryph. "Do you mind? Those are my fingers."

"He's a voracious fellow," said Sam.

"So he is."

"It will pass, in time," said Uzrath. "The wolves of the Black Arrow are similar in nature."

"How many wolves does the tribe have?" asked Hayley.

"About two dozen. They are stalwart hunting companions."

"I'm surprised you don't use them in the rangers," said Skulnug. "They are quite useful at tracking."

"True," the High Ranger replied, "but we spend a lot of time in cities. I'm not sure their presence would be welcome."

"What about the army?" asked Ayles. "Ever thought of using them in battle?"

"Albreda has occasionally used them," said Hayley, "but they're better suited to tracking and stalking."

"Yes," agreed Sam, "unlike those Kurathian Mastiffs."

"I wonder what Tempus would make of Gryph?" said Gorath.

"I think they'd get along," said Hayley. "Tempus may be big, but he's honestly just a big softy."

"A softy who can rip your throat out," said Ayles.

"Only if you upset him," added Albreda.

SEVEN

Weldwyn

Spring 965 MC

A nna slowed her pace, allowing Gerald to catch up.

"You're in a hurry," he remarked.

"It's not every day I get to visit my in-laws," she replied. "And without the inconvenience of a long carriage ride, I might add."

"The magic circles do have their advantages. Is Alric coming?"

"Of course. I could hardly visit his parents without him."

"Then where is he?"

"I sent him on ahead," she said. "Aubrey had to take Kraloch anyway, in order for him to commit the Summersgate circle to memory. Alric thought it expedient for him to accompany them. That way, he could announce our arrival."

"And now they're back?"

"Well, Aubrey and Kraloch are. My husband will remain there to help his parents prepare for my arrival."

"You seem to have everything thought out."

Anna smiled. "Thank you. It's what I do."

"You've always been a planner."

"Something I got from you."

"Me?" said Gerald. "I'd hardly call myself an expert in such things."

"You wouldn't call yourself an expert in ANYTHING, but you're the finest military commander in the history of Merceria."

"I'd hardly call myself that."

"No," she agreed, "you wouldn't, but I would."

A bark echoed from down the corridor, and then the heavy footsteps of Tempus followed, along with the maid, Sophie, rushing to catch up.

"Is he being trouble again?" asked Gerald.

"No," Sophie replied. "He's just full of energy. Do you think he knows we're going to Weldwyn?"

"No, I expect he's picking up on the queen's excitement."

"Well, why wouldn't I get excited?" said Anna. "After all, it's not every day we get to visit a foreign kingdom."

Gerald laughed. "I suppose that's true. Is everyone else ready?"

"Beverly will meet us at the casting circle, along with some guards."

"And Fitz?"

"I shall be leaving him behind this time. With Hayley away, I need someone I can trust to run the country."

"We'll only be gone a few days."

"True," agreed the queen, "but I shouldn't like to return to find trouble has been brewing in my absence. The nobles trust the baron, and I know he can keep them in line."

"It's too bad Albreda isn't back yet. She could keep him company."

"Aldwin will be here to help."

"I thought he'd be going with us?"

"Why would you think that?"

"He's Beverly's husband."

"He is," said Anna, "and ordinarily, I would agree with your reasoning, but he's doing something for me."

"Which is?"

"If you must know, he's designing the next magical circle."

"And where will that be going?"

"I haven't decided yet. I thought Eastwood, but Kingsford might be a better choice. Eventually, of course, I'd like to have one in every major town and city in Merceria, but we can't very well bankrupt the realm to do it."

"A valid point," said Gerald. "I hadn't considered that."

"That's what I'm here for. You take care of the army, and I'll take care of the rest."

"Works for me."

They halted, waiting as the guards opened the ornate doors that led into the casting room. Inside stood Aubrey and Kraloch, along with a series of chests and boxes.

"Good morning, Your Majesty," said the Life Mage.

"Aubrey," said the queen, nodding her head as she entered the room. "Master Kraloch, so good to see you."

The Orc bowed, appearing awkward in his ceremonial attire.

"*I see you've decided to wear your formal robes,*" said Gerald, using the tongue of the Orcs.

"*I have,*" replied the shaman. "*Is it not proper to do so?*"

"*It is. I'm just not used to seeing them outside of your village.*"

"*Indeed,*" said the Orc. "*I had to go through the gate to retrieve them.*" He glanced at his feet, which extended some distance beyond the bottom of his robes. "*It seems I have grown somewhat since last I wore them.*"

"Never mind," said Anna. "If this becomes a regular thing, I'll have some new ones sewn up for you, provided there is no objection, of course."

Kraloch bowed. "I would be most honoured."

"We took the liberty of taking some of the chests on our first trip," said Aubrey, "and I'll return later for the rest."

"I never realized how much baggage I've acquired," said Anna. "Things were so much easier in the old days."

"Don't worry," said Gerald. "If we do this often enough, you can just leave clothes there."

"A good idea. We'll have to set up an embassy, much as Leofric did here."

"I'm sure he'd be amenable to the suggestion."

"Lady Beverly is here, Your Majesty," called out a guard.

The red-headed knight entered, resplendent in her metal armour. She bowed. "I have brought the guards," she said.

Behind her were eight warriors, each in the heavy armour of the Guard Cavalry.

"Excellent," said the queen. She moved closer, examining each guard and chatting amiably. Gerald marvelled at her easy manner. She was a queen who had earned a deep devotion from her people.

Finally done, Anna turned to Lady Aubrey. "You're in charge of this trip," she said. "How would you like to split us up?"

"I'll take you, Gerald, Sophie, and Tempus first. Kraloch will follow shortly after with Beverly and the guards."

"You're sure he can accommodate that many?"

"Of course," said Aubrey. "The lack of horses makes it so much easier. Would you care to step into the circle?"

"Certainly," said Anna. She shifted her position, calling Tempus to her side. Moments later, Gerald took his own place, along with Sophie.

Aubrey moved to stand in the very centre of the casting circle, closing her eyes and taking a deep breath. Words of power tumbled from her mouth, and then the runes inlaid on the floor began to glow.

Gerald stood beside the queen, looking over at Kraloch and Beverly, who stood outside the circle, along with the guards, watching with great interest as the magic began to build. When the last rune lit up, a cylinder of light erupted from the floor, obscuring his view. The next moment the air changed, and as the bright light faded from view, he saw they were inside the Grand Edifice of the Arcane Wizards Council of Weldwyn, better known as 'The Dome'. And instead of Kraloch and Beverly, a trio of mages waited to greet them.

Tyrel Caracticus, their appointed leader, stepped forward, bending at the waist in a bow. "Your Majesty, welcome to Weldwyn."

"Thank you, Master Caracticus," said Anna. "Would you care to introduce your companions?"

"Certainly," the mage replied. "This is Aegryth Malthunen, our Earth Mage." He paused, waiting as the woman bowed. "And this"—indicating the second—"is Osbourne Megantis, a Fire Mage."

"I prefer Pyromancer," the man insisted.

Gerald noted Osbourne's lack of greeting but said nothing. He had heard Weldwyn Mages were notorious for being rude, although, in truth, he had met few. His main experience had been with the healer, Roxanne Fortuna, and she had been almost as polite as Aubrey. Perhaps that reflected the fact that she was a fellow healer.

"So pleased to make your acquaintance," said Anna. "We aren't blessed with Pyromancers in Merceria. Maybe you'd like to visit one day?"

"I should think that unlikely," the man responded. "My studies keep me quite busy, but I do appreciate the invitation."

"This is Gerald Matheson," said Anna, "marshal of my army and my very dear friend. In addition, I've brought Lady Sophie"—she waited as her maid bowed—"and, of course, my dog, Tempus."

"Ah, yes," said Tyrel. "The famous Kurathian Mastiff. I've heard much about him. I understand he caused quite a stir on his first visit?"

"He did indeed," said Anna.

"The king is expecting you," said Tyrel. "We'll send word to the Palace once the rest of your party arrives. In the meantime, can I offer you some refreshments?"

"That would be nice."

They cleared the circle, taking a seat at a nearby table as they waited. The doors opened, admitting a bevy of young men and women, each carrying a tray filled with food and drink.

"Servants?" said Gerald.

"In a sense," said Tyrel. "They're actually students who have come here to learn magic."

"You seem to have quite a few of them."

"It's out of necessity, I can assure you."

"Necessity?"

"Yes. They're all eager to learn the craft, of course, but many of them will lack the potential to become spell casters."

"A pity," said Gerald. "If only you could tell which ones had the potential." He looked at Aubrey, but the young Life Mage remained silent.

Anna lifted a chalice. "To your health, Master Caracticus."

"And yours," replied the Water Mage.

They each took a sip, then Gerald reached across, selecting a tasty-looking pastry from a plate. "This reminds me of the ones back in Uxley. Do you remember?"

Anna's eyes lit up. "I do," she said, reaching out to pick one up. She took a bite and let out a soft exclamation of satisfaction. "Mmm, this is delicious."

Tyrel Caracticus looked quite pleased. "It's a favourite of ours," he said. "Studying magic is an exhausting pastime, and diversions such as this are a welcome respite."

"I may have to take some of these back with me," said Anna.

"I'm sure that can be arranged."

The room was bathed in light as the floor runes began to glow.

"That must be Beverly and the others," said Gerald, selecting another morsel.

"Careful there, Marshal," said Anna. "You want to leave some room for dinner."

"It would be discourteous of me to refuse the hospitality," he countered.

She laughed. "You're becoming quite the diplomat, at least when it comes to food." She held out a pastry, allowing Tempus to gingerly take it. The action elicited a gasp from the Fire Mage, something that didn't fail to escape the queen's attention.

"Do you not like dogs, Master Megantis?"

"Arcanus Megantis," the man corrected her, "and no, not particularly. I find them to be rather unclean beasts, useful for little outside of guarding cattle."

Gerald let out a guffaw just as a cylinder of light shot up from the floor. He had meant to offer a reply, but the impending appearance of the rest of their party threw all such thoughts from his head. The light dimmed, revealing Beverly, Kraloch, and the guards.

"Now that you're all here," said Tyrel, "I will send word to King Leofric. Would your guards like something to drink while we wait?"

"Certainly," said Anna. "I assume you've already met Kraloch?"

"Yes," said Tyrel. "He arrived earlier to examine our magic circle."

"This is Dame Beverly Fitzwilliam," she continued, "Knight Commander of the Order of the Hound, and my personal bodyguard."

"It is an honour," said the mage. "Your fame precedes you."

"My fame?"

"Yes, everyone has heard of your part in the Battle of Norwatch."

"I wasn't the only one there," she protested.

"True, but you are a woman warrior. A rare thing in these parts."

"Rare indeed," agreed Anna. "Maybe I should speak to King Leofric about changing that."

"That is, of course, your prerogative," said Tyrel. "Would you like a tour of the Dome while we await word from the king?"

"That would be nice. Thank you."

"We are currently on the topmost floor," explained Tyrel, "with a circular corridor that runs around its perimeter. Beneath the casting circle is our primary library."

"Primary?" exclaimed Anna. "You mean you have more than one?"

"We do. Three, to be exact."

"Why three libraries?" asked Gerald. "Do you have that many books?"

"No," said Tyrel, "but the primary library is used by our students. We don't want them getting into more advanced topics until they're ready."

"I take it the others are kept locked?" said Anna.

"They are, Your Majesty."

"Fascinating." She turned to Gerald. "We must do something similar in Hawksburg."

"Hawksburg?" said Tyrel. "I don't believe I'm familiar with that place."

"It's my home," offered Aubrey, "and the future site of our magical academy."

The mage wore a look of surprise that was easy to see. "A tremendous undertaking," he said, "and one I wish you only the best of luck with, but I fear you shall quickly become disillusioned."

"Why would you say that?" said Aubrey.

"As I mentioned earlier, very few students hold the true potential to be a mage."

"Do you have any idea what the actual percentage is?"

"Less than one in twenty, I'm afraid, and you must remember, we only take students we feel carry the magic in their bloodlines. What of yourself? Was your mother a mage?"

"No," said Aubrey, "but my great-grandmother was."

"Ah, there you have it, then. You would have been sought out as a student had you lived here in Weldwyn."

"I managed well enough. Of course, I didn't know magic was in my blood. That didn't come out until well after I'd been apprenticed."

"Might I ask who discovered it?"

"It was actually Beverly who first noticed my affinity." Aubrey turned to the red-headed knight. "Cousin?"

"Yes, that's right," said Beverly. "I went to Hawksburg to stay for a while, and that's when I noticed her dexterity with her hands. She did exquisite needlework, you see, and was an avid reader."

"And so you assumed she was a mage?" asked Tyrel.

"Not at first, no. It was only later when I was travelling with Revi Bloom, and he mentioned how busy he was. I asked him why he didn't have an apprentice, and he claimed he had no time to train one."

"I'm afraid I don't see how that led to Lady Aubrey learning the arts."

"Oh," said Beverly, "I haven't finished yet. I then asked Master Bloom about magic, and he revealed that those with power often manifest certain traits."

"Ah, I see now," said Tyrel. "He mentioned mental discipline and dexterous hands."

"Is that how you seek out new students?" asked the knight.

"It is, or at least, it's one of the ways. We also research family trees and investigate reports of unusual events."

"Such as?" said Gerald.

"Oh, the usual things."

"Yes," added Aegryth. "I was discovered because of my affinity with animals. It's prevalent amongst Earth Mages."

Gerald looked at Osbourne. "What about you? Did you start setting fires at an early age?"

"I beg your pardon?" said the Fire Mage.

"You know," pressed the marshal, "to show your affinity for fire, I mean."

Gerald received a stern look in response. "I most decidedly did not. I'll have you know my family has been using magic for generations."

"How nice for you," said Gerald, biting his tongue.

"Come," said Aegryth. "Let's show them the library, shall we?"

"Of course," said Tyrel. "It's this way if you'd like to follow me?"

"Lead on, Grand Master," said Anna.

"Yes," said Gerald quietly, "before this fellow sets the world aflame."

They went out into a corridor where the windows were spaced at regular intervals, large enough to let in light, but with shutters to close up during inclement weather.

Master Caracticus led them down an ornate stairway. One of two, he told them, that allowed access between floors. They passed by at least a dozen students, each appearing to be in their teens.

"Have you no older students?" asked Aubrey.

"Older?" said Tyrel.

"Yes. Surely there are many potential users of magic who might have aged?"

"While that is true, our history tells us they seldom make good students. Too set in their ways, you see."

Gerald scoffed.

"You disagree with that?" asked their host.

"I train soldiers," said Gerald, "and it's usually the older types which are easier to deal with. You simply have to know how to communicate with them."

"I should hardly say magic is the same thing. Any old person can be taught to poke a spear."

"Is that what you think we do? Hand a spear and say go stick the other end into the enemy? I'll have you know soldiering is a difficult profession. We take it quite seriously back home in Merceria."

"I did not mean to give offence," said Tyrel. "I merely meant fighting is a more physical endeavour while magic requires a higher level of concentration."

Gerald opened his mouth, about to argue the point, but Anna gripped his arm.

"Tell us," she said, "how many actual mages do you have in Weldwyn?"

"I am one of five greater mages, and we have another seven in the various stages of their training."

Aubrey gasped. "Are you telling me that out of all these students, you've only managed to identify seven with potential?"

"Sadly, that's true. As I said, I wish you well with your new academy, but I fear you will have few students of your own."

"And if we did, somehow, manage to identify more, do you think your mages would be interested in assisting us?"

"I should think such a thing is not beyond reason, but training a mage takes many years."

"How many years?" asked Gerald.

"Ten to twenty, at least," said Tyrel.

"Then you are doing it wrong," offered Kraloch. He had remained quiet until now, but his remarks caused all three Weldwyn mages to stare at him.

"Why would you say that?"

"Our shamans usually learn their magic within a year, two at the most."

"That might be all well and good for the primitive magic of the Orcs," insisted Osbourne Megantis, "but we're talking of Humans here. It is a much higher level of learning."

"But we have taught Humans. I was telling our Magic Council of this very thing only a few days ago."

"What type of magic?" said the Fire Mage, his expression growing bored. "Working with trees, perhaps?"

"I must object," said Aegryth. "Magic of the earth is quite complex. Just because you use fire doesn't mean you can rub it in people's noses."

"I believe," said Aubrey, "that the Human in question was taught Fire Magic. Isn't that correct, Kraloch?"

"It is indeed," said the Orc.

Aegryth chuckled. "You should know better than to correct one of the elder races, Osbourne," she said.

"He's an Orc," counted the Fire Mage, "not an Elf or Dwarf."

Now it was Anna's turn to intervene once again. "The Orcs have an ancient tradition of magic, far more so than the Elves, if I'm not mistaken."

"That is true," said Kraloch. "In fact, it was the Orcs who gave magic to the first Humans."

"Ridiculous," said Osbourne. "Everyone knows it was the Elves."

"I shall not debate the issue," said the shaman, "but I think, if you dig deep enough, you will discover it unlikely."

"What makes you say that?"

"Simple," said Anna. "Elves are very secretive people. Have you ever known them to willingly share anything?"

"That's different. The modern Elf is merely a descendant of a once-great race."

Anna was about to speak. Indeed, her face betrayed a growing fury.

"An interesting theory," interrupted Gerald, "but a debate best saved for a different time."

He could tell Osbourne felt nothing of the sort, but then Tyrel Caracticus stepped in. "Quite right. Now, here we are, the library."

The mage threw open the door, revealing a massive room held within. Gerald knew it was only an illusion created by the rounded walls, but the shelves of books appeared to stretch on and on.

Anna was immediately enthralled. "I could stay here forever."

"Your Majesty is free to come and visit anytime," offered Tyrel.

"There was a time when nobles were not allowed in here," said Osbourne, a little perturbed.

"All that changed with our new alliance," added Tyrel. "It's the sharing of knowledge that has led to the golden age of magic in which we now find ourselves."

"I would hardly call it a golden age," said the Fire Mage.

Anna was too engrossed to bother adding her own thoughts.

"Her Majesty is an avid reader," explained Gerald, "and remembers everything she reads."

"A pity you don't have magical potential," offered Osbourne. "You would have made an ideal candidate for this grand edifice."

"Aubrey's quite the reader as well," said Anna. "And a dedicated student. How long did it take you to master Life Magic, Aubrey?"

Lady Brandon placed her hand to her chin, thinking a moment. "Let's see, Revi taught me my first spell back in 960."

"Why, that's only five years ago, and you've already mastered it?" said Tyrel. "Astounding. Master Bloom must be quite the mentor."

"Master Bloom only got me started; the rest I've had to learn on my own. It's all quite a long tale, actually. My biggest breakthrough was finding my great-grandmother's notes. Of course, since then, I've learned much from Master Kraloch, not to mention Albreda."

"Albreda taught you magic?" said Tyrel. "But she's an Earth Mage, isn't she?"

"She didn't teach me spells, but she did give me advice on how to unlock new magic."

"New magic?"

"Yes, how else would you develop new spells?"

Osbourne sneered. "Spells are passed down from generation to generation. They must be carefully learned. They are not the playthings of the young."

"If that were true," said Aubrey, "then who developed the first spells? You don't seriously think they were passed down from the Gods, do you?"

"I... hadn't thought of that," admitted the Fire Mage.

Aegryth was beaming. "Finally, someone has managed to shut him up. Come, Your Majesty, let me show you our history section. All of the books here are much too dull for someone like you." She took the queen's hand, leading her farther down the rows of books.

"We've lost her now," said Gerald. "She'll be in here for days."

"That's all right," soothed Aubrey. "Sooner or later, Prince Alric will get here. If there's anyone who can get her mind off of books, it's him."

"I find the Human tradition of books to be most interesting," said Kraloch. "My people pass things down from generation to generation, but it is an entirely oral tradition."

"But surely you have a written language?" said Aegryth. "Didn't you once have cities?"

"We did," the Orc replied, "and yet with their loss, so, too, went our written accounts. We live a simple life now, with no paper or parchment on which to write, even if we did possess the knowledge."

"We are changing that," added Aubrey, "although slowly. I've been teaching Kraloch the written language of Merceria. It's not Orcish, but at least it's a way in which to record things."

"Agreed, and yet I wonder what knowledge we might still possess if it hadn't been for the destruction of our cities."

"Did all your cities face destruction?" asked Aegryth.

"As far as we know. The last was the great city of Toknar-Ghul, but eventually, even it succumbed."

"And where was this great city?"

"No one knows," said Kraloch, "not even the Ancestors. It is as if they lost all their shamans."

"So it may still be out there somewhere," suggested Aubrey.

"Perhaps, but it is unlikely to ever be found. Still, it is nice to think at least part of our past survived unscathed."

"The past is important, of course," said Gerald, "but it's the future we must look to. We've come to talk to King Leofric about that very subject."

"I'm sure his delegate will arrive in due course," said Tyrel. "Truth is, I'm surprised he isn't already here."

A student looked up from his book. "But he is, Master Caracticus."

"What do you mean, 'he is'?"

"He was here in the library shortly before you arrived."

"Then where is he?"

"I don't know," the young man replied. "He muttered something about going up to the casting room. Did you not pass him in the hallway?"

"We most certainly did not. Are you sure that's what he said?"

"He did, right before he left by that door." The man pointed.

"Ah, that explains it. It appears he took the other stairs. I'll go and fetch him, shall I?" Tyrel turned his attention back to the student. "Who was it you saw?"

"The prince, Master."

A look of impatience flickered across the Grand Mage's face. "Which prince?"

"The youngest. I think his name is Alric?"

"You think? You're a student of the Dome, for Malin's sake. Have you not learned to be precise?"

"Sorry, I was rather preoccupied with my studies."

EIGHT

The Hollis Estate

Spring 965 MC

H ayley crouched by the edge of the forest, peering at the distant town of Beaconsgate.

"Not the prettiest of places," offered Gorath. "It's missing the symmetry of a Mercerian town."

"Symmetry?" replied the High Ranger.

"Yes. This is far more spread out and lacks a sense of organization."

"That's because Mercerian towns were founded in a time of war. The buildings are close together to help in defence."

"And yet these Norlanders are descended from your people, are they not?"

"They are," said Hayley. "Why?"

"Would they not adopt the same customs?"

"You must remember a Mercerian army has never set foot in Norland before. They've had little reason for such precautions."

"And yet they fight amongst themselves. That is the definition of a civil war, is it not?"

"It is," said Hayley. "Tell me, have the Orcs ever fought amongst themselves?"

"No," said Gorath. "At least not that I'm aware of. It might have been so in the days of the great cities, but that is far in the past. These days, the Orcs are scattered. Very seldom will two tribes find themselves in the same hunting grounds."

"And if it does happen, do they fight?"

"I doubt it. Kraloch tells us he knows of only one area where tribes coexist, and interestingly enough, there are three of them."

"Three tribes? All in one area?"

"Yes, it's likely the largest concentration of our people for generations."

"What about here?" asked Hayley.

"What about here?"

"There are a lot of Orcs in our army."

"True, but the tribes' homes are still scattered. The nearest tribe to us would be that of the Black Raven."

"I thought the Orcs of the Greatwood would be closer," said Hayley. "I saw them at Norwatch, you know."

"Ah, yes," said Gorath. "We call that the Netherwood. They will, no doubt, be helping King Leofric when he finally marches."

"I somehow doubt that. I don't think the Weldwyn king feels comfortable using outsiders in his army. They were certainly shocked by the presence of Orcs in Norwatch."

"Even though they came to his aid?"

"Even so, I'm afraid," said the ranger. "Still, perhaps the queen can change their minds. You mentioned this other tribe, the Black Ravens?"

"Yes. They live in the foothills far to the north and east of here. At one time, they occupied one of the cities of our Ancestors, but it was destroyed by the elves."

"Are the ruins still intact?"

"I believe so, but a great Human fortress was constructed overtop of them."

"A castle?"

"An entire city, in fact, a place called Ravensguard. They even took the tribe's name. The queen promised us she would bring this to the Norlanders' attention when she visited their late king."

"Yes," said Hayley. "I remember her mentioning it. I wonder if they would have eventually relinquished their claim over it?"

"I doubt it. It's not the Human way to surrender such things, and the city has been there for generations now. Would you abandon Wincaster if you discovered it was built on a ruined city?"

"No, I suppose not. Still, if we win the war, we can force them to do so."

"I doubt it will come to that," said Gorath. "In any event, we are talking of things that are beyond our control. For the present, we must decide on our course of action here, at Beaconsgate."

"True enough," said Hayley. "What do you think is our best way around?"

"To the west, as there is less traffic there, and our best option is to travel at night. That way, we can be past the city by first light."

"That leaves us stumbling around in the dark."

"You forget," said Gorath, "we Orcs have superior vision to you Humans."

"You can see in the dark?"

"Not absolute darkness, but provided there is enough moonlight, we shall be fine."

"The sun will soon be setting," said the ranger. "We'd best get back to the others, and let them know we'll be moving soon."

They exited the woods at dusk, heading north. Hayley had suggested Albreda remain mounted, but the Druid balked at the idea, insisting instead that the remaining horse be set free. Thus it was that they found themselves crossing open terrain at night. The town of Beaconsgate lay off to their right, lit windows clearly indicating its location, but by midnight all the lights had been doused, leaving a dark countryside with little to help them navigate.

Urzath led the way across the darkened landscape. The others followed in single file, each only about an arm's length behind the person in front, moving slowly to avoid stumbling in the twilight gloom.

As the night wore on, Hayley found herself tiring. Her arm ached from carrying Gryph, yet she refused to allow anyone else to take him. Snarl padded along at her side, sticking close to the young pup as if sensing his vulnerability.

By the time the moon was high, they had halted to take a rest. They were well clear of the town by now, with little chance of being overheard, and yet no one talked above a whisper.

Hayley lay down on the long grass, placing Gryph on her stomach. The young wolf was asleep, and she found herself longing for a nice comfortable bed. She closed her eyes for only a moment, but Albreda had other ideas.

"How do you want to proceed once we reach the estate?" the Druid asked.

Hayley opened her eyes to see Albreda standing over her.

"I can't really answer that until we see the place."

"I can call for some help," offered the Druid.

Hayley sat up, causing Gryph to slide off her stomach. She snatched him up instinctively, holding him close. "What did you have in mind?"

"I shall call one of my winged friends."

"In the dark?"

"Yes, an owl, to be precise, provided one is close at hand."

"Close at hand? Don't you just conjure them?"

"Of course not. I can't create a complex creature like that from thin air. Rather, I summon one from the area in which I find myself."

"How long will that take?" asked Hayley.

"The spell is over very quickly, but it may take some time for the creature to fly to my location. Shall I proceed?"

"By all means."

Albreda stepped back, giving herself a little space. Her eyes closed, and she took a few shallow breaths, then paused, her body going rigid. Moments later, she whispered something, and then the air around her rippled out in a ring, expanding from her location. Hayley watched it go straight through her body but felt nothing. Gryph, on the other hand, woke up, letting out a small yip.

"There," said the Druid. "It is done."

"I suppose we'll have to wait and see if it was successful or not."

"Not at all," said Albreda. "We can continue on our way. An owl will be able to find us easy enough in the moonlight."

"I know owls have night vision, but just how well do they see?"

"You'd be surprised," replied the Druid. "They can hunt insects in nearly complete darkness. It's their eyes, you see; they're built differently from ours."

"I suppose they're more like the Orcs in that regard."

"A very keen observation."

"That spell," asked Hayley, "does it specifically target owls?"

"In a sense," said Albreda. "I originally created it to summon mammals, though I later discovered I could summon birds with only a slight modification."

"You created it?"

"Yes. Don't be so surprised. I'm a wild mage, remember?"

"Why mammals?"

"Why not?"

"No," said Hayley. "I mean, why did you create it specifically for mammals?"

"I didn't, actually. I wanted a spell to summon Fang." Albreda chuckled.

"Did it work the first time?"

"Yes, a little too well. The entire pack responded. After that, I managed to refine it a little. It wouldn't do to summon every mammal within range after all. Later on, I modified it further, allowing me to summon specific types of mammals. Now it works on bears, deer, and all sorts of other creatures, but I mainly use it for the wolves; they're my family." She cocked her head, her eyes searching the sky. "Ah, I believe we have a respondent."

"That was quick," said Hayley.

As Albreda held out her arm, a small shape plunged out of the darkness, coming to rest on her outstretched wrist. The small owl, only a dagger's length in size, sat there, staring at the Druid. "She must have been hunting in the area."

"What now?"

"I shall tell her what we are seeking," said Albreda. She moved her face close in, and the bird placed its forehead against hers. They stood that way for a moment, and then the owl flew off into the darkness.

"That was quick," said Hayley.

"The connection is much more efficient than words."

"Does that mean you can see through her eyes? I've seen Revi do that with Shellbreaker."

"Not quite," said Albreda. "The owl is not a familiar. She will seek out the estate and fly over it. Upon her return, I shall communicate once more, seeing the images in her mind. In the meantime, I suggest we continue our journey. We need to reach the edge of the Lingerwood before daybreak, else we stand the risk of discovery." She held out her hand.

Hayley grasped Albreda's hand, pulling herself to her feet. Having taken an interest in the exchange, the others had already risen and were gathering their things.

"Come," said Albreda. "It's time we were moving."

"Aren't you tired?"

"No, I am quite recovered from my earlier ordeal, and the Lingerwood is no place to dawdle."

They continued north, led once more by Urzath. The Orc hunter never seemed to tire, something the Humans amongst the group found quite annoying. She kept a brisk pace, crossing the countryside almost at a run. Finally, with the sun just starting to make its appearance, the edge of the Lingerwood came into view.

Soon they were amongst its boughs, watching the land behind them as it was bathed in the warmth of a new day.

The Humans collapsed to the ground, utterly exhausted, but Snarl's ears pricked up. Albreda, on seeing this, stood, holding out her arm. The tiny owl sailed down to land, once more, on her perch. The Druid placed her forehead to that of the owl, closing her eyes. The two of them stood thus for some time, then the owl flew off, leaving Albreda with a smile on her face.

"I have it," she announced. "It's close by." She looked towards the east. "No more than half a morning's travel by my reckoning."

"You call that close?" complained Ayles.

"We'll push on after a brief rest," announced Hayley. "Get some food into you, but no fires. I don't wish to give away our presence."

Albreda began clearing away a section of the forest floor.

"What are you doing?" asked Sam.

"Making room," the Druid responded. "I shall sketch a map of the area on the ground here. We can plan while we rest."

"But if we're planning," noted Ayles, "we're not resting, are we?"

When everybody shot him a look of annoyance, the man shrank back, falling silent.

With a suitable area cleared of debris, Albreda now selected a stick and began drawing a square. "The estate is bounded by a wooden fence," she said, "although it is not much of an obstacle. There are three buildings that lie to the north, right up against the forest's edge. The largest structure is the house itself, rather a grandiose affair I would liken in size and layout to the Royal Estate at Uxley."

"Never been there," said Ayles.

"Nor have I," said Sam.

Albreda was about to snap out with a nasty reply but instead took a breath, calming herself. "It's a two-storey building, with at least three entrances that could be seen. To the west lie the stables, though how many horses are held within is unknown."

"You said there was a third structure?" said Hayley.

"Yes, there is, one that looks something like another house, maybe a barracks."

"A barracks?" said Ayles. "You mean there are soldiers there?"

"So it would appear," said Hayley. "The big question is, where will we find the king's granddaughter?"

"I would suggest we observe the place for a day or two," said Sam.

"To what aim?" said Skulnug.

Sam, finding herself the object of everyone's attention, fell silent.

"Go on, Sam," said Hayley, "speak your mind. We're all rangers here."

"It seems to me," continued Sam, "we need to get some idea of the routine of the place."

Hayley nodded. "A good idea. It may also give us some indication of how many troops are stationed there."

"Yes," Sam continued, "and with a bit of luck, we might spot our target."

"What makes you say that?" asked Ayles.

"Common sense, I suppose. I can't see them keeping this girl locked up all day. She is a princess after all."

"I'm not sure I follow."

"They'll likely take her out for a walk occasionally, don't you think?"

"What kind of claptrap is that?" said Ayles. "Take her for a walk? She's a prisoner, remember?"

"We don't, in truth, know if she's a prisoner or not," said Hayley, "but the fact is, she's still a royal. If Lord Hollis wants to use her for political gain, he'd have to treat her with at least some semblance of respect. I'm told even our own queen was allowed out from time to time—when she was a little girl, I mean."

"So we sit and wait?" asked Skulnug.

"Yes," said Hayley, "but we won't be completely bored. We still have to get the lay of the land. After all, we'll be approaching on foot, not flying in on an owl's wing." She turned to Albreda. "Can you find us a good hiding spot that's nearby?"

"Snarl can do that," the Druid replied. "I'll send him off ahead of us."

"Good. Once we arrive, we'll break into teams of two and watch the place. By this evening, I'd like a better estimate as to how many soldiers are present."

"And if we spot our target?" said Ayles.

"We'll make no move just yet," said Hayley. "We're only going to get one chance at her. I'd rather not risk revealing our presence until we're ready."

Hayley looked at Albreda. "Anything else you'd care to point out?"

"No," the Druid replied. "There's not much more I can tell you."

"In that case, let's get moving. We've work to do."

They started on their way, Snarl in the lead.

By noon, they had taken up a position to the north of the estate. Urzath and Sam were sent to keep an eye on the western side of the place, whereas Skulnug and Ayles went east. Hayley and Gorath took turns watching the manor house while Albreda rested, conserving her strength.

The day wore on with little excitement. It was almost dinnertime when Gorath finally spotted some movement.

"This is interesting," noted the Orc.

Hayley put Gryph down, then came forward, crouching and parting the bushes to reveal the distant targets. From the western side of the manor house had issued three individuals, one clearly being a young woman.

"She can't be much older than the queen," said Hayley.

"Agreed," said the Orc. "Perhaps even a little younger. The other two appear to be guards."

"They certainly look alert."

"Do you think they suspect our presence?"

"No," noted Hayley, "their attention is on the girl."

"That would seem to indicate she is a prisoner rather than a guest."

"An acute observation, my friend. I see she has something in her hands."

"Yes, I noticed that too," said Gorath. "It's a crossbow."

"Strange that a prisoner would be allowed a weapon?"

"Not really. It's slow to use, and there are two guards. In any event, I doubt she'd get far even if she did escape, and then where could she go?"

"True," said Hayley. "She doesn't know about us. Let's see what she does, shall we?"

They watched in fascination. The young woman walked over to a pile of hay, then counted off a number of steps while the two guards watched and waited. Eventually, she turned, then began the process of loading the crossbow.

"Target shooting," said Gorath.

"Yes," Hayley agreed. "I wonder how good a shot she is?"

"We'll know in a moment, it seems."

The young woman raised her weapon, taking careful aim, then let her quarrel fly. It struck the hay pile, disappearing into its mass.

"Not bad," said Hayley.

"It's very large," said the Orc. "What she really needs is a proper target."

The practice continued until a dozen bolts had sunk into the target. The exercise complete, the young woman moved closer, digging through the hay to retrieve her bolts.

"I wonder if this is a regular occurrence?" said Gorath.

Hayley looked towards the sun to judge the time. "Yes, I think we've found our opportunity." She turned to the Druid. "Albreda, how long would it take you to cast your recall spell?"

"It's a ritual," the Druid replied, "and cannot be rushed."

"Is there any way to cast it faster?"

"No, not unless you want to end up in the middle of a tree."

"I think I can safely say no to that," said Hayley.

"Then the answer is still no. Great precision is required."

"Understood," said Hayley.

"I suppose that means we will have to act quickly," said Gorath.

"What are you thinking?"

"Two archers on each guard," said the Orc. "Then two more to make contact with the girl. We leave Albreda back here. She'll be needed for the recall spell."

Hayley nodded. "A good plan. The others will soon be returning. We'll see what they think."

"And if they agree?"

"Then that's the way we'll proceed, assuming the princess cooperates, that is."

"Princess?"

"What else would you call the granddaughter of a king?"

"I suppose I hadn't considered that," said Gorath. "Tell me, what makes this girl so valuable to us?"

"Whoever marries her will become the King of Norland," said Hayley.

The Orc shook his head. "You Humans have such strange customs."

"You have chieftains. That's not much different from a king or queen, surely?"

"Chieftains are chosen by the tribe," said Gorath, "and can be removed if they do not serve its interests. You Humans, on the other hand, seem incapable of taking action when a ruler becomes selfish."

"All true."

"Then what is it that makes these people into rulers?"

"Their bloodline."

"So let me see if I have this correct," said Gorath. "You believe the right of a leader to rule is passed down through the blood?"

"Yes," said Hayley, "it's considered divine."

"Divine?"

"Yes, chosen by the Gods."

"But your kingdom was founded by mercenaries. Surely your Gods were not involved?"

Hayley paused a moment. "I suppose you're right. I hadn't given it much thought. In any event, it's now the way of things, and who are we to argue?"

"I suppose it led to Queen Anna taking the crown," said Gorath, "and that has been a good thing for both our races."

"True. It also narrows the field quite a bit. Without it, there'd be all sorts of trouble every time a king died."

The Orc nodded. "Ah, I see now. It prevents arguments."

"Do you have such problems?"

"We had a chieftain who led us down the wrong path once."

"You don't mean Urgon?"

"No, his predecessor. He allied with the Duke of Eastwood when he rose up against your king."

"Yes," said Hayley. "I was there when we defeated him."

"As was I," said Gorath.

"Strange to think we were on opposite sides. But tell me, if his choice was unpopular, why not simply remove him?"

"We did. That's how Urgon became chieftain, but by then the damage was done. We had already been committed to the fight. If it hadn't been for the actions of Redblade, we would have fought to the death."

"Ah, yes," said Hayley. "Redblade. I'd forgotten that's what you call Beverly."

"It's an honourable name," said Gorath, "for an honourable warrior."

NINE

Summersgate

Spring 965 MC

Anna entered the room, Alric at her side, to see King Leofric already seated. He rose at her entrance as did his advisors.

"Greetings, Your Majesty," she said.

"Welcome to Weldwyn," said the king. "I trust your journey was pleasant."

"It was. The library at the Dome was most impressive."

"Yes," agreed Alric. "It took all my powers of persuasion to convince her to leave. Luckily, the marshal here backed me up."

The king chuckled. "Then we must count ourselves lucky to have him along. May we dispense with the formalities? I'm eager to get to work."

"By all means," Anna said, waiting as a servant pulled out the chair. She sat, watching as Alric and Gerald took their seats. As was her custom, Beverly stood behind the queen while Tempus took up his usual spot beneath the table.

King Leofric leaned down, looking at the great mastiff. "I hope he's not going to grow any larger, or else we'll have to get higher tables."

"I think we can safely agree he's quite finished in that regard. Now, where would you like to start?"

"I assume you've been considering the push into Norland for some time. I think it's best if you tell me what you've got in mind."

"I'll let Gerald handle that," said Anna.

Sophie stepped forward, handing the marshal a large, rolled-up scroll.

"Thank you," he said, placing it on the table. He used a cup to anchor one end, then unrolled it, revealing a map. The area of Merceria was very detailed, but north of the border, things were scarce. "We have little information about Norland other than those areas close to the border. We've sent out scouts to gather what knowledge they can, but we have, as yet, received no replies."

"What do you know of the political situation?" asked Leofric. "Alric tells me they may have fallen into civil war. Is this true?"

"As far as we can tell," said Gerald. "When we visited their capital last year, we met with a noble named Lord Creighton. He and Lord Hollis were at odds over the question of succession. The real question is how the other lords are aligned."

"And where are Lord Creighton's lands?"

"Here"—Gerald pointed—"in a place called Riverhurst. It lies just to the northeast of the Greatwood. You'll note the estimated position on the map."

"What are the approaches like?"

"There's a road that runs from Beaconsgate to Riverhurst, while another heads up to Galburn's Ridge."

"I understand that's their capital?" said the king.

"It is," said Anna, "though it would likely prove difficult to siege."

"Why is that?"

"It's up a steep cliff," said Gerald. "Our best hope is to attack from the east, but even that has its difficulties."

"I can well imagine," Leofric said. "The terrain looks formidable."

"It is," admitted Gerald. "I've seen it first-hand."

"Still, before we can even consider the idea of a siege, we must get our armies there in one piece. Have you considered the line of march?"

"We have. The plan is for a Mercerian army to cross the river at Wickfield, then push up the road as far as Oaksvale."

"Won't that leave your flanks exposed?"

"That's where we thought your army might be of use, Your Majesty."

"Go on," urged the king.

"Our thought was you could cross into Norland territory here"—he stabbed out with his finger once more—"just north of Bodden. From there, you could march to Beaconsgate."

"That's a sensible enough plan. What would come next?"

"That would depend on what opposition we encountered. Either you would advance up the road to Galburn's Ridge and reinforce our attack, or march northwest to Riverhurst and aid Lord Creighton."

"And what will you do if we go to Riverhurst?"

"We shall sweep eastward," said Gerald, "and threaten the eastern reaches of Norland."

They sat in silence for a moment. Gerald struggled to tell if King Leofric approved of the plan or not. Finally, unable to stay silent, he spoke. "Is there something you disagree with, Your Majesty?"

"It seems a reasonable enough plan, but what of the troops in Galburn's Ridge. Wouldn't they threaten your supply lines?"

"We've thought of that," said Anna. "Part of the army would remain in Oaksvale as it controls the key roads in the area. If the enemy counterattacks, we can quickly get word to either Gerald's army or your own."

"So we'll have three armies on the march?" asked Leofric. "An ambitious plan. Who will lead this third army?"

"Baron Fitzwilliam," said Anna, "Dame Beverly's father."

"He's a very competent leader," added Gerald. "One of our best, with lots of experience fighting Norlanders."

Leofric nodded. "Very well. When do you expect to start?"

"Not till the summer," said Gerald. "We're still replacing losses sustained last autumn."

"That works for me. I have to finish concentrating my own forces, then march them all the way to Almswell."

"Might you be able to give us some idea as to its strength and composition?" asked Gerald.

"Of course," said the king. He turned to Lord Edwin Eldridge, the Earl of Farnham. "Would you do the honours?"

"It would be my great pleasure, Your Majesty." Eldridge dug through some papers, extracting the necessary notes. "We have prepared an army of roughly sixteen hundred men. Seven hundred of that force are cavalry, the rest being two-thirds foot and one-third bow."

"Might I ask what type of cavalry?" asked Gerald.

The king smiled. "Three hundred light and three hundred regulars."

"And the rest?"

"Heavy," Leofric said, triumph in his voice, "in metal plates, much like your own Guard Cavalry."

"Heavy?" said Anna. "I didn't know you had such troops."

"We formed them from the cavaliers," said the king. "It was Lord Jack's idea."

Anna looked at Alric, but her husband merely grinned.

"That's excellent news," said Gerald.

"It is," said Anna, "but what did you use for horses? My understanding is that you don't have Mercerian Chargers."

"We don't," admitted the king, "but we do have some large breeds that proved suitable to the task."

"So that gives you how many?" asked Gerald.

"One hundred," said Anna. He looked at her in surprise. "I did the math," she explained.

"It is the largest single army ever assembled in Weldwyn," said the king. "What of your own forces?"

"Each of our two armies," explained the marshal, "will number between eight hundred and a thousand, but they will be much more diverse."

"I'm not sure I follow?"

"He means," said Anna, "our army includes Orcs, Dwarves, and Trolls in addition to the Kurathians we took into service some time ago."

"Oh, yes," said the king. "I'd forgotten about those. I trust they've been useful?"

"They have," said Gerald. "In fact, they've been able to train our own light cavalry in a number of tactics. You also have a higher percentage of horsemen in your army, whereas we tend to favour foot and bow."

"You still have your heavy cavalry, don't you?"

"Yes, of course, nearly two hundred, if you include the Guard Cavalry."

"Actually," said Alric, "you should also add in my two companies of horsemen."

"Are you sure?" said Anna. "That's your personal guard."

"They're warriors," he added. "I don't think they would look kindly upon being left behind."

"We're also gifted when it comes to experienced leaders," said Anna, "allowing our forces to operate in much smaller brigades."

"Brigades?" Leofric said. "I don't think I'm familiar with the term."

"Baron Fitzwilliam came up with it, years ago," said Anna. "I believe you might call them battalions, or sub-armies?"

"Ah, I see what you mean. I like the sound of that. I might have to adopt the method myself. I'd very much like to learn more about this idea."

"I can fill you in later, Father," said Alric. "I've spent a lot of time with Marshal Matheson."

"Thank you, I shall look forward to it." Leofric returned his attention to the queen. "You say you have experienced commanders. Who are they? Aside from Gerald here, I mean."

"Well," said Anna, "there's Baron Fitzwilliam, who I've already mentioned and, of course, Beverly."

"Dame Beverly?" said Lord Edwin. "I know she led the skirmish at Norwatch, but are you sure she's capable of leading an entire army?"

"Dame Beverly commands all the Mercerian horse," said Gerald, "and is one of our most capable leaders. I would have no hesitation placing her in charge of a brigade, or even the whole army if it were necessary."

"How curious," said Lord Edwin. "I wouldn't have thought her old enough to gain such experience."

"You forget," said the king, "these are Mercerians. Their traditions are different from ours. Please continue, Your Majesty."

"Certainly," said Anna. "There's also our High Ranger, Hayley Chambers, whom you've already met. She was with us when we first came to Weldwyn.

"Oh, yes. She's an archer, isn't she?"

"She is," said the queen. "We also have another Knight of the Hound, Sir Heward, at our disposal, along with Chief Urgon."

"Urgon?" said Leofric. "What kind of a name is that?"

"He's an Orc," offered Gerald, "and an outstanding tactician."

"Fascinating," said the king. "Tell me, have you many spell casters? We can lend you some if you like."

Anna blushed. "I think we might have more than you," she said. "Master Tyrel indicated you have five fully trained mages."

"We do," said the king. "How many do you have?"

"Six," said Gerald. "Three Life Mages, assuming you include Kraloch, two Earth Mages, and an Enchanter."

"By the Gods," said Lord Edwin. "You've been busy since we first met."

Anna smiled. "We have," she admitted, "and we have plans to add a great deal more."

"And how do you intend to accomplish that?" asked Leofric.

"We have something in mind, but I'd rather not talk of it just yet. We still have some details to work out. Of course, we'd be happy to share the technique should it prove successful."

"This is all very intriguing, but I don't want to step on the toes of the Grand Arcanus."

"You mean Master Tyrel?" said Gerald. "I thought the mages all worked for you?"

"Oh, no. The independence of our mages was established long ago by the very mage who gave our kingdom its name. In return, they pledged to never claim title nor lands within the realm. It is an arrangement that has served us well since the founding of our realm."

"It's a far different case in Merceria," said Anna. "Magic languished without the support of the Crown. It was nearly eradicated by the time of my predecessor. They were down to one Royal Life Mage."

"Good gracious," said the king. "It's a good thing you stepped in when you did, or magic would have disappeared entirely."

"There were other mages," offered Gerald, "but they were in hiding."

"We must give some thought to communication," added Alric. "The campaign should be properly coordinated."

"I've given that some thought," said Anna, "and I think I have a solution."

"What is it, pray tell?" pressed Leofric.

"We are blessed with two Earth Mages, and you have Lady Aegryth. I propose we use their magic to transmit messages by bird."

"Can they do that?"

"Aubrey assures me they can," Anna said, "but the messages would have to be short."

"I thought Aubrey was a Life Mage?" said Alric.

"She is, but her understanding of how magic works is quite deep, and she's spent a lot of time with Albreda."

"How would these messages be borne?" asked Lord Edwin. "I can't imagine a bird carrying a letter."

"We use a small metal cylinder that we attach to the bird's leg. Inside of this device, we could place a short note, perhaps only a sentence or two."

"A sentence or two would hardly carry a meaningful message."

"Yes," continued the queen, "but the overall plan would already be known, don't you see? We would number areas on a map that we would both possess copies of, then all the message would need to indicate was what numbered location the army was reaching. Anything more complicated would require riders."

"And how would we attract these birds?" asked Leofric.

"Yes," added Lord Edwin, "and how would they know where to find us?"

"That's where the Earth Mages come in," explained Anna.

"You appear to have given this some thought," noted the king.

"It's her way," explained Gerald. "She spends countless days planning for eventualities."

"It must be very taxing."

"It can be, on occasion," admitted Anna, "but it's usually worth it."

"Well," said Lord Edwin, "it looks like you've thought this through quite extensively. Might I suggest Their Majesties leave the details to Marshal Matheson and myself? I shouldn't like to bore them."

"A grand idea," declared Leofric. He stood, causing everyone else to do likewise. "We've prepared a little gathering for you, Queen Anna. Nothing too grandiose, you understand, but you made quite an impression last time you were here, and we have several people of note who wish to pay their respects."

"I should be delighted," said Anna. She turned to her marshal. "I'll leave the rest to you, Gerald. Don't stay up too long."

"I won't," he replied.

Anna took a step, then realized Tempus wasn't following. She glanced down to see him beneath the table, fast asleep.

"I'll look after him," said Gerald. "You go and have some fun."

"Very well. Alric?"

The prince moved closer, taking her arm. "This way, Anna, I'll show you to our room."

"Our room? I thought we were going to meet people?"

"We are," he added, "but I thought you might like to freshen up first. Maybe even have something to eat?"

"We had food at the Dome. Did no one tell you?"

Alric wore a surprised look. "No they didn't, as a matter of fact."

"I'm sorry. I didn't realize. Well, if we're going to our room, you can grab something to eat there."

"We can always find you some food," offered Leofric, "but don't take too long. The queen is keen to see you both."

"Would she care to join us?" said Anna. "We can have a little chat before we greet the others."

"A marvellous idea. She'll like that. I'll send her along as soon as I can find her."

"Excellent," said Anna. "I look forward to it."

Dame Beverly stood with her back against the wall, her eyes alert as dancers moved about the floor with stately grace.

"Not exactly the Bodden Jig, is it?" said Sophie.

The knight looked at her. "No, I suppose it isn't."

"Tell me, does Lord Aldwin dance?"

She smiled, returning her gaze to the dancers. "Not like this, no. What of Sir Preston?"

Sophie reddened. "What of him?"

"Come now, it's pretty obvious he's sweet on you. He even carried your favour into battle at Uxley."

"The truth is," said Sophie, "I don't know whether he dances or not. And in any event, I'm only a maid, an unsuitable match for such a gallant knight."

"You're anything but a mere maid, Sophie. You're the queen's confidante. She did introduce you as Lady Sophie, you know."

"Still, I'm common-born."

"So is Gerald, and I don't see anyone looking down at him. Nobility isn't everything, you know."

"How do I know he's genuinely interested in me?"

Beverly was about to laugh but then took notice of the serious look on the maid's face. "I think I can safely vouch for Sir Preston's interest in you. If he hadn't been needed at the border, I would have suggested bringing him with us here, to Weldwyn, then you could have danced at court."

Sophie's face grew sombre. "You don't think he's in any danger, do you? Being on the frontier, I mean."

"He's with a large contingent of forces at Wickfield. I doubt the Norlanders have anything that could threaten him."

"He's likely spending time with some country girl," said Sophie.

This time Beverly did laugh. "If that's what you think, then you don't know him very well."

"What do you mean?"

"Sir Preston is one of the most honourable men I've ever met. I doubt he's so much as talked to another woman with you in his heart."

"I wish I could be sure," admitted Sophie. "I have so many doubts. Was it like that with Aldwin?"

"No, but then again, I'd known him for years."

"And did you know, in the beginning, you would marry him?"

"Not right away, no," said Beverly, "but it didn't take long. Of course, in those days, I had no hope of actually marrying the man. Our stations wouldn't have permitted it, you see. Thankfully, things are different now, and people can marry whom they please. The queen saw to that."

"Did your father object?"

"Yes, he was quite adamant on the matter."

"What changed?" asked the maid.

"During the war, he heard I was killed. When I showed up alive, he was so overjoyed, he said it didn't matter anymore whom I married."

"Now that you are married, will Aldwin become baron?"

"Not precisely," said Beverly. "When the queen opened up the lines of succession to women, it changed everything. When my father dies, I will become Baroness of Bodden. Aldwin will still be a lord, of course, but he won't be THE baron, not in any real sense."

"I'm not sure I follow."

"Some things still have to be worked out as it's all very new. I imagine he'll be addressed as Baron, but he won't wield any of the power."

"How does he feel about that?"

"I think he'll manage just fine. He's never been one to worry about such things. He's more interested in furthering his craft."

"How does that make you feel?" enquired Sophie. "Knowing he's spending all day at a sweaty forge."

Beverly blushed slightly, a smile coming to her lips. "It's fine by me."

A young man, with the barest wisp of facial hair, approached, bringing an end to their discussion. He bowed deeply, looking directly at Sophie.

"Might I have the honour of this dance?" he asked.

Sophie looked at Beverly for guidance. "Should I?"

"That's entirely up to you."

The maid returned her gaze to the young man. "I'm afraid I must decline." She straightened her back. "I'm already spoken for."

"I was asking you to dance," the man said, his manner terse, "not trying to bed you."

He turned to leave, but Beverly grabbed him by the shoulder, stopping him in his tracks. He wheeled around, his face in a furious rage. "How dare you!"

Beverly's voice was calm. "You have insulted Lady Sophie of Wincaster," she said. "I could challenge you for that."

The young man turned pale. "I…"

"I think you'd better apologize for your rude behaviour." She could see his rage returning. "Of course, I could simply tell Her Majesty, the Queen of Merceria, of the insult. I'm sure she would be interested to hear of it."

His jaw clamped shut, and he gave a curt nod. "Very well," he finally squeaked out. "I apologize, madam."

"That doesn't sound very sincere," said Beverly.

"What do you want from me?"

Beverly moved closer, placing her mouth by his ear. "You will treat women with the dignity they deserve, you little guttersnipe, and if I ever hear otherwise, I shall seek you out and cut off your manhood. Do I make myself clear?"

He turned his head, looking at her in fear. "Very well. I do apologize most sincerely, Lady Sophie."

"Thank you," replied the maid, "and do carry on."

Now dismissed, the man quickly fled.

"Sometimes people have to be put in their place," said Beverly. "I've seen his type too many times before." She broke into a chuckle.

"What's so funny?"

"I was just thinking on what you said." She mimicked Sophie's voice, "'Do carry on.' Priceless!"

"I thought I handled that very well."

"So do I," said Beverly. "I wish I'd thought of that one when we first visited Weldwyn."

"Did they pester you much?"

"It was mostly Lord Jack. He thought he was the Gods' gift to women."

"He courted you?"

"He tried to, but I wouldn't have any of it. My heart had already been given to Aldwin, you see."

"Did you dance," said Sophie, "when you first came to Weldwyn?"

"Only once, in Riversend."

"With Lord Jack?"

"No, with Gerald, if you can imagine."

"He means so much to the queen. He was really her first friend you know, unless you count Tempus."

"Yes, I know," said Beverly. "And he's like an uncle to me. He was the one who trained me to fight. I don't think I've ever met a more honourable man, and he was born a commoner!"

"Thank you," said Sophie.

"For what?"

"For showing me I have value despite the circumstances of my birth."

"We're all in this together," said Beverly. "And if you should ever come across anyone else pestering you, you let me know, all right?"

"I will," the maid promised, "assuming Sir Preston isn't around, that is."

Beverly smiled. "As it should be."

TEN

Captive

Spring 965 MC

"I see her," said Sam. "She's just left the house."

"With only the two guards?" asked Hayley.

"Yes," added Gorath. "The same two we saw yesterday."

"Time to move in. Skulnug, you lead the way. Urzath, you follow."

"And the rest of us?" asked Sam.

"Keep your bows at the ready." She looked down at Gryph to see him snuggled into Snarl, fast asleep. "Time to go," she said.

The two Orcs silently crept forward, their weapons at the ready. In the distance, the princess had begun loading her crossbow while her two guards stood nearby, watching.

Hayley waited until her rangers were halfway to their target, then began moving forward. Her bow was nocked, her string half-drawn, ready to let fly with an arrow at a moment's notice.

Skulnug was within a few paces of his target when they spotted him. One of the guards gave a shout of alarm, then drew his sword and rushed to the princess's side. The other, too surprised by the sudden turn of events, had little time to do anything. He turned his head to his companion at the same moment Urzath rose from the ground. The Orc rushed the last few paces, striking out with her long knife, catching the man under the chin and cutting deep. With a gurgle, he fell to the ground, thrashing for only a moment before falling still.

The first man grabbed the princess by the arm, hauling her back just as Skulnug rushed forward. Hayley let fly, her arrow narrowly missing, and then the melee was on.

Skulnug slashed out with his knife, slicing across his foe's forearm. The guard gave a yell, then struck back, a neat stab that punctured the Orc's chest near the shoulder.

Hayley saw the Orc's weapon fall as his hand lost its grip. The guard's sword struck again, and Skulnug fell onto his back, black blood oozing from his neck.

Another arrow flew, this time from Sam, striking deep into the man's thigh. He called out in alarm, pushing the princess towards the door. The young woman paused, looking unsure of what to make of this strange turn of events.

Urzath, now finished with her own foe, ran towards the second soldier, shouting in Orcish. The Norlander gripped his sword tightly as he turned to face this new threat, parrying her first strike, then slashing out with a backhand swipe, cutting across her forearm. The Orc retaliated with a quick thrust, feeling the knife's tip puncture the man's chainmail shirt and dig into his chest.

He brought up his elbow, driving it into Urzath's face, causing black blood to explode from her nose. She countered by ramming her own forehead into his. When the stunned guard staggered back, she quickly plunged her knife in again, this time sinking the entire blade up to the handle. His breath came out in a rush, then his eyes rolled up into his head, and he fell forward. Urzath stepped back, pulling her knife out to let the body fall at her feet.

Having witnessed the encounter, Hayley was now running across the field as fast as she could, Albreda struggling to catch up. The princess, having kept her wits about her, had used the time to reload her crossbow. Now she held it to her front, aiming a bolt at the Orc.

"Stand back!" she commanded. Urzath retreated, using her hand to try to stem the flow of blood from her nose.

Hayley slowed, holding her left hand in the air well away from her bow. "We mean you no harm," she called out.

"No harm?" replied the princess. "You've killed two of my guards!"

The ranger struggled to find the words. The woman before her was young, likely only fifteen or sixteen, yet she carried herself with the grace and dignity of someone much more mature. "My name is Hayley Chambers," she said at last. "We're here to rescue you."

The young woman turned her crossbow on Hayley. "Who sent you?"

"I am here at the behest of Lord Creighton."

"A bold claim, but how do I know you speak the truth?"

"It's true, I swear it." A thought suddenly occurred to the High Ranger. "I have a letter that bears his seal." She fished through her tunic, retrieving a crumpled note and holding it out. "See for yourself."

"Put it on the ground, and back up," the woman responded.

Hayley did as she was commanded. The princess advanced, stooping to retrieve the letter but keeping her crossbow trained on the High Ranger. Her task complete, she backed up, unfolding the paper with one hand, a clumsy endeavour made all the more difficult by her determination to keep the crossbow held steady.

"This is likely a forgery," the young woman said.

"It is not, I assure you."

"Exactly what an enemy of Lord Hollis would say."

"Your life is in danger here," pleaded Hayley. "Lord Hollis means to use you to claim the throne."

"And what of it? I am a princess of Norland. It is my fate to be used thusly."

When shouts echoed from within the house, Albreda quickly cast a spell. Vines exploded from the ground, reaching out to hold the door in place. "We must hurry," the Druid insisted. "I cannot hold them forever."

"Please," said Hayley. "You must come with us."

The princess stiffened. "Must! Who are you to dare speak to me in such a manner? I am Princess Bronwyn of Norland!"

"Lord Hollis will dispose of you once you bear him an heir. Can't you see that?"

"I see no such thing. Besides, you would have me in the hands of Lord Creighton. How is that any different than my current fate?"

"No," protested Hayley. "We'd take you to Merceria to keep you safe."

Bronwyn fell quiet, although whether it was to consider her options or simply surprise was anyone's guess.

"We haven't much time," said the High Ranger. "You must decide now."

"Listen to her, girl," added Albreda. "Would you spend the rest of your life having Lord Hollis grunt over you until your hips can no longer bear children?" The Druid lowered her hands, looking briefly at the results of her spell. "It is time we left," she announced. "If this young woman wishes to remain a prisoner, then so be it."

The door began to tremble as it was pushed from within. Bronwyn cast her eyes to the door, then back to the group of strangers.

"So be it," said Hayley. "It's time to leave."

Urzath lifted Skulnug and began running back to the trees, joined by Albreda. Hayley alone remained, watching Bronwyn for any sign of a decision. Finally, she, too, turned and fled, crossing the field as quickly as she had come.

Bronwyn watched them go. Moments later, the door burst open, spilling soldiers into the garden. If there were any doubts about her freedom, it was soon put to rest by the snarl that erupted from their leader. He pointed at her, yelling, "Secure the prisoner."

For the first time, she recognized the look of disgust, the utter contempt in which she was held, and something inside of her snapped. As a princess of Norland, she was used to not having control of her future, but now, at this moment, she finally realized she was nothing more than a common prisoner. Calmly, she took aim, then loosed a bolt, sending it into the chest of one of her captors, who fell to the ground, a stunned look upon his face.

Bronwyn turned and ran, pumping her legs as fast as she could, hampered as she was by her dress. Ahead of her, the Mercerians were disappearing into the edge of the woods. She called out in desperation.

Hayley turned, loosing off an arrow at the pursuing guards. Bronwyn tossed aside her crossbow, using her hands instead to lift the hem of her dress—the better to run. Her heart was pounding, and for the first time in her life, real fear gripped her.

Past the ranger she ran, her breath coming in ragged gasps. She heard an arrow thud home and then the sound of someone falling behind her. Stumbling into a clearing, she spotted the old woman standing with her arms outstretched while the others stood around her, their weapons trained south towards the estate.

Bronwyn froze, her fear getting the better of her. It suddenly occurred to her she was trapped between two worlds. Grabbing the princess's arm, Hayley tugged her towards the Druid as words of power began to charge the air with magical energy.

Bronwyn turned, watching in horror as the guards drew closer. One of them raised a crossbow, taking aim at her, and she screamed as the bolt flew forth. An instant later, a cylinder of light erupted from the ground, and then everything around her began to blur to be quickly replaced by stone walls.

She looked around in awe. "Where are we?" she managed to stammer out.

"In Wincaster," said Albreda, "the capital of Merceria."

"Impressive," noted Hayley. "I thought we agreed to recall to Hawksburg."

"I was concerned that we get Skulnug to a healer."

"It is too late," announced Urzath. "He has joined the Ancestors."

"Saxnor's teeth," said Hayley. "I thought he was just wounded."

"He lost too much blood."

"I'm so sorry."

"There is nothing to apologize for. Skulnug died doing what he loved best—serving his people."

Bronwyn stared, her mind trying to make sense of things.

Albreda moved closer to the princess, pointing her finger in a most accusing way. "He died trying to help you," she said. "Do not let his death be in vain."

"I shall see to the disposal of his remains," said Urzath. The Orc lifted her dead companion, carrying him from the room.

Bronwyn looked around, noting the gold and silver runes on the floor. "What is this place?"

"A casting circle," said Hayley. "It enhances the power of magic."

"I've never heard of such a thing."

"Have you no mages in Norland?"

"None that I'm aware of," said Bronwyn. "How long have you had such power?"

"Magic is an ancient tradition," said Albreda. "One that has been carried on for generations."

Guards entered, drawing their swords as they noted the new arrival.

"Put away your weapons," commanded the Druid. "This is Princess Bronwyn of Norland. She will be staying with us for a while. Please show her to the guest rooms and make sure you show her the respect due her station."

The soldiers looked at Hayley for confirmation, but she merely nodded. Satisfied, they scabbarded their swords.

"This way, Your Highness," said the leader, "and we'll show you to your rooms." They all watched as their new guest was escorted out.

Albreda turned to Hayley. "What was all that about?"

"What?"

"That attitude, from the guards?"

"Oh, that," said Hayley. "I'm usually the steward when the queen is away. They only wanted confirmation of the order."

"And what's wrong with my word?"

"You're not one of the queen's inner circle, that's all."

"My dear," said Albreda, "I am far more powerful than any noble."

"Yes… well… I'll have a word with them about that. It shan't happen again. I promise you."

"It had better not! Now, will you take this pup of yours? I can't have him hanging around my feet all day. I have things to do."

Hayley moved closer, picking up Gryph. "Come on, then, let's show you home."

"I will return to the High Ranger's office," said Gorath. "I have things to attend to."

"What about us?" said Sam.

"Yes," agreed Ayles. "What are we to do?"

"Gorath will sort you out," offered Hayley.

"And where will you be?" the man asked.

"I'll be at Revi's house. I have a wolf to look after."

"Do you think that wise?" said Albreda.

"Of course, why wouldn't I?"

"Think about the state of Master Bloom's house. It's an absolute disaster. Young Gryph might start chewing on his books, and I don't think the Royal Life Mage would appreciate that."

"No," said Hayley, "I suppose he wouldn't." She cast her eyes around, looking for inspiration. "I've never had a pet before. Where should I take him?"

"I would suggest the Palace gardens," said Albreda. "It's where Tempus likes to spend time."

"It's as good a place as any, I suppose."

The Druid smiled. "I shall check in on you both later, but first, I must see Richard."

"Richard?"

"Yes, Baron Fitzwilliam?"

"I know who Richard is. I'm just surprised you need to see him."

"Why?" asked Albreda. "He's in charge during the queen's absence after all."

"How do you know the queen hasn't returned from Weldwyn?"

"Snarl says her scent is a few days old. That would seem to indicate she has left, but not yet returned."

"Are you going to stroll through the Palace with Snarl?"

"Of course, why wouldn't I?"

"He's a wolf!"

"Yes, and I'm a mage. What is your point?"

Hayley shrugged. "I suppose you're just going to walk down the street with him as well?"

"Yes. Why, does that bother you?"

"No, but what will the people of Wincaster say?"

"I couldn't care less," said Albreda. "I gave up caring what other people said decades ago." She left the room, Snarl padding along after her without a care in the world.

Hayley saw the look of amusement on the faces of Sam and Ayles. "Haven't you two got something better to do?"

"Yes, ma'am," they both echoed, then quickly walked from the room, eager to put space behind them.

Hayley scratched Gryph's head. "I wonder what Revi will make of you."

Baron Fitzwilliam stepped outside, taking in a deep breath of the afternoon air. It had been a busy day, and he had grown tired of the dusty offices that had claimed so much of his time. A pleasant stroll through the gardens was exactly what he needed.

He wandered around, stretching his legs as he thought things through. The queen loved her gardens, something in which she took a personal interest, and the result of her efforts was a quiet, reflective place, very different from the Palace's dusty halls. He rounded a hedge to see Hayley Chambers sitting on a bench, a small wolf pup running around her feet.

"What have we here?" he called out.

When the High Ranger looked up, her face appeared haggard. "Oh, hello, Lord Richard."

"Something wrong?"

"We lost a good ranger today."

"Ah, yes, I heard. Albreda filled me in earlier. Might I sit?"

"Be my guest."

He took a seat beside her. "It's not easy being a leader," Fitz began. "We are often called on to make decisions that cost lives."

"How do you deal with it?" she asked.

"You do what you can to keep them as safe as possible, but you must realize death is the nature of war. No matter how careful you are, you can never guarantee someone won't die."

"But it's my fault."

"I doubt that. From what Albreda told me, there was little you could have done differently."

"I should have sent in more people," said Hayley. "As it was, I used only two rangers."

"Had you sent more, the alarm would have likely been raised even earlier, and then where would you be?"

She nodded. "I suppose I can see your point."

"You know, you remind me of someone I used to work with quite closely. He thought he wasn't very good at command as well, but you'd never know it today."

"Oh? Who?"

"Gerald, of course."

"That's high praise indeed," said Hayley.

"I meant every word of it. You are an accomplished woman, Lady Hayley. Don't let one small setback upset you."

"But someone died!"

"He did," said the baron. "And you should never forget that, but he died doing something he loved. His memory should be cherished not dwelt on to belittle your own accomplishments."

She nodded again. "Very well."

"Now tell me about this little fellow?"

"His name's Gryph. We found him all alone in the Whitewood after the rest of his pack had been killed."

"Oh dear," said the baron. "I can't imagine Albreda was very happy about that."

"No, she was furious. You should have seen what she did to those Norlanders."

"I can well imagine. The packs are her family, you know. In a sense, they raised her."

"Truly?"

"Well, in a manner of speaking," said Fitz. "She had a father, of course, but he died in the wars. I think she was about thirteen when she found herself in the Whitewood for the first time. The wolves there befriended her. Did she ever tell you that?"

"She did mention something to that effect, yes."

"I can well imagine her rage. If I had come home to Bodden to find my family slaughtered, I shudder to think what I would have done."

"And yet you did, didn't you?" asked Hayley. "You thought they'd killed Beverly during the uprising."

The baron nodded. "Yes, that's right. I actually raised the red flag of rebellion. I'd had quite enough of the wretched fool who sat on the throne, so I suppose my reaction wasn't that far off from Albreda's."

"But you didn't kill the king," said Hayley.

"I gladly would have had he been within my reach. We all have family, Hayley, whether it's by blood or not. Family are those who you hold close to your heart. You and Beverly are family, as is Aubrey. The three of you are almost like sisters, no?"

"Yes, I suppose so."

"Well then, there you have it. You fight for your family. In the end, there's nothing more important."

"Thank you, Lord Richard. You've given me much to think of."

"Don't mention it, and please call me Fitz. No one else will."

"All right, I will. I promise."

"There now, that's better. Now, what's this I hear about you and Master Bloom?"

Her face brightened. "We're to be married."

"Congratulations!"

"Thank you, although I have no idea when we'll finally get around to it."

"We must have a celebration once Beverly gets back. What do you say, eh? We'll celebrate at my Wincaster home."

"I would like that."

"Good, then it's all settled. Now, I must get back to work. This kingdom won't run itself, you know."

"I can give you a hand if you like. I usually act as steward in the queen's absence."

"I shall take you up on that offer."

She rose, then remembered her pup. "What shall I do with Gryph?"

"Bring him along," said the baron. "We'll have someone dig up a cushion for him. If Tempus can lie around the Palace, why not this little fellow?"

She felt a great weight lifted from her shoulders. "Very well, Baron, after you."

The circle glowed, and then a cylinder of light lit up the confines of the Wincaster casting room a moment before dissipating, revealing Anna and her entourage.

The queen stepped from the circle, clutching Alric's arm. "You were quite impressive at the Palace," she said. "Now tell me more about this cavalry of yours. I was under the impression it was more ceremonial in nature."

"It was, originally, but I had a word with Beverly. She passed on some ideas regarding training."

"And now you have your own heavy cavalry?"

"Not quite," he replied. "I'd call them medium cavalry. They lack the heavier armour your own troops possess."

"Perhaps we should arrange some smiths to correct that deficiency?"

"No, I think their strength lies in their speed. They are faster than your own heavy horsemen yet more able to withstand battle than the lighter horse."

"Medium cavalry it is, then. I suppose this means you want your own command during the invasion?"

"I am content to place myself under Gerald's command."

"Spoken like a true diplomat," said Anna. "Now, shall we retire to our rooms? It's been a busy day."

"I think that's an excellent idea."

The queen turned to her bodyguard. "You can dismiss the guards, Beverly. We shan't be needing them anymore today."

"Of course, Your Majesty."

"Shall I stand by?" asked Aubrey.

"No, you and Kraloch have done all you can for now. We may have to send a messenger through come tomorrow to sort out minor details, but until then, you are free to spend time as you wish."

"Very well, Your Majesty."

"Anna?" said Gerald. "I need to talk to you about troop strengths. There are decisions to be made."

"We can deal with that tomorrow. Take some time off, have a nice meal, go for a walk if you like. You've certainly earned it."

"That's a splendid idea," he said. "I think I will. Can I borrow Tempus?"

Anna looked at her mastiff to see his tail wagging excitedly. "Well, now you've done it. You can't very well leave him behind now."

"Come on, then, Tempus, old boy. Let's go and stretch our legs, shall we?"

The great mastiff let out a loud bark that echoed throughout the chamber, then they all started filing from the room.

"I shall just go and ready your room," said Sophie.

"Nonsense," said Anna. "We're quite capable of doing that ourselves. Take the night off, Sophie, and see what that knight of yours is up to."

"He's in Wickfield, Your Majesty."

"Then write him a letter. I think he'd like that."

She smiled. "That's a wonderful idea, Your Majesty. I think I shall."

"Go on, then," the queen urged. "Off with the lot of you."

Anna waited until it was only the two of them. "Now," she said, clutching Alric's arm tighter, "let's go and see to that room, shall we?"

They strode out of the casting room and down the hall with a slight spring to their steps. Everything looked like it was going to end quite nicely, but then the Master of Heralds appeared, bringing them to a halt.

"Is something wrong?" asked the queen.

"We have a visitor, Your Majesty. Princess Bronwyn of Norland."

"Ah," Anna said, her face revealing her disappointment. She turned to her husband. "I'm afraid our private time will have to wait, my love."

Alric kissed her on the forehead. "For you, I would wait forever."

ELEVEN

Plans

Spring 965 MC

Bronwyn stood as the queen entered, followed by an older man. "Your Majesty," she said.

"Greetings," said Anna. "I hope you don't mind, but I asked Lord Fitzwilliam to join us."

"The Baron of Bodden?"

"You know of him?"

"Only by reputation," the young woman replied. "His tenacity is legendary. For years Lord Hollis has raved about his inability to crush Bodden."

Fitz smiled. "It's nice to know I'm appreciated."

"Might I ask why I've been brought here?"

"I can assure you it's entirely for your own protection."

"Then I can leave if I wish?"

"You may," said the queen, "but I would hope you would choose to remain amongst us, if only for a few days."

"And why would I do that?" asked Bronwyn.

"To understand us."

"Yes," added the baron. "This war was not of our making. We were hoping you might present us with a path towards peace."

"Me? I hardly see how."

"You have influence, Your Highness, though you may not realize it."

"I am a mere woman, nothing more."

"You are much more than that," said Anna. "You represent the future. The great lords of Norland will do anything to get you on their side. You give them legitimacy."

"There is a fine line between being influential and being a pawn."

Fitz turned to the queen. "A highly astute observation."

"Might I enquire as to your age?" asked Anna.

Bronwyn bristled. "I am sixteen. You?"

"Eighteen, though I suspect you are wiser than your years might suggest."

The Norland princess turned crimson. "Am I to be insulted now?"

"Not at all. It was merely an observation."

"You are very much like the queen," added Fitz. "I rather suspect your upbringing was of a similar nature."

"How?" said Bronwyn. "Wasn't she raised at court?"

"Actually, no," said Anna. "I was hidden away from society, kept at a remote Royal Estate."

The baron noted the look of surprise on their visitor's face. "Was it, perhaps, the same for you?" he asked.

There was a slight pause before Bronwyn replied. "Yes, my upbringing was quite similar, though maybe for different reasons."

"Would you care to explain?"

"Everyone knows Your Majesty is illegitimate," said Bronwyn. "Had you been born a man, you would, no doubt, have been branded a bastard."

"Not precisely," said Anna, keeping her calm demeanour. "The king was not my father, but the queen bore me."

"Then your claim to the throne is even weaker than we Norlanders thought."

"On the contrary, she who wears the warriors crown rules Merceria."

Bronwyn smiled. "I am merely trying to present the facts as I see them."

"For someone who's just been liberated from imprisonment," said the baron, "you have a funny way of showing gratitude."

"Gratitude?" said Bronwyn. "I wanted to make myself understood, nothing more. She was hidden away out of shame, whereas I was kept safe for my own protection."

"And yet you still ended up in the hands of Lord Hollis," said Fitz.

"Yes, but I could expect no less. As the granddaughter of the king, it is my husband who shall inherit the throne. In that regard, Lord Hollis is no worse than the other lords of Norland."

"Might I ask how this turn of events came about?" asked the queen.

"As you probably know, my father died some years ago. I was raised in the court of Galburn's Ridge until the death of my mother."

"How old were you when she passed?"

"Seven. I was then sent to Chilmsford by my grandfather. His health had been ailing, and he wanted me away from the politics of court. There, I was tended to by servants loyal to the Crown."

"But something changed that?" suggested Fitz.

"Yes," the princess continued. "As I aged, certain elements of Norland society began to exert more influence at court."

"You mean Lord Hollis?"

"I do. He began to put pressure on my grandfather, insisting I be properly trained in those skills required by women. The result was that I was placed in the care of Lady Hollis and sent to Beaconsgate to receive a proper education."

"And how long ago was this?" pressed Fitz.

"Three years, give or take a couple of weeks."

"And he treated you well?" asked the queen.

"Lord Hollis had little to do with me initially, but as I've neared my age of majority, he's begun to take more interest in me."

"Age of majority?" said Fitz. "You've reached that, surely?"

"No," said Bronwyn. "Our tradition calls for a woman to have reached her seventeenth year before she can wed. That is still some months away for me."

"And what then?"

"I suppose he will marry me."

"But he's already married, isn't he?"

"He is," replied the princess, "but I'm sure Lady Hollis would gladly step aside if it would elevate her husband to the throne. Our marriage would be nothing more than political expediency."

"And now we've brought you to Wincaster," said Anna. "I'm just sorry it couldn't have been under happier circumstances."

"What will happen to me now?" asked Bronwyn. "Have I simply traded one form of captivity for another?"

"We do not view you as a prisoner, rather as our guest. For now, I shall assign you a guide. You will have free roam of the Palace aside from my private areas, of course, and you can even travel into the city if you wish."

"So I am not under arrest?"

"No," said Fitz, "though guards will be provided for your own protection."

"And how long am I to remain here?"

"Until such time as we can return you to Norland and guarantee your safety." The queen rose, leading the baron to follow suit. "I shall leave you now, for I have much to see to. Baron Fitzwilliam will keep an eye on you while I'm otherwise engaged. Welcome to Merceria, Bronwyn. I hope you'll come to appreciate the risk we've taken in bringing you here."

The Norland princess stood, bowing respectfully. "Thank you, Your Majesty."

Queen Anna exited the room, followed closely by Baron Fitzwilliam, with guards closing the door behind them.

"Well?" said Anna. "What did you make of her?"

"She has a proud bearing," said Fitz, "not unlike yourself, if you'll permit me to say."

"I'll take that as a compliment. Do you think she'll come around?"

"I suppose it depends on your definition of 'coming around'. I think she'll be comfortable enough here once she gets used to our way of doing things. The real question is whether or not she'll eventually choose to return to Norland."

Anna halted, causing the baron to overshoot her location. He turned, looking back at her. "Is something wrong, Your Majesty?"

She resumed her steps. "Do you think a woman could ever rule Norland?"

"What are you suggesting? That we conquer and annex it?"

"No," said Anna, "though we might be forced to by circumstances. No, I was wondering if it might be possible to put Bronwyn on the throne."

"As the Queen of Norland?"

"Yes, why not? It worked for me, didn't it?"

"It did," agreed Fitz, "but I might remind you it was a long and difficult road."

"That does not rule out the possibility. What if we could? Would you favour the idea?"

"I'm not sure. The truth is we know remarkably little about the character of Princess Bronwyn. We could end up placing her on the throne only to find she turns against us."

"That is an excellent point, Baron. I shall make it your task to get to know her a little better over the coming days."

"Me? Why in Saxnor's name would you give that task to me?"

"You raised Beverly," said Anna, "so you're used to dealing with young women."

"I would hardly put Bronwyn in the same category as my daughter."

"True, but you're also the consummate diplomat."

"Gerald would be more appropriate to the task, I should think."

"Perhaps," said Anna, "but I need him by my side. And in any event, I don't feel like sharing him."

"Ah," said Fitz. "So I am to be considered surplus to requirements?"

"Not at all. You are a valued member of my inner circle, and I know I can trust you to represent the interests of the Crown."

"I am, as ever, at your disposal," said Fitz.

"Good, then I shall retire for the evening in the knowledge that things are well taken care of."

They halted at the door to the Royal Suite.

Baron Fitzwilliam bowed. "Goodnight, Your Majesty."

"And to you, Lord Richard."

Early morning found Gerald in the kitchen, searching out something to eat from the cook. He had returned late and, as a result, had been forced to look after Tempus overnight. The great mastiff now trailed in his wake, sniffing the floor for any sign of dropped food.

"See anything you like?" asked Linette.

"Ah," said Gerald. "I was looking for something filling."

"I can cook you something if you like?"

"You're a cook now?"

The young woman beamed. "I am. Now tell me, what can I get for you?"

"Is there any of that ham left from yesterday?"

"There is, as a matter of fact, and we've got some porridge on the boil if you're so inclined."

"That would be marvellous. Thank you."

"Take a seat over there, and I'll have it for you shortly."

"Thank you, Linette."

He moved aside as a servant struggled past, bearing a large silver tray.

"Company?" he called out.

"Yes," said the cook as she carved off a slice of ham. "Didn't you hear?"

"Oh yes. Is that for the Norland princess, then?"

"It is. Have you met her yet?"

"No," said Gerald. "What's she like?"

"I can't say. I haven't met her either, though I have to admit she can be quite particular when it comes to food."

"Particular?"

Linette carried over a plate of meat, placing it before him, then tossed a slice onto the floor that was quickly gobbled up by Tempus. She looked down at the great beast. "We don't need to clean the floor with you around, do we?" She looked back at Gerald. "I'll just get your porridge."

"You were saying something about our visitor being particular?"

"Never mind what I said," she replied. "It's not my place to talk of such things."

"Nonsense," said Gerald. "You know the queen would want you to speak your mind."

"Well, it's just that she insists that everything she eats be covered in some sort of sauce."

"What kind of sauce?"

"Any, apparently. It's like she has no spit of her own."

"I suppose that makes her a saucy wench?" said Gerald with a chuckle.

Linette screeched out a laugh. "That was a good one, sir."

The cook made her way over to a large pot and began ladling porridge into a bowl. Her task complete, she gathered up the food, placing it on a wooden tray. "There you are, all set."

Gerald rose. "Thank you, Linette. Your efforts are greatly appreciated." He grabbed the tray, carrying it from the room, Tempus leading the way.

The marshal's office was only a short distance away, and in no time, he was seated at his desk. He tossed a piece of ham to Tempus then took a spoonful of porridge, relishing the thick, pasty goo. No sooner was it in his mouth than the door opened, and Baron Fitzwilliam poked in his head.

"Where's your aide?" he asked.

"You mean Hill? Still in bed, I would expect," said Gerald. "It's early yet. Something you want to see me about?"

"As a matter of fact, there is." The baron entered, taking a seat.

"Do you want some ham?"

"No, thank you," said Fitz. "We just received word from Hawksburg, thanks to Kraloch."

"I thought he was here, in Wincaster?"

"He was, but he popped back there last night to see how the rebuilding was going. That's when he came across this." Fitz passed over a note. "It's from Sir Heward."

Gerald looked at the note held before him, then at his food. "I'm still eating," he said. "Summarize it for me, if you would."

"Certainly. He reports a rather strange encounter north of the river near Wickfield."

"You have my interest," said Gerald. "What does he mean by strange?"

"It appears some troops belonging to Lord Hollis took it upon themselves to attack a group of villagers. A sort of militia if you will."

"Oh?"

"Yes," said the baron. "Sir Heward got wind of it through our Kurathian scouts. He took cavalry north and intervened."

"So fighting has broken out?"

"If you can call it that. He reports no casualties on our side but sent the earl's men running."

"And what of the villagers?" the marshal asked.

"Yes, well, that's the sticky part."

"What do you mean, 'sticky'?"

"He decided to bring them back to Mercerian soil."

"To what end?"

"To keep them safe, apparently," Fitz said, "but many of them wish to take up arms."

"I'm not sure what you're suggesting. Are you saying they wish to fight us?"

"No, against Lord Hollis and his allies. It seems they've had enough of his predations."

"I doubt they'd get far," Gerald said. "The earl's troops are well equipped."

"So, too, are these militia, now."

Gerald paused, a spoon of porridge about to enter his mouth. "Now?"

"Yes. Heward thought it expedient to take the weapons and armour from the earl's men. He's passed it over to the militia."

"I see. What does he intend to do with them?"

"Train them, I think," Fitz said. "He's asked the queen for assistance."

"An interesting development."

"Will the queen agree, do you think?"

"I'm sure she will," Gerald assured him. "Who did Heward ask for?"

"Beverly. He can't really spare any of his own men, you see."

"I'll take it to Anna, but I'll need numbers."

"It's all right here," said Fitz, tossing the note onto the desk. "Heward is extremely thorough in his reports. He's managed to arm about fifty of them using the weapons recovered from the battlefield, but they'll need more."

"Weapons we have in plenty; Uxley saw to that. What we don't have is men, but this may help us."

"Are you suggesting we incorporate them into the Army of Merceria?"

"No," countered the marshal. "I'm suggesting we allow them to form their own faction, as allies."

"Who would lead them?"

"What about this new princess?"

"She is a mere slip of a girl," said Fitz. "And with no military experience that I'm aware of."

"Yes, but if she were placed in command, we could assign her an experienced general."

"Surely you're not suggesting me? That would throw our entire campaign into chaos."

"No, not you. You're too important to our plans. I had another leader in mind, one I know is quite capable." Gerald smiled.

"You mean Beverly, don't you?" said Fitz.

"You know she's right for the job."

"I do," the baron agreed, "but I'm not sure I like the idea of her being at the mercy of a bunch of foreign troops."

"We'll send some of the heavy cavalry with her," said Gerald, "ostensibly to reinforce our allies."

"Ah, but actually to keep her safe. I like it."

"Good. Now all I have to do is convince the queen."

"I doubt that will prove too troublesome. She values your opinions. You are, after all, the marshal of her army."

"True, but she can be stubborn at times."

"Funny you should say that," said Fitz. "I was just thinking the same of Bronwyn."

"Oh? In what way?"

"They are both quite set in their ways. You and I both know the queen does not suffer fools gladly."

"And yet she often seeks advice," said Gerald.

"Yes, but only from those she trusts."

"And the princess doesn't trust us."

"Precisely," concurred Fitz.

"What do you make of this Bronwyn?"

"She's still young, only sixteen. Oh, she has a certain maturity in some things, but there's a streak of rebelliousness in her that might prove troublesome."

"You think she could cause trouble for us?" the marshal asked.

"I think that depends entirely on how we treat her. One thing is for sure, she won't like being controlled."

"But we're not controlling her."

"We are, in a sense," said Fitz. "Putting her in charge of an army and then placing Beverly to keep an eye on her might not go over well."

"We have to do something."

Fitz nodded. "Aye, we do. I suppose we must make the best of a difficult situation, politically speaking. Do you think Beverly could win her over to our side?"

Gerald fell silent, his food forgotten. His hand began stroking his beard, a sure sign he was deep in thought.

"Something come to you?" Fitz asked.

"It did, as a matter of fact."

"Do tell."

"What if we made her think it was her idea? Bronwyn's, I mean."

"And how do we do that?"

Gerald smiled. "We arrange a little trip to Wickfield."

"To what end?"

"We let her meet the Norlanders we've taken under our wing. Maybe seeing the plight of her fellow countrymen will entice her to take up their cause?"

"That's a splendid idea," the baron said. "Shall I talk to Beverly?"

"No, not yet. I'd best talk to Anna first."

The ruling Queen of Merceria leaned forward, resting her elbows on the table and cradling her chin. "Just how many troops are we talking about?"

"Several hundred," Gerald replied, "if Heward's reports are to be believed."

"And their composition?"

"That largely depends on how we equip them. I would be inclined to make most of them footmen, with a smattering of light cavalry."

"Well," said Anna, "after the Battle of the Deerwood, we've plenty of horses to spare."

"Agreed. And as light cavalry, they would be trained to avoid combat while keeping their eyes and ears on the enemy."

"We also have to look at our timeline. Would they be trained up in time to march with the rest of us?"

"I would think so," Gerald said. "We'll have a better idea once we begin and see how they adapt to our methods. Of course, they won't be a match for our own troops, but they would certainly be a welcome addition."

"And the cost?"

"We would have to feed and pay them, but thanks to our recent victories, we have plenty of spare weapons."

"I think it's worth pursuing, but if we are going to do this, we must start as soon as possible."

"I can have Beverly on her way this very day."

"Very well," said Anna. "Oh, and I've made another decision."

"And what decision might that be?"

"I've decided on the location for our next magic circle."

"Which is?"

"Wickfield."

"Are you sure?" asked Gerald. "It's a very small village."

"Yes, but a strategic location in our border defences, and instant communication would help us a great deal in the coming campaign."

"How long would it take to construct?"

"Aldwin assures me he can have it completed by the end of the month."

"And who is to empower it?"

"That remains to be determined. It does drain a mage of their power to a certain degree. I shall pass word on to our Magic Council and let them decide. In the meantime, I'd like you to go north with Beverly and help her set up the training. I'm sure she's more than capable of looking after things, but the fact is you've been training soldiers for far longer than she has."

"She'll need a staff," suggested Gerald.

"That's your responsibility," said Anna, smiling mischievously, "but don't let her rob us blind of all our best soldiers."

He chuckled. "I'll do my best."

"You always do."

TWELVE

Training

Spring 965 MC

Beverly sat astride Lightning watching as a group of soldiers practiced their blocks.

"Keep the tip of your sword higher," bellowed the sergeant. "You're blocking, not thrusting!"

His student, unused to fighting on foot, grunted an acknowledgement and made the correction.

"Sergeant Gardner," called out Beverly. The sergeant turned and, spotting the knight, revealed the slightest of smiles.

"Commander Fitzwilliam," he said. "What brings you to Wickfield?"

"I'm here to see you."

The man looked stunned. "Me?"

"Yes. How would you like to join my staff?"

"I thought only the marshal had a staff."

"No," the knight replied, "all the senior officers do now. It's far more efficient."

The sergeant moved closer. "And what would this entail?"

"We're going to be training the Norlanders. And your experience with the Wincaster Light Horse would be most beneficial."

"I hope you're not sticking me with another bad captain?"

"No, you'd be working directly for me. Interested?"

"Of course! When would I start?"

"Right now," Beverly said. "I've already talked to your captain."

"How did you know I'd accept?"

"Come now, Sergeant, I've known you for years. How long has it been since we first served together?"

"Eleven years," said Gardner.

She leaned down from her saddle, offering her hand. "Welcome aboard, Hugh."

"Thank you, Commander."

"Grab your horse, and meet me over by the headquarters. I need to talk to Sir Heward."

"Yes, ma'am."

Beverly turned Lightning around, urging the great horse northward. Through the village she rode, observing the work with great interest. The wooden walls were progressing nicely and would be completed by summer, but the towers would take considerably longer. At least they could be used as lookout points for now.

The guards on the building watched her approach, nodding as she dismounted. She dropped the reins knowing he would remain there, untethered, until he was needed.

Stepping inside, she spotted Sir Preston giving orders to an Orc, who then turned and jogged past Beverly, intent on his destination.

"Trouble?" she asked.

"What?" said Preston, looking up. "Oh, it's you, Dame Beverly. No, he just made a report. He's one of the rangers, you see."

"Anything new?"

"Yes, we've received some more refugees."

"How many?"

"Twelve in the last week alone," Preston informed her. "It looks like word is getting out."

"And how did that happen?"

"Sir Heward might have had our horsemen spreading the word north of the border."

"How would he do that?" Beverly asked. "It's not as if he can send riders into the towns."

"True, but the farms are easy enough to find. You'd be surprised how eager a person is to spread rumours when a few coins are sent his way."

"I've stolen one of your men," she said.

"I'd been warned you might. Who did you take?"

"Sergeant Hugh Gardner from the Wincaster Light."

"Well, at least it wasn't the captain," said Sir Preston. "They're hard to find, you know."

"Still?"

"Yes, and I blame you."

"Me? Why in Saxnor's name would you blame me?"

"You're the one who made a name for the heavy cavalry. That's all a horseman dreams of now, riding down the enemy atop a Mercerian Charger. Nobody wants to be a light horseman anymore. It's a good thing we have the Kurathians."

"Yes, that's another thing," continued Beverly. "I may have to borrow some of them too. At least until we get the training well underway."

"Are there any men you're not going to steal?"

"Don't worry, I'll leave you enough to carry out your duties."

"Heward will be relieved."

"Have the reinforcements arrived from Hawksburg yet?"

"No," said Sir Preston, "but a shipment of assorted weapons came in this morning. Oh, and Heward wanted me to inform you there are some bowmen in amongst the Norlanders."

"Archers? Are you sure?"

"Yes, he had a talk with them. It appears a number of them have some hunting skills. With any luck, you might be able to scrape together enough for a company."

"That's excellent news," said Beverly. "Where is Sir Heward?"

"North of the river. He likes to accompany patrols from time to time. He should be back later this afternoon. Did the marshal come with you?"

"No, he'll be along later today. He got held up in Hawksburg. Where do I find these Norlanders?"

"East of the village," said Preston. "There's an old abandoned farm there that serves as their barracks."

"Very well, I shall head over there directly. Give Sir Heward my regards, and let him know I'll catch up on things later this evening."

"I will," said Sir Preston. "It's good to see you."

"And you, my friend," said Beverly. She turned to leave, then paused, looking back over her shoulder. "Did you hear from Lady Sophie?"

The man turned crimson. "I did. Why? Is something wrong?"

"No, not at all," she said, a smile escaping her lips as she stepped outside.

Sergeant Gardner was already riding up the street, a fact that surprised Beverly. "That was quick," she said.

He grinned as he pulled up beside Lightning. "No sense in delaying the inevitable. Where would you like to start?"

"I thought we'd ride over to these Norlanders, though now I think of it, we might want to give them another name."

"Why?" asked the sergeant. "That's what they are, isn't it?"

"Yes, but it's confusing when our enemies bear the same label."

"I see what you mean. What would you propose?"

"I suppose there's enough of them to make a decent detachment."

"What was that word the general liked to use?"

"You mean my father?" asked Beverly.

"Yes. You used it once before, at Eastwood, if I recall."

"You mean brigade?"

"That's the one. You could call them the Norland Brigade."

"That still sounds like our enemy," said Beverly. "How about the Rebel Brigade? They did rise up against Lord Hollis."

"There you go," the sergeant agreed. "That's it."

"Good, then that's settled. Now, have you seen much of our new command?"

"Only from a distance," said Hugh. "And what I did see didn't exactly leave me quaking in fear."

Beverly laughed. "They're villagers, not warriors, at least not yet."

"Yes, I know, and that's half the trouble."

"What is?"

"Well, it's our job to make them into soldiers, isn't it?"

"It is," she replied.

"And how do we go about that?"

"Don't worry, help is on the way. For now, we just have to take stock of what we have."

"To what end?"

"We need to ascertain what skill sets they might possess. Once that's done, we can organize them into companies. There'll likely be a few experienced ones amongst them, Hugh. Do you think it would be better to group them together? Or do we spread them out amongst the others?"

The sergeant scratched his head. "That's a good question."

They passed through the village's outer perimeter, where cut logs lay stacked, ready to be utilized on the walls.

"I see they're making fine progress," noted Beverly.

"The reinforcements helped. We have twice the manpower we had a month ago."

Beverly nodded at the archers, who stood watch high atop the unfinished towers. "I wish we had more rangers."

"So do I, but we can't have everything, I suppose."

They began crossing a large open area full of tree stumps. "I see where they got all the wood from," said Beverly.

Sergeant Gardner laughed. "Yes, it's quite a sight, isn't it? Do you think they'll ever grow back?"

"I'm sure they will, in time. Maybe we should get Aldus Hearn up here? I'm sure he could convince them to grow faster."

She saw the confusion on his face.

"He's an Earth Mage," she explained.

"I thought Albreda was the Earth Mage?"

"She is, and he's another one."

"How many do we have?"

"Just the two."

They cleared the stumps and set out across a field of long grass. It had been badly trampled for the most part, evidence of a lot of activity in the area. The noise of the camp soon drifted to their ears.

They were greeted by a young man no more than eighteen years of age. He stood guard with a fairly rough-hewn spear, its tip dented and scratched.

"Have you come to help us?" he asked.

"This is Commander Beverly Fitzwilliam," said Gardner. "You address her as Commander, or ma'am, is that clear?"

The young man looked suitably chastised. "Yes, sir."

"You call me sergeant."

"Yes, Sergeant."

"Good. Now where are the rest of you?"

The youth pointed. "Over there, behind the ruins of the house."

"Have you no shelter?" asked Beverly.

"No, ma'am."

She turned to Gardner. "Make a note, Sergeant. It's just one of the many things we'll have to see to."

"Aye, Commander."

She urged Lightning forward, clearing the edge of the burned-out building. Beyond, lay quite a flat stretch of land that reached down to the riverbank at its northern end. A number of people were gathering water for horses, while others sat around, sharpening a wild assortment of weapons.

Beverly halted. "My goodness. There's certainly a lot more of them than I expected."

"Where would you like to start?"

"We'll find out who's in charge, then work from there."

Gerald slowed his horse, waiting as the wagons rolled past. The afternoon was wearing on, but with any luck, they would reach Wickfield before nightfall. He spotted Aldwin atop a wagon that bore a heavy load of stone.

"Are you sure you're going to need all this?" he called out.

"Of course," the smith called back. "I can't construct a magic circle out of wood!"

Gerald pulled his horse up beside the wagon, matching its speed. "How long do you think it will take to get it up and running?"

"That depends on whether or not we have a suitable building to house it in. Assuming we do, I should think a week would be all I need. That's not counting empowering it, of course. You'd have to talk to a mage about that. Have they decided who's going to undertake that responsibility?"

"Yes," said Gerald. "Aldus Hearn."

"I'm surprised. I would have expected someone else."

"Really? You do realize he's from these parts."

"Is he?" said Aldwin. "I had no idea."

"Well, from Mattingly, actually, but it's in the same general area."

"In any event, I shall do my best to be finished with my work as quickly as possible."

"Good, because we'll need your smithing skills to help equip those Norlanders."

Aldwin looked back at the other wagons. "We certainly have enough weapons."

"Yes, but have you seen the state of them?"

"I have, as a matter of fact. I think the smiths will be quite busy for the foreseeable future."

"Do you think we have enough?"

"I believe so," said Aldwin. "Though we'll have to borrow some from the other companies for the short term." He looked at Gerald. "Do you honestly think you can prepare these Norlanders in time?"

"You'd have to ask your wife that. She's the one in charge of their training."

"You did tell her I was coming?"

Gerald smiled. "No, didn't you?"

"How could I? I only found out after she'd left."

"Then it will be a nice surprise for her."

"I hope she won't be too upset."

"Why in Saxnor's name would she be upset?"

"Well, maybe distracted might be a better word."

"Listen," said Gerald. "The two of you will be far too busy to be distracted by each other. Look at it this way, after a hard day of work, you'll be able to spend time with your wife."

"That will be nice," said Aldwin. "It's been so busy of late."

"I must say I was a little surprised you had to work on a new circle. I would have thought the old design was good enough."

"It certainly was, but the amount of silver and gold required cost a fortune."

"How is that any different for here?"

The smith grinned. "I came up with a more efficient way of laying the runes that won't require as much metal."

"And will that save us much?"

"Yes, it should carve off at least half the expense."

"I'm impressed."

"You should be," said Aldwin. "It took me months to make the calculations."

"Calculations?"

"Yes. I had to measure each rune, then determine how much gold or silver was required for the symbol. Albreda informed me that precious metals are required to hold on to the magic when it's empowered. She said you could make one of wood, but the magic would only last a day or two."

"Wasn't Revi's mirror made from wood?"

"That's what Albreda said," said the smith, "but it was something called shadowbark. Unfortunately, it doesn't grow in these parts."

"That means at least there's something else other than silver and gold that can hold magic."

"Don't forget sky metal. That's what I used to make Nature's Fury."

"So you did. I don't suppose there's any left, is there?"

"No, and I doubt we'll see another deposit in our lifetime."

"It's that rare, then?" asked Gerald.

Aldwin nodded. "The Dwarves are aware of it, but as far as I know, the piece I discovered was the first and only example to fall within our borders."

"And it chose to come to us in our greatest time of need," said Gerald. "Some might say it was sent by the Gods."

"Herdwin told me it's also known as godstone, and I can see why. It is, I believe, the rarest of all metals."

Gerald spotted the roofs of Wickfield off in the distance. "It appears we're almost there. I'd better ride on. I'll catch up with you later, Aldwin."

"Of course, my lord."

"Now, now, it's Gerald. None of this 'my lord' business."

Aldwin laughed. "Very well, Gerald. I'll look you up once I've sorted this lot out." He indicated the pile of stone in the back of his wagon.

Gerald galloped ahead, passing by a gate that was half under construction. The workers paused, noting his arrival, then resumed their work.

The village was a busy place, the soldiers easily outnumbering the locals. Each wandered about on their own business, respectful of others. Gerald had worked hard to instill a sense of pride and discipline in the army, and he was pleased to see the results. Too often in the past, soldiers had taken advantage of their hosts, a situation that had led to unrest and discontent. There was none of that here. Instead, he saw a peaceful and content populous.

He halted at the new headquarters, easily identifiable by the Mercerian flag that hung over its door. The simple red-and-green banner was a constant reminder of their past. The red was a recent addition, denoting the rebellion that led to Anna being crowned queen.

"Marshal," came the voice of Sir Preston. "We've been expecting you. I trust your trip was uneventful?"

"It was," said Gerald. "How have things been here?"

"Relatively peaceful of late. We did have some more Norlanders join us."

"That seems to be a common occurrence these days."

"It helps that Commander Lanaka is spreading the word north of the border," said Preston. "I hear you've come to whip our allies into shape."

"That's Beverly's job. I'm only here to advise." He peered back down the street. The wagons were trundling past the gate creating quite a racket with their squeaking axles.

"Pig fat," said Sir Preston.

Gerald looked at him in surprise. "Pardon?"

"They need to grease the wheels with pig fat."

"The axles, you mean?"

"Yes, it keeps the noise down."

"How in Saxnor's name do you know that?"

"My family made their fortune in shipping."

"We have no ships in Merceria."

"No, I mean overland shipping. You know, wagons."

"You mean your family drove wagons?"

"No," corrected Sir Preston, "they made them. They were wainwrights, you see."

"Fascinating. I thought they were nobles."

"They were," the knight confirmed, "but they still needed an income. Not that they made the wagons themselves, of course. They had skilled craftsmen for that."

"You are a constant source of surprise, Sir Preston."

"If you were looking for Sir Heward, I'm afraid you're out of luck. He's on patrol north of the river."

"I suppose that means I'll have to come back later. Can you point me in the direction of these Norlanders we're helping?"

"To the east," the knight replied. "There's a large open field by an old farm the invaders torched on their way through last year."

"I hope they didn't destroy all the crops."

"No. Luckily, the harvest was in before they struck. Of course, they used up most of the stores when they took Wickfield, but we brought plenty of food with us when we returned."

"Are these Norlanders going to put an undue strain on us?"

"I'll admit it's kept us on our toes, but we have sufficient supplies for the time being. I'm assuming the army will bring more when we march north?"

"Naturally," said Gerald. "I wouldn't expect you to feed everybody."

"I suppose that means we'll need more wagons."

"More are coming"—he grinned—"but you might want to stock up on pig fat."

Beverly watched as Sergeant Gardner put the men through their paces. They had only received rudimentary instructions, but she could already spot those who had potential. The rebels had been organized into groups of twenty, then armed with spears to begin their training. At the moment, this consisted of little more than thrusting their weapons in unison and marching around without tripping, but there was no doubt they were enthusiastic. Those who weren't practicing watched, eager to pick up any tidbits of information that might help them master these new skills.

The vast majority of them would form companies of spearmen. In Mercerian terms, they would be classified as light infantry, men who would stand in a line of battle and defend their position but would not be used aggressively. And, if armour could be obtained in a sufficient quantity, they might upgrade them to a heavier contingent, but she doubted the cost would be worthwhile. After all, when all was said and done, these were still foreign troops. The expense of armour was something the Crown was quite willing to bear, but priority must first go to the soldiers of Merceria.

Gardner dismissed the men, taking a break before beginning with the next group. It was proving to be a warm day despite that it was still the early days of spring, and he wandered over, wiping sweat from his brow.

"That lot has some potential," he said.

Beverly cast her gaze over the remaining rebels. "And the rest?"

"Don't worry, I'll have them trained in time."

"You can't do it all by yourself."

"Nor do I intend to," admitted the sergeant, "but I won't hand them over for training until I've had the measure of them."

"They appear to handle spears well enough."

"Yes. They're eager to make their mark. If it were up to them, they'd march across the river today, but they have no idea what a real battle looks like."

"Are there no veterans amongst them?" Beverly asked.

"One or two, but they're old. Still, I might use them as sergeants. That would help speed up the training."

"Once you've finished with these basic moves, we'll figure out how to organize the companies. I'd like to put the most promising men together into a heavier company."

"You think we can get armour?"

"We already have some captured armour," Beverly informed him. "I'm hoping our smiths can salvage something useful, even if it's only one company's worth."

"So what are we looking at, do you think? Five companies?"

"I think we can manage that. I'd like to get together some horsemen if we have enough riders and some archers."

"I'll keep that in mind," said Gardner, "as I take them through their paces. I suppose I'd best get back to it. They won't train themselves."

"More weapons are due in soon from Hawksburg," said Beverly. "I'll ride back to Wickfield and see if they've arrived yet."

She turned Lightning around, ready to gallop off, but the sight of Gerald's approach soon put an end to such thoughts. "Looks like we've got company."

"It's the marshal," said Sergeant Gardner. "I didn't know he'd be here so soon. We haven't even finished assessing the rebels."

"I'm sure he understands. I'll talk to him while you get back to our troops."

"Yes, Commander." Hugh returned to the Norlanders, who had been watching the discussion. "All right, then, let's get the next group out on the field, shall we?"

"You're late," called out Beverly.

"No I'm not," said Gerald, grinning. "I'm the marshal. I arrived exactly when I wanted to." He pulled up beside her. "Let's dismount, shall we? I've been in the saddle all day."

They climbed down from their horses, then moved closer to observe Sergeant Gardner at work.

"How are they?" asked Gerald.

"Not as bad as I thought they were going to be, if I'm being honest."

"Still, a lot of work, isn't it?"

"It might be easier if I had a better idea of how we were going to employ them."

"From my perspective, they're untried troops," said the marshal. "Which means I have no idea how trustworthy they'll be. I think the best option, for now, is to form them into an independent force. Once you've got them trained, we'll send them on a small expedition and see how they do. Don't worry, we'll support them with Mercerian troops."

"A test of battle?"

"Precisely."

"Where?"

"We'll worry about that later. You've got training to complete first."

"I'll need more weapons," said Beverly.

"Now, that I can take care of. We brought spears from Hawksburg. How does that sound?"

"I can work with it. Any chance of getting more armour?"

"I doubt it," Gerald said. "We haven't the time. Even if we could get some smiths on it, there wouldn't be enough completed to form a whole company, let alone all these people. What if you trained them in close order tactics, like the spears of the Orcs?"

"They'd need longer spears, wouldn't they?"

"Yes, but wooden spears are easier to work with than swords. We could simply remove the heads from the spears we have and put them on new shafts."

"We'll keep them on the shorter spears for now," said Beverly, "but if training goes well, I'll consider your suggestion. Did you bring any horses?"

"I did, enough to outfit a company. I wasn't sure if you'd have the riders, but I know the Norlanders love their horses. I even brought spares for our own men."

"The advantage of our recent victory," said Beverly. "It's a pity they aren't a heavier breed."

"True enough, but more than up to the task of scouting. You were looking at training horsemen, weren't you?"

"Of course," said Beverly. "Every army needs its light horse."

He chuckled. "Oh, you're an army now, are you? Aren't you getting a little presumptuous?"

"If the rebels are going to fight as an independent force, I have little choice."

"Rebels? Is that what we're calling them?"

"Yes. Sergeant Gardner and I came up with the name. It's better than calling them Norlanders. That might lead to confusion."

"I like it," said Gerald. "It reminds me that we, too, were rebels before Anna became queen."

"Do you truly think this will work?" said Beverly. "Arming and training them, I mean?"

"If I didn't, you wouldn't be here. Look, Beverly, if anyone can do this, it's you. You've already trained men. Look what you've done with the Guard Cavalry."

"Yes, but this—"

"This is not much different," Gerald said. "I tell you what, I'll send over the Wincaster Light Horse. They can help out."

"I could use some archers."

"The Greens are garrisoned in Wickfield. I'll see if they can spare some men. Anything else?"

"Tents?" she asked.

"Have they no shelter?"

"None whatsoever."

"Well, that won't do. I'll talk to Heward and see if we can't get some huts built."

"Sorry to be such a bother," said Beverly. "I didn't know what to expect."

"It's no bother. It's all part of running an army. It's not unlike being back in Bodden, you know. Except with more people to train."

"Yes, a LOT more people."

"Just remember," Gerald said, "you're not alone here."

"I appreciate that."

"Oh, there was a couple of other things."

"Yes?"

"Princess Bronwyn of Norland will be visiting."

"What?" said Beverly. "Here? In Wickfield?"

"Not for some weeks yet. Plenty of time for you to whip this lot into shape."

Beverly's eyes narrowed. "And the other thing?"

"Oh, didn't I mention it?"

"No, you most certainly did not."

"I could have sworn I did. Are you sure?"

"Come on, Gerald. Out with it."

"Well, the queen has decided to construct a magic circle here in Wickfield. Aldwin accompanied the wagon train."

Her face lit up. "Aldwin's here?"

"He is," replied Gerald with a straight face, "but you'd best get back to work if you want to see him. There'll be no fraternizing till the day's work is done!"

"Then you should be on your way, Marshal. You're taking up too much of my time!"

THIRTEEN

Hawksburg

Spring 965 MC

A ubrey stood in the centre of the circle. "All right, here goes."
She began casting, feeling the arcane power surge through her as the magical words issued from her lips. The energy built, and then she released it, causing a ripple in the air.

"I can't seem to contain it," she complained.

Kraloch entered the circle. "You almost had it, even I could feel it. It was as if the very fabric of the air was being twisted."

"Perhaps it's just too much?"

"No, I think you are close. If you are successful, you will be able to peer into the spirit realm and see auras. To do that, you must call a portion of that realm to ours."

"I'm just not sure if it's even possible."

"My people can communicate over great distances," said Kraloch, "using something we call spirit talk. I think, if I teach this spell to you, you might be able to adapt its effects to this task?"

"It's worth a try, I suppose."

"Very well. Now come, sit, and I will explain how it works." They sat, cross-legged, on the floor, facing each other. "The spell will only work with those you know. The better you know them, the easier it is to make contact."

"And if they are far away?"

"It makes no difference. Distance has no meaning in the spirit realm."

"But surely—"

He held up his hand. "You must clear your mind of your preconceptions. They are what limit you."

"Very well," said Aubrey. "What's next?"

"Every person has a spirit, a manifestation of their spiritual being. This spell calls that manifestation to you, allowing you to communicate."

"I'll be able to see into the spirit realm?"

"Not exactly, no. The spirit will appear before you, like a ghost if you like. As the caster of the spell, you will be the only person capable of seeing this image, but you will be able to talk as though the person were actually in the room with you."

"Will others hear the spirit?"

"To observers, all will be quiet. Of course, you could cast the spell on others, allowing them to participate in the conversation, but that only appears to work with shamans. That is, other spell casters."

"Why is that?" asked Aubrey.

"It's quite simple, really. They need to call on their inner power to do so. Those unable to wield magic are incapable of calling forth such power."

"That makes sense."

"Now," said Kraloch, "before I show you how to cast, you must understand something."

"Go on."

"This spell is a sacred ritual amongst my people. It should not be shared with outsiders."

"But aren't I an outsider?" said Aubrey. "This won't get you into trouble, will it?"

"No, you have proven yourself to be a great friend of the Orcs. No one will object to your learning this technique."

"I'm honoured. Who shall I contact? Revi?"

The Orc chuckled. "That would never do. He is not versed in the spell."

"Then who?"

"For now, you will use it to contact me."

"But you're right in front of me?"

"So I am, but remember, in the spirit realm, distance is immaterial."

It was Aubrey's turn to chuckle. "Isn't everything immaterial in the spirit realm?"

The Orc stared back at her, unable to understand the jest.

"Sorry," she said. "I was just being silly." She cleared her throat. "Please, continue."

"The spell is similar in nature to spirit walk, a spell you have already mastered. Note, however, the different cadence to the words. You'll also see that the last part of the spell differs to a marked degree. Are you ready?"

Aubrey nodded, fascinated with the whole idea. Kraloch closed his eyes, incanting the spell. The words flowed from his mouth quietly as was the Orcish custom. She felt the room buzz with magical energy, then the shaman's eyes glowed with a white light.

"There, you see?" he said.

"I see your eyes glowing, but no sign of a spirit."

"That is because you have yet to master the spell."

"Who did you contact?"

"A fellow shaman of a distant tribe, named Shaluhk. Her tribe lies far to the east."

"And you can see her?"

"I can, as well as talk to her. Would you like me to ask her something?"

"I wouldn't know what to ask. This is all so unexpected."

"This is interesting," said Kraloch. "It appears there is a great conflagration in the east."

"Conflagration?"

"Yes," said the Orc, "a war."

"I hope the Orcs are not in any danger," said Aubrey.

"Not as yet, but they are concerned the war may eventually reach their lands. They, like us, have allied with Humans in order to stay safe."

Kraloch's eyes returned to normal as he dismissed the spell.

"How far away is this other tribe?"

"I do not know for sure, but night has already fallen upon their village."

"But it's only early in the evening here," said Aubrey. "That would put them thousands of miles away, wouldn't it?"

"You would know more than I. Such things are beyond my reckoning."

"And yet you contacted this shaman—what did you say her name was?"

"Shaluhk, of the Red Hand," said Kraloch. "Remember, distance—"

"Has no bearing. Yes, I remember."

"Now, are you ready to learn the spell?"

"I am."

"Very well, repeat the words after me…"

It was dark by the time Aubrey was confident enough to attempt the spell herself. She stood, shaking the cramps out of her legs.

"I don't know how you can sit for so long," she complained. "I feel as though I've seized up."

Kraloch stood, patiently waiting. "Are you ready?"

"I think so."

"No, you must be sure. Indecision will only cause problems."

"What sort of problems?"

"An inability to concentrate," Kraloch explained. "Then you would have expended your energy for nothing."

She closed her eyes, taking a cleansing breath. In her mind, she pictured Kraloch, then began reaching out to him mentally as the arcane words spilled from her mouth. The power flowed through her, and then she imagined a flash of light. Aubrey opened her eyes to see the room bathed in a soft glow. Kraloch still stood in front of her, but it was as if his spirit were standing in the same spot, creating a double image.

"So," said Kraloch, his voice echoing through his spirit, "did it work?"

"It's a little unsettling," said Aubrey. "I can hear an echo."

The Orc chuckled. "The spell is not typically cast when the target is in the same room. Hold on a moment." His physical form turned, taking the stairs up to the outside. His spirit, however, remained in place. "There, is that better?"

"This is incredible. Tell me, how do you walk and talk at the same time?"

"Can you not walk and talk at the same time in the physical realm?"

"I suppose I never thought of it that way."

Kraloch's spirit looked around. "I am walking through town," he said, "and people are watching me."

"Why?"

"To them, it appears I am alone, yet I am talking to you."

"I imagine they find it as strange as I do."

"The Orcs are familiar with the technique, but you Humans are… what is the word? Ah, yes, fascinated."

"I can see this spell will be quite useful."

"Yes," agreed Kraloch. "We use a variant of it to talk to the Ancestors."

"This would make it much easier to coordinate armies."

"So it would, but the gift must be carefully guarded."

"I can see why. It's extraordinarily powerful. Can any mage learn it?"

"No, only those skilled in what you would call Life Magic. You are the only Human to ever learn it, as far as I know."

"I shall keep it to myself," promised Aubrey.

Kraloch nodded. "As you should. Now, I think it time we end the spell. We have much to do."

"We do?"

"Yes, and Master Hearn will be arriving soon. He'll need the magic circle."

"Very well." Aubrey dismissed the spell, feeling a small tug as the energy dissipated.

Moments later, Kraloch came back down the stairs. "There, now you have mastered spirit talk."

"I feel quite tired, yet strangely energized. How is that even possible?"

"It is the excitement of mastering a new spell. Your magical energy reserves have been taxed, even though your mind is clear. In time you will grow more familiar with the connection, and then it will require less power."

"So it gets easier with practice?"

"Familiarity is key. Were you to contact someone you barely know, it would require more energy. You and I have worked together many times, so the connection is relatively strong. Eventually, you will be able to contact me with hardly any effort at all."

"Your people fascinate me," said Aubrey. "You have such an affinity for the spirit realm. I'd love to learn more."

"And so you shall. But for now, let us rest."

"Agreed, and maybe get something to eat?"

Kraloch smiled. "You have learned to read my mind."

Aldus Hearn stepped from the circle. The air in Hawksburg was cooler than the capital, something for which he was thankful. He breathed in the fresh scent of nature, relishing in the sensation despite the fact he was still indoors. An Orc stood above him, looking down from the steps with spear in hand. As guardians of the gates, they took their responsibilities seriously, but the old Druid was well known to them.

"Welcome," the guard said.

"And to you," replied the old man. "Tell me, is Mistress Aubrey here somewhere?"

"She is," said the Orc. "Up at the main house."

"Then I shall seek her there, thank you." He made his way up the steps and then out into the open air. A cold breeze ruffled his beard, reminding him it was still early in the year. His eyes sought out the manor house, revealing a large number of wagons, and as he drew closer, he spotted Arnim Caster.

"What's all this?" asked Hearn.

"Timber," said Arnim, "for Wickfield."

"Don't they have enough?"

"Not as yet. The palisade might be nearing completion, but there's lots more work to be done. Our sawmills have been quite busy for some time, and now that Hawksburg is rebuilt, we can afford to ship the excess north."

"Not for the palisade, surely?"

"No, for buildings. We have barracks to build, plus a new stable, not to mention replacing some of the older structures."

"I'm surprised they would bother," said Hearn. "Wickfield is always the first city to be overrun."

"Not anymore," said Arnim. "The marshal wants it fortified."

Hearn shook his head. "All those trees," he muttered.

"Pardon?"

"Oh, nothing, just the ramblings of an old man. Carry on, Lord Caster, I shouldn't wish to hold you up. Have you seen Lady Aubrey, by chance?"

"Inside," said Arnim.

"Very well, I shall seek her there." He turned towards the house, noting the relatively large Orcs who stood guard. They towered over him, each with a spear clutched in their grip. Aubrey was just inside, standing over a small table, examining some sketches.

"What have you there?" he asked.

She looked up, revealing a smile. "Aldus, so good to see you. I trust everything is well in Wincaster?"

"It is," he replied. "I'm on my way to Wickfield to empower the new magic circle."

"I hadn't heard it was finished."

"Nor had I, but it's been some time, and I can wait in Wickfield as easily as I can in the capital. What have you been up to?"

"Oh, you know, the usual sort of thing."

"Still rebuilding?"

"Most of Hawksburg is restored, but you know how it goes. The queen wants a proper garrison. That means building barracks, stables, and a new headquarters."

Hearn frowned. "I don't see why. The army of Merceria has stood for almost a thousand years without all of these new buildings."

"In case you hadn't noticed, we're changing things."

"Yes, but is it all really necessary?"

"Times change," said Aubrey, "and with them, organization and tactics."

"That's all well and good, but look at the cost."

"The Crown can afford it."

"No, I mean all the wood! Do you realize how many trees you had to cut down?"

Aubrey stared at him, unsure of how to respond.

"All this building of yours must have levelled an entire forest by now."

"It will grow back," said Aubrey.

He pouted. "I suppose it will, in time."

"Are you always this morose, or are we just lucky?"

"What was that?"

"Nothing, I was just saying you're quite plucky. Excited, are we? It's not every day a mage gets to empower a magic circle."

"Ah, yes," said Hearn. "That's what I wanted to see you about."

"Of course. What would you like to know?"

"You cast the first empowerment ceremony in Wincaster. I was wondering if you had any pointers."

"Yes, make sure you get lots of sleep the night before. Oh, and make sure you have a nice breakfast. You'll be starving by the time you're done."

"It's quite a complex ritual," said Hearn.

"I have it written down," said Aubrey. "Take the lectern from the circle here. It'll make things much easier."

"Will you be joining us?"

"Of course," she said. "Kraloch and I will both be there. We'll have to commit it to memory after all."

Hearn took a breath, letting it out slowly. "I must admit to some trepidation."

"Over what?"

"The empowerment. I understand it will consume part of my power."

"It will, but you'll be able to build it back up in time."

"How long did it take you to recover?"

"About six months, but then again, I'm a pretty active caster."

"True. I suppose I'll be weakened for much longer, seeing as I'm quite a bit older."

"It's not age that has that effect," said Aubrey, "it's the casting. The more you employ your magic, the quicker you'll recover."

"Can you explain that?"

"It's quite simple, really. As a mage, the more you practice casting spells, the stronger you get. Imagine you were a horseman who hit his head. You might lose some of your skill, but with patience and a lot of practice, you could relearn those skills."

"I see now," said Hearn. "Yes, that makes it much clearer. I'm quite looking forward to it, you know. I've never attempted such a thing before."

"I found it quite tiring, but it was well worth the experience. Hopefully we never have to worry about Air Mages."

"Air Mages? I don't understand?"

"You will be empowering the circle with the power of the earth," said Aubrey.

"And?"

"And air is the opposing element. Did you not realize that?"

"Oh yes," said Hearn. "I'd forgotten about opposing schools. I suppose that means an Air Mage would be unable to use it?"

"Yes, though at the moment we don't have one, so it's of little consequence."

"But the circle in Wincaster is of Life Magic, is it not?"

"It is," Aubrey replied, "meaning it can't be used by a Necromancer."

"Yes, of course. That makes perfect sense."

"Are you continuing on to Wickfield right away?"

"I shall wait until the next caravan heads out."

"I believe Lord Caster is taking one tomorrow morning."

"Good, then I shall accompany them if he doesn't mind."

"I'm sure he'd appreciate the company."

"Tell me," said Hearn, "is Lady Nicole with him?"

"No, she remains in the capital with the twins."

"Of course, that makes perfect sense. Well, I'd better get some rest. It'll likely be a long day tomorrow."

"Very well. Goodnight, Aldus."

"Goodnight, Lady Aubrey."

The morning mist was still draped over the land as Aldus Hearn made his way out of the manor. Outside waited the wagons, loaded up and ready to go. He climbed up to sit beside Lord Caster, then smiled. "It will be fine weather today, don't you think?"

Arnim looked skyward. "With these darks clouds? I doubt it."

Hearn shrugged. "Well, what harm is there in a little downpour every now and again?"

A horse snorted, then Aubrey and Kraloch rode by, their mounts at a gallop.

"I didn't know Orcs could ride," said Hearn.

"Why shouldn't they?" asked Arnim.

"I don't know. I suppose I just assumed they didn't know how. Do they have horses in their villages?"

"I have no idea, but these Orcs live here in Hawksburg now. Many of them have taken to the saddle."

"Next thing you know, you'll be telling me they fight from horseback."

"Not as far as I know," said Arnim, "but it's an interesting thought." He flicked the reins, and his team of horses began moving, pulling the wagon along with a rumble.

They sat in silence as the mist burned off. Finally, with the wide-open fields visible, Hearn turned to his companion. "What are you going to do in Wickfield?"

"I serve the queen," the man replied, "and I go where needed. Right now, that means Wickfield."

"So I gathered, but I was curious as to what those duties might entail?"

"Leading troops, I would imagine. You'd have to ask the marshal."

Again the discussion came to an end. Desperate to keep the conversation going, Hearn looked around, seeking something to talk about. "Interesting plants they have in these parts," he finally said.

"If you say so," said Arnim.

Hearn gave a sigh. "It would be nice if you could maintain a conversation."

"It would help if you picked something of interest to talk about."

"Very well. How's your family?"

"They are well," said Arnim.

"And?"

"And what?"

"Is that it, 'they are well'? Haven't you got anything else to say?"

"They're fine?" offered Arnim.

"I give up," said Hearn, lapsing into silence once more.

The wagons stretched out for miles, forming a caravan that took half the morning to get underway. In addition to lumber and weapons, it carried saddles, rope, canvas, and all sorts of other goods desperately needed by the army.

At the tail end came the horses, herded by experienced riders. Most of them had been captured from the Norlanders, but a number of Mercerian Chargers had joined the herd to serve as remounts. Hawksburg was famous for its rich pastures, the ideal breeding ground for such creatures, but now the war called them north as the army prepared for its eventual march into Norland.

After her initial charge into the countryside, Aubrey had settled in for the trip, falling back to follow the great Mercerian Chargers for which her family was so well known.

"Beautiful, aren't they?" she said.

"They are indeed," replied Kraloch. "How long has your family been breeding them?"

"The breed was first established back in 602, but they'd been working on larger horses for years."

"Why is that? You didn't have knights back then, did you?"

"That's true, we didn't," said Aubrey, "but it was thought a larger mount would be more dangerous in battle. They were bred for their stamina more so than their strength."

"And have they changed much since then?"

"A little. If anything, they're a bit larger. My father was quite proud of his breeding program."

"And now you carry on the tradition," said the Orc. "How do you find the time?"

"I do very little in that regard. It's the horse breeders who do all the work."

"Remarkable."

"Have your people ever used horses?"

Kraloch looked down at his horse. "No, this is new to us."

"For something you've never done before, you appear to be exceedingly comfortable in the saddle."

He shrugged. "It is not difficult, and we have worked with animals before."

"Wolves?"

"Yes, our tribe uses them on the hunt. The relationship has been beneficial to both races."

"We use dogs, but you already knew that."

"I did. I have seen Tempus, remember? Not to mention the other Kurathian Mastiffs. Will they be joining us in the coming campaign?"

"I doubt it," said Aubrey. "The queen is concerned we can't replace losses. She wants their handlers to start a breeding program, but we're still waiting on breeding stock."

"And where do you get those?"

"From the Kurathian Isles, and before you ask, I have no idea where those are."

"A long way from here, I would gather. How do these breeders intend to get here?"

"By ship, out of Riversend."

"I can't imagine the men of Weldwyn will like that. They have no love for the Kurathians."

"They're already on their way, but we haven't heard anything back yet."

"Perhaps they will return by summer?"

"We can hope," said Aubrey. "In the meantime, they'll remain in Queenston, under constant supervision."

"They are savage beasts in battle," noted Kraloch.

"They are," agreed Aubrey.

"But something about them bothers you."

She looked at him in surprise. "Yes, it does. How did you know?"

He grinned. "We have worked together for some time, and I have begun to recognize your moods. Tell me, what is it that troubles you so?"

"It's their training methods. I find them harsh and distasteful."

"It makes them effective on the battlefield."

"There's no denying that," said Aubrey. "I just wish they didn't have to treat them with so much violence. Albreda says there are other ways to train them, but she's been far too busy to look into it any further."

"I suppose an Earth Mage could talk to them, though I don't know what they would say in response. How do you ask an animal to be vicious?"

"I have no idea, but luckily, it's not our job to worry about such things."

"And yet you do," said Kraloch.

"I have a soft spot for animals," said Aubrey. "I suppose it comes from spending time with Albreda."

"It is your inner essence."

"Essence?"

"I suppose you might call it a conscience."

"Well, whatever it is, it appears I have it in droves."

"That is good," said the Orc. "It is what makes you an effective Life Mage."

"I sometimes wonder what life would have been like had I not taken up magic."

"It is a waste of effort. You were destined to be a mage, as was I."

"How did you know you wanted to be a shaman?"

"It runs in my family, much as it did yours."

"So your parents were shamans?"

"No, but my aunt was. She demonstrated an even deeper understanding of the spirit realm than I ever could. It is said she was touched by the Ancestors."

"Is she still alive?"

"No, she died some years ago, long before the current alliance."

"Do you think she would have approved?"

He smiled, revealing his ivory teeth. "I doubt it. She never truly embraced change. The truth is, if it had not been for Lady Beverly's performance at Eastwood, we never would have considered such a thing."

"Ah, yes," said Aubrey, "the famous Redblade. My cousin will never live that down."

"You make it sound bad," said Kraloch, "yet her very actions that day led to a lasting friendship between our people."

"So it did," said Aubrey, "and for that, I am truly thankful."

FOURTEEN

The Netherwood

Spring 965 MC

Mazog looked across the fire, observing the shaman who was deep in concentration as they sat in a small clearing, surrounded by lean-tos and other temporary shelters as was typical for an Orc hunting party. They were deep in the Netherwood, an area where game was found in abundance, but there was an ominous feeling of late as if a great shadow had fallen over them.

Andurak opened his eyes, looking across at his chieftain with a face devoid of expression.

"What is it?" asked Mazog. "Is something wrong?"

"They have not answered the call."

"I do not understand."

"I can not communicate with the Ancestors."

Mazog scrunched up her face. "Could something be interfering with your magic? Or maybe the milk of life is tainted?"

In answer, the shaman looked down at the bowl of milky white liquid. "There is nothing wrong with this. I prepared it myself."

"Then what?"

"I do not know. The spell worked, but none have answered the call."

"Has this ever happened before?"

"Never!" said Andurak. "Nor have I heard tell of such a thing in our past."

The chieftain looked worried. "We can not proceed without the guidance of our Ancestors."

"I know," said Andurak, "and yet they do not answer my call. What would you have me do?"

"This is terrible news." Mazog's eyes scanned the area as if the very trees might hold an answer. All around them, their fellow hunters went about their business, unaware of the great calamity that had befallen them. "Maybe," she said at last, "we are in an area of the forest where your magic is dampened."

"Dampened? It has never been so in the past."

"Could you find a place of greater power, where the magic flows to the surface from deep below the ground?"

Andurak nodded his head. "A confluence." The shaman noted the look of ignorance on his chieftain's face. "An area where lines of magical energy converge."

"You know of such a place?"

"I do," the shaman replied, "although it is a long way from here."

"Then you must leave at once and seek this place," insisted Mazog. "We can not afford to be cut off from our Ancestors."

"Agreed," said Andurak. He stood, his staff firmly in hand. "I shall gather food and set out this very day."

Mazog stood, then moved closer, placing her hand upon the elder Orc's shoulder. "Be careful, my friend. You bear the fate of the tribe on your shoulders. It is not a burden to be carried lightly."

"I shall heed your warning, Mazog of the Wolf Clan. Look for me when the moon once more is at its brightest."

Mazog lowered her arm, watching as the shaman made his way to his shelter. There, the old Orc retrieved a small satchel, placing it around his shoulder.

Andurak rooted through his bag until he was satisfied with its contents, then looked once more at his chieftain. He nodded his head, then turned, disappearing into the forest.

Mazog watched him depart, wondering what these strange developments portended. Was this the end of her tribe?

The sun was high but barely trickled through the canopy of the forest. To another race, the effect would have been dark and foreboding, but to the eyes of an Orc, there was little cause for concern.

Andurak had started heading north mid-morning and by noon was well on his way. He occasionally halted, taking his bearings, using his inner magic to 'feel' the lines of force. The barest tingle of power told him he was some distance off yet. He knew this power crisscrossed the land, laying out a grid of sorts. His plan was simple: Find the line that ran north-south and follow it until it converged with one running east-west. Here the power would be at its greatest, allowing him to reach further into the past. Hopefully then he could succeed in contacting an Ancestor who might be of help.

By nightfall, he finally felt the power beginning to grow. Now all he had to do was follow it until he found a point of confluence. Picking out a soft patch of leaves, he lay down and closed his eyes. Tomorrow he would be entering a part of the Netherwood he had never trod, and he wondered briefly what he might find.

For five days, Andurak kept up his northern trek, then he beheld an unexpected sight. A great ravine crossed his path as if some ancient power had split the very dirt beneath his feet. He gazed across at the other side, but there was little he could do to gain access to it.

Although trees grew right up to the edge of the gap, no branches were long enough to reach the other side. Andurak sat down at its edge, pondering the sight. It stretched to his left and right as far as his eyes could see. Down below, the canyon teemed with vegetation and even had a little stream running through it.

Perhaps, he thought, it might be possible to climb down? He set about looking for a path and soon found a steep incline where a tree had toppled over the side, the roots pulling up the dirt to leave a gaping hole on the ledge. He climbed down, taking care to secure his footing with every step. With his staff in hand, he descended, wishing, not for the first time, he had thought to bring a master of earth, for such a power would have made his efforts all the easier.

Farther and farther he descended while the cliff grew less steep until a small ledge appeared. He placed his back against the wall and continued, moving sideways. Eventually it widened, and then he stepped into the greenery of the ravine floor.

All around him, he heard the sounds of wilderness, from birds chirping to the distant cry of a wolf. Onward he went, driven by the need to find answers. His tribe was counting on him, and he was determined not to fail in his duty.

By now, the sun had reached its zenith, flooding its light into the ravine. Andurak took a moment to orient himself, then started heading north towards what he hoped was the far wall.

He longed for a breeze, as the air down here was humid and stale with the smell of rotting vegetation drifting to his nose. Soon the noises ceased, and he paused, aware he was no longer alone. Off in the distance was the sound of scrambling feet as if something was climbing into the ravine. Was he now the prey?

Andurak froze, listening intently. His heart was beating heavily now, his breath coming in laboured gasps. Something made a sound off to his right, and he was reminded of someone cutting through vegetation with an axe or long knife.

He turned, ready to face this new threat. Closer came the noises until he thought he could see movement through the tall ferns. Moments later, a pale-grey visage peered out at him, its face appearing flattened as if the nose had been cut off; instead, there were just two slits that presumably served as nostrils. The eyes staring back at him were large and its limbs gangly, but still, it was Humanoid in shape. It held a strange-looking weapon within its grasp, a short spear with a blade on one side that used up half its length. Uttering something incomprehensible, it suddenly rushed forward, weapon held on high.

Andurak raised his staff, manoeuvring it before him to ward off the attack. The creature's blade dug into the wood, carving off a splinter, the shock travelling up the Orc's arms.

The shaman countered by twisting his weapon, striking out with the end and hitting the strange being on the head. It backed up, temporarily stunned, and he moved in closer, striking again. Down went his foe, and then Andurak turned and ran as fast as his legs could carry him.

With the sounds of pursuit drifting to his ears, he briefly considered turning to fight, but with a quick look behind, the numbers appeared to be against him. He burst into a small clearing, pausing for a moment to catch his breath. His pursuers had fallen behind, limited, no doubt, by their smaller stature. Gulping in air, he cast his eyes around, trying to get his bearings. In his mad dash to escape, he had fled deeper into the lush, green vegetation, but now, with the sun once again visible overhead, he realized his mistake.

Turning back to the north, he continued his flight, but then something whistled past his ear, and just in front of him, the top of a plant fell to the forest floor. Andurak didn't stop to examine what it was, but as more flew through the air, he instinctively ducked. He found himself wishing for the energy of his youth as he ploughed through the underbrush, and then without warning, the cliff wall was directly in front of him reaching far above.

Tucking his staff into his belt, he sought out a handhold and began climbing. Roots came loose in his fingers, and the dirt collapsed as he took hold, but slowly, ever so slowly, he began easing up the side of the ravine.

Sounds of chatter erupted below him, and then a round, sharp-edged piece of metal embedded itself into the dirt, narrowly missing his hand. The close call urged him onward, and he felt a burst of energy, sending him into a frenzy of motion.

Still frantically scrambling up, the sound of falling rocks caught his attention, and he looked down to see two of the creatures mimicking his actions, pulling themselves up the face of the cliff. His hand gripped a stone, and he halted, prying it loose before tossing it below and having the satis-faction of watching it bounce off a creature's back, causing the thing to lose its grip and fall.

Andurak glanced up, noting the root of a tree hanging over the ravine. His fingers reached out, but he felt something tug at his foot just as he touched the wood. Looking down, he saw a grey face grinning back at him as his second foe began crawling up his leg.

The shaman kicked out, trying to shake his enemy free, but it clung on with a tenacious grip. Andurak pulled himself upward, heedless of the extra weight and managed to get his hands around the root. He held on tight, then swung out over the ravine. The strange creature clung on even harder, but then Andurak swung back, smashing his legs against the wall of dirt and stone. An anguished cry rang out as his enemy released its grasp, falling with a scream to disappear into the greenery below.

The shaman hung for a moment, catching his breath, then hauled himself upward to perch on the root. From there, it was a simple matter to crawl along it to the top of the ravine. Thankful his ordeal was over, he collapsed on the forest floor, once more amongst familiar surroundings.

For two more days, Andurak travelled, putting his strange encounter well behind him. The forest here was thick with underbrush, a far cry from the deeper parts of the wood he had already traversed, and he wondered if he might finally be coming to the very edge of the Netherwood. Eventually, he had to resort to using a knife to cut his way through the plants, even having to backtrack on several occasions, so thick did the vegetation grow.

By noon of the second day, the land rose, and he found a high spot with a view of the surrounding countryside. Looking out upon the forest, it appeared to stretch on forever, and he grew despondent. Was he to wander the woods for the rest of his life? Then his eyes caught sight of a distant hill upon which sat an ancient structure, and in that instant, he knew he had found what he was looking for: a pair of large stones stood upright, with a third lain across their top, forming a crude arch.

He breathed a sigh of relief. It looked like his quest had not been in vain after all. With renewed purpose, he descended the hill, confident he would reach his objective by nightfall.

Andurak sat, his back resting against one of the stones. As the sun slowly set in the west, it cast a warm red glow over the top of the Netherwood, reminding him again how vast this area was. He closed his eyes, opening himself to his inner magic, sensing the power flowing beneath him. It was said great rivers of magical energy rushed below the ground, creating the very fabric that made magic possible. Those who had the gift could harness their own internal version of this same power, using it to manipulate the substance of reality.

Opening his eyes, the shaman gazed up into the starry night. From the Ancestors' teachings, he knew that ages ago, the God Hraka had given life to the race of Orcs, along with the gift of fire, theirs to share or keep as their own. This had set them apart from the creatures of the Underworld who had already spread across the land. Those creatures were eventually sent back to their home by the magic of the Gods, leaving a pristine world for the elder races. The Orcs had long since given up worshipping Hraka, yet they still acknowledged his contribution. However, it was to the Ancestors they had turned, using their arcane skills to seek wisdom from forefathers and mothers. Could he now seek to contact those very same predecessors?

Pushing himself to his feet, he walked around the stones, examining the ancient runes. To his surprise, he recognized a number of them as being Orcish in origin. Could this strange structure have been built by the Ancestors he sought to contact? Running his fingers over the symbols gave him a sense of wonder. What ancient knowledge might he unlock by tapping into these primeval forces?

Andurak halted, facing the stones. He held his arms out to either side, his staff firmly gripped in his right hand. Magic words spewed from his mouth, and then a tingling ran up his spine as the air began buzzing with energy. The power built until he felt he could contain it no longer. His arms went higher still as he spoke the final words that would call forth the Ancestors he sought. Energy surged through him, and then a ghostly figure appeared before his eyes.

"Who has called me?" the figure asked.

"It is I, Andurak of the Wolf Clan. Identify yourself."

"I am Granag Hornbow, Grand Chieftain of the Crimson Hawks. Why have you summoned me thus?"

"I seek your guidance, mighty one," said the shaman.

"Then speak while you have my attention."

"Many times, I have contacted the Ancestors," said Andurak. "And always they have answered, until now. For the last few ten-days, they have failed to heed my call. Tell me, oh wise and powerful Granag, why have they abandoned us?"

"They have not," replied the ghostly image. "But they no longer wander the realm of spirits."

"What magic is this?" said the shaman. "It must be powerful indeed to pull the Ancestors from their spirit home."

"They have been pulled to the physical realm," said Granag. "There to be bound by dark magic to serve a new mistress."

"This is terrible news. What is to be done?"

"For that, you must seek answers elsewhere, for it is beyond my understanding. Indeed, it is beyond any of our race. Only the Humans will have the answers. Go east, my descendant, and search for she who is known as the Witch of the Whitewood. Only there will you find the answers you seek."

"And will she be able to undo this great evil?"

"I can not see, for the future is in turmoil. Heed my words, Andurak of the Wolf Clan, for the entire future of our race is in your hands."

The image faded, leaving the shaman pale and shaking as he gazed east, wondering what the future might bring.

FIFTEEN

The Circle

Spring 965 MC

Aubrey watched as Aldus Hearn moved to the centre of the magic circle, where a book sat on a lectern. The Druid quickly scanned its contents before closing his eyes and gathering his thoughts. The process of empowering would be a lengthy one, and Aubrey knew first-hand just how exhausting it could be. She stepped into the circle, taking up a position on the other side of the tome.

Hearn slowly exhaled, then dropped his eyes to the pages before him. He began reading the words aloud, his voice falling into the rhythm that was so common for spells of this nature. On and on he droned until the air came alive with energy. Aubrey flipped the page, allowing him to continue with the ritual uninterrupted. She glanced at Kraloch, but the Orc's eyes were glued to Hearn.

The old man kept up the litany, the individual words becoming almost indecipherable to all but the most experienced mages. Aubrey heard an audible pop and then tasted metal in the back of her mouth as one of the floor runes began to glow. She thought back to Wincaster and her own empowerment ritual when runes had finally lit up with an intense light, but here the colour was more muted as befitted a less powerful circle.

She turned the page again as Hearn continued the ritual, the words tumbling forth at a faster and faster pace. Another rune lit up, and the air resonated with an audible hum. Time felt like it had come to a standstill, and Aubrey looked around the room to see if anyone else had noticed.

Aldwin was there with Beverly, but her cousin had nodded off, while her husband took it all in with intense interest. Looking back at Aldus Hearn, she noticed him straining with the effort. He had broken out into a sweat, his face beginning to look drawn and haggard.

When another rune came to life, the Druid appeared to get his second wind. He straightened his back, slowing the incantation for a moment as he paused, reaching to the floor where a cup stood waiting. A sip of water was all he needed, and then he resumed as he set it back down.

Aubrey, caught up in the display, almost missed her cue and rushed to turn the page. Hearn looked at her, a smile playing across his lips, but still, the words poured forth.

The liturgy continued in cycles with the Druid slowly fading, only to be re-energized each time a rune locked into place.

As the final rune lit up, the room became hazy when a ring of mist emanated from Aldus Hearn to spread out from his location, engulfing the room, and then the magical symbols began to pulse with light.

She watched as Hearn's voice grew louder, now shouting, using the last of his energy to release his magic. When a clap of thunder echoed off the walls, the strange mist settled into the runes as they slowly dimmed. The magic circle was now empowered and ready for use.

Hearn collapsed to the floor, and Aubrey knelt at his side. He was quite still, his breathing shallow, and she immediately began casting a spell of healing.

Kraloch soon joined her, using his fingers to pry open the man's eyelids. The Orc looked up from where he worked to meet her gaze. "He must rest. He is exhausted, nothing more."

Aubrey breathed a sigh of relief, letting her spell dissipate. "That was close."

"It was," the Orc agreed. "It is not something I would care to see repeated."

"We must find some way of lessening the burden."

"Perhaps there is a way," he said with a far-off look.

"What are you thinking?"

"It can wait," said Kraloch. "We must first see to Master Hearn."

Beverly was soon there, looking down at the stricken Druid. "Is he all right?"

"He'll be fine," said Aubrey, "but the casting was a strain on his body. Rest is all that's required now."

"I don't understand," said the knight. "You were weak when you empowered the circle in Wincaster, but you didn't pass out."

"True, but Aldus is far older than I."

"But isn't he more powerful?"

"In casting terms, yes, but the release of one's power in this manner wears on the physical form."

"I hope this isn't going to happen every time we empower a circle," said Beverly.

"We can agree on that," said Aubrey. "Now, give us a hand, will you? We need to get him to a bed."

Beverly leaned over Hearn, lifting him by the armpits while Kraloch took his legs. They carried him from the room, disappearing from sight.

"Well, that was quite an interesting display," said Aldwin. "I hope it wasn't my circle that caused him so much strain."

"No," said Aubrey. "The ritual worked just as it was supposed to. I'm afraid it was his advanced years that worked against him."

"Just how old IS Aldus Hearn?"

"I'm not sure," she replied, "but if I had to guess, I'd say he's at least sixty. Whatever age he is, he's the oldest mage we've got."

"I thought Lord Greycloak was older?"

"He is, but Elves don't age the same. And in any case, the Lord of the Darkwood is no longer interested in participating in the work of the Mages Council."

Aldwin stared at the floor, noting the inlaid runes. They were no longer glowing, but the gold and silver caught what light there was, throwing strange reflections against the wall. "I suppose now I'll have to get to work on the next circle."

"I think that can wait," said Aubrey. "We have to find some way to make the ritual less taxing."

"I can see why," said the smith. "By all appearances, that almost killed Master Hearn."

"Yes, and we have few enough mages as it is. There has to be a better way!"

"Listen, Beverly and I are having a little get-together tonight. Why don't you come along?"

"Surely you don't want me getting in the way?"

"Nonsense. We've had plenty of private time, and it would be nice to have family over. Assuming you don't have to return to Wincaster, of course."

Aubrey smiled. "I'd like that."

"Very well, we'll see you later." He turned to leave.

"Wait," she called out. "I don't know where you're staying?"

"We have a tent," he replied. "It's set up just behind the church. We'll see you there."

"I look forward to it."

Aldwin took another bite, the juice dripping down his chin.

Beverly laughed.

"You're lucky he doesn't have a beard," noted Aubrey. "I'd hate to think how messy that would be."

"It's the forge," said Aldwin through a mouthful of food.

Aubrey wore an expression of confusion and looked to her cousin for clarification.

"Beards can burn," explained Beverly. "That's why he keeps himself clean-shaven."

"The look certainly makes him appear younger."

Beverly smiled. "I know. I quite like it, don't you?"

Aubrey laughed. It was good to be able to relax with family, something she did far too infrequently.

As if reading her mind, Aldwin spoke. "We should do this more often."

"I agree," chimed in Beverly.

"I'm in," added Aubrey, "but I can't guarantee we'll all be available at the same time."

"Well," said Aldwin, "having a circle in Wickfield will certainly make a difference. Beverly can pop back to Wincaster whenever she likes now."

"Yes, or Hawksburg, for that matter," added his wife.

"Easier said than done," noted Aubrey. "You'd still need a mage."

"Yes, but there'll be mages using recall daily now, I expect. The queen will want to be kept informed of our progress. She might even visit us herself. I doubt we'd have to wait long to see her."

"I suppose that will make me even busier now," complained Aubrey.

"You need to get that academy of yours going."

"Thanks for reminding me I have even more work to do. As if I didn't have enough on my plate."

"We're all busy, Aubrey. These are tough times. There is a war on after all."

"I know, I'm just feeling overwhelmed."

"You know what would help?" asked Aldwin.

"No, what?"

He leaned back in his chair, reaching into a box that was on the floor.

Moments later, he produced a bottle with a flourish. "How about a little Hawksburg Red?"

Aubrey smiled. "Where did you find that?"

"In Wincaster."

Beverly laughed. "Is this how you've been spending your time in Wincaster? Searching through wine cellars?"

The smith blushed. "It was your father's fault. He's the one who sent me down there."

"I didn't know your father had such a thing," said Aubrey.

"Oh yes," said Beverly. "He considers himself an expert on such things." She looked at the label. "I'm surprised he let you take that. It's one of his favourites."

Aldwin looked quite pleased with himself. "He suggested it, actually."

"Well, don't just sit there," said Aubrey, "pour it!"

He filled her cup, then turned to his wife, but she held up her hand. "No, thank you, I've had quite enough for one night. And besides, I've got a small army to train tomorrow."

"Maybe we should save it?" suggested her cousin.

"No, no. You go right ahead, Aubrey. You deserve it."

Aubrey's head was pounding. She opened her eyes to see her red-headed cousin staring down at her. "What time is it?" she muttered.

"Past daybreak," said Beverly. "I would have let you sleep, but there's someone here to see you."

"There is?" The young mage sat up, instantly regretting the move as the room swam and her eyes ached.

"I'm not sure I'm fit for company."

Kraloch's voice drifted into the tent. "Perhaps I can be of assistance?"

"I'm not sure what you can do," said Beverly. "I'm afraid this is all my fault."

"How so?" asked the Orc.

"I insisted she have that wine last night."

The Orc gestured. "May I come in?"

"Of course."

He stepped into the tent, coming to stand beside Aubrey. One look at her eyes was all the examination he required. "You say it was wine?"

"Yes," said Beverly, "although I think it was more the quantity than quality that did her in."

"It is a simple enough problem to deal with, so long as you don't mind me casting a spell?"

"It's fine by me, but you might want to ask my cousin."

Kraloch looked at Aubrey, who was squinting in a vain effort to keep the daylight from her eyes. She nodded. "Go ahead."

The shaman closed his eyes, calling on his inner magic. The air buzzed, and then his hands began to glow with a faint blue light. He gently placed them on Aubrey's temples, and then the colour flowed into her, concentrating on her head for a moment before dissipating.

"Well?" said Beverly. "How do you feel?"

Aubrey stood, stretching. "Like I just awoke from a nice long nap." She turned to the Orc. "What spell did you use?"

"Neutralize toxins," said Kraloch.

"I'm surprised. I thought that only worked on poison."

"In a sense, it does. It detects and eliminates things foreign to your body."

"Best not talk of it," warned Beverly, "or you'll find yourself in demand. Any mage who can cure a hangover would never have time to do anything else."

"I shall bear that in mind," said Kraloch.

Aldwin stepped into the tent, already sweating from working at the forge. He looked at his wife. "Still here? I thought you had training to do?"

"I do," said Beverly. "I'm just on my way out." She looked at the Orc, then her cousin. "Thank you, Master Kraloch, and I'll see you later, Aubrey."

The mage smiled. "I look forward to it, but maybe next time we hold back a little on the wine?"

Beverly chuckled. "Very well."

Aubrey watched as the knight left, then looked at Aldwin. "How is it you're not hungover? You drank even more than I did."

He shrugged. "Who's to say I wasn't? The difference is I was up early this morning, sweating it off at the forge. In any event, I just came in to get something." Aldwin began rooting through a chest, then pulled forth a pair of tongs. "There they are. I knew I had them in here somewhere."

"Strange place to keep them, in with your clothes, isn't it?" asked Aubrey.

"I travel light when it comes to clothes," said Aldwin. "Now, I'd best get back to work before the forge begins to cool."

He disappeared through the tent flap.

Aubrey turned her attention back to Kraloch. "You wanted to see me about something?"

"I did," said the Orc. "I've been thinking on what we talked about yesterday."

"I'm afraid you'll have to remind me."

"We were both concerned with the toll that empowering the circle took on Master Hearn."

"I take it you have some thoughts on the matter?"

"I do, but there is a complication."

"Of course," said Aubrey, "things always have to get more complicated. What is this idea of yours?"

"As you remember, we combined our magic to seek an answer to Master Bloom's infirmity. I propose a similar technique be utilized to empower circles."

"Would that even work?"

"It is unknown, but it is worth investigating, is it not?"

"It certainly is. You mentioned a complication?"

"Yes," said Kraloch. "The mages combining their power would likely have to be of the same variety. You and I both utilize the power of Life Magic, for example."

"I suppose that only makes sense," said Aubrey. "But that doesn't help us much. The only other school of magic in which we are blessed with more than one mage is that of the earth."

"What if we called on the mages of Weldwyn to lend a hand? Do you think they would be willing to assist?"

"Possibly," said Aubrey, "but even then, we might not have enough."

"They have an Enchanter, do they not?" asked Kraloch.

"They do, a woman named Gretchen Harwell, but I have no idea if she'd be willing to work with Kiren-Jool. The people of Weldwyn have little love for the Kurathians."

"It is worth a try, at least."

"True," agreed Aubrey. "And they have an Earth Mage who could work with either Albreda or Master Hearn, so that might help."

"It is a pity we have no more Elementalists. A nice master of flame would be useful."

"Agreed, or a Water Mage, for that matter. We lack both."

"I shall give it further thought," said the Orc, "but there is far too much to keep us busy at present."

"There is?"

"Yes," he continued. "Now that the Wickfield circle is working, we have messages to carry and people to ferry back and forth to Wincaster."

"In that case, I'd better get some food into me," said Aubrey. "It looks like it's going to be a busy day."

Gerald entered the casting room to see Master Kraloch waiting.

"*Good morning,*" he said, using the Orcish tongue.

"And the same to you," said the shaman. "Are you ready to depart?"

"Yes," replied the marshal, "but we must wait on Dame Beverly."

"I had no idea she was travelling with us."

"The queen wants a report on how well her training is going, and I thought it best she gets a first-hand account. She'll only be a moment. I ran into her on the way over here."

"How are the preparations for the invasion going?" asked Kraloch.

Gerald frowned. "Not as well as I would have liked. It feels like every time we make progress, something else sets us back."

"Is there anything I can help with?"

"Not unless you can keep wagons rolling."

"I'm afraid I don't understand. Do we lack horses?"

"No," said Gerald. "We have plenty of those, but the wagons we use to haul supplies are getting a little long in the tooth."

Kraloch gave him a quizzical look. "Are long teeth not desired?"

"Sorry, my friend, I meant they're getting old. We had two broken axles just yesterday, and some of the wheels look like they might wear out given another few days of use. I don't suppose your tribe might have someone who can fix such things?"

"I am afraid not," said the Orc. "Though if we did, I am sure Chief Urgon would happily give them to you."

"Ah, well," said Gerald. "It's just one more thing to add to the list of never-ending problems."

"Is it serious?"

"Don't worry, we'll sort it out in time. In any event, we won't be marching north for some time yet."

"Are the problems that severe?"

"No, but we're still awaiting word on maps. Only a fool goes blundering into enemy territory with no clue what it looks like."

"That explains the absence of the Kurathians," said Kraloch.

"An astute observation. I wish all my troops were as observant."

The guards outside called out a challenge.

"It sounds like Beverly's here," said Gerald.

Sure enough, the door opened, revealing the red-headed knight.

"Not bringing your horse?" he asked.

"Why would I need Lightning? We're going to the Palace, aren't we?"

"Of course," said Gerald. "I was only making conversation. Got every-thing you need?"

She produced a rolled-up scroll. "It's all here for the queen's perusal."

"Good," he added. "You may proceed, Kraloch."

SIXTEEN

Bronwyn

Spring 965 MC

B ronwyn stared at the guards. "This will not do," she declared.
"I'm sorry?" said Fitz.

"These guards are common," she clarified.

"Yes, they're all over the Palace, in fact."

"No," said the princess. "I mean they are of common birth. They are most unsuitable for one of Royal Birth."

"Ah, I thought that might end up being the case. Allow me a moment if you will?"

He poked his head outside the door. "Come in, gentlemen."

Two warriors entered, each wearing the plate and chain armour that was becoming so common in Merceria.

"Allow me to introduce Sir Greyson and Sir Hector, Knights of the Sword."

Both men bowed, Sir Greyson with much more of a flourish. Sir Hector, the younger of the two, added "Your Highness," to his response.

"These men are both distinguished members of the nobility, Highness. I trust that will suit you?"

"Perhaps," said Bronwyn as she moved to stand in front of Sir Greyson. "Tell me about yourself," she demanded.

"I come from Shrewesdale," the knight replied. Noting the look of confusion, he decided to expand upon his answer. "It lies to the south, Your Highness, near to the Great Swamp."

"And was your master the Earl of Shrewesdale?"

"All knights are sworn to the queen," interrupted the baron.

"I worked closely with the earl," added Sir Greyson, "if that's what you mean. I was in that fair city for three years, until Lord Montrose was executed by the Crown."

Bronwyn looked at the baron for an explanation.

"It's a long and complicated story," offered Fitz.

"I see." She stepped to the side. "And this one? Sir Hector, was it?"

"Yes, ma'am," said the knight.

"Where do you hail from?"

"Kingsford, my lady."

"Your Highness," corrected Bronwyn.

"Sorry, Your Highness," Sir Hector repeated.

"And where is Kingsford?"

"It lies on our western border, across the river from Weldwyn."

She turned to the baron. "These two will do nicely, I should think. You may leave us, Baron."

"As Your Highness wishes," said Fitz. He bowed, then backed up, turning to exit the room.

Bronwyn made her way across the room to look down at a bottle of wine. She cast her eyes about, seeking a girl to do the work, but remembered she was without servants. Lifting the bottle, she poured herself a drink, then turned to face the guards once more.

"Tell me, Sir Greyson, what think you of your queen?"

"We are sworn to her, Your Highness."

"Maybe I should be more precise. What do you think of the idea of a queen as opposed to a king?"

"It's a difficult idea to wrap one's head around," offered the knight.

"I disagree," said Sir Hector, then remembered his place. "Sorry for interrupting, Your Highness."

"Not at all," said Bronwyn. "Please continue. Are you saying you find the idea pleasurable?"

"I wouldn't say pleasurable is the right word, but she is a fair and just ruler."

Sir Greyson's frown revealed his true thoughts.

"You don't agree?" said Bronwyn, turning her attention to him.

"She is young," said the knight, "and, as such, is subject to influence by her advisors."

"Not true," defended Sir Hector. "She is a wise ruler and seeks consensus on issues, but still has her own mind."

"I sense you are loyal to her cause," said Bronwyn. "Tell me, do the other women in her inner circle receive such devotion? What of the old woman?"

"Old woman?" said Sir Greyson.

"Yes, I believe she was called a witch?"

"You mean Albreda?" asked Sir Greyson.

"Yes. I found the woman to be quite rude."

The knights both laughed.

"She's rude to everyone," added Sir Hector.

"Is she indeed? Then why does the queen tolerate her?"

"She is the most powerful mage in the realm, Your Highness. In any event, the queen values her views on a wide range of subjects. She's willing to overlook such behaviour in exchange for honest advice."

"And this Albreda," pressed the princess, "is she a noble?"

"Not as far as I'm aware," said Sir Greyson. "But then again, neither is her marshal."

"Her marshal? Isn't he the Duke of Wincaster? I've heard Lord Hollis speak of him."

"He is," said Sir Greyson, "but it was not always so. He was awarded that rank only after the civil war."

"Some might say he earned it," added Sir Hector. "He is an experienced warrior, Your Highness."

"And he is not the only commoner to be rewarded for their service," added Sir Greyson.

"Can you be more specific?" asked the princess.

"The woman who found you, Dame Hayley Chambers—"

"Lady Hayley Chambers," corrected Sir Hector.

Greyson grimaced. "Whatever you want to call her, everyone knows she was born to a poacher. You can put a person into high office, but you can't take away the stench of their birth. And let's not forget the Royal Life Mage, Revi Bloom."

Bronwyn waved away the subject. "Practitioners of magic are of no consequence to me, but this Hayley Chambers, what office does she hold?"

"She is Baroness of Queenston," said Sir Hector, "and occupies the position of High Ranger."

"I'm afraid I'm not familiar with that role."

"The rangers keep the Queen's Roads safe from brigands and wild animals. In wartime, they supplement the queen's archers."

"Fascinating," said the princess. "How did she come to gain the confidence of the queen?"

"She was a Knight of the Sword," said Sir Hector.

"No she wasn't," argued Sir Greyson.

"Yes she was. Don't you remember? She brought back the body of Prince Alfred, and King Andred knighted her on the spot. It was only later when the princess was allowed to create her own order that Dame Hayley became a Knight of the Hound."

"Oh, yes," said the older knight. "She was recruited by Dame Beverly."

"Dame Beverly?" said Bronwyn. "Am I to be confounded by even more names?"

"The daughter of Baron Fitzwilliam," said Sir Hector.

"And she is a knight? Why haven't I heard of her?"

"Quite frankly, Your Highness, I'm surprised you haven't heard her name mentioned. She fought Lord Hollis's champion in Galburn's Ridge."

"And lost," added Greyson.

Bronwyn noted the hostility between the two knights and smiled. It looked like there were significant differences between them. Perhaps this weakness might be exploited?

"You said she was a Knight of the Hound, yet you are both Knights of the Sword, are you not?"

"We are," said Sir Hector.

"What's the difference?"

"Knights of the Hound is a more select order of knighthood," he explained. "They were started by the queen before she was crowned but are considered the more senior order."

"And yet," countered Sir Greyson, "the Order of the Sword has been in existence since King Arnulf created them back in 583."

"And the Hounds are commanded by the queen?" asked the princess.

"No," said Sir Hector. "The Knight Commander of the order is Dame Beverly."

"A disgraced knight," spat out Greyson. "She was dismissed from the Order of the Sword by King Andred."

"You would be wise to pick your words carefully," warned Sir Hector. "You tread close to treason."

"Is it treason to speak my mind?"

Bronwyn smiled. "Gentlemen, I appreciate your candour. I seek only to learn of your land, not divide it. In any event, I think it best if you take up your positions outside my door."

As the two knights filed out quietly, she noted the look of hatred that passed between them. It appeared her stay in Wincaster would be far more interesting than she had thought.

. . .

Bronwyn sat at the table, staring at the food on her plate. It was apparently called Mercerian Pudding, but to her mind, it lacked a sauce, something she was finding quite common amongst these southerners.

"How are things in the north?" asked the queen.

The princess looked up, ready to speak, only to realize the question had been put to Lord Matheson, the marshal. The old man looked over at Bronwyn with concern on his face.

"You can speak openly," the queen added. "We have no secrets here."

"Things are coming along nicely," he replied. "The training of our new recruits is going well. They should be ready to march by month's end, just in time to join the offensive."

"You mean to invade Norland?" asked Bronwyn.

"I might remind you that it was we who were invaded first," said the queen. "We are merely returning the favour."

"I had thought to take the mastiffs," offered the marshal. "They could prove quite effective against the enemy cavalry."

"I think not. They took losses in their last engagement, and without a breeding program in place, they are irreplaceable."

"Any word back from Kurathia yet?"

"I'm afraid not, but you must remember it's quite a long trip. We likely won't hear anything till late summer, possibly even autumn. What about the Trolls?"

"Tog already has them moving," replied the marshal. "I received word that they arrived in Kingsford a week ago. They're likely halfway to Hawksburg by now."

"Trolls?" said Bronwyn.

"Yes," said the queen. "They are a large race. Easily a head or two taller than most men, with grey skin that's hard as stone."

"Now you're pulling my leg," said the princess. "Such creatures are the stuff of bedtime stories."

"I can assure you they are quite real."

"Yes," added the old man, "and quite terrifying to face on the battlefield."

"Have you any other news, Gerald?"

"Herdwin has brought more troops from Stonecastle."

"Stonecastle?" said Bronwyn. "Is that the Dwarves?"

"It is," he replied. "Why? Do you know of it?"

"No, but the name sounds Dwarvish."

The queen put down her fork. "Do you have Dwarves in Norland?"

"No, but we are aware of them. They occupy a fortress in the gap."

"The gap?" said the marshal.

"Yes. It's a flat area of land that runs through the mountains near Holdcross."

"Where does it lead?" asked the queen.

"No one really knows. The Dwarves of Ironcliff have a fortress on its northern side, but no Norlander has ever ventured past it."

"Could it lead to the Continent?"

"The Continent?" said Bronwyn.

"Yes," said the queen. "What we like to call the old country. Our Ancestors came from there many generations ago. Surely you know of it?"

"I do not. My knowledge of history only goes back to the origins of our realm. Perhaps you'd care to enlighten me?"

The queen smiled, obviously relishing the thought. "Our Ancestors were mercenaries," she began, "and they came to this land after betrayal at the hands of their final employers."

"What kind of betrayal?"

"The books don't say, but it led them to the coast where they seized ships, hoping to sail away to an untamed land. Eventually, they made landfall on what is now the southern coast of Weldwyn. That's Westland to you."

"Is that where Weldwyn comes from? Our common Ancestors?"

"In a manner of speaking, but not the way you might think. The land was already inhabited by Humans, though a unified kingdom did not exist. Instead, they lived as clans or tribes, similar in some ways to how the Orcs are organized. When our forefathers landed, the tribes united against us. They had the advantage of numbers, whereas we were few. We fled eastward, across the river to found the city of Kingsford. That was the start of Merceria, or Mercenaria, as the men of Weldwyn used to call it. From there, we spread eastward until we came up against the mountains. Along the way, we battled Elves and Orcs."

"Who now serve you," said Bronwyn. "I suppose that's the price of being conquered."

"What makes you think they were conquered?" asked the marshal.

"Why else would they serve you?"

"They're our allies."

"Allies? Aren't you worried they might turn on you?"

"Turn on us?" said the queen. "Why would they do that?"

"Elves are not Human. To believe they would see reason would be a grave mistake. The comparison gets even worse when you consider the Orcs."

Anna's face turned to stone, her voice growing cold. "They might look different, but inside they are much like us. They live, they love, and they see reason. Is that not enough?"

"Do not tell me such nonsense," said Bronwyn. "I saw black blood on that Orc. They are as different from us on the inside as out."

"Why do you hate them so?"

The princess was taken aback. "What makes you think I hate them?"

"You see them as monsters," said the queen. "That much is clear."

"And you do not? They are savage brutes, capable only of murder and mayhem."

"Is that what you think?"

"Of course, don't you?"

"Not at all," said the queen.

Bronwyn turned to the marshal. "You must make her see reason, Lord Matheson."

"I have no reason to disagree with her," the man replied. "The Orcs have proven to be solid, reliable allies. They came to our aid during the war when we could offer them little in return, and even helped us rebuild Hawksburg after the king burned most of it to the ground. They are a people to be admired."

Bronwyn's face betrayed her disgust. "Spoken like the commoner you are. The queen might see fit to dress you in finery, but you will always be of low birth!"

"That's enough!" shouted Anna, rising to her feet and slamming the table with her fist. "I will not have you speak ill of Gerald."

The two royals stared at each other, neither willing to back down. The moment stretched into eternity.

Bronwyn's mind was racing. What was this strange connection between this young queen and her marshal?

The door opened, revealing Prince Alric. "Is everything all right in here?"

The queen sat, taking a moment to compose herself.

"A slight disagreement," explained Gerald.

Bronwyn noted the lack of respect given to the prince. Just who was this man?

"Come. Join us, Alric," said the queen. "Perhaps your presence will have a moderating effect."

"I should be delighted."

The old man shifted his chair down the table, allowing the prince to take his place. It appeared they knew each other well, yet there was something the young princess was missing.

"We were just talking of Lord Matheson," said Bronwyn. "Do you know him well?"

Alric smiled, warming the room. "I first met him some years ago when he visited my home. I thought him a bit rough at first, but I've come to appreciate his qualities."

"And what qualities are those?"

"He cares greatly for the queen. She's like a daughter to him." '

"Oh?" she said, feigning only moderate interest. "Do tell."

"Gerald lost his own family some years ago," explained Anna, her composure now fully restored. "Through a series of unfortunate circumstances, he found himself assigned to the Royal Estate at Uxley. That's where we first met."

"Assigned? Was he then a servant?"

"He was actually a soldier. He'd been injured in Bodden and was sent to Wincaster to recuperate."

"But you just said he was assigned to a place called Uxley. Is that here in town?"

"No, it's a country estate. He was eventually assigned there as a groundskeeper."

Bronwyn sneered. "Then it's worse than I thought."

Alric picked up on the tension. "Lord Matheson is more of a father than King Andred ever was," he said. "Would you insult the Royal House of Merceria?"

She stubbornly clung to her belief. "He is no royal."

"Nor are you at the moment."

Bronwyn stared daggers.

The prince continued. "You are the granddaughter of the late King Halfan, but there's no king on the throne of Norland at present as the earls fight over it. While there is war, there is no Royal House. The victors will dictate who is royal and who is not."

"And what would you know of such things?"

"My father is the King of Weldwyn, my elder brother, the heir."

The princess hid her surprise. She had assumed he was a prince by way of his marriage to the queen, but this revelation painted an entirely different picture. "Tell me," she continued, "what do you think of these creatures?"

"Creatures?" said the prince.

"Yes, the Orcs and Elves."

"They are people," objected the marshal, his voice betraying his agitation.

Alric held up his hand to halt any further harsh words. "While it's true the army of Weldwyn includes only Human warriors, it might surprise you to know we count Elves and Dwarves amongst our populace."

"Surely not in positions of authority?" said Bronwyn.

"Oh, yes. In fact, an Elf, Lord Parvan Luminor, is the Baron of Tivilton, though maybe he's not the best example."

"Do Weldwyn women hold titles like they do in Merceria?"

"Only one," said Alric, "and only because she's a widow. Of course, here, it's much more common. Have you met Lady Aubrey?"

"I can't say I have. Tell me about her."

"She's the Baroness of Hawksburg. She assumed the title upon the death of her parents."

"But won't that change when she marries?"

"Not under Mercerian law," added the queen. "And if you want another example, consider the woman who rescued you."

"Yes," said Bronwyn. "I understand she is a Knight of the Hound."

"More than that," added the marshal. "She is the Baroness of Queenston."

"Wasn't she born to a poacher?" asked Bronwyn.

"I see the Palace guards have been talking," noted the old man. "I shall have to have words with them."

"It wasn't Palace guards," added the prince. "I spoke with Fitz earlier. He assigned two Knights of the Sword to her protection."

The marshal's frown flooded Bronwyn's mind with possibilities. Was there dissension within the Palace halls?

"I value people based on their abilities," said the queen, "regardless of race or gender. Perhaps your own kingdom would be better served if your fellow Norlanders did likewise."

"My people value the art of war," insisted Bronwyn.

"MY kingdom was built by such men, yet I am not the first queen to rule Merceria. The last time a woman wore the warriors crown, it heralded in a golden age."

"Yes," said the prince, "Queen Evermore." He blushed, then looked at Anna, who was smiling. "I've been reading up on your history."

"I don't think I'm familiar with her," said the marshal.

"I am," said the queen, "but I'll let Alric share what he knows."

The prince smiled. "Her actual name was Georgette. She was the widow of King Ansel the Second, only taking the name of Evermore when she accepted the crown. I believe her reign lasted twenty years, but at that time, it was the longest Merceria had ever been at peace. She is particularly remembered for encouraging the arts. That's when the great bard, Califax, came into his own. She was succeeded by her son, who was still in the womb when she was crowned."

"Would her son not have been named king after he was born?" asked Bronwyn.

"That would have been the normal course of events," said the queen, "but she was determined to remain on the throne."

"Did I hear you mention Califax?" asked Bronwyn. "I've heard of him."

"I did," said the prince. "You're familiar with his work?"

"Such books are hard to come by in Norland," said the princess, "but I have read *Autumn's Twilight*."

"A fine story."

The queen laughed. "Before you came to Merceria, you'd never heard of the man."

"True," said Prince Alric, "but I've come to appreciate his works since coming to Wincaster. The books are good, of course, but to truly experience them, you must see them on the stage."

"Stage?" said Bronwyn.

"Yes, at the theatre. Don't you have those in Norland?"

"I have heard of no such thing. Explain it to me if you will?"

"It would be far better to show you."

"That's a tremendous idea, Alric," said the queen. "What's playing at the Grand?"

"Something by Madrusen," the prince replied. "*The Golden Mask*, I think. They had *Autumn's Twilight* last month; it's a favourite amongst the populace. What if you demanded a Royal Performance?"

The queen sat back, contemplating the idea. "Very well, but I shall make it a request, not a command."

"You are the queen," said Bronwyn. "Surely they must obey your commands?"

"I rule on behalf of my people, not over them. It is the obligation of the nobility to protect the people, something I learned many years ago." She looked at her marshal with a smile. "A wise man once told me that."

"Shall I arrange things?" asked Prince Alric. "I thought we might make an event of it, invite all the people of influence."

"If the master of the Grand is agreeable," said Anna. "How long do you think it would take?"

"I suspect he'll need a week or two to organize things."

"What is there to organize?" asked Bronwyn. "Do they not merely show up and read the book?"

"No," said the prince. "They act out the story, each performer taking on a singular role. I suspect they'll need time to review their lines."

Bronwyn couldn't quite grasp the concept, her face revealing her confusion.

The prince was quick to notice. "Let's just say preparations will have to be made, shall we? I'll get Jack onto it right away."

The princess allowed the smallest of nods. "Very well, I shall look forward to it."

SEVENTEEN

Autumn's Twilight

Spring 965 MC

After the carriage rolled to a stop, Bronwyn waited until her guards climbed down, then the door opened, revealing Sir Greyson. "We are here, Your Highness."

Bronwyn took his hand as she exited, leaning on him perhaps a little more than necessary to keep her balance. It had the desired effect, eliciting a smile from the older knight.

They were now standing in front of a rather nondescript building with an archway serving as the entrance. Inside, doormen waited, no doubt aware the queen was visiting this day. They bowed as she entered, and then the princess beheld a young woman dressed in fine clothes.

"Good afternoon, Your Highness," the woman said. "My name is Lady Aubrey Brandon. I've been asked to escort you to the queen's box."

"Box?" enquired Bronwyn.

"Yes, a private seating area for the enjoyment of the play. If you'll allow me?"

"Of course. Lead on."

The princess followed the young woman up the stairs, halting before a door. Outside stood a red-headed woman wearing armour, a sight that made her look at Sir Greyson. Sure enough, the man was scowling.

"This must be Dame Beverly," said Bronwyn. "Knight Commander of the Order of the Hound."

The knight nodded. "Your Highness, welcome to the Grand Theatre. Her Majesty is inside, along with her other guests."

"Other guests?"

"Yes, Prince Alric and the marshal."

"The marshal? Does he accompany her everywhere?"

"No, but this theatre is one of his favourite places, as it is the queen's." Beverly turned, opening the door a crack and peering inside. "The princess is here, Your Majesty."

"Show her in, Beverly," came the reply.

The knight stood back, opening the door fully and bowing slightly. Bronwyn strode through the door into the small space beyond, barely big enough for the five chairs it held. Situated high on the side of a large room, it thankfully had a low wall to keep them from falling.

Queen Anna had risen, as had the rest. "You may take a seat and get comfortable, Your Highness. Once you are ready, I shall give the word for the play to begin."

Bronwyn looked from the seats to the queen.

Anna immediately understood the younger woman's dismay. "Your guard will have to wait outside, I'm afraid."

"Very well," said the princess, turning around.

Sir Greyson nodded. "Your Highness." He cast a glance at Dame Beverly, then took up a position on the other side of the door from her in the small hallway.

Bronwyn settled into her chair while Lady Aubrey took a seat behind her.

"The queen tells me you've never seen a play before," noted the lady. "I hope you like it."

"It will be a new experience for me," Bronwyn said in a rather neutral tone.

The queen nodded at someone below, then took her seat. Bronwyn noticed Prince Alric taking the queen's hand in his own, giving it a slight squeeze. Was this a normal sign of affection, or was he trying to tell her something?

The princess looked down to where a large curtain had been drawn across the back of the room. Men appeared below, snuffing out candles, plunging the audience into darkness. Moments later, the curtains began to part. Candles were lit on the front of the stage, their metal coverings shielding them from the audience and pushing the light back towards the curtain.

Bronwyn watched in fascination as the curtains revealed a scene of carnage. Dead and dying men littered the stage, and for the briefest of moments, she wondered if something had gone terribly wrong. A man strode out amongst them, then paused to kneel, taking the hand of a wounded man.

"Oh, woe is me to suffer such a loss," he keened, "for the entire kingdom lies in ruins. How did such a thing come to pass?"

The Norland princess found herself drawn into the scene, and she felt a lump in her throat, her mind struggling to make sense of things. In her heart, she knew this was only a story, yet the scene below her evoked such a strong feeling of loss.

The man stood, moving to the front of the stage, speaking directly to the audience, lamenting how the kingdom had risen to such heights. Never again would the realm see such a golden age until another queen wore the warriors crown.

Bronwyn was suddenly taken aback. She had read *Autumn's Twilight* many times, yet she could not recall this reference. She looked at the queen for an explanation and saw only delight on her face. Her attention turned back to the stage in wonder. What else would they change?

The curtain came down to tremendous applause.

Bronwyn looked around in confusion. "It's done?" she said. "Surely they don't mean to end it so soon?"

"It's merely a break," said Lady Aubrey, "to allow the audience to stretch their legs. Shall we go and seek some refreshments?"

"Yes," added the queen. "Alric has arranged for food and drink to be served in the foyer." Anna rose, the prince on her arm, and right on cue, Lady Beverly opened the door.

For a brief moment, Bronwyn wondered how the knight knew such was expected of her, but then reason told her it was the clapping that had given it away. She let the queen and her husband exit, then followed. Once outside the door, she looked at Sir Greyson.

"Would you accompany us?" she asked.

A smile creased the knight's features. "I would be delighted, Your Highness."

They took their time descending the steps, allowing Bronwyn to see the people crowding the foyer. Amongst them, she spotted several Orcs. So engrossed in their appearance was she that she was taken by surprise by the queen's remarks.

"Lord Herdwin, it's so good to see you again."

Bronwyn snapped her head around to the sight of a short-statured man, his face covered by a thick beard and with unnaturally stocky limbs, and then she realized he was a Dwarf.

"Lord Herdwin is an old friend," said the marshal. "We go way back."

"Aye, we do," said the Dwarven lord. "And mighty pleased I am to see you today, Your Majesty."

"Allow me to introduce you to Princess Bronwyn of Norland," said the queen. "I believe you know of her?"

The Dwarf bowed, a comical sight to the young princess. She fought back her laughter, showing, instead, a slight bow of the head. "Pleased to make your acquaintance, Lord Herdwin."

"If you'll excuse me," said Lord Matheson. "I'd like to have a word or two with Lord Herdwin."

"Of course," said Anna. She turned to Bronwyn. "No doubt they'll talk of army matters. Herdwin commands the Dwarven contingent."

"It must be strange having foreign warriors in your army. Whom do they obey?"

"They fall under the command of the marshal," offered the prince.

Bronwyn fought the impulse to criticize. "Is this the normal way of doing things in Merceria?"

"It is now," said the queen, "but it was not always so."

"You have me intrigued."

"Under the reign of King Andred, only Humans served in the army. Then the Dwarves came to our aid, much as the Orcs did and ever since, we've worked to integrate them into our army. After all, an army should reflect its people, don't you think?"

"It's not something I've given much consideration," said Bronwyn. "Is Lord Herdwin related to the King of Stonecastle?"

"No, he's a smith," said the queen. She turned, displaying an ornately crafted scabbard with a sword in it. Grasping the weapon's hilt, she pulled it forth, offering it to the princess. "Herdwin made me this many years ago. What do you think?"

Bronwyn took the blade, marvelling at how well-crafted the weapon was. Swinging it around, it caught the light, revealing runes on its surface. "Is this a magic sword?"

"No, but it's of Dwarven construction."

"This must have cost you a small fortune, Your Majesty."

"Actually," said the queen, "it was a gift."

"No doubt, he sought your favour."

"No, I was only a little girl at the time. He took me for a commoner."

"And he gave you this? I find that hard to believe."

"He's an old friend of Gerald's. Mind you, at the time, Herdwin took me for his daughter."

"I hope you corrected him."

"Not in the least. I was quite proud to be considered thus." Anna noted the look of distaste on Bronwyn's face. "Come now, there's more to life than power."

"Is there? I have been taught otherwise."

"How can you be so serious all the time?" asked the queen. "Have you never had someone who you could confide in?"

"Never. It is the way of royalty."

"It most definitely is not," said the queen. "If it were not for my friends, I would not be on the throne."

"I somehow doubt that."

"Would it surprise you to know I have taken steps to give up some of my power?"

"Give up?"

"Yes," said Anna. "I believe it was Califax who once said 'Power, in the wrong hands, can turn the truest heart to darkness.'"

"It is part of this very play," added Lady Aubrey, "though we will not see it till late in the second half."

"I do seem to recall reading those words," said Bronwyn, "but I suppose I never truly understood their meaning. Surely as a queen, you wish to hold more power? In that way, you can govern your people as you see fit."

"Our history shows otherwise," replied the queen.

"And yet you give more power to the nobility? Look what that did in Norland? Now we have the earls fighting over the throne."

"It's not to the nobles I have given the power, rather it is to the people."

"I don't understand."

"Look at it this way," explained Anna. "Do you wish to concern yourself with the daily chores of running a kingdom? I know I don't. Is it not better to have them look after themselves, confining your own power to matters of state?"

"But they are commoners! It is their lot in life."

"Why?" said the queen. "To protect the power of the nobility? Every Mercerian deserves the right to live free of such restrictions."

"Are you proposing to ban the nobility now?"

"No, of course not, but they have enough on their plate without worrying about the everyday lives of their people. For too long, the nobles of Merceria have preyed on the commoners. Under my reign, that will cease."

Bronwyn frowned. "How does the Baron of Bodden feel about that?"

"He is in favour of it," said the queen, "as he has always been. In some ways, he is the one who started all this."

"He did?"

"Yes, it was his teachings that inspired Gerald, and through him, me. I have come to realize it's not our right to rule. It's our obligation."

"Yes, you said all that before," said Bronwyn, "but I suppose I didn't quite see what you meant. This play seems to have put things in a new light for me."

"Speaking of the play, Your Majesty," interrupted Lady Aubrey. "We'd best return to our seats. You know the rest of the crowd will do nothing until you set the example."

"Very well. Lead on, Aubrey."

They made their way back up the stairs to the balcony. The marshal soon joined them, looking a little worse the wear for rushing to catch up to them. They all took their seats as the lights were once again extinguished.

The curtain descended one final time, bringing tremendous applause. Below them, Orcs were pounding their fists on the bench seats, confusing Bronwyn. She leaned closer to Lady Aubrey.

"What are they doing?"

"They are showing their appreciation," the young woman replied.

"By hitting their seats?"

Aubrey chuckled. "Normally, they pound the ground with their fists, but the wooden floor does not lend itself to such expressions."

"You appear to know a lot about them."

"And so I should. As Baroness of Hawksburg, I've worked with them quite extensively."

"Do you not find them difficult to work with?" asked Bronwyn.

"Difficult? No, quite the reverse, actually. I wish we had more of them."

"That surprises me. Aren't they primitive creatures?"

"Primitive? I suppose I can see how you might think so, considering the huts they live in, but no, I've found them to be quite civilized. Even more so than us, in some regards."

"How so?"

"Crime is almost non-existent amongst them. There is no theft, for example, nor do they covet what is not theirs."

"That's not true," insisted Bronwyn. "The Orcs of Ravensguard have given us no end of trouble for generations."

"Wasn't Ravensguard built on the ruins of one of their cities?"

A slight flicker of annoyance crossed the face of the princess. "I suppose it was."

"Would you be content if your cities were occupied by outsiders?"

"When you put it like that, I suppose I must concede the point. Why? Are you intent on conquering Norland?"

"Merceria wishes to liberate," said Lady Aubrey, "not conquer. I know the same could not be said of our predecessors, but I give you my word all we desire is a lasting peace."

Prince Alric joined the conversation. "We of Weldwyn once thought the same as you. Merceria was always our greatest enemy."

"What changed your mind?" asked Bronwyn.

"Anna," he replied. "She was only a young princess at the time, of course, but she came to Weldwyn on a diplomatic mission."

"And so your marriage was arranged for political expediency? It is not so different for me."

"No, you misunderstand. I was the one who asked my father to arrange the marriage. At first, I was quite annoyed by this young foreign girl who so upset our ways, but in time I came to see the real Anna, and that's who I fell in love with."

"Love?" said Bronwyn. "How can you love someone who won't share the crown?"

"Do men of Norland share power with their wives?"

In answer, she cast her eyes downward. "No, I suppose they don't. Tell me, is there no way for you to be king? Do you not seek it?"

"No, I am content as a prince. Anna is the queen, and I accept I shall never rule here."

"I'm not sure I understand. If she were to die, wouldn't you inherit the throne?"

"No, not at all. In that case, it would pass to our child, but until we have one, it would fall to the marshal."

"The marshal? Surely not! He cannot rule. Such a thing would never be tolerated in Norland."

"It was not so long ago that the same words were uttered in Merceria, yet here we are."

The queen smiled, revealing that she, too, had been listening.

"What changed?" asked Bronwyn.

"I took the throne," Anna said, "with an army to back me up. An army led by Gerald, in fact."

Bronwyn looked at the marshal with newfound respect. "So you would be a maker of kings, or queens, in this case. Is there no end to your quest for power?"

"I never coveted the crown," he replied. "I did it all for Anna." He coughed, trying to hide his discomfort. "I mean the queen."

"And so you fought a war just to please her?"

"No," said the queen. "WE fought a war to bring justice to the realm."

"And how did that work out for you?"

The queen smiled. "It's not perfect, but things are much better now than they used to be, barring the war, of course. The realm suffered under my predecessors, and it takes time to implement changes."

"And yet you rule supreme, do you not? Can't you simply dictate whatever changes you want?"

"No. We have laws preventing such acts. I am but a queen, and no one is above the law, not even me."

Bronwyn was intrigued by the concept. "The Lords of Norland are absolute in their power."

"As kings were here, at one time," the queen continued. "But that power corrupted them. It would have led to the downfall of the realm."

"But rank and power go hand in hand. You made your marshal the Duke of Wincaster. Is that not great power?"

The queen chuckled. "You don't know Gerald. I'm sure others might see it so, but he believes, as do I, that we are here to serve the people. It is a sacred duty."

"Would that my countrymen felt the same," said Bronwyn.

"Perhaps, in time, they will see the wisdom of it, but for some, change is difficult to embrace. It has not been an easy trip for me, nor, I suspect, will it be any easier for you."

"Me?"

"The future of your kingdom may very well depend on your actions, Bronwyn. I have no control over your future. Only you have that power."

"And yet, I am your captive."

"No, you are my guest. Say the word, and I shall have you returned to your native soil."

Bronwyn stood quietly for a moment, letting it sink in. This was all so overwhelming, yet at the same time, so appealing. She must strive to learn more. Finally, she returned her gaze to the queen. "With your permission, Your Majesty, I should like to remain in Wincaster a little while longer."

EIGHTEEN

The Capital

Spring 965 MC

Bronwyn sat down across from the queen, sinking into the soft chair. The High Ranger, Hayley Chambers, had joined them for this afternoon's meeting. The room was quiet. The princess looked at Baron Fitzwilliam, but he, too, appeared distracted.

"Tell me," said Anna, directing her conversation towards Bronwyn. "How has your stay been thus far?"

"Passable," the princess replied. "The theatre was most pleasant, but I still miss my home. Have you any news from Norland?"

"Not much, I'm afraid. We've heard of some fighting north of the border, but it's sporadic, and our reports are lacking any details."

"Then it's true," said Bronwyn. "A civil war is upon my people. It is a terrible thing to fall into such chaos."

"And yet it was of their own making," said the queen.

"Do not blame the people of Norland for the actions of its earls. It is the nobility who has brought this war to the land."

"It's the nobles of which I speak. If you were in charge, what would you do?"

"Do? What could I do? I am but a woman. Under Norland law, I have no power."

"You are not in Norland now," said Anna. "And not subject to the limitations of those laws. Tell me, if you had the power, what would you do with it?"

"I would destroy the earls who brought about the death of my grandfather."

"How?"

"I beg your pardon?" said the princess.

"It's a simple enough question," said the queen. "Assuming it was within your power, how would you go about taking such vengeance?"

"I would carry the war to Lord Hollis first. He is their ringleader, though I must admit to having no experience with such things."

"What if a leader were provided?"

"What are you suggesting?"

"It's quite simple, really," Anna said. "We are at war with your country. Lord Hollis saw to that when he invaded us last year. Preparations are now underway to march into Norland and defeat what's left of his army."

"And then you'll take the crown," said Bronwyn, her voice bitter.

"No," said Anna, "our fight is with Lord Hollis and his allies. We have no desire to rule Norland."

"I have heard that several times. I wish I could believe it."

"Whether you believe it or not, it's true. It might interest you to know that a number of Norlanders have fled your country, seeking us here, in Merceria."

"To what end?"

"They wish to fight to retake the crown."

Bronwyn snorted. "It is nothing but a dream. No one can defeat Lord Hollis."

"That's where you're wrong," said Anna. "We have, in fact, defeated not one, but two armies who marched into our territory."

"Was Hollis with them?"

"We're not sure," offered Fitz. "If he was, he managed to evade us."

"He is a master strategist," offered Bronwyn. "Even with his forces depleted, he is a dangerous foe. He also has strong allies."

"Ah, yes," said Anna. "You mean Lords Rutherford and Thurlowe?"

"I do, and you could never take Galburn's Ridge, let alone Ravensguard."

"I can understand your belief in the capital," said Fitz. "Our marshal has indicated as much, but what's the significance of Ravensguard?"

"It is one of three great fortresses that protect the south."

"Then what is the third one?"

"Riverhurst," said Bronwyn. "With those three cities under his command, Lord Hollis can hold you at bay."

"Good thing he only has two, then," said the queen.

Bronwyn looked at her in shock. "Are you claiming to have captured Riverhurst?"

"No. I am saying the Earl who rules there is one of our allies, or rather, we are his ally since conquest is not our ultimate goal here."

"Still, that leaves two great fortresses. I hope you have plenty of siege engines."

Fitz frowned. "She has a good point there."

The door opened, revealing a young woman.

"Yes, Sophie?" said Anna.

"The marshal is here, Your Majesty, along with Dame Beverly."

"Show them in, and send for some drinks if you would be so kind."

"Yes, ma'am." The maid backed away, closing the door behind her and leaving Bronwyn staring at the queen.

"If you would be so kind? Do you ask favour from even the lowest of servants?"

"A ruler doesn't need to be harsh to command the respect of her subjects," said Anna. "And in any event, Sophie is a good friend of mine."

"Royals have no friends," said Bronwyn.

"I would disagree with that."

The door opened again, this time revealing the marshal, along with Dame Beverly. They both bowed respectfully.

"Come and sit, the both of you." Anna patted the chair, looking at the old man.

"Thank you, I will," he said, taking the indicated seat. "The truth is, I think I've been run off my feet this morning."

"It looks like your marshal is feeling his age," said Bronwyn.

"He is," agreed Anna. "But all the same, he's the finest military leader in the three kingdoms, four, if you include the Twelve Clans."

Bronwyn frowned. "And what, might I ask, is Dame Beverly doing here? Isn't she your bodyguard? Or am I to assume she's here to convince me women make competent warriors?"

Anna smiled, sinking back into her seat. "Dame Beverly has been busy on the frontier, carrying out a very special task on my behalf."

"What? Dancing with Lord Hollis?"

"I shall let her tell you herself," said the queen. "Beverly, if you'd be so kind?"

The red-headed knight looked at her queen. "Are you sure, Your Majesty?"

"Quite."

"Very well. For the sake of the princess, I shall start at the beginning. Some weeks ago, we became aware of two armies preparing to do battle north of the border. One flew the flag of Lord Hollis, but the other consisted of common folk, simple villagers by the look of them. A Mercerian force was sent to investigate, resulting in quite a few Norland refugees making their way to Wickfield. Those men and women expressed a desire to fight back against the oppression of the Earl of Beaconsgate, so we have begun equipping and training them to do just that."

"How many people are we talking about?" asked Anna.

"About two hundred fifty warriors, along with assorted family members and such. I've organized them into companies of about fifty, placing them under the command of the few veterans who were scattered amongst their number."

"So the entire army is led by Norlanders?"

"Other than training officers, yes," replied Beverly.

"Would you care to break down the organization of this army?"

"It's mainly foot, Your Majesty, but we have managed to cobble together a company of bowmen, along with one of light horsemen."

"Light horsemen?" said Bronwyn. "I don't believe I am familiar with the term."

"They are riders trained in scouting and screening the army, Your Highness, as well as being used to carry messages. The Norland army uses them in abundance."

"I don't believe you," said Bronwyn. "Are you trying to convince me that you willingly gave close to fifty horses to my people?"

"Not at all," said Beverly. "They were, in fact, Norland horses, captured at the Battle of the Deerwood."

"How has their training progressed?" pressed the queen.

"They're still in the early stages as yet. We've managed to arm them all, but it takes time to turn them into disciplined warriors."

Gerald leaned forward. "Beverly assures me they will be ready when we march across the border."

"You can't be serious," said Bronwyn. "You would sacrifice the lives of my countrymen?"

"Would you do any less to put a rightful ruler on the throne?"

The room fell silent until a soft rumble reverberated throughout.

"What's that?" asked Bronwyn.

Anna chuckled. "That's merely Tempus, my dog. He's sleeping."

"You have a dog?"

"Yes. He's around here somewhere."

"How can you misplace such a large creature?" asked Fitz.

"He's behind the chair," offered Gerald. "I can feel his breath on the back of my legs."

Anna called him by name, and the Kurathian Mastiff rose, letting out a large yawn. Bronwyn's eyes went wide as the great hound padded around the chair and put his massive head in the queen's lap.

"He's honestly quite sweet," offered Anna.

"I've never seen such a beast," said the princess. She shifted slightly in her chair, then began to relax as she realized there was no threat.

"Would you like to see your countrymen?" asked Anna.

"See them? Why? Are they here in Wincaster?"

"No, but we can take you to them if you like."

"Using the same magic that brought me here?"

"Yes," said the queen. "We could have you there by dinnertime today."

"And you would let me talk to them freely?"

"Naturally."

Bronwyn cast her eyes around, looking for any signs of deception, but no one avoided her gaze. "Very well," she said at last. "Take me to my countrymen."

Anna rose, looking at the High Ranger. "Make the arrangements, Hayley, and gather a small group of your rangers to escort her."

"Yes, Your Majesty. Will you be accompanying us?"

"Not this time, but I may follow in a day or so. I'm putting you in charge of her safety until then."

"Very well," said Hayley.

Now dismissed, the High Ranger left the room. The other Mercerians stood as well, then, at a nod from the queen, filed out of the room, leaving the two royals alone with the great mastiff.

"You might want to change," suggested Anna. "I hear it's a little chilly in Wickfield."

Bronwyn stood defiantly. "I am well aware of the climate of Norland."

"Then I shall leave you to make whatever preparations you deem necessary. I will send someone for you when it's time to leave."

Hayley stood at the doorway, peering down the corridor. "Where is she?" she mused.

"She is making us wait," said Gorath, "likely to establish her dominance."

"Dominance? Surely not?"

"Well," said the Orc, "maybe dominance is not the right word."

"Speaking of dominance, look who's just arrived." Hayley pointed down the hall.

Gorath leaned out the doorway, only to see Albreda's approach. The

Witch of the Whitewood was walking briskly, causing her dress to billow out behind her. In her wake came Kraloch, rushing to keep up.

"Ah, Hayley," said the Druid. "I rather gather you're coming with us."

"I didn't know you were going to Wickfield?"

"How else am I to commit the new circle to memory?"

"I suppose that makes sense."

"Now," Albreda continued, "how many others are going?"

"Only a few. The same group who retrieved Bronwyn."

"Are you sure that will be enough?"

"Enough for now," said Hayley. "Others will join us once we've arrived. Aubrey has already left, taking Gerald and Beverly with her."

"I see," said the Druid. "And where is Gryph?"

"He's inside."

"Then I suppose we must be on our way."

"We can't."

"Why ever not?"

"We're waiting on Princess Bronwyn."

"Very well," said Albreda, sweeping into the room, "though I cannot, for the life of me, see why she couldn't be here on time."

The answer came a moment later as Baron Fitzwilliam appeared. "She's almost ready," he called out. "There was a slight problem with her guards."

"What kind of problem?" asked Hayley.

"She insisted she be escorted by those two knights we assigned to her. She seems to have grown rather fond of them. In any event, it's all settled now. Is everyone else ready?"

"We are, Richard," called out Albreda. "Are you sure you won't accompany us?"

"I'm afraid I'm far too busy for such a trip. I'll leave you lot to have all the fun."

"Fun," said Gorath. "An interesting word."

"Here she comes now," said Fitz.

Princess Bronwyn finally appeared, led by Sir Greyson and Sir Hector, their armour highly polished.

"I'll leave you to it," said Fitz. He then turned, bowing to their Royal Visitor.

Bronwyn returned the compliment, nodding her head in acknowledgement.

"All set, Your Highness?" asked Hayley.

"You may proceed," the princess replied, letting the High Ranger lead her into the casting circle.

Kraloch was already waiting, as were Sam, Ayles, and Urzath. The shaman handed Gryph off to Gorath and then began preparing himself for casting.

"You may begin," said Bronwyn.

Sergeant Hugh Gardner watched as the rebel cavalry reached the end of the field and began their turn. Their formation quickly devolved when some of the riders went the wrong way, throwing the entire manoeuvre into chaos. Gardner shook his head, wondering if they were ever going to get it right.

"There were fewer mistakes that time," noted Beverly, "and they were doing fine until they came to that turn."

"Tell me, did you have this problem when you were learning to ride?"

"You forget, I learned at a very early age. Not everyone can claim such an advantage."

"How early?"

"I was four. Not that I really rode in those days, mind you, it was more a case of sitting in the saddle while someone walked my horse."

"Still," said Gardner, "it's safe to say you've spent a lifetime around horses."

"Yes, I have. What of it?"

He gazed back at the rebels. "You've led cavalry into battle, right? What do you REALLY think of these horsemen?"

She watched as the distant riders slowly reformed into a semblance of order. "I think they have potential."

"Truly? I think they look terrible."

Beverly smiled. "I could have said the same of the Wincaster Light Horse when I first took command. I seem to recall a sergeant being instrumental in bringing them around."

"Yes, but it was different back then."

"How?"

"What do you mean, 'how'?"

"How was it any different? Come now, you're the one making excuses. I'm merely curious as to how you think the current situation is any different."

The sergeant was at a loss for words but tried to press on. "It just is, that's all."

Beverly laughed. "I see no reason why you can't repeat your magic here, unless you feel you're getting too old for this sort of thing?"

"Too old?" said the sergeant, turning indignant. "Who said I was too old?"

"Oh, no one in particular."

"Well, I'll show them!" He stomped off across the field towards the waiting horsemen.

Beverly heard the bellowing commence, a sure sign Gardner had returned to his old self. Satisfied all was well in order, she made her way over to the archers.

Captain Wainwright, of the Greens, had set up a row of targets. Fed by an almost limitless supply of arrows, the rebels took their time, lining up their shots in a leisurely manner. Wainwright and his two sergeants wandered up and down the line, offering words of encouragement. He happened to glance up just as Beverly approached, so he made his way towards her, lest Lightning scare his trainees.

"Commander," he said. "You honour us with your presence."

"How are things going, Captain? Making progress?"

He glanced at the targets. "Yes, surprisingly well. Not many of them have any experience, but they are picking it up quite quickly. I've kept them with the shorter bows. They lack the strength for anything more powerful."

"Have they practiced volleys yet?"

"No, I'm letting them get used to individual target practice. Once they're comfortable with their new weapons, I'll start forming them into ranks."

"And how long do you think before you can do that?"

The captain gazed once more at his charges. "I'm tempted to start this very afternoon."

"That's the first good news I've heard today. I wish the same could be said for the cavalry."

"How are the footmen doing?"

"We have them constructing a new barracks under the guidance of Sir Preston."

Captain Wainwright looked past Beverly. "Looks like we have company."

Beverly turned to see a small group approaching. She recognized Hayley immediately, and then her eyes fell on Bronwyn and her two knights. The Norland Princess was wearing a thick blue cloak to ward off the chill, but her head was bare, revealing her regal countenance. Hayley raised her hand in greeting, and Beverly nodded.

"Her Highness would like to talk to the rebels," the ranger said.

"Of course," the knight replied. "Would you like me to assemble them?"

They all looked at Bronwyn. The princess gave them an icy stare, then nodded. "Very well."

"Captain Wainwright, please assemble your men on the common."

Wainwright snapped to attention, then bowed his head slightly. "Yes, Commander." He turned and began walking through the archers, calling out commands as he went.

Beverly wheeled Lightning around and trotted off towards the distant cavalry. Hayley scanned the area, taking everything in, then pointed to the empty field.

"They'll likely be assembling over there," she said. "Would you like a chair?"

"My horse will do just fine," said Bronwyn. "But I think the spot to my left would be better."

The High Ranger looked at the indicated patch of ground. It was no different than the common, and she struggled to see what advantage it offered. Returning her gaze to the princess, she was ready to speak but was cut off.

"I must insist on that spot," said the princess. "Or are the men of Norland to be herded like sheep?"

Hayley bit back a retort. "Very well, I shall send word to Dame Beverly."

"I'll go," offered Sam. The young ranger trotted off towards the horsemen.

"Captain Wainwright," called out Hayley. "It appears we have a slight change of plans. Your men are to assemble"—she pointed—"in that spot over there."

"Yes, ma'am," the captain replied as if the change in location was of little consequence.

Bronwyn watched the entire display with detached interest, a slight smile creasing the corners of her lips.

It took some time to assemble all the rebels, a task made all the more complicated by their lack of discipline. Beverly had intended to have them form up by companies, but in the end, they gathered into one large mass of people, standing around waiting.

"I am Princess Bronwyn, of the Royal House of King Halfan," the princess announced. The crowd grew quiet at the mention of their late king. Bronwyn hesitated, and Beverly could see sweat breaking out on the brow of the princess.

"I have come here today to give you hope," the princess continued. "Hope that you will someday regain that which you have lost."

The crowd stared at her expectantly.

"I know you have suffered, as have we all." Bronwyn winced, noticing she was losing them as they started to turn away. "But I give you my word I shall not rest until Lord Hollis and his cronies have been driven from the field, and the true bloodline of Norland restored to its rightful place on the throne."

She took a breath, then plunged onward. "Come with me, and together we shall defeat this menace to the great land we call home. Let us march into Norland and reclaim that which is rightfully ours!"

The rebels let out a cheer that appeared to please the young woman. She held her fist in the air. "To victory!" she shouted.

"To victory," they echoed, though to Beverly's ears, they were not overly enthusiastic.

Bronwyn turned her horse around, riding over to where Beverly sat astride Lightning.

"Make me an army," she commanded. "An army the likes of which has never been seen before."

"They are but few in number," warned Beverly.

"Yes, but their numbers will grow as we deliver defeat to our enemies. Do this for me, Dame Beverly, and when the crown is mine, I shall see to it that you are richly rewarded."

The knight looked drawn in by the intense gaze. "I shall do all I can, Your Highness. I promise."

NINETEEN

Leofric

Summer 965 MC

S pring finally bloomed its way into summer, and with the warmer weather, the armies began to assemble. In the east, the Mercerians gathered at the border, while to the west, the army of Weldwyn was about to start the long march into Norland.

A lone rider broke away from the assembled Weldwyn troops, galloping across the tournament field to come to rest before his liege king. Wearing the colours of a herald, he bowed respectfully before delivering his news.

"The Army of Weldwyn is ready to march, Your Majesty."

King Leofric nodded his head in acknowledgement, then let his eyes drift over the warriors lined up before him in three battalions. The vanguard consisted of the cavalry, which numbered some seven hundred strong. Behind them would follow the centre, the footmen who would stand in lines to oppose the enemy. Bringing up the rearguard were the archers, numbering nearly four hundred.

Weldwyn tradition had always stressed the importance of their horsemen, something on which the realm prided themselves. It had been the cavalry who had blunted the invasion from Merceria back in 583, and although that was centuries ago, the king still looked on it with pride. Their recent brush with the Twelve Clans was still fresh in everyone's mind, and he was eager to prove to his new allies that the army of Weldwyn still had teeth.

Nodding to Lord Edwin for the march to commence, Leofric listened as a series of orders echoed out across the tournament grounds. The cavalry marched off the field and onto the road, leading the way towards the city's east gate. Leofric watched as they rode by, their heads held high, their spirits matching. The king was filled with pride at the sight, confident in their ability to bring defeat to their enemies.

The new heavy cavalry raised their swords in salute as they passed, and Leofric was overcome with emotion. These men were willing to give their lives in service to their sovereign king, part of an army the likes of which had never before been seen on Weldwyn soil.

Casting his eyes to his left, Leofric caught sight of the footmen marching towards the road. The lighter troops led the way, carrying spears and shields, but little more. They would guard the camp and be the army's eyes and ears, while the heavy fighting would be left to the armoured men who followed in their wake.

"They are well underway, Your Majesty. Shall we ride to the head of the column?" Lord Edwin's voice brought him out of his musings.

"Yes, of course." They spurred on their horses, galloping beside the army as it made its way eastward. Soon they were at their proper place, leading an army of some eighteen hundred men who stretched out behind them.

The gate came into view, its doors wide open. Atop the battlements stood Queen Igraine with Prince Alstan at her side. The prince would rule in his father's absence, although Leofric knew, in his heart, it would be his wife making most of the decisions. The king's eyes met those of his queen's for a moment, and they both smiled. This was a glorious day indeed.

The route to Falford was long and tortuous. Unused to prolonged marching, the troops suffered in the summer's heat, forcing the king to order frequent stops. In theory, the army of Weldwyn was an impressive sight, but the strain of feeding and watering eighteen hundred men soon began to wear.

Lord Edwin had stockpiled stores in Summersgate, but as the capital fell farther and farther behind, the lack of transport became more pronounced. The trip to Falford had been calculated at ten days, but it was over two weeks by the time the exhausted troops finally arrived.

Leofric permitted the army a mere two days rest while his captains rushed about, snatching up any wagons they could. By the time the march resumed, they had tripled their supply capacity, but the journey had only just begun.

Next came the route to Hanwick, and then Almswell, marching to the far northeast corner of the realm. From here, they would cross the river and be within enemy territory, but first, they must get there. The road to Falford had been wide and well-kept, but the path north was little more than a trail, meandering through patches of trees and around hills.

King Leofric sent the cavalry on ahead, leaving only a small force of horsemen to keep an eye on the rest of the army. The summer grew hotter still, and the heavily armoured footmen suffered the most, their chainmail armour and padded undershirts causing no end of torment.

Finally, after three days of such punishment, the king had seen enough. He ordered the troops eastward until they found the banks of the River Alde that formed the border with Merceria. Now, with an ever-present source of water, the speed of the march improved.

Two more days brought them to the village of Almswell, where the army took a well-deserved rest.

Riders were sent north and east, seeking any sign of the enemy. Within the week, word had returned from Bodden, the Mercerian stronghold that lay to their east some seventy miles away. Allied patrols reported no enemy activity to their north, so finally, the army of Weldwyn crossed the river into Norland territory.

Leofric looked towards the west, where the ever-present spectre of the Greatwood cast its long shadow. The Orcs of that region had lived there for generations, and he wondered if they watched as the Weldwyn army marched past.

Queen Anna had suggested he use Orcs as auxiliary troops, but Lord Edwin had been adamant it would cause only trouble. Few in Weldwyn spoke the language of the greenskins, and everyone at court knew the common tongue of man was far too complex for the Orcs to master.

Hearing a splash, he looked eastward to spot a group of horsemen entering the river, crossing at the ford that had been marked out for them by his advanced scouts. Immediately behind the horsemen came wagons loaded with timber. The king's plan was to build a bridge, allowing the supply wagons to keep up with the pace of the army's advance. Everything appeared to be going to plan.

Lord Edwin rode up beside him, a large smile splayed across his face. "Your Majesty," he said. "'Tis a fine day."

Leofric looked skyward. "It is indeed. Have you news?"

"I do," the man continued. "Our advance riders have reached the outskirts of Harrowsbrook. They report no sign of the enemy as yet. Another two days, and we shall be safely encamped within its walls."

"It has walls?"

"No," said Edwin. "Forgive me, it was simply a turn of phrase. I merely meant we shall be able to take shelter out of this sun."

"Still," said the king, "it raises a difficult possibility, one I'm afraid we didn't take into account."

"Which is?"

"We have no siege engines. Should we find ourselves up against any sort of prepared defences, we will be at a disadvantage."

Lord Edwin smiled. "You may rest assured the situation is well in hand, Your Majesty, for I have thought of that very thing."

"And yet, I see no catapults?"

"They would only slow us, my lord. Instead, we have brought siege engineers, experts in that type of warfare. Should the need arise, they can see to the construction of such engines of war."

"It looks like you have thought of everything."

Edwin smiled. "I do my best, Your Majesty."

"Come now, Edwin, aren't we being a little formal? You are my closest friend."

"I am," the man replied, "yet here, in front of the men, it is important I pay you the respect due your station."

Leofric chuckled. "Very well, I can see I have been outmanoeuvred on this. How much longer till the crossing is complete?"

"At this rate, well into the evening. I've arranged a camp to be set up on the other side. We'll march from there first thing tomorrow."

"And the bridge?"

"The men will labour all night to ensure its completion."

"That's excellent news," said the king. "We can march into this Norland village and use it as a supply centre. Any word from our allies?"

"No, Your Majesty. They were due to cross the border anytime now, but we have had no confirmation as yet."

"Where is our Earth Mage?"

"She's with the wagons," Edwin said, "along with our healer."

"Have her send word to the Mercerians that we shall be in Harrowsbrook in two days."

"Certainly, Your Majesty. Anything else?"

"Yes. See if you can find us a decent vintage of wine. We have much to celebrate."

"We do?"

"Yes," said the king. "This is the first time an army of Weldwyn has crossed into Norland territory."

"I suppose it is, isn't it?" agreed Edwin.

Leofric gazed once more at the Greatwood. "I feel as though we're being watched."

"Nonsense. The hunting grounds of the Orcs are more than a hundred miles to the west."

"Still, I have an uneasy feeling." Leofric looked towards the south at the distant peaked roofs of Alsmwell. "Take a good look, my friend. It will be a long time before we see it again."

"Yes," said Edwin. "But return we shall, and covered in glory!"

They rode into Harrowsbrook to faces of resentment. King Leofric had the new heavy cavalry lead the way. Made up of cavaliers, they were the finest warriors in Weldwyn, and provided a sight that the townsfolk must have found quite intimidating.

They took over a large house near the town's centre, and Leofric set up court there, billeting several of his men close by. By next morning the king was sitting at a table, sifting through reports. Riders had gone further north and east, seeking signs of enemy movement, but so far, they had discovered little.

The entrance of Lord Edwin made him look up. "Trouble?

"Nothing that can't be dealt with, Your Majesty. Some of the locals are offering resistance to our presence."

"They're not fighting, are they?"

"No," said Edwin, "but they are expressing discontent with us taking their food. I had to send several warriors to make a show of force and seize their granaries."

"I see," said the king. "Was there much grain left?"

"More than we had expected, to be honest. It will go a long way to help feed our army."

"And the locals?"

"They backed down under the threat of force. It means having to leave a garrison behind, but we'd already decided on that."

"That is good news," said Leofric, waving his troubles away. "And as for this... resistance, I'm sure we'll hear no more of it. Is there something else you came here to see me about?"

"There was, in fact. I want to talk to you about the garrison. How many troops do you want to remain here?"

Leofric put down the paper he was scanning, looking at his friend with a smile, knowing full well Lord Edwin had already decided on what was needed. "What do you recommend?"

"I would propose a modest force, say a hundred and fifty?"

Leofric nodded. "And what type of troops would you recommend?"

"Equal numbers of horse, foot and bow."

"Not our best cavalry, surely?"

"No, I would recommend our light horsemen. What think you, Your Majesty?"

"I would concur. Oh, and let's not leave our best footmen either. We shall eventually need them if we are to bring Lord Hollis to battle."

"Very well," said Lord Edwin. "I shall make all the appropriate arrangements."

Aegryth Malthunen looked skyward to where a hawk circled. Closing her eyes, she released her magic, calling to it, only to see it begin spiralling down towards her. She stretched out her hand, and the creature landed, revealing the slender metal cylinder attached to its leg.

Her words soothed the feathered creature as she removed the tiny package. Another word dismissed it, and it flew off, leaving Aegryth to open the tube. Carefully she withdrew the note, examining its contents.

Satisfied with what she had read, she returned to her horse, pulling herself into the saddle in a single, smooth motion. A word to her horse was all it took for the mount to start galloping back towards the army.

The guards paid her no mind as she entered the building. Walking with purpose, she held the note tightly in her hand as she approached Leofric's office. Ignoring the two guards standing sentinel, she knocked.

"Come," came the king's voice.

Pushing open the door, she took a moment to bow as he looked up. "Ah, Aegryth. I take it you have news?"

"I do, Your Majesty. Word has just come from the Mercerians."

"And?"

"They have crossed the border at Wickfield and Mattingly." The king wore a troubled expression. "Is this not the news you expected, Your Majesty?"

"It's good news, to be sure," agreed Leofric, "but we should have been further along by now. I had hoped to reach the estate of Lord Hollis by the time our allies commenced marching. As it is, we are well behind our original schedule."

"Shall I send a reply?"

"No, not yet, but don't go far, I might need you. I have riders out to the northeast, and if they make contact with the enemy, we shall need to inform our allies."

"Shall I send a scout of my own?" asked Aegryth.

The king looked at her in surprise. "You have your own scouts?"

"Yes, Lord King. A bird can spy out the enemy as easily as carry a message."

"Yes, but how intelligent is a bird? How are they to know the difference between a cow and a soldier?"

"Their intelligence is of no matter," said the mage. "The bird merely views the target, then returns. It is my mind that will assess what it has seen."

King Leofric shook his head. "The world of magic is such a mystery to me. Very well, Aegryth Malthunen, send your bird. Let us see if we can't find the army of the elusive Lord Hollis."

"As you wish, Your Majesty."

TWENTY

Across the Border

Summer 965 MC

F itz watched as the rebels made their way across the river, Beverly at their head. Bronwyn had insisted on accompanying her countrymen, a move that had quite surprised the baron. As the last of the rebels reached the far side, he turned to Sir Preston.

"Ready?"

"Ready and eager, my lord."

"Very well. You may begin, but leave a suitable gap between the rebels and yourselves. We don't want to crowd them."

"Aye, sir." The Knight of the Hound rode off to join the heavy cavalry.

"He's eager," said Alric.

"Yes, but he knows his business. Once he's on the far bank, you may take the footmen across, Your Highness. The Dwarves will follow under Herdwin's command."

"Very well, General."

"Please, call me Fitz."

Alric smiled, for, like Gerald, this had become a bit of a game. "Of course, sir."

The prince was about to rejoin his men but turned back around, waiting for the baron to acknowledge his presence.

"Something wrong?"

"Yes, sir. It's the Dwarves."

"What about them?"

"It occurs to me that they might have trouble fording the river, on account of their shorter stature."

The baron was about to reply, then paused. "I hadn't thought of that. What are you suggesting?"

"If I were to split my personal guard, I could send half of them upstream and the rest downstream. It would help break the current, and if any of them do flounder, those downstream could assist in their recovery."

"That's an excellent idea, but if Herdwin asks, it's simply a sign of respect. We don't want them to feel awkward."

"Awkward?"

"Yes, I don't want them feeling as if they're being treated like children."

Alric smiled. "I understand, sir."

"Good. Well, you'd best be off, Your Highness. We haven't got all day." The prince turned, finally riding off towards his assembled troops.

Fitz moved closer to the river's edge, casting his eyes over his troops. They were a sizable force, over nine hundred strong, not including the rebels. Beverly's troops added another three hundred, although he had to confess, if only to himself, their reliability might come into question. In theory, they were under the command of Princess Bronwyn, but the baron had no doubt it would be his daughter bearing the brunt of command, as it should be. She was, after all, far more experienced in such things.

"What are you thinking, my lord?" came the familiar voice of Sergeant Blackwood.

Looking back, Fitz recognized the grinning face of the old veteran who had served him in Bodden for years. Indeed, when Gerald Matheson left for Wincaster all those years ago, it had been Blackwood who had replaced him as Sergeant-at-Arms. The man was no Gerald but had proven loyal and reliable in battle.

"I was wondering how Beverly might fare today."

"With the rebels?" said Blackwood, shaking his head. "I don't know that I trust them."

"We'll see. I've given them first crack at capturing Brooksholde. If they don't have it in their hands by nightfall, it'll be up to Prince Alric."

"Are you sure that's wise, my lord?"

"Yes, why wouldn't it be?" Fitz stared at his sergeant, noticing his look of trepidation. "Out with it, man. You can be honest with me."

"Well, it's only that Prince Alric has little experience in battle."

"I might remind you he has seen extensive action in both Weldwyn and Merceria. He also came to our aid during the civil war, you know."

"I realize that, my lord, but he is commanding a mixed force here, not just some cavalrymen."

"Ah. I see why you have reservations, but I can assure you he has been under the tutelage of Gerald, and you know how thorough he can be. In any case, I doubt his troops will be needed. Beverly's rebels should be more than capable of taking the village."

"If you say so, my lord."

Beverly halted when the village of Brookesholde came into view. It was small, almost as tiny as Wickfield, but with no sign of prepared defences. She glanced at the rebel brigade, noticing the eager looks on their faces. Many of them called this place home. Would they be up to the challenge of reclaiming it?

"You may proceed with the attack," declared Bronwyn.

"Yes, Highness," replied the knight. As she issued the orders, the footmen began forming a line, behind which the archers took up their position. The small rebel contingent of cavalry had been bolstered by a company of the Wincaster Light Horse, so she placed the rebel horses on one flank with the Mercerian troops on the other. This day, their job was to cut off any stragglers from escaping, not fight in the streets of the village.

The men deployed quickly, eager to be about their business. She waited for Sergeant Gardner to nod, indicating they were in position, then gave the command to advance. This was a straight forward assault against an undefended village. There would be no fancy manoeuvres this day.

The first sign of opposition appeared as they neared their target. A volley of arrows sailed forth, doing little damage, but causing the rebel footmen to falter. Gardner halted them, taking a moment to straighten their line, then resumed the advance. Behind the front line, other sergeants scolded the men for their lack of discipline, keeping their minds occupied. It was an old trick and one she had seen Gerald do many times, back in Bodden.

More arrows flew, and then one of the rebels went down. The men stepped past the fallen warrior while others, at the rear, waited as the army advanced past him. Once that was done, they rushed forward, pulling him to safety and seeing to his wounds. They might not have Life Mages, but Beverly had insisted on implementing some steps to see to the wounded.

When Beverly shouted out a command, the archers all halted, drawing back their bows, angling the arrows high over the heads of their comrades.

"Loose," she called out.

The volley flew from their bows, raining down on the enemy troops.

There was little sign of actual damage, but the Norland archers slackened their pace, and now the rebels were within fifty paces of the village. Gardner gave the command, and the men surged forward with a triumphant yell.

Beverly wanted to rush to their aid, to use Nature's Fury to drive through the enemy, but her duty this day was to keep watch over her command, a responsibility she took seriously. She looked at both her aides who sat nearby, each with a collection of flags.

"Advance the flanks," she ordered, and two blue flags unfurled. Moments later, the cavalry began to advance, enveloping the village and cutting off any chance of escape.

Suddenly, Bronwyn spurred her horse forward, catching Beverly by surprise. The knight swore as she urged Lightning into a gallop, desperate to keep the princess in sight. The aides, caught unawares, fumbled to pack away the flags as quickly as they could before following her lead.

The attack had flooded in between the buildings now, all semblance of organization lost. Into this melee rode Bronwyn, her cloak billowing out behind her as she went. Beverly let Lightning have his head, and the great beast surged forward, all caution to the wind. An arrow came out of nowhere, narrowly missing Bronwyn as it caught in her hood. It would have been comical had it not put the royal's life at risk. Beverly pulled up beside her charge, raising her shield to protect the princess, and not a moment too soon as another arrow sailed forth, striking metal before falling harmlessly to the ground.

Spotting the archer perched atop the bell tower, Beverly urged her Mercerian Charger into a gallop, closing the distance as fast as she could. Nature's Fury swung out, striking the corner of the building and smashing through a timber. Two more times she struck, each one faster than the last. Bits of wood and daub flew off into the air, and then the timber support gave way with a groan.

It didn't topple the tower, but the archer, realizing what was happening, fled his position, rushing across the peak of the roof to jump the short distance to another building. Beverly watched him land, and then a group of rebels swarmed onto the roof, their work inside obviously complete.

The sounds of fighting began to slacken and then grow quiet, leaving only the moans of the wounded. The knight sought out Bronwyn, making her way over to her side as quickly as possible. The young princess had dismounted and was now congratulating her men on their great success.

"Ah, there you are," said Bronwyn. "Is this not a great victory?"

"Indeed, Your Highness," said Beverly, plucking the arrow from her hood and holding it out. "You should take more care. A tad closer, and you would have been skewered."

"Nonsense, I'm a royal. The Gods will protect me."

The red-headed knight bit back a retort. Was there no end to this woman's sense of entitlement?

The rebels were ecstatic, and why not? Mere months ago, they had been but simple villagers, yet in their minds, they had bested professional soldiers, raising their confidence by a considerable degree.

"You may inform Baron Fitzwilliam the village is secure," said Bronwyn.

Beverly sought out an aide. "You heard her. Send word to my father."

"Yes, ma'am." The horseman turned, riding off.

"Now," said Bronwyn, "we must prepare for the next stage of our liberation."

The words caught Beverly off guard, for she knew full well their only objective was taking Brooksholde. "The next step, Your Highness?"

"Yes, we shall march on to Oaksvale."

"That is for the rest of the army. Our job is done."

"By the Gods," said Bronwyn. "I didn't expect cowardice from someone with your reputation."

Beverly reddened. "It is not cowardice, Your Highness, but a matter of distance. By our estimation, Oaksvale is several days from here. Rushing there will leave us dangerously overextended."

"Nonetheless, come morning, I want the rebel forces marching north. Am I clear?"

"Of course," said Beverly.

"Good. Now have someone find me a place to rest this evening. That house over there will do nicely."

The knight looked at her remaining aide. "You heard Her Highness."

The man nodded, then pushed his way past the victorious rebels. This was going to be a long night.

Darkness had fallen by the time Sir Preston finally made his way amongst the troops. As cavalry commander, he had taken it upon himself to check the pickets, thus ensuring no Norland raiders could sneak into camp and create havoc this night.

A challenge caught his attention, and then there was a shout of alarm. Alerted, he drew his sword, making his way towards the altercation. Expecting to encounter a Norland patrol, he was surprised to see a group of his men surrounding an Orc.

"Problems, gentlemen?"

"This Orc came from the west," replied one of the sentries. "He could be a spy."

"Don't be ridiculous," said the knight. "The Orcs are our allies."

"Still, it's a bit strange, don't you think? All our Orcs are further east, crossing at Mattingly. What's this fellow doing here?"

"Did you ask him?"

"I did," admitted the guard, "but he seems to have difficulty understanding our language."

"Don't any of you speak Orcish?"

They all shook their heads.

Sir Preston looked at the Orc, expecting to see weapons, but all the creature had was a gnarled staff covered in strange symbols.

"I am Sir Preston," he said, his voice slow and measured.

The Orc stared back. "Andurak," he said, thumping his own chest.

"Ah, that's your name. Welcome, Andurak." He bowed. "If you'll come with me, we'll find someone who can speak your language."

"I speak a little," the Orc replied. "Lead on, and I shall follow."

Sir Preston led him through the camp to where Baron Fitzwilliam had erected a command tent. The guards on the door looked on in fascination but took no actions against their strange visitor.

"Is Lady Aubrey here?" asked the knight.

"Inside," answered one of the guards.

Sir Preston pushed the tent flap aside. Baron Fitzwilliam was within, along with Herdwin, Prince Alric, and Lady Aubrey, all looking at a map laid out on a table. Close by sat Albreda, absently petting a large wolf.

"My lord," said Sir Preston. "We encountered a visitor, someone by the name of Andurak."

"I know that name," said Alric. "Come in. We can't see anything with him standing out there."

Andurak entered the tent, breaking into a smile as he spotted Alric.

"We meet again," said the Orc.

"You're a long way from home," said the prince.

"Perhaps I might assist?" offered Aubrey. She switched to the Orcish tongue. "*Master Andurak, you honour us with your presence.*"

The Orc smiled, revealing his ivory teeth. "*It is nice to meet someone fluent in the language of my people. Honour be to your Ancestors.*"

"*And to yours,*" replied the mage. "*You are a long way from home, Master Andurak. What has brought you so far east?*"

"*I seek the Witch of the Whitewood.*"

Aubrey looked at Albreda. "He's here for you."

The Druid stood, coming closer. "Me? Are you sure?"

"*This,*" said Aubrey, "*is Albreda, Mistress of the Whitewood.*"

Andurak bowed. "Greetings, most noble of shamans."

"It appears he has found his tongue," said Sir Preston.

"Hello," said Albreda. "How may I be of help?"

"The Ancestors," said the Orc. "They no longer answer our call."

The Druid's face betrayed her puzzlement. Aubrey, however, immediately grasped the importance of the situation.

"Are you sure?" she said. "We've had no word of it here."

Andurak looked around the tent, reverting to his own tongue for clarity. "*I see no Orcs here.*"

"*There are none,*" said Aubrey, once again in Orcish. "*They are further east, but I can contact Kraloch if you like. He is Shaman of the Black Arrows.*"

"*Then do so. I fear this calamity has affected us all.*"

"What did he say?" asked Sir Preston.

"I need to contact Kraloch," replied Aubrey. "I shall have to cast a spell."

"Do what you must," said Fitz. "We have to get to the bottom of this."

Aubrey closed her eyes, digging deep to bring forth her magic. She uttered words of power, and then the ghostly image of Kraloch appeared.

"Aubrey," said the Orc. "This is rather unexpected. Is something wrong?"

"It is. We have encountered an Orc by the name of Andurak. Do you know him?"

"I know of him," said Kraloch, "though we have never met."

"He says he is unable to contact the Ancestors. Is this something new?"

"I do not know. We have not consulted them for some time. Shall I try now?"

"If you would be so kind."

"Very well. I shall contact you shortly." The shaman's image faded away.

"Who were you talking to?" asked Sir Preston.

"Kraloch," said Albreda. "Didn't you hear her say she was going to?"

Sir Preston, duly chastised, fell silent.

"What did he say?" asked Fitz.

"He's going to try contacting the Ancestors. He'll cast spirit talk once he's done."

"Spirit talk?"

"Yes," said Aubrey. "It's a spell we use to contact each other over great distances."

"That's new," said Albreda.

The Life Mage blushed. "I'm afraid I was sworn to secrecy."

"And rightly so," said the Mistress of the Whitewood. "We can't have everyone knowing about it."

"Master Andurak," said the baron. "Can I offer you something to drink?"

"That would be most appreciated," said the Orc.

"Might I ask you a question?" said Sir Preston.

"Most certainly."

"When the guard first accosted you, why did you not speak?"

"Our interactions with Humans have always been strained. I thought it best to wait until I met with someone in charge."

"I suppose that makes sense."

"Well," said Aubrey, "you must admit until recently, our relationship with the Orcs was not very friendly."

"I would agree," added Alric. "Andurak is quite right to be cautious. I'm afraid my countrymen are wary when it comes to the Orcs."

"A pity," mused Aubrey. "They have so much to offer."

Baron Fitzwilliam looked at their new visitor. "Lady Aubrey is our resident expert on your people. She works very closely with them."

Aubrey's face stared off into the distance.

"Is something wrong?" said Fitz.

Albreda was the one who answered. "I think she is being contacted by Kraloch."

"Understood," said Aubrey. "I shall let them know. Anything else?" She paused, obviously listening to a reply none of the others could hear. Her eyes turned to Andurak. "Is there anything else you can tell us?"

"Yes," replied the shaman. "I travelled through the Netherwood to a place of great power. There, I used my magic to contact the ancient spirit of Granag Hornbow, Grand Chieftain of the Crimson Hawks. She told me our Ancestors were being pulled to the physical realm and bound by dark magic to serve a new mistress."

"Necromancy!" said Aubrey.

"Yes," agreed Albreda, "and I sense the hand of the Dark Queen. It appears we are not so easily rid of her."

"But to what end?"

"Think of it, an army of spirits. The very prospect is quite frightening."

"Are you suggesting," said Fitz, "that Penelope is raising an army of the dead? Are we to be overrun by living corpses?"

"No," said Albreda. "Something far worse, a ghost army."

"How does one fight ghosts?"

"They can be defeated much like any other foe. It's just harder."

"Harder, how?" asked Sir Preston.

"Spirits are, as you said, essentially ghosts, mere images of what they were in life, but even ghosts have to materialize in order to attack. It is at this point that they are most vulnerable."

"So they can be killed?"

"Not precisely," said the Druid, "but their anchor to the physical realm can be disrupted. You also have to remember they have no weak spots."

"I'm not sure I follow," said Fitz.

"Think of it this way," Albreda continued. "If you were to stab out with your sword, you might kill a man with one strike, but you might just as easily inflict a flesh wound. Spirits have no heart to pierce, no stomach to puncture, no brain to smash. You must wear them down until their physical form can no longer contain their essence. Even then you must strike at the right time."

"And what's the right time?" asked Fitz.

"As they, themselves, strike, the spirits will flicker between their ghostly form and a more physical manifestation."

"Which they have to do in order to attack?"

"Precisely."

"That doesn't sound particularly easy."

"I don't imagine it is, Richard."

"How do you know all this?" asked Sir Preston.

"I read about it years ago," said Albreda, "in the Library of Kendras in Shrewesdale."

"And you remember all that?"

"It was a rather chilling read, I could scarcely forget it. Of course, I didn't give it much credence at the time."

"How many spirits are we talking about here?" asked Fitz.

"Yes," added Alric. "And where might we find them?"

Andurak offered an answer. "Based on our inability to contact our Ancestors, I would estimate that thousands were affected."

"It gets worse," warned Aubrey.

"Worse?" said Fitz. "We're talking about an army of ghosts. How can it get any worse?"

"This is Necromancy."

"Meaning?"

"Meaning," explained Aubrey, "every time they defeat an enemy, they can claim the spirits of the slain."

"Malin help us," said Alric. "That means their army will only get larger with time."

"Yes," said Albreda, "and worse yet, we have no idea where they're assembling."

Aubrey relayed all the information to Kraloch while the rest waited patiently for the Orc's reply. She eventually waved her hands, dismissing the spell, then looked at her companions. "When someone passes to the Afterlife, the location of their death forms a bridge of sorts. It's quite likely a Necromancer's powers would be most effective in such a place."

"So an ancient battlefield, perhaps?" said Fitz.

"Yes," said Aubrey, "or a graveyard."

"That would not account for so many Ancestors," said Andurak. "With the exception of Norwatch, my people have not fought in battles for many years. Are you suggesting these Necromancers have infiltrated the Netherwood?"

"I can't say for certain," said Aubrey. "None of us can, really. Death Magic is largely an unknown area of expertise for us."

"Then what do we do?" asked Sir Preston.

"Do?" said Albreda. "There's nothing we CAN do. We must carry on with our present military campaign, and hope word reaches us of this Spirit Army before it can wreak too much damage."

TWENTY-ONE

The East

Summer 965 MC

U rgon looked across the table to where Gerald sat, pondering the situation. Joining them were Kraloch, Hayley Chambers, Aldus Hearn, and the Royal Life Mage, Revi Bloom. Only Sir Heward and the Troll leader, Tog, were absent, their duties keeping them busy elsewhere.

"How serious is this threat?" asked Gerald.

"We are unsure at this time," said Urgon, "but Master Kraloch and I estimate they could easily number in the thousands."

"How many thousands?"

"I cannot say, but they will likely be limited by how many Necromancers they have," offered Kraloch.

"Why is that? You yourself can conjure spirits, can you not?"

"I can," the Orc shaman replied, "but only for short periods of time. Death Mages bind spirits to this mortal realm by anchoring them."

Gerald frowned. "I'm not sure I understand."

"It's quite simple, really. The Death Mage, or Necromancer as you Humans like to call them, must surrender a part of themselves."

"You mean like Albreda did when she created Nature's Fury?" said Revi.

"Yes, in a manner of speaking, but this power isn't permanently expended. It's merely borrowed by the spirit, anchoring them to this world, hence the term. The more powerful the mage, the more spirits they can anchor."

"So to raise a large army," continued the Royal Life Mage, "they'd have to be extremely powerful?"

"Yes, or have a large number of Death Mages who could use the spell."

"And if a Death Mage were killed, what would happen to their anchored spirits?" asked Gerald.

"They would be released," explained Kraloch, "and return to the spirit world."

"So all we have to do is kill all the Necromancers?"

"Yes, but that will be difficult. They will likely be able to control their army from a distance."

"Does that mean they could be anywhere?"

"They would have to be reasonably close. Otherwise, they could not adapt to battlefield conditions."

"Meaning," asked Gerald, "they'd have to be within visual range?"

"Precisely."

Gerald sat silent, pondering the situation.

Hayley was the first to speak. "What do we do?"

"Do?" said the marshal. "There's little we CAN do at this point."

Revi leaned forward. "You're not suggesting we ignore this threat, are you?"

"No, of course not, but until we learn more about it, we have little choice but to continue on with the campaign."

"Speaking of which," said Urgon, "we've heard back from our scouts at Hammersfield. It appears the earl is massing for a battle."

"Good," said Gerald. "I'd much rather fight him in the open than have to pry him out of a fortress." He turned to the High Ranger. "Any idea of his numbers?"

"Our Kurathian scouts report a force of some five hundred," offered Hayley.

"That gives us the advantage, for once," said Hearn.

"Yes," agreed the marshal, "but we can't be sure he won't be reinforced. Where is the Earl of Ravensguard?"

"Last reports put him farther east," said the Orc chieftain.

"What do we know of the Earl of Hammersfield?" asked Hayley. "You met him at Galburn's Ridge, didn't you?"

"I did," replied Gerald, "but we have little knowledge of his military ability. The real unknown factor here is Lord Thurlowe, the Earl of Ravensguard. Will he sit in his fortress and watch everything fall to pieces around him, or will he come to Rutherford's aid?"

"Thurlowe?" said Hayley. "Didn't you say he was the one who accused you of murdering King Halfan?"

"He was, which proves he wants war, but once again doesn't give us any indication of his intentions."

"What would you do," asked Urgon, "if you were Lord Thurlowe? Would you march to the assistance of your ally or remain safely behind your walls of stone?"

"I would probably attack," said Gerald, "but that would depend on what I knew about the enemy. There's no sense marching to battle if you have no chance of winning."

"We know they lack communication between their forces," offered Urgon, "and Lanaka's scouts have cut off any chance of them gathering information about our army."

"True," agreed Hayley, "but he also knows they suffered defeat at Uxley and Eastwood. He's likely heard something from the survivors by now."

"In which case, he knows we took heavy casualties even though we won," said Revi. "I suggest we attack Rutherford's army with all haste while keeping an eye out for Thurlowe. If he is out there, he'll likely be coming down the Ravensguard road. I'll send Shellbreaker to look out for him."

"That's very helpful," said Gerald. "Thank you, Revi."

"Not at all. It's the least I can do."

"So we are finally marching to battle," said Urgon. "How would you like us to proceed?"

"Your Orcs are faster than the rest of us," said Gerald. "You march north at first light. If you see any sign of the enemy, take up a defensive position. I'll have Heward follow with the rest of the army, including the Guard Cavalry."

"Where would you like my rangers?" asked Hayley.

"You'd best follow the Orcs. They may need your extra bows."

"And the Trolls?"

"I'll keep Tog's troops in reserve. I have a feeling we're going to need them once we get to Ravensguard." The marshal gazed down at what passed for a map. "It's important we coordinate this with Fitz. His job will be to tie down Hollis at Oaksvale. If he can do that, we have a good chance of knocking Rutherford out of the war entirely." He looked around the room, noticing their intense stares. "We have an opportunity here to deal a devastating blow to the enemy. Treat your troops with care and respect, and they'll do what they have to in order for us to win through. Now, you'd better all get some rest. There'll be lots to do come morning."

They began filing out, save for Urgon. The Orc chieftain waited until he was alone with Gerald before speaking. "I have news from Ravensguard."

"Oh?" said the marshal.

"Yes, the Orc shaman there sent word to Kraloch. They stand ready to assist when the time comes."

"That's welcome news, but I'm not sure what they can do. Ravensguard is a fortress. It'll likely require a long and difficult siege."

Urgon smiled. "It is built upon the ruins of an ancient Orc city."

"I had heard that," said Gerald, "but I still don't see how that helps?"

"There are hidden pathways into the ruins known only to my people."

"Enough to get troops into the city?"

"A select group of warriors, yes," said Urgon. "Maybe even enough to seize a gate tower."

Gerald smiled. "Then it's definitely worth looking at, but we must first deal with Rutherford."

"Of course," said the Orc, "but I thought it best to bring this to your attention."

"And much appreciated it is. If we can take Ravensguard without a protracted siege, it could shorten the war by months."

"That was my thought as well." Urgon made to leave.

"One more thing," said Gerald.

The Orc halted, turning to look at the marshal. "Yes?"

"Let's not tell anyone else about this quite yet. They have enough on their plates."

"On their plates? Are they eating?"

Gerald chuckled. "No, it's a Human expression. It means they have a lot to think about at the moment. We'll keep this between you, I, and Kraloch, of course."

"Very well," said Urgon. "I shall do as you ask."

Two days later, Sir Heward topped a rise, halting to gaze down at a distant field awash with Norland troops.

"It appears our estimates have been wrong," he noted.

"So it would seem," replied Hayley. She looked over her shoulder to where the Orcs were marching up behind them, then her gaze returned northward. "What would you estimate their numbers at?"

"At least seven hundred. Much larger than we thought."

"That still gives us the advantage."

"Yes, but only a slim one. At least they don't have a lot of cavalry."

"They likely lost most of it invading Merceria. Look at those archers over there." She pointed. "Do you see what I see?"

"Those look like crossbows. I didn't know Norland used them. Did you?"

"No. They're just full of surprises today."

"We'd best get word back to the marshal," said Heward. "He won't be happy about their increased numbers."

"Agreed," said Hayley. "Let's hope Thurlowe's army is still some distance off."

"What can you tell me of the landscape?" asked Gerald.

"It's mostly flat," reported Hayley, "with a stream running east-west. There are two hills on the northern side, along with a smattering of trees."

"Anything else?"

"Yes," said Revi. "I had Shellbreaker fly over. The stream to the east is flooded out. It would be tough to cross."

"Can cavalry get through it?"

"I doubt it," said the mage, "and just to the north is a small copse of trees. I imagine they could put some archers in there and play merry havoc with anyone foolish enough to enter the swamp."

"Hardly," said Gerald. "That would be a waste of resources."

Master Bloom looked insulted. "Why would you say that?"

"No general in his right mind would send soldiers through a swamp. It's a death trap."

"Then how do you propose he'll fight?"

"He'll likely anchor a line using the two hills. A typical tactic would be archers on the flank and footmen forming the line."

"What of his horse?" asked Hayley.

"I'd put them on his western flank. It gives them room to manoeuvre."

"How do you propose to counter this?" asked Urgon.

"With a straightforward attack. We'll send in the army in two waves, foot interspersed with bowmen. Hayley, I'll want your rangers on the right, along with the Trolls. Heward, you take your cavalry left, to counter the Norland horsemen." He looked at Revi. "Any sign of Thurlowe's army?"

"They're marching to join the battle as fast as they can. I would estimate their numbers at about six hundred."

"Saxnor's balls!" said Gerald. "We've lost the advantage."

"Should we defend instead?" asked Heward.

"No, we strike while we can. If we defeat Rutherford's forces before aid arrives, we can pivot to the east and stop Thurlowe in his tracks."

"I have an idea," said Hayley.

"Go on," urged Gerald.

"This flooded area, what you called a swamp, presents a significant obstacle, but the Trolls can move through it like it was an empty field."

"Even Trolls can't stand up to an army alone," protested Revi.

"True, but they can slow them down."

Tog bent his massive head. "It is true. My people will see it as no obstacle. We can carry the rangers across, allowing them to get into the trees that lie to the north. That would buy you time to deal with the army of Rutherford, would it not?"

"It's worth a try," said Gerald.

"Do we assault the entire line?" asked Heward.

"No, we'll concentrate on their eastern end. That'll keep our right flank up against the edge of the bog. Tell me, is there much cover there?"

"In the swamp?" clarified Revi. "No, it's mostly long grass and weeds. Not even a swamp in the true sense of the word, more like a flooded riverbank."

"Still, it'll act as a deterrent."

"Where would you like me?" asked Aldus Hearn.

"We'll keep you in the second line, along with the Mercerian foot. You know better than I how and when to use your magic. Revi, I'd like you in the second rank as well. Stay close to me, and keep Shellbreaker airborne as long as possible. Knowledge of Thurlowe's whereabouts will be crucial to the battle."

He took a measured breath, then plunged back in. "Remember, the Orcs march faster than the rest. That means they'll reach the enemy lines before we can bring up the second wave. I'm afraid that also means you'll bear the brunt of it, Urgon, until we can reinforce you."

The Orc chieftain smiled. "Understood. Do not worry. We shall not fail you."

"I know you won't. Now remember, preservation of the army is still important. We can't afford another victory like Uxley; it almost destroyed us. From that perspective, the battle is theirs to lose. If they simply wear us down, they'll have accomplished their objective. We can't let that happen."

"If we break through," asked Heward, "do we pursue?"

"No. If by some miracle that comes to pass, then you double back and take the enemy from behind, understood?"

"Understood, sir."

"Tog, I'll leave you and Hayley to sort out how to deal with the bog, or swamp, or whatever it is you want to call it."

"Very well," said the Troll.

"Now, get to your troops and pray to Saxnor, or the Ancestors, to guide us this day."

"The Ancestors will not answer," said Urgon, "but it matters little. My hunters will fight regardless."

"I know that, my friend, but let's hope their sacrifice is not in vain."

. . .

When the door opened, Lord Rutherford looked up from where he sat at his desk, sorting through dispatches. Finlad, the aide to Lord Hollis, stood there, a triumphant smile upon his face.

"You have come from your master?"

"I have," the man replied. "He is sending troops from Oaksvale to reinforce your position. They should arrive by late afternoon."

A smile crept over the earl's face. "This is excellent news, most excellent indeed."

"I trust this fits with your plans, my lord?"

"It does. With Thurlowe at hand and the addition of your troops, we shall thoroughly thrash these invaders. I'm told the Mercerian marshal leads the army himself. Once we have him in irons, their plans will be crushed. Tell me, how many warriors does Hollis propose to send?"

"Two hundred armoured cavalry, my lord. Enough to turn the enemy's flank, no doubt."

Rutherford grimaced. "I had hoped for more. Is that all he can spare?"

"He is threatened himself, else he would be here in person."

"I understand," said the earl. "I shall have to make do with what I have."

"Have you any message in reply, my lord?"

"Yes. Tell him I am preparing to engage the enemy and should have them fleeing by nightfall."

"Yes, my lord."

TWENTY-TWO

Hammersfield

Summer 965 MC

Urgon urged on his Orc hunters as they crossed an open field, the enemy visible on the distant hill. Bolts began to whizz by, doing little damage at such an extreme distance, but he knew they were merely gauging the range. Once he gave the order, his hunters began loosing off their own arrows while his spears kept up their advance. Sure enough, the enemy switched targets, sending volleys at the archers in a vain attempt to prevent them from continuing their rain of death. The Orc chieftain smiled, knowing it was a mistake that would cost the Norlanders considerably. Now free of the troublesome bolts, his spears began crossing the stream.

To the west, Sir Heward swung his contingent wide, keeping the enemy cavalry in sight. The Norland lighter horse was directly north of him, but their armoured cavalry stood to the inside of the westernmost hill. He counted saddles as best he could, estimating the Norlanders to have close to two hundred arrayed against them. Accompanying the knight were two companies of Mercerian heavy horsemen, including the famed Guard Cavalry. Heward was confident they could defeat whatever the enemy threw at them.

Tog knelt, allowing Hayley to clamber onto his back. The great Troll then stood, towering over the other rangers. He began advancing with a lumbering gait that looked awkward, but his long strides soon had the effect of quickly closing in on the flooded ground off in the distance.

Hayley risked a peek to her left, spotting Sam who, with her legs wrapped around the neck of a Troll, was trying to nock an arrow. The whole scene looked ludicrous to the High Ranger's eyes, but she had to give the new ranger credit for trying. Right as she was about to dismiss it, she was struck by the idea that crossbows would prove quite useful in such a situation. She shook her head. No one was going to convince her to give up her trusted longbow.

The Trolls continued their advance with little evidence the extra weight was having any effect.

Gerald watched the advance with keen interest. The Orcs were just beginning to cross the stream despite sporadic volleys of crossbow bolts. Tearing his eyes away from the scene before him, he sought out Revi Bloom, who sat atop his horse, his eyes closed while his head bobbed around as if he were flying.

"See anything?" the marshal asked.

"Yes, Thurlowe's army," the mage responded. "But they're still some distance off. Their horsemen are in front, advancing in two columns along the Ravensguard road, exactly as we thought."

"And our Trolls?"

"They should reach the flooded ground long before the Norland reinforcements."

"Keep an eye on them, Revi, and be sure to tell me if anything changes."

"I will."

Urgon heard the crash the moment his Orc spears smashed into the Norland line. The enemy had managed to form a shield wall right before impact, but the Orcs' initial contact forced them back at least five paces, disrupting the defence. The longer reach of the Orcs' weapons allowed them to strike over the defenders' heads to the second line of defence.

Drawing his own sword, its blade glowing with the faint blue colour of magic, Urgon moved to just behind the first rank of Orcs. When he saw a tribemate go down, he leaped into the gap, his sword striking out, the blade scraping across a shield. Quickly, he raised it again for an overhead swing that cut through his foe's helmet. The man went down, leaving a small gap in the enemy line that the great chieftain rushed through, his sword lashing out in rapid succession. Two more men went down, widening the opening to allow the Orcs to flow in, their spears dealing death to the enemy.

Feeling a Norland sword scrape across his chainmail, Urgon kicked out, forcing his opponent back. The man fell, tumbling into the warrior behind him, and the Orc chieftain struck again, thrusting his sword through the man's belly as he let loose with a primal scream.

~

The distant Norland riders held their ground, refusing to advance. Sir Heward began to wonder why they sat so still in plain sight of his troops. Slowing his advance as his horsemen splashed across the stream, he looked to his right. There, the Orcs were pushing into the Norland line, the sounds of combat drifting to his ears.

Turning back to the enemy before him, he watched as his men drew closer and closer, but still, they didn't react. Throwing caution to the wind, Heward ordered the charge. His great Mercerian Charger exploded into action, forcing him back against his war saddle.

All around him, the Guard Cavalry spurred onward, drawing their swords as they called out to Saxnor. Heward spared them a quick glance, proud of their tight formation, a perfect display of their discipline and training. The Guard Cavalry was the best in the entire land, and he had the honour of leading them this day. He swore he would not disappoint the queen!

Closer they drew until the Norland horsemen began to show signs of unease, their mounts shifting on their feet, and then suddenly they turned and fled northward.

Heward cursed and began looking around, concerned he had been drawn into some sort of trap. Sure enough, rounding the woods to his west, came a large force of armoured cavalry. He slowed his men, turning the formation to face this new threat.

~

Hayley kept her eyes on the distant treeline as Tog splashed through the water, the mud sucking at his feet as he made his way north. Behind them trailed the rest of the Trolls, each with a ranger perched high atop their shoulders.

A deer sprang from the woods, rushing east, no doubt startled by the sight of the great grey creatures and their strange companions. Tog's eyes tracked the animal, watching it as it rushed across the plain.

"Such strange animals," he said.

"Have you never seen a deer before?" asked Hayley.

"Our home is in the swamp," the troll replied, "and such creatures are rare in those parts."

"Luckily, they are more common here, and the appearance of one is a good sign."

"Is it?" said Tog. "I had no idea they had such power."

Hayley chuckled. "They don't normally, but this fellow tells us the trees over yonder are not full of enemy troops. It appears we shall be arriving to an empty woods."

"Good. It will make our job all the easier."

Gerald shifted his men to the left, coming up alongside his Orc allies and watching in satisfaction as they charged into battle. These were hardened warriors, the cream of the Mercerian army, and they would bring swift and terrible retribution to the enemy.

Protecting the flank were the archers who began pouring volleys into the Norland bowmen who held the westernmost hill. With little room left for further manoeuvres, the men were committed. Now it was a test of arms, of sword against axe, of men tearing at each other in an effort to wear them down.

Gerald could see little of the battle other than his immediate vicinity. The flanks, both out of sight, were hidden by the mass of troops who fought tooth and nail. It was up to others now, and he must trust they would do what was necessary to win the day.

Feeling the tip of a spear sink into his leg, Urgon struck out, carving a vicious cut across his foe's face. His opponent fell back, dropping his weapon and disappearing into the swirling mass of Humans and Orcs.

The chieftain stepped forward, ready to slash out with his sword, but his leg buckled, no longer able to bear his weight, sending him crashing to the ground.

The enemy, sensing victory, mustered the courage to surge forward, pushing aside the long Orc weapons to get in close amongst their enemy. The Orcs, no longer able to strike back, discarded their spears and drew their axes. Blood flew, red and black, soaking the ground as the two forces rained down blow after blow on their enemies.

In the middle of the melee, a Norland warrior stomped upon the prone chieftain's head, stunning him. Looming over his victim, the man stabbed down with his sword, piercing through the Orc's chainmail and into his stomach.

Grunting, Urgon tried to ignore the pain, but his head was ringing, his senses confused. He was helpless to defend himself, but then an axe crashed down into the Human's skull. The warrior fell beside Urgon, to lie still, his eyes staring at the Orc with a permanent look of surprise.

Someone grasped the chieftain's hand, and then he was hauled back from the fight. Shaking his head, Urgon tried to clear the fog from his mind as the face of Kraloch finally swam into focus.

"Be still, my chieftain," said the shaman. Words of power spilled from his lips, and then glowing hands were pressed against Urgon's stomach.

The chieftain felt a warmth spreading over him as the pain dissipated and his head stopped pounding. He removed his helmet to gasp a breath of air, absently noting a huge dent, and then he suddenly understood why his head had spun.

"Thank you," he said. "You have pulled me from the firepit."

"As you would me," said Kraloch. "Now, let us be done with this." He began casting once more, calling forth the spirits of long-dead hunters to drive the enemy back.

Urgon watched as the shaman invoked the spell, but it was soon evident something was wrong. Kraloch finished and turned to his chief in disgust. "They will not answer," he said. "It is worse than we feared."

"We are the Orcs of the Black Arrow," said Urgon. "We do not need the spirits of the past to defeat our enemies." He held his sword in a tight grip, staring at his friend.

"Very well," said Kraloch. "We shall do this in 'the old-fashioned way' as our Human allies would say."

Urgon grinned. "So be it!"

～

Heward cursed his misfortune. He had regrouped his horsemen, ready to countercharge, but the armoured riders of Norland had been too quick. They thundered across the field, crashing into the Mercerians before they could respond. The knight soon found his men surrounded by the enemy, attacked on all sides.

Striking out with his axe, the knight cleaved through someone's arm. The rider went down with a scream, his horse bolting away. Again and again, Heward swung, feeling his axe bite with every attack. All around him, his men fought desperately while still remembering their training and working in pairs. When he spotted an enemy light horseman in amongst the fray, he realized the very men who had drawn them in had turned to join the fight.

The heavy horsemen of Merceria kept together, forming a rough circle. So far, they had managed to keep the enemy at bay, but numbers would soon tell. He watched as one of his men went down, held fast by his dying mount. The man screamed as the weight of his horse crushed the life out of him.

Heward let out a curse, then forced his own horse into the gap. Standing in the stirrups, he raised his axe on high, letting out a scream of defiance. Metal scraped along his breastplate, and then his weapon came down, cleaving a man's skull.

He struck again, cutting into a rider's chest. His victim fell, his blue surcoat torn apart by the attack. As Heward watched him drop, he noted his newest victim wore the colours of Lord Hollis. Norland reinforcements had arrived from the west!

Hayley jumped off as Tog knelt. They had waded through the bog, little more than a flooded field, and now her rangers were rushing in amongst the trees, seeking cover.

"I shall wait here," said Tog, "unseen behind these small woods. Once the enemy is closer, we shall engage them."

Stringing her bow, Hayley made her way into the trees where her command waited.

"Sam, pull back," she called out. "You're meant to stay hidden. Ayles, keep low until you see the enemy."

The High Ranger made her way through the crouching archers, giving them words of encouragement and keeping their minds occupied. Many had seen battle before, but there were enough new recruits, like Ayles and Sam, that she worried about them. In the distance, she could make out a small dust cloud, a sure sign Thurlowe's army was nearing. Soon it would come down to their volleys' accuracy, something for which the rangers had spent months training.

The enemy banners drew closer until Hayley could make out individual companies of men marching under their officers' command, led by the armoured cavalry. Following were crossbowmen mixed in with the footmen.

Picking out her own position, she then began removing arrows from her quiver, planting them tip down into the ground, the better to draw them quickly. Ayles was to her left, looking pale.

"Remember your training," she said. "All you have to do is fire arrow after arrow, but wait till I give the command. The first volley is the most important."

"And then?" the man asked.

"Then you begin firing as fast as you possibly can. When they're all bunched together, you just fire in the general direction, but as they draw closer, take your time to pick your target. That's when every arrow must count."

He nodded, then began planting his own arrows as she had done.

Gerald watched the battle carefully, looking for any break in the enemy line. It was difficult to make out friend from foe, except where the green-skinned Orcs fought to gain a toehold. He saw his own men wavering, their casualties mounting and sent more footmen to fill in the gaps.

"Marshal," said Revi, "Heward is in danger."

Gerald glanced westward, but all he could see was a swirling mass of cavalry.

"More Norlanders have arrived," continued the mage, "from the west."

"Saxnor's balls," swore Gerald. "Is there no end to them?" He cast his eyes around, desperately seeking some spare footmen. His gaze finally rested on Hearn.

"Aldus," he called out, pointing. "Heward is hard-pressed. Can you buy us some time?"

"I shall do what I can," he called back, "but it will not hold them for long." The Druid closed his eyes, calling on arcane powers.

Gerald sought out his aide. "Hill, get together as many archers as you can. I want them formed up facing west as quickly as possible."

"Yes, sir," the man answered, riding off.

The marshal returned his attention to Aldus Hearn. The Druid had completed his spell, summoning a pack of wolves. Now they raced across the field of battle towards the distant horsemen, who fought a desperate struggle for survival.

Urgon took down his foe with a final swing of his sword. All around him, the Black Arrows surged forward, a renewed energy spurring them on. He was about to join them when Kraloch grabbed his arm.

"You must oversee the army. This is not the time for personal glory."

Urgon stared at him, fighting against his urge to return to the fray. Finally, he shook his head, then grimaced. "You are right, my friend. Can you make out how the battle progresses?"

"I cannot," said Kraloch, "but the crossbows on that hill are still causing us trouble."

"Then we shall drive them from their perch. Call up the hunters. They shall put down their bows and attack with axes and knives. Let nothing stand before them."

Kraloch waved the archers forward, seeing their dark-green faces break out in toothy grins. The moment had come for these hunters to be tested. The shaman was confident they would not disappoint. Joining them as they rushed up the hill, Kraloch drew his own axe, holding it high. They roared as they ran, calling on the Ancestors to give them victory.

At the top of the hill, the Norland crossbowmen took their time, reloading and then carefully picking their targets. They had been under tremendous pressure during the initial assault, but once the Orc spears had reached the point of melee, the threat to their flank had lessened. That all changed when they saw the green swarm climbing up the hill.

It was rare for bowmen to fight bowmen in a general melee, but the Orcs were no ordinary archers. They screamed out their challenge as they drew closer, their axes ready to cut down all who opposed them.

The crossbowmen, not used to such ferocity, broke and ran, streaming to the north in an effort to avoid a terrible fate.

Heward smashed down with his axe, cleaving into the neck of a horse. It stuck, and when the horse fell, it threatened to take his weapon with it. Giving the axe a hefty tug, he felt it come free, but his shoulder ached with the effort.

The Norlanders fought with determination, but the heavy horsemen of Merceria used their well-practiced strokes to tremendous effect. One after another, the enemy fell until the ground was littered with the bodies of men and horses.

When a blow caught Heward in the upper arm, he felt the crunch of bone, and then his arm went limp, his axe falling from his grasp. Only the loop of leather around his wrist prevented him from losing it. He twisted, shoving the edge of his shield into this new opponent and had the satisfaction of collapsing the man's visor and driving it into his face.

A horse beside him went down, its body careening against his own mount. The mighty charger shifted, trying to keep on its feet, but the corpses littering the field made such an action difficult. The great steed stumbled, and Heward fought to remain in the saddle. Another blow struck him from behind, glancing off his backplate, but it was enough to unhorse him. As he tumbled to the ground, the wind was knocked out of him, but he quickly rolled out of the way as his own horse collapsed.

Iron-shod hooves stamped around him, and he pulled his shield tight to his body in a desperate attempt to avoid being trampled.

∿

Hayley watched as the Norland troops marched by. "We must time this right," she said. "Wait until the first few are past us."

Drawing back her arrow, she picked out a target but held steady. The enemy, unaware of their presence, continued on their trek westward, desperate to reinforce their brethren who were fighting for their lives.

"Now!" she shouted, and a flurry of arrows exploded from the woods. At least a dozen Norlanders fell, and then the rangers began loosing off arrows in their own time.

Hayley picked out someone on horseback, possibly a captain, and let fly. The arrow struck him in the centre of the chest, and he slumped forward, then slid from the saddle.

The Norland company, now bereft of their captain, looked about nervously. Some began cranking their crossbows while others looked for safety. Sam took down a sergeant, and then Urzath, not to be outdone, took down another mounted man. The enemy archers were falling into chaos.

A few random bolts flew their way, but the rangers had used the cover of the woods effectively, and none took any hits.

Behind the Norland crossbowmen, though, was a more significant threat, for the footmen had been trailing. Now they began making for the woods, closing the distance with surprising speed.

∿

Gerald watched as the wolves closed with the enemy. Some of the Norland cavalry turned to face this new foe, but being so low to the ground, the pack was difficult to hit. The wolves attacked the horses' legs, doing little actual damage, but frightening the beasts. The cavalrymen, trying to fight under such circumstances, were overwhelmed.

Aldus Hearn gave a yell, his voice carried out across the field by magic. The wolves turned, running back towards him as Gerald's archers finally let loose with their first volley. Aiming low to avoid hitting their own men, their arrowheads sank into horseflesh and armour, devastating their ranks.

After another volley sang out, some of the Norland horse began to retreat, while a small group turned to face the archers, breaking into a trot. Hearn called out again, and the wolves turned once more to face the horsemen.

The horses balked, refusing to close the distance. Their riders finally turned aside, resigned to giving up the ground this day.

Urgon spotted the Earl of Hammersfield beneath his distinctive banner, urging his men to hold the line, a bloodless sword held high. The chieftain called six of his finest hunters to his side.

"That," he said, pointing, "is the enemy general. Kill him, and we have won the day." They gripped their spears with a look of determination. "Follow me, and we shall gain glory in the eyes of our Ancestors!"

Rushing towards the enemy with his fellow Orcs at his side, Urgon aimed for the weakest point of the line where his own troops had pushed back the enemy to form a bulge in their formation. Spears reached out, impaling Norlanders and pushing them aside.

"For glory!" shouted Urgon.

The Orc hunters took up the call and fought with a renewed vigour, forcing the enemy even farther back. The Norlanders were taking frightful losses, yet still, they held their ground.

Urgon stabbed out, taking a warrior under the chin, just as an Orc spear pierced the man's chest. The great chief ignored his victim's cry of anguish, pulling his blade free and pushing on. Three more times he reached out, and then they finally broke through.

Rutherford sat on his horse, watching the scene of death and destruction with detached interest. As Urgon and his hunters rushed through the line, the man's eyes widened in shock, his face growing pale. Bodyguards leaped to his defence, but the Orcs cut them down.

Urgon smashed one in the face, using his fist while his sword arm recovered for a moment. His foot slipped on a body as it rolled to the side, and then the Orc stabbed out with the point of his sword, driving it into another man's groin.

All around them, the enemy died in scores defending their leader. The Orc chieftain wondered what type of man could command such loyalty. Taking down his last opponent, he ran forward, but it was too late. Lord Rutherford was riding like the wind for the town of Hammersfield.

∾

Heward got to his feet, desperate to avoid being crushed by the swirling mass of horsemen. A hoof struck his shield, knocking him back while sending a jarring sensation up his arm. He pivoted, desperate to avoid a second blow, but it never came. Peering over the edge of his shield, he saw the Norland horsemen fleeing in all directions.

They had won against impossible odds, and yet the victory was bittersweet. Casting his eyes over his diminished command, he realized that out of a hundred riders, less than twenty now sat astride their great chargers. The Guard Cavalry, the finest horsemen in Merceria, had paid a terrible price.

Heward knelt and wept.

∾

To the east, Thurlowe's men closed in on the woods. As they approached, the rangers changed their tactics, resorting instead to volley fire, much more effective against the tightly packed troops. Norlanders fell under the barrage, but still, they came until their naked swords were ready to reach out and bring death.

Even as they prepared for the final surge, a mighty bellow issued forth from Hayley's right. The branches parted, and the grey-skinned Trolls exited the woods, closing quickly with their foes.

The attack caught the enemy completely by surprise. Few men had ever heard of a Troll, let alone seen one, and now, with their stone-like skin and towering height, they shook the enemy to their very bones.

Tog struck out with his massive club, smashing a man in the chest and knocking him from his feet to send him flying into two of his companions. The attack was quickly followed by his fellow Trolls, and a gap was soon cleared. Onward they pressed, feeling little as swords scraped across their hardened skin.

Hayley watched in fascination as she bore witness to the terrible carnage they inflicted.

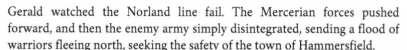

Gerald watched the Norland line fail. The Mercerian forces pushed forward, and then the enemy army simply disintegrated, sending a flood of warriors fleeing north, seeking the safety of the town of Hammersfield.

The men of Merceria paused while sergeants jostled them back into a semblance of a line. With the companies still mostly intact, they resumed their advance at a moderate pace.

Gerald looked at Revi. "What's happening in the east?"

"The Trolls have made contact," the mage replied. "Thurlowe's army is disengaging and withdrawing to the northeast. Should we pursue?"

"No. We might have beaten them this time, but we took a pounding." He turned to his aide. "We need to send word to Commander Lanaka. He'll have to pull his men back. The losses to our own horse have been too great, and we'll need him to screen the army."

"Yes, sir," said Hill. "I'll send someone immediately."

The marshal surveyed the battlefield, feeling a lump in his throat at the thought of so many dead.

"Are you in need of a heal, Gerald?"

He looked at Revi. "No, thank you."

"I should think you'd be pleased. We've dealt the enemy a terrible blow."

"We may have given Rutherford a good thrashing, but Thurlowe escaped. Now he'll retreat all the way to Ravensguard and hide behind its strong walls."

"Still," said Revi, "he no longer has the ability to roam freely. You've seen to that."

"Yes, but now we have to dispatch a force to keep him bottled up. That means fewer men with which to press forward with the war."

TWENTY-THREE

Fitz
_____

Summer 965 MC

"Where's Hollis?" demanded Fitz. "His army was supposed to be at Oaksvale!"

"It appears they tricked us," offered Alric, "and snuck off in the night."

"I can see that," the baron roared. "What I want to know is how?"

Herdwin straightened himself. "They set false campfires. A tactic Gerald and Beverly used when they fled Galburn's Ridge last year."

The baron was not amused. "I'd give my left leg to know where he's gone."

"My guess would be east," said Alric. "Likely to join forces with Lord Rutherford."

"That would put him in a position to attack the marshal's flank," warned Sir Preston.

"Could he get his whole army there in time?" asked the prince.

"No," said Fitz, "though his cavalry might be fast enough."

"In other, more encouraging news," interrupted Albreda, "I've heard from Aegryth. King Leofric is advancing on Beaconsgate. By my reckoning, he should be there, in force, on the morrow."

"At least that makes our west flank secure," said Fitz.

Everyone looked at him expectantly.

"What do we do now?" Alric finally asked.

"We secure Oaksvale, then send a force east to see if we can find the army of Lord Hollis."

"I've heard from Kraloch," added Aubrey. "They've defeated a large contingent at Hammersfield."

"Finally," said Fitz, "some good news. Any word on whether or not Hollis was there?"

"Only his horse, the rest of his army appears to be in the wind. Our forces did manage to deal Rutherford's army a killing blow, but unfortunately Thurlowe escaped eastward. They think he's heading to Ravensguard."

"What were our losses?"

"I'm afraid Gerald's forces took quite a pounding. The Guard Cavalry has been decimated, and they're now short of horsemen. The marshal is calling in the Kurathians to screen."

"Should we send him aid?" asked Alric. "I could take my Weldwyn guard."

"I shall consider it," said Fitz, "but I won't make a decision until I have a better idea of the whereabouts of Lord Hollis. The man fooled us once. Let's not let him do it a second time. Lord Herdwin, your Dwarves will secure Oaksvale once we've reached it. Alric, your group will deploy to the east, but keep a close eye on things. Hollis may reappear at anytime." He turned to Albreda. "Can we call on your flying friends for help?"

"Of course. I take it you want to find the enemy?"

"If we can. I rather suspect they're in a bit of a mess. Gerald's army has taken Hammersfield, and that traps our friend Hollis on the road between here and there. What do we know of the terrain?"

"The road goes through the Deepwood," said Albreda. "It's a thick forest, so they'd be forced to stick to the road."

"Can Gerald trap them at the other end?" asked Fitz.

"I doubt it," offered Aubrey, "and especially not with the losses they've sustained. They'll likely remain stationary until Lanaka returns from the north."

"Then we'll remain in Oaksvale until we either make contact with Hollis or hear from King Leofric. If he can secure Beaconsgate, it will free us up to move eastward."

"Weldwyn has a heavy cavalry contingent," suggested Alric. "Maybe my father can lend us additional troops?"

"Possibly," said Fitz, "but I've got a feeling he'll need them himself. We've been fighting here, in the south part of the country, but we really have no idea what's going on farther north. We'll have a better understanding of the situation once we contact Lord Creighton."

"What of the princess?" asked Sir Preston.

The baron looked at him in surprise. "What about her?"

"What do you want her warriors to do?"

"Have them march to Oaksvale and wait there," said Fitz. "If the population submits, she might see fit to recruit there."

"And if we have to fight?"

"Then we shall have to storm the place, but let's hope it doesn't come to that. We're going to need all the troops we can muster for Galburn's Ridge."

Beverly slowed Lightning as she approached Bronwyn.

"Your Highness," she said. "Oaksvale is up ahead, just beyond that ridge."

"Is there any sign of resistance?"

"None that we can see, but it still flies the flag of Lord Hollis."

"Is Oaksvale walled?" asked Sir Greyson.

"No," Beverly replied, "but that doesn't rule out the possibility of makeshift defences. We'll know more once our horsemen get closer."

Greyson turned to Princess Bronwyn. "Your Highness, allow me the honour of leading the attack."

"Attack?" said Beverly. "Aren't you being a bit premature? We don't even know if there are any warriors there yet."

Bronwyn, who appeared to relish the confrontations between her advisors, smiled. "Dame Beverly is right. We must seek answers before we act, but I will remember your words, Sir Greyson. Should an attack prove necessary, I would have you lead it."

"Your Highness is too kind," he said, bowing his head.

"What do you suggest we do, Dame Beverly?"

"The light cavalry has already cut off any chance of escape, Your Highness. I would suggest deploying our troops in a line of battle and then offering to parley. Let's hope they might be convinced to give up without a fight."

"Do you fear battle?" demanded Sir Greyson.

Beverly kept a calm face despite the outrageous accusation. "I might remind you, Sir Greyson, our objective here is to enlarge our forces, not whittle them away to nothing simply to soothe your ego. A battle would leave hard feelings, making recruitment much more difficult. If we are to win this campaign, we must be seen as liberators, not oppressors."

"You make an interesting point," said Bronwyn. "Very well, we shall follow your advice. Anything else you'd like to add?"

"Yes, Your Highness. It's important the troops under your command behave themselves when in Oaksvale, whether we are forced to fight or not."

"Meaning?"

"I would like to issue strict orders to the men. There will be no raping or pillaging."

"Oh, come now," said Sir Greyson. "Is that truly necessary? We all know the men will expect to slake their thirst on the enemy if it comes to a fight. It's expected."

Beverly ignored the knight's presence, turning her attention directly to the princess. "These are your people, Your Highness. How you act towards them will have far-reaching consequences. Will you put yourself on the throne of Norland to be despised or loved?"

"A leader must be feared," countered Sir Greyson, "or they will be thought of as weak."

"Not true. You only have to look at Merceria to see that. Do you think Queen Anna weak?"

"You make a compelling case," said the princess, "but I wonder if you would feel it necessary to do the same were the troops Mercerian."

"I would, Your Highness," said Beverly, "and, in fact, the marshal insists on it for every city assault."

"And if the men misbehave?"

"It is under penalty of death."

Bronwyn turned her attention to Sir Greyson. "Is this true?"

The Knight of the Sword did not look pleased. "It is, Your Highness."

"But you disagree with the order?"

"I do, but not for the reasons you might think."

"Then do, please, elucidate."

Sir Greyson cleared his throat, his nerves, perhaps temporarily getting the better of him. It was one thing to disagree, quite another to lecture a royal. "When a town is besieged, Your Highness, it frequently leads to a brutal fight. The threat of mistreatment at the hands of the enemy is an incentive to surrender rather than resist."

"What do you make of his remarks, Dame Beverly?"

"These are not foreign troops, Your Highness, but your fellow country-men. As I said earlier, you must make a decision as to what type of ruler you would be."

"Be ruthless," insisted Sir Greyson. "That will make the enemy fear you."

"Do that," said Beverly, "and you can forget about recruiting more troops."

The princess's eyes flickered between her two advisors. "It's an interesting dilemma. What would Queen Anna do if she were here?"

"I have no doubt she would agree with me," said Beverly.

"Of course she would," said Sir Greyson. "She's weak."

"Weak? She took the Crown of Merceria, despite attempts by your fellow knights to stop her!"

"That's enough!" shouted Bronwyn. "I have made up my mind." They both stared at her, waiting for further details. The princess took her time, relishing the combative relationship of the two knights. "We shall do this as would the Queen of Merceria. You may carry out your plans, Dame Beverly."

"Aye, Your Highness." Beverly rode off, kicking up dust as she went.

"Are you sure that's wise?" asked Sir Greyson.

Bronwyn smiled. "We need a bigger army, and we cannot do that by killing my own countrymen. Do not worry. Your time will come, my brave knight."

Sir Greyson smiled, his ego soothed.

Sir Hector approached from the rear, his horse breathing heavily, causing them both to turn in acknowledgement.

"You have news?" asked Bronwyn.

"I do, Your Highness. The baron wishes us to remain in place. The Dwarves are to secure Oaksvale."

Bronwyn turned her gaze towards Beverly, galloping off to her troops. "Return to the general and ask for clarification," she commanded.

"His orders were quite clear," noted Sir Hector.

Bronwyn turned, her face full of fury. "Do as I command!"

"Yes, Your Highness." Duly chastened, he bowed his head before heading off.

Sir Greyson smiled. "A clever move, Your Highness. By the time he returns, the town will be ours."

"Yes," she replied, "and if anything goes wrong, we can blame Dame Beverly."

Sir Preston noted the approach of a horseman. "It appears we have company, my lord. It's Sir Hector."

"He can't be back already!" said Fitz. "Whatever is he doing?"

They waited as the knight drew closer.

"Something wrong, Sir Hector?" asked the baron.

The knight slowed, coming to a halt before them. "I have come from Princess Bronwyn, my lord. She seeks clarification of your order."

"Clarification?" said Fitz. "What is there to clarify? I gave an order for her to halt. Surely that was put to her clearly?"

"It was, my lord, and yet she commanded me to return to you."

"What is she up to?"

"I believe she means to press the attack," said Sir Preston. "Her request for clarification is simply a delaying tactic on her part."

"By the blood of Saxnor," said Fitz. "I shall have none of this under my command. The marshal put me in charge of this army, and I mean to keep it in one piece. We have already lost troops at Hammersfield; we cannot allow the same to happen here."

"What shall we do, my lord?" asked Sir Hector.

"I would call her back," said Fitz, "but she's likely already begun the assault."

"Is there no way to stop her?" asked Sir Preston.

"Shall I ride back?" offered Sir Hector.

"No," said Fitz, "your horse is too tired. Sir Preston, find Prince Alric. Tell him I need his horsemen up front to support the attack on Oaksvale. How far back are the Dwarves?"

"Too far to make the town before nightfall," replied Sir Preston.

"I swear I shall have nothing but grey hair by the time this campaign is over."

"I'm afraid it's a little late for that, Richard," came Albreda's voice.

A flicker of annoyance crossed his face. "Where did you come from?"

"I was conferring with Lady Aubrey, if you must know. Why? What's gotten you in so foul a mood?"

"It's that cursed Norland princess. She's decided to take matters into her own hands and attack Oaksvale."

"And?"

"And?" said Fitz. "Don't you see? She's blatantly ignoring my orders. This is a catastrophe in the making."

"Really, Richard, you must take a deep breath. Who commands Bronwyn's troops?"

"You know full well Beverly does."

"And do you trust her as a commander?"

"Of course I do."

"Then let her do what she does best. You know she wouldn't risk lives unnecessarily."

"Yes," said Fitz. "I suppose you're right, but what of the princess? I can't have her ignoring my orders."

"Let me deal with Bronwyn," said the Druid.

"You?"

"Yes, I can hardly have her setting you off like this again."

"What makes you think you can control her?"

"She's a mere slip of a girl. Do you honestly think I would find it difficult?"

"She is a royal," he warned.

She smiled. "When has that ever stopped me from being blunt?"

"Very well. I will leave it in your capable hands."

"Good, then I shall have a nice long talk with our new ally once this battle is over."

Beverly watched as the rebels advanced. After their recent victory at Brooksholde, they were in high spirits, but she knew one good drubbing could easily cause them to fall apart. Some activity at the edge of the town drew her attention; a small group of horsemen rode towards them, none of them equipped with armour.

She halted the troops, then rode forward, joined by Sergeant Gardner. They quickly reached the halfway point, then halted, waiting as the delegation approached.

"What do you make of them, Hugh?"

"They certainly don't look like warriors. Merchants, maybe?"

"That was my thought," Beverly replied. "Do you think they're here to surrender?"

"What else could it be?"

The riders drew closer, then halted. One of them raised his hand in greeting. "Good day," he called out, his voice betraying his nervousness. "We have come to negotiate the safety of Oaksvale."

"Negotiate?" replied Beverly. "Don't you mean surrender?"

"I do not. The leaders of the town are fully aware of the conflict that has arisen between our two kingdoms. We are proposing we pay you to leave us out of it."

Beverly looked at Sergeant Gardner, but all her aide could do was shrug. She returned her attention to the man before her. "Whatever makes you think we would be interested in doing such a thing?"

"Come now," the man continued. "Surely a noble such as yourself has expenses. What better way to avoid unnecessary bloodshed?"

"You seem to be under the impression I serve Merceria," she said. "The truth is these troops belong to Princess Bronwyn of Norland."

The man's face turned pale. "The princess? Here in Oaksvale? But I thought she was under the protection of Lord Hollis?"

"She was," said Beverly, "but she has regained her freedom and now seeks to take the throne. Do you intend to help or hinder her?"

"We wish only to remain neutral."

"I'm afraid it's much too late for that. Armies are moving, my friend, armies who care little for those who would sit on the fence. The time has come to hop off your perch and choose which side you will support. Which will it be? Opposition and bloodshed? Or support and ultimate victory?"

The man looked past Beverly to the waiting troops. "Your army is not large," he remarked. "It would cost you greatly to take the town."

"Not at all," said Beverly. "The truth is we don't need the town at all, only the road. I'd be just as happy to put the whole place to the torch."

The man quickly put up his hands. "Let us not be too hasty," he said. "I'm sure we can come to some other arrangement."

"Surrender your town, and I promise you we will treat you with the utmost decency."

He conferred briefly with his companions, then turned his attention once more to the negotiations. "What assurances have we you won't let your soldiers loose on the townsfolk?"

"I am Dame Beverly Fitzwilliam," she said, "and I give you my word, as a Knight of the Hound, that the property and lives of your fellow townsfolk will be respected."

"I've never heard of you," countered the man.

"Then maybe you've heard of my father, the Baron of Bodden?"

The man hurriedly turned once more to his companions. To Beverly's eyes, they huddled for an eternity. The original spokesman, possibly overcome with fear, relinquished his position to a tall, thin man.

"We agree to your terms," he declared.

"Good," said Beverly. "Now tell your men to lay down their arms, and we shall enter the town."

"Give us till nightfall."

"I shall do nothing of the sort. If my men are not safe within the town by noon, I will commence an attack, and all promises will be forgotten."

"Noon? But it's almost noon already. That doesn't give us any time to prepare."

"There's nothing to prepare," said Beverly. "On second thought, I shall accompany you back to Oaksvale. Only then can I see that you have not betrayed us."

She urged Lightning forward, only to see their defiance completely collapse.

"Very well," the man said.

She ordered Sergeant Gardner to return to the lines, then followed them into Oaksvale.

.   .   .

Bronwyn smiled as she led her men towards the town. The locals had turned out to watch the spectacle, likely drawn more by her presence than that of the soldiers.

Dame Beverly had promised her the town was secure, and so she took the additional step of riding out front, the better to appeal to the masses for volunteers. With any luck, she could double her men in a week, although she was fully aware training would take significantly longer.

She spotted Dame Beverly at the edge of town. The red-headed knight was sitting astride her great charger beside the important men of Oaksvale. As Bronwyn rode by, Beverly drew her sword in salute. The princess, ever the gracious royal, nodded her head and waved to the crowd, which appeared pleased with her entry. And why not? In one fell swoop, they had taken the town without bloodshed. The town elders should be pleased with themselves.

"I wonder," said Sir Greyson. "Would these townsfolk be so eager to change sides if we were to leave?"

"Are we leaving?" asked Bronwyn.

"Eventually, and when we do, the army will have to assign a garrison as Oaksvale controls the crossroads. The question will be who they'll put in charge?"

"I might suggest you," said the princess.

"Me?"

"Yes. You don't like that?"

"No, Highness. My place is at your side."

"Ah," said Bronwyn, "but were you to remain here, you could look after recruitment and training. Assuming you're up to the task, that is."

"Aren't there others better suited?"

"Possibly, but none I could trust more than you, Sir Greyson. Remember, these are Norlanders, not Mercerians, and their loyalty should be to me, not the queen who sits in Wincaster. Does that thought offend you?"

"No, Your Highness. I pledge my life to you."

Bronwyn smiled. "I am glad of it, but this is something we best keep to ourselves for the time being. I doubt the Baron of Bodden would be pleased to hear of your loyalty."

Sir Greyson bowed. "Most certainly, Your Highness."

She stared at him a moment longer. "You know, you've just made me think of something."

"What is that?"

"How many Knights of the Sword are there?"

"I don't know the exact count," said Sir Greyson, "but at one time, before the civil war, there were close to a hundred. Why do you ask?"

"I can't imagine they're too happy about being relegated to second place amongst the hierarchy of such things."

"They are not, Highness."

"Then maybe I should start my own order of knighthood. What do you think?"

"I think it a marvellous idea."

"Then I shall give it further consideration. Of course, they'd have to give up their oath to the Mercerian throne. They CAN do that, can't they?"

"Aye, Highness, though renouncing their oath may prove an unpopular choice for some."

"And what of you, Greyson? Would you do it?"

"For you, Highness, I'd do anything."

TWENTY-FOUR

Reinforcements

Summer 965 MC

G erald held the map higher, the better to see it in the waning light.

"This is not much of a map," he complained.

"It is the best we have," replied Commander Lanaka. "It appears map-making is not a particularly valuable skill in Norland."

"This road here"—he pointed—"are you sure it goes all the way to Ravensguard?"

"It does indeed, my friend. My men have ridden all the way to the outskirts of the fortress."

"And how far is that, would you say?"

The Kurathian thought for a moment before answering. "A hundred miles, at least, but the terrain is mostly flat with little cover, making an ambush quite unlikely. Getting to Ravensguard will not be the problem, but getting inside of it? That's a task I don't relish."

"And yet we must," said Gerald. "The mere presence of enemy troops there threatens our campaign in the east."

"Could we not just keep them inside their fortress?"

"No, that would require too many troops."

"Can we lure them out?"

"I like the idea," said Gerald, "but I think Lord Thurlowe is far too smart for that. He'll dig in and let us waste our men against the wall."

"What of our mages? Have they nothing that can help?"

"You tell me. What are the walls like?"

"They are tall," said Lanaka, "and dominate the entire countryside. The fortress itself extends out from the side of a mountain."

"I don't suppose we could get above it?"

The Kurathian grinned. "I thought of that, my friend, but it looks like the Saints have not seen fit to give us that advantage."

"Your Saints are no better than our Gods in that regard," noted the marshal.

"Then what are we to do?"

"We may have another option, but it's quite a risk."

"Go on," urged Lanaka.

"Urgon and Kraloch think the Orcs of the Raven can get us inside, or at least a small group of us."

"Who can then capture the gate?"

"That was the idea."

"I have seen the gate," admitted the commander, "and I do not fancy the thought of taking it."

"What makes it so tough?"

"There are two towers that project out on either side. Anyone rushing the gate would be exposed to a hail of arrows."

"Still," said Gerald, "if the gate were seized…"

"It would be costly, and we have little information on what the inside of the fortress looks like. Even if we did manage to secure the gate, there's no guarantee there are no other defences."

"That's easy enough to determine. Once we're closer, I shall have Revi send in Shellbreaker. I'm sure an aerial view of the place would tell us what we need to know. I think the real question is how close the Orcs can get us to that gate. I really need to see it for myself."

"You can't possibly mean to enter Ravensguard yourself?"

"I must," said Gerald, "else I can't plan the attack."

"But if you were captured, the result would be catastrophic!"

"The army would be able to function well enough without me."

"I do not like it, my friend. There is much that could go wrong."

Gerald chuckled. "You don't have to like it. That's my job."

The marshal's aide appeared, hurriedly closing the distance.

"Something wrong, Hill?"

"Troops have been spotted, Marshal."

"Where?"

"To the south."

"Those are likely our reinforcements. Fetch my horse, and we'll ride out and meet them. Lanaka, you're with me."

"Yes, Marshal," Hill said.

They mounted up and headed south, into the gathering darkness. Soon the lights of the camp fell behind them, and the glow of the moon illuminated the landscape, giving it an eerie feeling. Gerald brought them to a halt as they topped a rise. In the distance, torchlight flickered, dancing around like faerie lights.

A distant howl drifted up to them, causing Gerald to smile. "I know that sound," he said. "It's Tempus."

"That can mean only one thing," said Lanaka. "The queen has come north."

"Then we'd best not keep her waiting," said Gerald, spurring on his horse.

They raced down the hill, the distant torches growing closer. He called out a greeting, and then they passed by the sentinels, small green lizard men who clutched peculiar spears with bone tips.

"Saurians," exclaimed Lanaka. "I had no idea they were joining us."

"It's an idea I had discussed with the queen some time ago, but we weren't sure if they would agree to fight." Gerald spotted a tent and angled towards it, the Kurathian by his side.

A woman's voice rang out in the night, and then he spotted Sophie standing at a tent flap talking to those inside. Moments later, a Kurathian Mastiff raced out, releasing a howl of utter delight.

Gerald dismounted, waiting for the huge beast to find him. Tempus halted before him, a great stick in his mouth, his tail wagging furiously. The marshal placed his hand upon the great hound and was about to say something when a familiar voice came to his ears.

"Gerald! I didn't expect you to greet us in person. You must be so busy."

"Nonsense," he replied. "And what kind of a marshal would I be if I didn't greet my queen?"

Anna stepped closer, embracing him. It was only once she stepped back that she noticed the Kurathian.

"Commander Lanaka," she said. "I trust all is well?"

He briefly looked at his marshal. "Well enough, I suppose."

The queen immediately picked up on the glance. "I think you'd best come inside," she said. "It looks like we may have things to talk of."

Guards opened the tent flap, allowing them entry. Inside were Lily and Hassus, the High Priest of the Flame, both old acquaintances. They were joined by Sophie, who poured wine and passed out goblets.

Gerald fidgeted, unable to meet Anna's eyes.

"Well?" she said.

"I feel I must submit my resignation," he solemnly admitted.

"Why? What's happened?"

"Several days ago, we encountered a Norland army," he began, "and fought them just south of Hammersfield."

"But you must have defeated them," said Anna, "or else you wouldn't be here now."

"We did, but our losses were high. I regret to inform you the Guard Cavalry has been decimated. I had to recall Lanaka's horsemen to provide cover."

"Tell me more of this battle."

Gerald took a deep breath before beginning. "The enemy was arrayed in a defensive position between two hills, their cavalry on their western flank. Sir Heward took our own horsemen to the west, hoping to push them back."

"What happened?"

"Lord Hollis had managed to send reinforcements from the west, and they quickly surrounded Heward's forces."

"And the rest of the army?"

"They assaulted the line, finally breaking through to threaten Lord Rutherford, but our losses were higher than expected. It seems these Norlanders have learned how to fight."

"And you blame yourself?"

"I should have seen the trap for what it was."

"Nonsense," insisted Anna. "You made the best decision you could with the information at hand. You are my marshal, Gerald. Nothing changes that, not even these losses."

"But—"

"No more buts. I shall hear no more of it. Instead, let us discuss our next steps. What do we know of Rutherford?"

"His army is scattered," said the marshal, "with many of them in our custody. Lord Thurlowe, on the other hand, has fled eastward, towards Ravensguard."

"And Lord Hollis? Have you any news of him?"

"Kraloch has been in contact with Lady Aubrey. She reports Fitz was unable to pin him down. We dare not renew our advance until we have a better idea where his forces are hiding."

"We have sent out scouts," added Lanaka, "but they have, as yet, failed to make contact."

"How many reinforcements did you bring?" asked Gerald.

"Two hundred Saurians," said Anna, breaking into a smile. "Along with a little surprise."

"What kind of surprise?"

"Come with me, and I'll show you." She reached out, taking his hand, and for a moment, it was as if the little girl from Uxley had returned.

Leading him outside, she headed south through the camp. A loud snort echoed in the distance, making Gerald pause. Anna, detecting the hesitation, pulled him forward. "It's all right. They're not dangerous."

"What isn't?"

She paused, then swept her arm rather dramatically. "These."

Before them stood massive beasts, easily three times the size of a horse. Each had a large, bony head, from which protruded two massive horns. Another, smaller horn grew above its mouth, making the entire head rather dangerous. Its thick, flat feet shook the ground as they walked, and their hide reminded Gerald of the skin of Trolls, though here it was green rather than the grey that decorated the elder race. Saurians scuttled about, using small sticks to guide them.

"What are those things?" he said. "They look terrifying."

"The Saurians call them three-horns, and they live in the Great Swamp."

"What do they hunt?"

"They don't," said Anna. "They eat plants, if you can believe it."

"They're frightening," said Lanaka.

"They're honestly quite docile. The Saurians ride them."

"With saddles?"

"Not exactly. They sit astride the creature's neck, behind that strange bony frill."

"How do they guide them? It's not as if they could use stirrups?"

The queen called out to one of the Saurians. The diminutive creature ran over with something in his hands.

"They use these sticks," she continued. "Note how the ends are covered in resin, forming a ball."

Lanaka took one, examining the tip. "It's quite hard."

"Yes, they tap the three-horn on the side to tell it which way to turn."

"Then how do they stop it?"

"By tapping it on its frill. To make it go forward, they tap its back."

"What do these creatures do?" asked Gerald.

"They're primarily used as beasts of burden," said Anna.

"They're larger than the drake we fought at Tivilton."

"Yes, and with a thicker hide, I'd wager."

"But you say they're docile?"

"They are," Anna confirmed. "Come, I'll show you." She took the stick from the Saurian and moved closer while the three-horn continued grazing, ignoring their presence. Anna placed her hand on the creature's leg. "Feel the skin. It's like stone."

Gerald reached out, touching the rough hide. "Remarkable."

Anna used the end of the stick to tap behind the creature's knee, and it raised its leg, allowing her to climb up it like a set of stairs. She soon settled in on the back of its neck.

"You've done this before," noted Gerald.

"Of course. I've been travelling with them for weeks, and you know I can't pass up a new experience. What do you think? Shall I get one of these to ride around Wincaster?"

He laughed. "I doubt the streets would be wide enough. What do horses think of these things?"

"They get a little skittish when the three-horns are near, but as long as they keep their distance, everything is fine."

"I can think of several ways to use these creatures on the battlefield," mused Lanaka.

"We cannot risk them," said the queen. "We only have a dozen."

"They could be used as a deterrent," suggested Gerald. "Even the sight of them would be intimidating. Imagine if they came out of the mist?"

"Ah, yes," said Lanaka. "I forgot about the Saurian's mist. Another ploy we can take advantage of."

"Tell me about these Saurians," said Gerald. "They look different than they did at Uxley."

"Yes, they've been digging through their ancient records. They now have woven vests to help protect them, and this group has been training with spears. I wouldn't stand them in the line of battle, but they should suffice quite nicely as light footmen."

"Do Saurians see well in the dark?" asked Lanaka.

"Only in moonlight," replied the queen. "Put them in a dark room, and they're as helpless as the rest of us."

"Aside from being able to produce mist," offered the commander.

"Only some of them have that power. Lily tells me that in ancient times they had a strict caste system. They don't follow it anymore, but descendants still have dominant traits like being able to create mist."

"Any other traits I should know about?" asked Gerald.

"As a matter of fact, there is," Anna said. "You remember Hassus? He's able to control the Saurian gates. That's another thing which is handed down from generation to generation. I need to talk to Aubrey about it as I think it might be a form of magical ability."

"Are you saying Hassus is a mage?"

"I'm saying he might have the potential to become one. And if that's true, there's likely more where he came from."

"That's all well and good for the future," said Gerald, "but we must still deal with the present."

"You're right, of course," said Anna. She climbed off of the great beast and returned the guiding stick to the Saurian. "Let us return to my tent, then we can discuss what's to be done."

They made their way back to the queen's pavilion, where Sophie had managed to acquire them some food.

"Come, sit," said Anna. "Let's discuss where we go from here."

"I had thought to march on Ravensguard," said Gerald, "but we must find Lord Hollis first."

"What have we got to work with?"

"Not much. Lanaka has his light horse, but they're spread awfully thin at the moment."

"Where was Hollis last seen?"

"His horsemen were at Hammersfield," said Gerald, "but the rest of his troops haven't been seen since Oaksvale."

"And the baron is sure he hasn't ridden north?"

"Quite sure. He's had Albreda sending out birds to watch for him."

"That likely means Hollis has fled into the Deepwood," suggested Anna.

"That was Fitz's best guess too. If he's there, he'll be hard to find. It's difficult terrain."

"How long ago was the battle?"

"Three days," said Gerald.

"Then he's likely through the woods by now. Are my husband's men still with the rest of the army?"

"As far as I know."

"Good," Anna said. "Then have the baron send them eastward along the Deepwood's road. I'll deploy the Saurians to watch the eastern end of the woods. If Alric's cavalry comes through unchallenged, we know Hollis has fled, and we'll concentrate our search in the north."

"You don't suppose he could be going through hills, do you?" asked Lanaka. "He might try using the same route you took when you escaped Galburn's Ridge last year."

"He'd have a hard time of it," said Gerald. "We destroyed the rope bridge as we left. If he's not in the woods, he's likely trying to march up the eastern side of the hills. If I remember, there's a town there."

"Yes," said Lanaka. "A place called Anvil."

"How poetic," said Anna. "He's caught between a hammer and an anvil."

"I might remind you the Norlanders control Anvil," said Lanaka. "He'll likely fortify the place."

"Your men have seen it," said Gerald. "What's it like?"

"Close-set buildings, mainly of stone. They refine the raw materials from the mines nearby. I suppose that's why the place is called Anvil."

"But it's not walled?" asked Anna.

"No, but it wouldn't be too hard to build up the defences."

"Do you think he could be trying to draw us towards the Shadow Army?" asked Lanaka.

The queen wore a puzzled look. "Shadow Army?"

"My apologies," said Gerald. "You wouldn't have heard as yet. Do you remember Andurak?"

"The Orc shaman from the Greatwood? Of course, why?"

"He stumbled into the baron's camp a week ago. Said something about not being able to contact the Ancestors."

"Did he say why?"

"Yes, he said their spirits were being bound by Necromancers or some such thing. You'd have to ask Kraloch for more details. The general consensus is they're being used to create an army."

"An army of ghosts?"

"Yes," said Gerald, "but we don't know where. And at this point in time, we haven't the resources to investigate further."

"Is Andurak still with the baron?"

"I believe so. Why?"

"If we can bring him here, he can help coordinate our forces."

"But we already have Kraloch," said Gerald.

"Yes, but if you march to Ravensguard, Kraloch will need to go with you. If Andurak stayed here, with the rest of us, we could stay in communication."

"I'll send word as soon as I return," said Gerald. "The camp is only a short distance from here."

"Very well," said Anna, "but you can't go yet."

"I can't?"

"No."

"Why not?"

"Sophie's gone to a lot of trouble to find you some sausages. I'd hate to see them go to waste."

"Well," said Gerald, breaking into a grin. "I can't let that happen."

TWENTY-FIVE

Beaconsgate

Summer 965 MC

K ing Leofric watched as the Weldwyn cavalry thundered past. The enemy line was breaking, worn down by the massed volleys of his archers. His footmen had followed up with an assault, and now weakened, the enemy was ready to break.

"They are in fine form, Your Majesty," announced Lord Edwin.

"Agreed," said the king. "Yet I fear this was only a skirmish. The earl's main army is elsewhere."

"Still, we shall have his seat of power by nightfall. No small feat."

"True, and definitely a victory to be celebrated. Has there been any attempt to surrender?"

"Not as yet, no. Do you wish me to raise a flag of truce and ask them?"

"No," Leofric said. "Let the cavalry have their day. Once they've broken through the lines, we might find these Norlanders more amenable to the thought."

They watched in silence as the horsemen engaged the enemy, their thunderous charge striking the line like a massive wave, pushing everyone back until, from this distance, friend could no longer be distinguished from foe.

Lord Edwin saw the resistance beginning to collapse. "We have them, Your Majesty. See how they run?"

Leofric turned to an aide. "Send in the light horse. Make sure no one escapes."

"Yes, Your Majesty." The man rode off at a gallop, eager to do the king's bidding.

The battle began winding down, now concentrated in small pockets of resistance, which the Weldwyn troops quickly overwhelmed.

A cough drew the king's attention. He pivoted to see a rider astride a grey horse, the man covered in dirt and wearing livery he didn't recognize.

"Yes?" Leofric said.

"Your Majesty," the man began, bowing, "I have come from Lord Creighton, Earl of Riverhurst."

"Go on."

"He sends you his felicitations and tasks me with giving you this." He held out a sealed letter.

Leofric took it, breaking open the seal to examine the contents. Lord Edwin watched as the king perused the letter. His Royal Majesty finished his read, then looked at the courier.

"How long ago did he write this?" asked Leofric.

"Five days, Your Majesty."

The king looked at his friend. "It appears one of our allies is missing."

"Missing?" said Lord Edwin. "How can that be?"

"That has yet to be determined. Lord Marley, the Earl of Walthorne, has failed to rendezvous at Riverhurst."

"Could he have been attacked?"

"Your guess is as good as mine." Leofric's gaze swivelled to the messenger. "What can you tell us of this Lord Marley?"

"He commands great respect from Lord Creighton, Your Majesty."

"Has there been any indication of activity in the area, other than this missing rendezvous?"

"None that I am aware of, sire."

"Hmmm," mused the king. "I shall have to give it some thought."

"My lord wished me to express the importance of this message," the man continued. "Without the earl's assistance, we shall be unable to complete our strategy and isolate Galburn's Ridge. Shall I return with a message, Your Majesty?"

"No, get yourself some rest first. I shall call upon you in the morning once I've had a chance to consult with my allies."

The man's eyes bulged. "Allies, my lord?"

"Yes, the Mercerians. Surely you've heard of them?"

"Of course, Your Majesty."

Leofric returned his attention to the battle, or what was left of it. "You may give the command to enter the town," he said. "Once that's done, we'll detail out a garrison and then have Aegryth contact the Mercerians."

"An excellent idea," said Lord Edwin.

"And round up the commanders. I'd like a full report before we lose the light."

"Have you further information for our allies?"

"Not yet," said the king, "but we'd better alert them to Lord Creighton's situation. It may have a significant effect on our plans."

Aegryth Malthunen entered the tent to see her fellow mage bent over an injured man. "How are the wounded?"

Roxanne Fortuna looked up. "Nowhere near as bad as I thought they'd be. We got off rather lightly, although our enemy suffered terribly. I am tending to them now."

"The king used his forces wisely."

Roxanne frowned. "I still think this entire campaign could have been avoided. What has Weldwyn to do with the affairs of Norland?"

"You forget, they invaded our allies, the Mercerians."

"Defending a country is one thing, invading, quite another."

"If you are so opposed to this campaign, then why are you here?"

"I am a healer," said Roxanne. "And as such, it's my duty to go where I am needed, whether I believe in it or not."

"I admire your commitment to your craft."

"You are no different."

"I suppose that's true," said Aegryth, "but I don't have to deal with the injured and suffering. Such a thing must wear on you."

"I shall survive. Have you come bearing news?"

"I have. It appears we may soon be marching again."

"To link up with the Mercerians?"

"No, I rather suspect we shall be marching to help Lord Creighton."

"Creighton?" said Roxanne. "I don't believe I know the name."

"He's a Norland earl and an ally. I have sent word to the Mercerians that the king wishes to march to Riverhurst."

"Is King Leofric now under the command of the Mercerians?"

"No, but the original strategy was to march directly to Galburn's Ridge."

"I care little for such things," said the Life Mage. "We would all be better off for some diplomacy rather than marching armies."

"You should show a keener interest," said Aegryth. "After all, he is our king."

"Then he should know better than to involve us in a foreign war." Roxanne stood, wiping her bloody hands on her apron. "I'm sorry, Aegryth, but I find war so abhorrent. Why is it men cannot simply live in peace? Why must we always covet what others possess?"

"It's Human nature," replied the Earth Mage, "but then again, it's not only Humans. Albreda tells me the Orcs and Elves almost destroyed each other when they went to war."

"How long ago was that?"

"No one truly knows, but it was long before Humans came on the scene. The Mercerian Queen is particularly interested in such things."

"I can't see why. Of what possible use is such knowledge?"

Aegryth shrugged. "Wise men say we can learn from history and avoid the mistakes of the past."

Roxanne laughed. "Then our king should study his history. How many times have we fought Merceria? Or the Twelve Clans, for that matter? And yet still, we have conflict."

"The Mercerians are now our allies," Aegryth reminded her.

"Yes, so we have moved on to find a new enemy"—she waved at the wounded who littered the ground—"in these Norlanders."

Aegryth's gaze turned to the casualties. A man to her left let out a groan. Blood bubbled from his mouth, and then he lay still. "Is there nothing more you can do for these men?"

"I wish there was, but my energy is depleted. Things would be easier if we had more Life Mages."

"A common complaint amongst all the disciplines of magic. We train apprentices, but most of them never develop the talent for spells. What else can we do?"

"We could recruit the other races," said Roxanne, "as they do in Merceria."

"The king would never approve."

The Life Mage looked around the room at her charges. "Then let the king spend a day tending to the wounded. Perhaps then he'd see reason."

"I understand your frustration, but you should choose your words with care. They might be interpreted as treasonous."

"Treasonous? I'm not the one throwing lives away, and I might remind you I am the only Life Mage in Weldwyn. What can the king do, execute me? This is all too much for one person to bear." Her shoulders slumped, and Aegryth stepped closer, embracing her fellow mage.

"You are exhausted, Roxanne, and in no shape to continue. When was the last time you ate?"

"Not since sun-up."

"Then come, let us find you some sustenance, and then you can rest."

"What do you think?" asked Leofric.

Lord Edwin stared down at the rather crude map. "I fear we cannot continue with the current plan. If Lord Marley has failed to show, it means he's fought a battle, or he's switched sides. Either way, it spells trouble."

The king nodded in agreement. "Norland has seven earls, three of which are firmly against us."

"Yes, Lords Rutherford, Hollis, and Thurlowe."

"We also know Creighton is on our side and, up until now, took it for granted Lord Marley could be counted on. The unknown factors are the last two—what are their names?"

"Lord Calder, the Earl of Greendale, and Lord Waverly, Earl of Marston."

"Malin's beard," cursed the king. "We don't even know where Greendale is, let alone Marston! Do we, in fact, know there are only seven earls, or is this simply assumed knowledge?"

"The number is confirmed as seven," said Lord Edwin. "Queen Anna and her entourage met them all in Galburn's Ridge last year."

"And they have no lesser nobles? How do they rule?"

"I would imagine they appoint stewards to oversee the smaller towns and villages."

"Rather a strange way to run a kingdom, if you ask me."

"It is," agreed Lord Edwin, "and unlike Weldwyn, their earls hold all the power, instead of the king."

"It's no wonder their country has floundered. With no central authority, there's no one steering the ship."

"They have a king, or rather they did have, but he held little power."

"Then why this war?" said Leofric. "Aren't the earls better off by themselves?"

"It all comes down to greed, Your Majesty. They each seek power but are ill-equipped to wield it."

"So instead, they invade Merceria. What were they thinking?"

"I would suspect they know little of our ally, as we know little of Norland. I might remind you that until quite recently, we thought the same of Merceria."

"Yes," admitted Leofric, "I suppose we did. Strange how much things have changed of late. At least we are fighting on foreign soil now, rather than defending our own. What did you make of the Norland troops we fought?"

"I rather suspect they were not the most experienced of men."

"Naturally, Lord Hollis would have taken those with him."

"They were also quite short on cavalry," added Edwin.

"That's a result of their botched invasion. Alric tells me they captured hundreds of mounts at Eastwood. I suspect it's put back their breeding program by decades."

"Theirs was an ambitious plan, Your Majesty."

"Ambitious or foolhardy? I think the latter more likely."

"We have the benefit of hindsight," said Lord Edwin. "And at the time, the Mercerians were hard-pressed to halt them."

"You have a valid point, Edwin. Do we know who was behind that campaign?"

"We suspect Lord Hollis, but we really don't know for sure. I, for one, have my doubts."

"You don't think Hollis is capable of it?"

"The man has spent years raiding across the border. That hardly makes him an expert in commanding large armies."

"You seem to forget the accomplishments of the queen's marshal. He was only a sergeant, and yet he's led armies to victory multiple times."

"True, but he had the benefit of being trained by the Baron of Bodden."

The king smiled. "And how do we know it was any different for Lord Hollis? Perhaps he had a mentor as well?"

"Yes, but Merceria has been in a state of near-total war for generations."

"Let us not jump to premature conclusions. We know so little of Norland. They may have a northern neighbour who gives them trouble, much as they do to Merceria."

"I hadn't thought of that," confessed Lord Edwin, "though I've never heard tell of such a place."

"Or they could have been fighting Orcs, maybe even Elves."

"Not the Orcs, they would have told the Mercerians. It's said they can communicate over long distances. A skill, I might add, that would benefit us immensely."

"We shall not employ the greenskins," said Leofric. "As you pointed out before, it poses too many issues."

"That is, of course, your decision, Your Majesty. You did, however, mention the Elves. Considering the Mercerians' history with that race, I would say it's a definite possibility."

"Yes," said the king, "and if that were to prove true, we might have found a new ally. However, it's all conjecture at this point."

"Have you considered Lord Creighton's plea for help?"

"I have," said Leofric, "and I have decided to march to his aid. I have already informed the Mercerians of my decision. We shall leave a small garrison here, in Beaconsgate, along with a junior commander. The mages, we'll take with us."

"I fear our allies will be disappointed, Your Highness. They were expecting us at Galburn's Ridge."

"Galburn's Ridge is a fortress carved into the rock. The presence of our men would do little to force its surrender. In any case, if we march to Riverhurst, we can combine with Creighton's army, then travel upriver to that large lake—what's it called?"

"The Windstorm Depths," replied Lord Edwin.

"Strange name for a lake. Then again, they have no access to the sea. Once we reach the lake, we can loop around its northern shore and come down to Galburn's Ridge from the north. That should put an end to this war."

"And if Marley stands against us?"

"Then we shall defeat him in the field. Our army is the largest we have ever assembled, Edwin. Do you honestly think anyone can stand against us? Come now, let us be more reasonable. I doubt Marley has turned. He likely came up against the army of Lord Calder, and they're busy trying to outmarch each other. Our arrival will help tip the balance in our favour. You just wait and see."

"When will we march?"

"In two days," said Leofric. "That will be enough time to let our men rest up and get word to the Mercerians. I have sent word to Lord Creighton, telling him of my decision. He will expect us by the end of the week."

"The end of the week? Is that even possible?"

"We shall make it so. I want the cavalry in the lead. We must get to Riverhurst with all haste, the better to get apprised of the current situation. If we're lucky, we'll arrive to find Marley is already there."

"One can only hope," said Lord Edwin.

"You worry too much, my friend. Remember, Creighton's letter left Riverhurst five days ago. It will be at least a fortnight by the time we arrive in person. A lot can happen in that time."

"And in the meanwhile?"

"You need to make some decisions," the king advised, "regarding the garrison we leave here, in Beaconsgate. You'll also need to appoint a commander. Have you anyone in mind?"

"I was thinking of Lord Milburn."

"The Baron of Kinsley? I didn't even know he was with us."

"He came with the engineers, Your Majesty. As you know, he's rather a solitary man, but he's more than capable of looking after things here."

Leofric frowned. "The man has no experience with military matters."

"True, but he will be acting more as a governor than a soldier, and our victory here has secured the area for miles in any direction. The risk is minimal, and his appointment would free up the more battle-hardened commanders to accompany us to Riverhurst."

"You offer sage advice," said the king. "Very well, we'll do as you have suggested."

Two days later saw the army of Weldwyn stretched out on the road to Riverhurst. They were only awaiting the arrival of their king to signify the start of their march.

Aegryth Malthunen put spurs to her horse, galloping down the column looking to find King Leofric. She soon spotted him emerging from his tent even as others rushed to begin disassembling the structure.

"Your Majesty," she began. "I bring word from the Mercerians." She held out a small cylinder, handing it to her king.

Leofric unrolled the tiny note, holding it close to examine the fine writing. A smile soon creased his lips. "They send us greetings and wish us well on our endeavours, as I knew they would."

"But what of Galburn's Ridge?" asked Lord Edwin. "Won't it interfere with their own plans?"

"Their plans are on hold. It appears Lord Hollis has given them the slip."

"What if he marches to Beaconsgate?"

"Relax," said the king. "His troops have been spotted to the east. It appears he is trying to link up with his allies, not reclaim his home."

"That frees us up."

"It does indeed. You may give the order to commence the march."

Lord Edwin took his horse's reins from a nearby servant, and pulling himself into the saddle, he nodded to the king, then rode off, calling for the march to begin.

Aegryth looked once more at her king. "Have you any messages for me, Your Majesty?"

"No," he replied.

"Shall I send scouts ahead of us?"

"I hardly think that necessary, do you? We're marching in friendly territory, and I won't have the army wait while your birds fly over the area. You may take up your customary position at the rear of the column, along with the rest of the followers."

Aegryth watched as Leofric mounted his horse, too surprised to object to the king's command. Did he really feel there was no need for scouts?

Resolving to ignore the order, she sent out a falcon, for it was better to waste the effort than be caught unawares.

TWENTY-SIX

Albreda

Summer 965 MC

Albreda, Mistress of the Whitewood, walked down the streets of
Oaksvale, taking in the scene around her. Rebel warriors were everywhere, standing around as if they had not a care in the world. Farther up
the street, she saw a knight taking the new recruits through the basics of
fighting. The town had surrendered rather quickly, and Bronwyn had been
eager to take advantage of it. The Druid wondered if the Norland princess
had been given too much free rein.

She halted by a large house, where guards stood sentry, and considered
her options. It was clear the extra troops were useful to Lord Richard, but
Bronwyn's sense of independence could jeopardize the entire campaign.
Something had to be done, and Albreda felt she was the one to do it. Having
made up her mind, she took a step towards the house, but just as she did so,
Dame Beverly came out the door, a most fortuitous event.

"Beverly," said Albreda. "How are things in the camp of Princess
Bronwyn?"

The red-headed knight drew closer until they could talk in low tones.
"She can be stubborn at times, but she means well. Is this an official visit?"

Albreda locked her arm in that of Beverly's and began walking down the
street. "Let's go and have a chat, shall we? There are a few things I'd like to
discuss with you."

"Very well. There's a nice tavern down the end of this street."

"I think I would prefer somewhere a little more private, away from the ears of strangers."

"That sounds a tad serious," said Beverly. "I hope I haven't upset you?"

"No, of course not," said the Druid, "but I need to talk to you of the princess."

Beverly cast her eyes around, but no one was within earshot. "What, precisely, do you want to know?"

"Was it her decision to attack Oaksvale or yours?"

"I was under the impression my father had ordered it. Was it not so?"

"It most decidedly was not," said Albreda. "He had intended for the Dwarves to take Oaksvale."

"Had I known—"

"It wasn't your fault, and you should know he doesn't blame you in any way. In fact, once he realized you were leading the attack, he decided to let the assault continue. The bigger issue here is Bronwyn taking matters into her own hands. Tell me, you have her confidence. What is she up to?"

"I'm not sure I know, nor do I have her confidence. She's more than willing to let me lead her troops but has said little about her plans."

"Are you involved in training these new recruits?"

"No, she's placed them under Sir Greyson."

"Do you trust this man?"

"He's a Knight of the Sword," said Beverly, "so I have my reservations."

"Oh? You do not see them as honourable men?"

Beverly stared at Albreda. "You know my history with the order. Why would you even ask such a thing?"

"I'm sorry, I don't mean to be insensitive, but I recall you trusted Sir Preston. I merely wondered if Sir Greyson fell into a similar category."

"Most decidedly not," said Beverly. "He spent most of his time in Shrewesdale, under Montrose."

Albreda's face paled. "He wasn't one of your attackers, was he?"

"No, but he was in the city when it happened. Then again, so was Heward, and he's an honourable man."

"But you don't believe the same to be true of Greyson?"

"No, I don't. I can't explain it in so many words, but I have the feeling he's currying favour to advance his own position."

Albreda nodded. "Most likely he is. It's a common enough trait amongst the lesser nobility, yourself excluded, of course."

"Does my father consider him dangerous?"

"My dear, your father is a kind and generous soul who only thinks the best of people. I, on the other hand, don't trust the man for a moment. I've seen his type far too many times in the past."

"For what it's worth, he's doing well with the training."

"And where is Sir Hector in all of this?" asked the Druid.

"I must confess I've seen little of him. The last I heard, he was running messages between my father and us."

"Is he trustworthy, do you think?"

"He comes from Kingsford," said Beverly, "and Lord Somerset has always supported the queen."

"I think it best you have a chat with him, but keep it quiet. The more eyes that watch this Norland princess, the better."

"You think she might betray us?"

"Not intentionally," said Albreda, "but she may try something reckless. We've already suffered losses at Hammersfield. We can ill afford more."

"And if she gets out of hand?"

"I cannot tell you what to do, Beverly, merely remind you that the command of the rebel forces lies on your shoulders, not hers."

"Will you have a chat with her?"

"I shall," said Albreda. "Perhaps all she needs is a good talking to."

"I doubt she'll take kindly to that."

"Nor do I, but it must be done. I should have done it some days ago, but I have been kept busy of late trying to track down the elusive Lord Hollis."

"Have you had any luck with that?" asked Beverly.

"We have determined he is NOT in the Deepwood, but beyond that, we know little."

"Shall I send the rebel cavalry to assist?"

"No, you'd best keep them here, with the princess. You were coming out of her headquarters when I met you. Were you going somewhere in particular?"

"Only to check on the pickets," said Beverly.

"Then I'll let you get on with it. Any advice on how I should deal with Bronwyn?"

"You want MY advice? I find that hard to believe."

"Nonsense," said the Druid. "You're practically family. Why wouldn't I seek your advice?"

"I've never known you to ask anyone for help."

"Well, let's just say I'm trying to turn over a new leaf. I've been told I can be a little abrupt at times."

"Who told you that?" said Beverly. "My father?"

"Not in so many words. So, your thoughts on the princess?"

"She expects to be treated with deference. Other than that, she's not too difficult to deal with."

"I don't do deference," said Albreda.

"No, I don't suppose you do. Perhaps if you keep in mind she's our ally, things will be easier?"

"I shan't make any promises, but I'll see what I can do. Now, best you be off. Those soldiers won't look after themselves."

"Very well," said Beverly. "I'll drop by the headquarters later and see if you've utterly destroyed the place."

Albreda smiled. "If you must."

Bronwyn sat, staring at the letter before her. "Are you sure this isn't some form of elaborate trap?"

"I can make no guarantees," said Sir Greyson, "but I can assure you it's from Lord Hollis. Note the seal."

The princess lifted the letter, holding the seal closer to the flames, the better to see its details. "And he sent this to me?"

"He did, Your Highness. A rider came in this morning, dressed as one of our own. He made some enquiries that led to me. I assured the courier I would hand deliver the message."

"But how did he know I was here?"

"A lucky guess? He likely knows of your disappearance from his estate, and the presence of rebel soldiers amongst the Mercerians might have led to the conclusion you were here."

"There's another option," said Bronwyn, "and one I should have thought of sooner."

"Which is?"

"He has spies amongst our men."

"If that's true," said Sir Greyson, "there's little we can do about it. And in any case, your soldiers know nothing of the overall plans."

She looked at the letter, tapping it against her other hand. "What in the Afterlife can he want?"

"Maybe you should open it and find out?" he suggested.

Bronwyn drew her slim dagger and used it to pry up the seal. Her task complete, she unfolded the note, perusing it as her knight watched. "He wants to meet."

"Is that wise, Your Highness?"

"It is if we are to discover what he desires. Perhaps he's willing to negotiate peace?"

"More than likely he wants to capture you and force you into marriage. He's still after the crown."

"No," said the princess, "it's more than that. I have an army now. It might be small, but it could be used to swing the battle at a critical time."

"He wants you to betray the Mercerians?" suggested Sir Greyson.

"I am merely speculating. His note indicates nothing of the sort."

"You don't mean to take him up on this offer, do you?"

"I think it a wise decision to do so, don't you? After all, we should at least hear what he has to say. And if he does want to surrender, it would be wise to do so to me, rather than our allies, don't you think?"

"I don't like this, Your Highness."

"Don't worry, we'll take precautions. I'll need you to select only the most trustworthy of men, Sir Greyson, and tell no one else of this letter."

Someone knocked at the door, causing Bronwyn to quickly hide the letter by placing it beneath the many papers that littered her desk.

"Who is it?" she called out.

"It's the Druid, Albreda," came the voice of a servant. "She wishes an audience with you, Your Highness."

Bronwyn looked at Sir Greyson. "We shall speak of this in more detail later. For now, let us talk to Albreda, but no word of what has transpired, understood?"

"Yes, Highness."

"You may let her in," she called out.

The door opened, allowing Albreda entry. The Druid was wearing the green-and-brown mottled dress for which she was best known, and her hair hung down her back in a long ponytail, giving her the look of a country matron.

"Mistress Albreda," said Bronwyn, "what brings you to my office?"

"I bring greetings from the general, Baron Fitzwilliam. He asked me to look in on you and see if everything is to your satisfaction."

"That was nice of him," said Bronwyn, "but doesn't he have more important things to worry about?"

"Your troops distinguished themselves taking Oaksvale," Albreda continued. "Did you find much in the way of opposition?"

"Not at all. In fact, they welcomed us as liberators. Even as we speak, we are training three more companies of footmen."

"Remarkable. At this rate, you'll soon have more troops than Merceria."

"I doubt that," said Bronwyn.

"Well, perhaps if we don't count the Dwarves and Orcs. Regardless, the men under your command have done well for themselves. I trust Dame Beverly has been up to the task of leading them?"

"Actually, I have been considering making some changes."

"Of course you have," said Albreda.

Bronwyn frowned. "What's that supposed to mean?"

"Nothing at all, simply a turn of phrase. Why? Does it bother you?"

"I am a princess of the Royal Line of Norland. You will address me as 'Your Highness'."

"I shall do no such thing," said the Druid.

"Do you show the queen such disrespect?"

"Queen Anna has earned my respect. You, on the other hand, are nothing but a spoiled child."

Sir Greyson's hand went to the hilt of his sword. "How dare you speak that way to the princess."

Albreda turned her gaze on the knight. "Draw that sword, and it will be the last thing you ever do."

"I could strike you down long before you could cast your spell."

"Is that what you think? I am a wild mage, you fool. Spells are second nature to me. I could destroy you with the merest flicker of my eye."

Sir Greyson paled as he looked at his princess, but her eyes were locked on the Druid.

"What do you want, witch?" Bronwyn demanded.

"You're new to being in charge, so I'll forgive your rashness, but you are part of a much larger campaign to free your country."

"Don't you think I know that?"

"I imagine you do," said Albreda, "but you most certainly don't act like it. You had a victory today, but it might as easily have turned into a disaster. An army is like a chain, held together by discipline and training. If one link breaks, it can destroy everything we've worked for. Is that what you wish for your countrymen? To be plunged into the hands of a despot?"

The Druid stopped for a moment, staring intensely at the princess, then continued. "I know you see yourself as the liberator of your people, but there can be no victory without a careful and deliberate plan, and your actions threaten that. You need to earn the respect of your allies, Bronwyn, not dictate it. Listen to your advisors. They know what they're doing, and for Saxnor's sake, don't start taking matters into your own hands like you did here at Oaksvale."

"That was not me," said Bronwyn. "It was Dame Beverly who took matters into her own hands."

"Do you honestly expect me to believe that?"

"It's true," added Sir Greyson. "I heard her give the commands myself."

"I see," said Albreda. "Yet you did nothing to persuade her otherwise?"

"It's not my place," said the knight. "She outranks me."

The Druid fixed her gaze on the princess. "You and I both know the truth of things, Bronwyn. Show the general you can act like a true leader, and stop this outrageous display of bravado. Only then will the people of Norland accept you as their queen."

"I'm already their queen," insisted Bronwyn, though her voice shook with emotion. Albreda held her tongue, her eyes boring into the young princess.

"I will be Queen of Norland," added the princess.

"Then act like one, and work WITH your allies, not against them."

"And how do you propose I do that?"

"Ask yourself what the Queen of Merceria would do?"

"She would lead the army herself," said Bronwyn, her voice now defiant.

"No," said Albreda. "She would trust in her leaders to do that, just as you must. You are not a warrior, Bronwyn, and you have little experience in such matters. On the other hand, Dame Beverly has spent her entire life learning how to lead men into battle. Trust her in military matters, and trust in her father to make the best use of your men."

"I thought Marshal Matheson was the great Mercerian leader?"

"And who do you think taught him everything he knows?" said Albreda. "Lord Richard, that's who. You would do well to remember that."

Bronwyn's face was flushed. "I... didn't know that."

"Well, now you have no excuses. I shall expect you to follow orders from now on, not send Sir Hector scrambling off to clarify a very straightforward order. Is that understood?"

"It is," replied the princess.

Albreda stared for another moment or two, then took a breath. "Good, then that is all I have to say. Now, I shall leave you to your work, Princess, in the hopes you may consider my advice. Good day to you."

She turned, striding from the room with but a cursory glance at Sir Greyson.

"She has the manners of a cur," he remarked once she left.

"True, but they say she's the most dangerous mage in all the lands."

"I still think I would have been justified in striking her down for her insolence."

"Justified, maybe," said Bronwyn, "but I doubt you would have survived the encounter. And how would we have explained it to our allies?"

"Perhaps it's time we acquired new allies?"

Bronwyn's eyes dropped to her desk where the earl's letter lay hidden. "Perhaps it is."

Sir Preston reached across the map, pointing with his finger. "They were here, my lord. Approximately two hundred of them."

"Did you engage?" asked Fitz.

"No," replied the knight. "As per your orders, we maintained our distance. They were heading north, keeping to the edge of the hills to their west. I think they mean to reach the town of Anvil."

"That would match up with Gerald's assessment."

A deeper voice cut in. "What about Galburn's Ridge? Are we to leave it unattended?"

The baron looked over at Herdwin, the Dwarven leader. "No, of course not, but we lack the troops to assault the place. The strategy is to isolate them, then starve them out."

"That could take years," complained the Dwarf.

"If we secure the area around their capital, they will have little choice but to surrender."

"Might I suggest we move troops up to cut off any reinforcements?"

"Now, that," said Fitz, "I would consider. How many would you require, do you think?"

"My Dwarves will be sufficient, although I'd be much obliged for the loan of some cavalry."

"I shall send Sir Preston and his horsemen. I'd also like to send the rebels. Hopefully, their presence might convince the Norlanders to cross over to our side."

"Not to say ill of the leadership of Dame Beverly," said Herdwin, "but can we trust these troops to behave?"

"You will act as regional commander," said Fitz, "and they'll take their orders from you. I'll make sure my daughter understands that, but you may wish to consult with her. She was inside Galburn's Ridge last year with the queen's delegation."

"Good to know," replied the Dwarf. "I'll see if we can't work up a floor plan of the fortress."

"I'm told it's quite impressive."

"It's not of Dwarven construction," argued Herdwin. "It can be defeated. We merely have to figure out how."

"If you run into any trouble, send word immediately. The rest of the army will remain here, just north of Oaksvale, ready to move where needed."

"Very well, General, I'll have my troops on the march before midnight."

"You can wait for tomorrow," suggested Fitz.

"Nonsense," said the Dwarf. "My people can march just as well at night, and in any case, it'll be cooler than marching in the sun. Now, with your permission, I'll get right to it."

"By all means, and good luck, Commander."

Herdwin smiled. "I don't need luck, General. I have Dwarves."

He moved towards the exit, halting as he almost collided with Albreda, who was just entering.

"Pardon me," said the Dwarf.

Albreda nodded her head. "Greetings, Lord Herdwin. I trust all is in order?"

"It is, but you'll have to excuse me, Mistress. I have things to attend to."

"Of course." She stepped aside, allowing the Dwarf to exit.

"How did it go with the princess?" asked Fitz.

"About as well as I expected," she replied. "She can be stubborn, but I think she got the message. I doubt she'll trouble you again."

"I certainly hope not. We shall need them in the coming days."

"Oh? For what?"

"We're sending them to cut off the Norland capital."

"And you trust Bronwyn to do that?"

"No, not at all, that's why they'll be put under Herdwin's command. Beverly won't mind. She's known him ever since they escaped Wincaster together. He's also a good friend of Aldwin."

"Sometimes, Richard, I wonder if you don't think more of your son-in-law than you do your own daughter."

"Don't be ridiculous," countered Fitz. "It's only that he needs more guidance. Beverly will always be my favourite."

Albreda laughed. "Don't fret, my dear, I'm only teasing. I know how important your daughter is to you."

TWENTY-SEVEN

The Hammer

Summer 965 MC

"Are you sure about this?" asked Hayley. "It means splitting our forces."

"It's a calculated risk," said Gerald, staring down at the map, "yet I believe it has the best chance of success."

"But you can't take Ravensguard with less than five hundred troops. You'd need at least four times that number."

"We're counting on some help from the inside," he revealed.

Hayley turned her attention to the queen. "Surely you don't agree with him, Your Majesty?"

"I have complete faith in Gerald," replied Anna.

"And the rest of the army?"

"Sir Heward," she continued, "will take the Mercerian foot north, towards the town of Anvil. Their job will be to shadow the troops heading there."

"I need you with us," said Gerald, "along with Tog and his Trolls. The plan is to form an Orc brigade."

Sir Heward spoke. "Are you sure, my lord? Won't the presence of the Orcs only make things worse?"

"That is precisely the effect we're going for. I can't say more at this time, but if their attention is on the besieging army, it will only work to our advantage." Gerald looked around the room, seeing the nervous expressions of those gathered. "I know this is a gamble, but I'm confident it will work."

"And if it doesn't?" asked the knight.

"Then we are no worse off than we are right now. We won't assault the gates unless we think we have a high chance of success. You know I won't waste the lives of our troops."

"Very well," said Hayley. "Where do you want my rangers?"

"We'll need them out in front and to the sides. We won't have any cavalry to screen for us."

"What about the Kurathians?"

"Commander Lanaka and his light cavalry have been given the task of tracking down Hollis. Once they locate him, it'll be up to the rest of you to bring him to battle."

"I'm not sure I'm up to the task," said Sir Heward, his voice choking. "My last battle resulted in the loss of my command."

"Nonsense," said Gerald. "You have suffered a defeat by a superior enemy. No one faults you for that."

"Shall I accompany Lanaka?" asked Revi. "With Shellbreaker, I could greatly increase the range of detection."

"No," said the queen. "You shall accompany Sir Heward." She looked over at the aged Druid. "Master Hearn, I would like you to march with the Saurians if you would be so kind."

"I should be delighted, Your Majesty, though I can't for the life of me see why."

"You have the power of nature. It may prove beneficial in communicating with the three-horns."

"Three-horns?"

"Yes," added Gerald. "The beasts of burden that the Saurians use. Haven't you seen them yet?"

"I fear I have not, nor have I even heard of them."

Anna chuckled. "We've kept them some distance to the south. They have a tendency to frighten horses."

"Are they vicious brutes?"

A mischievous smile appeared on the queen's face. "You'll see."

Gerald turned to the massive Troll. "Tog, will your people be ready to march at daybreak?"

"They will," he promised in his deep baritone.

"Good. The actual order of march will be left to Chief Urgon since his people will be forming the bulk of this brigade." He looked at the Orc chieftain.

"We'll set out at dawn," began the Orc, "with the rangers spread out in front and to the sides, as the marshal indicated. I would prefer our Troll allies to bring up the rear. The Orcs march quickly, and I shouldn't like to slow them down."

"Understood," said Tog.

"Master Kraloch will accompany us," the Orc continued. "His presence will prove crucial to the success of this operation."

"What about the rest of us?" asked Sir Heward. "We'll be short a Life Mage to help with communication."

"That has already been arranged," said Anna. "You shall be joined by Lady Aubrey."

"Then who will remain with General Fitzwilliam?"

"An Orc named Andurak."

"Yes," added Kraloch. "He is a shaman from the Wolf Clan, located in the Netherwood, what you call the Greatwood."

"What do we know of this fellow?" asked Sir Heward.

"He was of great help to us in Weldwyn," said the queen. "And he's the one who warned us about the Spirit Army."

"I have been in communication with him," added Kraloch, "and he assures me he will cooperate in any way he can."

"Remember," urged Urgon, "you are allied with all the Orcs, not only one tribe."

"Excuse me," said Aldus Hearn, "but I wonder if you might clarify something for me?"

"By all means."

"We have always referred to your people as tribes, and yet you refer to Andurak's people as a clan. Why is that?"

The Orc smiled. "The people of the Wolf do not live in villages, preferring instead to travel around their land in small hunting parties, gathering only for special events. As is our custom, such Orcs are referred to as clans, rather than tribes, but it is a term used without malice. All of us, be they clans or tribes, are still considered Orcs."

"Did all Orcs used to live in clans?" asked the Druid.

"No, but after the fall of our great cities, many generations ago, our people were driven into the wild. As a scattered people, we lived in small groups, the better to avoid the wrath of the Elves. It was only later we began to settle down and once more establish permanent homes."

"But some of your people still wander?"

Urgon nodded. "Now you understand."

"It's getting late," said the queen, "and all of you have preparations to make. This meeting is adjourned."

She rose, prompting the rest to do likewise. As was the tradition, they all filed out, leaving her alone with her marshal.

"Well?" she said. "How do you think that went?"

"About how I expected," said Gerald.

"They're nervous."

"As they have a right to be. The odds are definitely against us."

"How many know the actual plan?"

"Very few," said Gerald. "Us, Urgon, Kraloch, and, of course, Lanaka. Without him, we'd have no chance of pulling this off."

"I feel bad about excluding the others."

"So do I, but one slip of a tongue could lead to disaster."

"Well, I, for one, am looking forward to it."

"You would," said Gerald. "It gives you something to do."

"What's that supposed to mean? I have plenty to do as the ruling monarch."

"Yes, but you've always seen yourself as the Warrior Queen. This gives you the chance to do just that."

"My part is small," she countered.

"But still crucial to success. And might I remind you, it was your plan that led to success at the Battle of Kingsford, back in 960."

"Was it truly that long ago?" said Anna. "It seems like only yesterday."

"Funny," said Gerald. "I would have said the opposite."

She laughed. "That's because you're old." Seeing him cringe, she quickly added, "Well, older than me, anyway. You're still a veritable child compared to Baron Fitzwilliam."

Now it was his turn to laugh. "You always know what to say to make me feel better."

"Of course, we're family. Why are we here if not to support each other?"

Gerald was up before sunrise, watching as the troops began their march down the road to Ravensguard. Sir Heward soon joined him, riding his great Mercerian Charger over to the marshal as the soldiers marched by.

"They are impressive," noted the knight, "but they've got a long march ahead of them, even farther than the rest of us."

Gerald smiled. "Don't worry, they'll get there in plenty of time. These are Orcs. They don't believe in resting; they're like Dwarves that way."

Heward noted the approach of the queen. "Is she really going to command the reserves here in Hammersfield?"

"That's the plan. Someone has to do it."

"I suppose, but aren't there any junior officers who are more than capable?"

"Really?" said Gerald. "And how many of them speak Saurian?"

"I suppose you have a good point." He moved his horse aside, allowing Anna to pull up alongside her marshal.

"Your Majesty," Heward said with a bow. "I'm surprised to see you up so early this morning."

"I couldn't let Gerald leave without wishing him well," she said. "And what of you, Sir Knight? Is all ready for your own expedition?"

"It is, though I fear we cannot leave until the marshal's forces have cleared the area." There was only one road leading north, and it branched off the Ravensguard road some twenty miles to the east of the city.

"I thought you would have taken the opportunity to sleep in a little longer," said Gerald.

The knight was about to object but then noticed the look of amusement on the marshal's face. "Very funny."

"You need more of a sense of humour," said the queen. "Perhaps you should spend more time at court?"

"And be besieged by eligible women? I think not."

Anna turned to her oldest friend. "It appears our gallant knight thinks a lot of himself."

"He can't help it," said Gerald. "It comes from his training as a Knight of the Sword."

Sir Heward grinned. "Am I to be insulted all morning?"

"No, of course not," said Gerald, "I'm leaving shortly. Of course, if the queen desires it..."

Anna held up her hand. "Fear not, Sir Heward, your reputation remains intact. I shall not speak of such matters anymore this day."

"Then, with your permission, Your Majesty," said the knight, "I shall be about my business."

"You may."

He rode off at a trot, angling towards the Mercerian troops.

"Is he up to this command?" asked Anna. "He suffered terribly at Hammersfield."

"His wounds have been healed," replied Gerald. "Kraloch saw to that."

"It's not his physical wounds that I'm worried about. He suffered a loss. Has he dealt with it?"

"I believe so. Heward is nothing if not resilient. He took a stand against the Earl of Shrewesdale. He won't let us down."

"Very well," said Anna. "I shall take your word for it. Does he suspect anything of our plans?"

"No," replied Gerald. "He believes you're staying here to command the reserves."

"Good," said the queen. "Then things are proceeding as we planned."

"Any news from Revi?"

"No, and that worries me. If we can't locate Hollis, everything could turn against us."

"We must have faith," said Gerald. "You're the one who always says we win when we're together."

"True, but in this case, we're not. You're marching off to Ravensguard without me."

"Yes, but we hatched this plan together, remember?"

"I could hardly forget," said Anna. "And it felt like a good idea at the time, but now, in the early morning, it somehow seems more foolhardy."

"It's merely nerves, that's all. I always get nervous before a coming battle, as you well know."

"Yes, but I'd feel safer if you had more soldiers."

"If I had more soldiers," he said, "the plan wouldn't work."

"I suppose there is that."

"Hey now," said Gerald, "you've got this backwards. YOU'RE supposed to be the one cheering ME up."

She forced a smile. "I know, but it's been hard being separated from all my friends."

"You're missing Alric, aren't you?"

"I am," Anna admitted. "I worry about him."

"He's an accomplished leader, and he's seen his fair share of battles and come through them unscathed."

"Yes, but he almost died at Riversend."

"That was years ago."

"It was more recent than the Battle of Kingsford."

"Exactly my point," insisted Gerald. "He fought with us all through the civil war and then helped fight off the Norlanders at Uxley. You have nothing to worry about."

"Don't I?" she said.

He could see tears forming in her eyes. "What is it?" he asked. "What's wrong?"

Her voice began to falter. "I had a dream," Anna admitted. "I saw Alric lying on a battlefield, covered in blood."

"Albreda's the one who has premonitions," said Gerald.

"What if that's not true?" she said. "What if it really is going to happen?"

"Do you really think Fitz would let that happen to a prince? Come now, Anna, it's only a dream."

"But I can't shake that image from my mind."

He could feel a lump forming in his throat. Watching her in turmoil wounded his heart. "Then go to him."

"I can't."

"Yes you can. You're the queen. You can do whatever you want. Put someone else in charge here, and ride over to Oaksvale and see for yourself that he's fine."

She used her hands to wipe away the tears. "No, I'm all right. It's nothing but a bad dream."

"I can have Kraloch contact Aubrey if you like. I doubt she's left yet, and I'm sure she'd be willing to check up on things."

"No, I'm the queen. I can handle this."

He stared at her a moment, seeing the determination creep back into her eyes.

"Very well," he said. "Make sure you look after Tempus. I won't be around to give him his evening walks."

She smiled. "Of course."

"And have Sophie make you your favourite meal. That always cheers you up."

"I will," she promised.

"Good. Now I must be on my way."

She reached out, taking his hand and squeezing it. "Be careful, Gerald. I want you to live to see your grandchildren."

He smiled. "I look forward to it." He was about to ride off when a thought struck him, causing him to return his gaze to Anna. "Have you had any trouble lately?"

"Trouble?" she asked.

"Yes, you know, with… being a woman?"

She wore a puzzled look. "What do you mean?"

"Well… I… that is…"

"Are you asking me if I might be pregnant?"

"The thought had crossed my mind. After all, you and Alric did manage to spend quite a bit of time together before we marched."

"I don't know. It's not something I've given much thought to."

"You should have Aubrey take a look when she gets here."

"Do you think that's necessary?"

"I do," he replied. "She can use magic to tell if you're expecting, can't she? I know Kraloch can."

"Very well," she said. "I shall do as you ask."

"And if you are?"

"Then you shall be the first person I tell."

"The first? Don't you mean the third?"

Anna's face betrayed her confusion. "Third?"

"Yes, Aubrey would be the first, and then Alric, as the father, should be next, don't you think?"

She laughed. "Very well, but you're next in line, agreed?"

"Agreed."

Halfway through the morning, Gerald spotted Hayley riding towards him. The Orcs had set a brisk pace, and the rangers had been hard-pressed to keep up. Now, with the sun rising steadily, the heat was beginning to become a factor, and he knew the Humans amongst them would be unable to sustain this pace for much longer.

"Hayley," he called out. "So good of you to join me."

The High Ranger pulled up alongside him.

"I take it your people are tired," said Gerald.

"They are," she admitted. "They need to rest."

"I thought as much. Have your rangers fall back and join Tog's Trolls."

"That will leave you unprotected," she protested.

"I'll have a word with Urgon. He can use his archers to screen."

She looked around at the Orcs marching with grim determination. "Don't they ever tire?"

"They do, but they know their cousins need their help at Ravensguard. They'd march till they dropped if we let them."

"I still don't know why you wanted the rangers. One company can't make that much of a difference? I would have thought cavalry preferable, at least for screening purposes."

"I have all the Orcs I need for the assault, but we're hoping to get people inside, and that means we need Humans who can pass for locals."

He saw the light dawning on Hayley's face.

"So you need us to seize the gate?"

"Yes, though we don't know what the inside looks like just yet. Once we arrive, Kraloch will arrange a meeting with the Orcs of the Raven. This used to be their home, you know."

"So I'd heard. Does that mean they have a way into the city?"

"That's what I've been led to believe."

"You don't trust them?"

"I trust the Orcs. I just don't know if they will be of any help."

"Wouldn't a secret entrance be a great advantage?"

"Yes," said Gerald, "but there's still the matter of navigating the city to get to the gate, not to mention taking out any guards who are present. It's a risky endeavour. Think your people are up to it?"

"That depends entirely on what these new Orcs tell us. Without knowing the details, we can't really plan anything."

"You see my problem, then. I'd like you present when we meet with Ghodrug."

"Is that their chieftain?"

"Yes, and Kraloch tells me she's had the confidence of the tribe for some time. Does that mean anything to you?"

"It does," said Hayley. "I've picked up quite a bit of Orc culture working with Gorath. They elect their leaders."

"Elect? How does that work?"

"When a chieftain dies, the tribe gathers to select their next leader. Each Orc then chooses who they wish to follow. Whoever gets the most stones wins."

"Stones?"

"Yes, they drop stones into a bowl, then count the total."

"Seems a strange way to pick a leader."

"I suppose it does," said Hayley, "but I'm told they've done this for centuries. It's the same method that brought Urgon to power."

"We must be thankful for that at least. He's proven to be a stalwart ally."

Hayley rode for some time in silence, deep in thought. Gerald looked at her, noting her troubled look. "Something wrong?"

"As you know, I'm the High Ranger."

"I am well aware of that," said Gerald. "You're the one who arrested me, remember?"

"I'm sorry about that. I was only doing my duty."

"I understand, and I don't hold a grudge, but you're getting off topic. You were talking about your position?"

"Yes. As High Ranger, one of my responsibilities is keeping the peace on the Queen's Roads. A good part of my day consists of combing through written reports from all over the kingdom."

"And?"

"And there has been a disturbing trend of late."

"Oh?" said Gerald. "Is banditry on the rise?"

"No, but there's a growing resentment against arming the Orcs, except in Hawksburg, of course."

"What kind of resentment?"

"People are scared that after the war, the Orcs will turn against us."

"What absolute nonsense," said Gerald. "They want peace and prosperity, nothing more."

"And I would agree with you, but I think someone is stirring up trouble."

"That wouldn't surprise me. We never did find out who collaborated with Montrose. Is it serious?"

"Not yet," said Hayley, "but the sentiment is growing."

"Saxnor's beard. Can they never give us peace? It feels like every time we face a foreign adversary, trouble has to brew up at home. The whole thing sickens me."

"I think it's Lord Stanton."

"The Earl of Tewsbury? That would make sense, I suppose. He's always been opposed to the queen. Still, we'd need undeniable proof if we're to arrest him. In any case, that would be for the queen to consider, not me. Why bring this up now?"

"Hey, now," said Hayley, "YOU'RE the one who asked ME, remember?"

He chuckled. "I suppose I did. Still, it's good that you brought it to my attention. You know, we should probably talk to Urgon about it."

"You think it wise?"

"If there's a growing sentiment against his people, I think he ought to know, don't you? Interesting that Hawksburg doesn't have that problem."

"Not so surprising if you consider the situation there. The Orcs helped rebuild the town, and it earned them a lot of goodwill."

"It did, didn't it. You know, if Stanton, or anyone else for that matter, has been throwing their coins around, there's a good chance they tried it in Hawksburg. I bet if your rangers investigated, they might find someone there willing to talk."

"Talk?"

"Yes, you know, reveal that someone was offering them recompense to spread rumours about the Orcs?"

"That's an excellent idea, Gerald. You would've made a good ranger."

"No, not really. My archery skills are crap."

"That surprises me. I thought you were proficient in all weapons?"

"I am, at least in theory, but I haven't used a bow in years. I'm quite happy to leave that work to you younger folk."

Hayley snickered. "Then, as a member of us 'young folk', I thank you." She spotted a hawk, winging its way northward, and watched it with interest.

"Thinking of Revi?"

She looked back at Gerald. "How did you know?"

"You were watching that bird, wishing it were Shellbreaker."

"How could you possibly know that?"

"You don't need to be a mage to read a person's face, just years of experience. Have you two set a date for your wedding yet?"

She frowned. "Not yet. He wants to wait until after the war."

"That's so much like him. He's always been a bit of an odd duck."

Hayley laughed. "Odd duck? Where did you get that one from?"

Gerald grew defensive. "It's a common enough term in Bodden."

"I'm sure it is, but I'd say it's quite rare anywhere else, dare I even say unknown?"

"If you're quite finished poking fun at my turn of phrase, perhaps you'd like to take care of your rangers before they pass out?"

"Very well, Marshal, I shall be on my way."

She turned her horse around, galloping off.

TWENTY-EIGHT

The Deepwood

Summer 965 MC

Sir Greyson halted, his hand going to the hilt of his sword. "We are here, Highness, although I see no sign of who we are to meet."

"Then we shall wait," Bronwyn replied. She stepped from the trees, moving into the clearing to better see her surroundings. It was late evening, well after dark, and the knight's lantern did little to illuminate the area. "Are you sure this is the correct place?"

"It is, I swear it. The instructions were quite clear."

The rustle of leaves caught Sir Greyson's attention, and he pivoted, his sword now half drawn.

"Put away your sword, Sir Knight," came a clear voice. "I am here to talk, not fight."

"How do I know you don't mean the princess harm?" demanded Sir Greyson.

"If that were my aim, I would hardly have alerted you to my presence." The man who stepped from the shadows wore a hooded cloak masking his features. He turned to face the princess, the dim torchlight revealing the countenance of Lord Hollis.

"So," said Bronwyn, "you came."

"As I promised," said the earl.

"Then speak," she demanded. "Tell me what it is you want."

"All I want is peace for the kingdom, but there's little chance of that while a foreign army marches upon its soil."

"That's all on you. You were the one who chose to invade Merceria."

"True. And it would have worked had the Mercerians not bought the allegiance of the other races."

"Get to the point," demanded Bronwyn.

"You and I have had our differences," said Hollis, "but in the end, we both want the same thing."

"Do we?"

"Yes, peace and prosperity for Norland."

"And yet we see things differently when it comes to who takes the throne."

He smiled, unsettling her. "And if I were to offer the crown to you?"

Bronwyn scowled. "Why would you do that?"

"It's now clear I cannot hope to win the throne for myself. I would rather see you sit upon it than another earl."

"So I am seen as the least threatening of your allies?"

"My allies? Yes, I suppose you are, but you can use that to your advantage."

"You seek power for yourself. You and I both know whomever I marry will become ruler of Norland."

"While that might be true," Hollis admitted, "it can still work to our mutual benefit."

"What are you proposing?"

"You have no desire to wed, yet without a marriage, there can be no official heir to the crown. What I propose is that you rule as queen until your natural death."

"Naming you as my eventual heir?" Bronwyn guessed.

"Yes, or my son, should you outlive me."

"And I am expected to believe THAT would be the end of it?"

"I give you my word."

"That still doesn't explain how such a thing would be accomplished. We are on opposing sides, you and I, or did you forget the current war?"

He chuckled. "The war is an inconvenience, I grant you, but something that can be rectified."

"Meaning?"

"Even now, the Mercerians have split their eastern force. Here, in the centre, they are required to divide their army to make up for the fact King Leofric has taken his men to Riverhurst."

"You appear remarkably well-informed of events," she accused.

"I make it my business to be so. Tell me, how goes the training for your new recruits?"

Bronwyn felt the heat rise on her cheeks, although in the darkness, it was hard to see. "What is your point?"

"Your forces are growing, Princess. Soon they will rival the army of General Fitzwilliam. I am fully aware you are advancing to Galburn's Ridge, along with the Dwarves. Were you to turn against them at the right moment, you could decimate their forces."

"And why would I do that?"

"To win this war for Norland!"

"The rest of the Mercerians would crush me."

"No they wouldn't. Don't you see?" he insisted. "Once you have destroyed the Dwarves, you could seek refuge within the fortress at Galburn's Ridge. What's left of Fitzwilliam's army would never stand a chance of prying you out of there. They would be forced to sue for peace."

"I think you overestimate the strength of my soldiers. They would be hard-pressed to defeat the Dwarves."

"Nonsense," said Hollis. "You would be within their lines. You could kill their leaders before they even knew what hit them."

"Dwarves are fierce warriors."

"They are, but without their leaders, they are like a wagon without a horse. All you'd have to do is inflict enough damage to throw their army into disarray. You can break this unholy alliance, Bronwyn, but the time to act is drawing nigh. Will you join me in defeating this invasion by the Mercerian horde, or become their lapdog?"

"I serve no master!" Bronwyn claimed.

"Then prove it! Destroy the Dwarves, and then take up your rightful place as Queen of Norland. Show the kingdom that the blood of your grandfather runs deep."

"I… shall think on it. What you ask is no small matter."

"No," said Hollis, "but small deeds do not win great rewards. Very well, I will leave it in your hands. I shall inform the garrison at Galburn's Ridge to allow you entry should you make up your mind to join us. In the meantime, I must depart, for I have preparations to make."

He paused, his eyes focused on her. "Consider my offer carefully before you reject it, Bronwyn of Chilmsford. It shall not be made again."

He turned and walked off, disappearing back into the darkness of the woods.

Bronwyn turned to Sir Greyson. "What do you think?"

"I'm not sure what to think, Your Highness. His proposal was quite unexpected. I suppose the real question is whether or not you believe him. This could be all part of a deliberate plot to ensnare you."

"I had thought of that. Were he to simply deny us access to Galburn's Ridge, we'd be left out in the open."

"Yes, and we rely on the Mercerians to feed and equip us. That's not an easy lifeline to abandon. Still, if he is to be trusted, it could put you on the throne. Is it something you're seriously considering?"

"I certainly will not dismiss it out of hand. In the meantime, I shall take a few precautionary measures to ensure the option is still open to me, should I choose to take advantage of it. Now come, we must get back to Oaksvale before the army marches."

Lord Hollis made his way through the darkness guided only by his inner senses. He soon found what he sought, a hooded figure dressed much like himself, with a goat tied on to the end of a thin rope.

"Did all go as planned, my lord?"

Hollis removed his hood, shaking out his hair in the cold night air. Words of power issued from his mouth, and then his features changed, his face elongating, his ears narrowing to a pointed tip. When the spell was complete, he wore his natural countenance again, that of an Elf.

He gazed down at the goat. "Is this all you could find?"

"It is, my lord. I'm afraid the army has rounded up most of the animals in the area. Will it suffice?"

"It will have to." He moved closer to his companion, standing directly in front of the man, facing him. The guttural sounds of dark magic spat from his mouth, the air around them becoming infused with a thick black ichor. On and on he droned until his very breath turned malodorous and vile.

The goat erupted in a spray of blood and flesh, and then the two individuals completely disappeared, carried away by the magic of death.

Beverly stepped into the room, coming to a halt before Princess Bronwyn. "You called for me, Your Highness?"

"I did," the young woman replied. "Your service to me has been greatly appreciated, Dame Beverly, but I think it's time we Norlanders took matters into our own hands. Your presence is no longer required here. Go with the knowledge you have served my line well."

"You're dismissing me?"

"That's correct."

"But you can't," insisted Beverly. "I was appointed by the queen."

"Need I remind you that my rebel troops are not Mercerians? Your queen has no power over them."

"But we are allies."

"And we shall remain so," said Bronwyn, "but the time has come to free you up for other duties. Sir Greyson will carry on as commander of my forces from this point onward. Is that understood?"

"And what is to become of me?"

"You may return to your father. I'm sure he has more than enough jobs to keep you busy."

"He won't like this," warned Beverly.

"No," said Bronwyn, "I don't suppose he will, but you must do your part to assure him I still intend to honour our agreement. I will have my troops march to Galburn's Ridge, as promised, and we shall follow the recommendations of our gallant ally, Lord Herdwin."

Beverly cast a glance at Sir Greyson only to see him grinning like a fox.

"Is there anything else?" asked the princess.

"No, Your Highness."

"Then you may leave."

Beverly wanted to speak out but knew it would do no good, for Bronwyn's mind was made up. The red-headed knight left, turning only to bow as she reached the door.

Sir Greyson waited until she was gone before speaking. "That was surprising," he said. "You might have given me a bit of warning, Highness."

"I was expecting more of an argument," she replied. "Dame Beverly surprised me. Is she always this meek?"

"Her reputation far exceeds her character," said the knight. "I've said it before, and I'll say it again, women don't belong in armour," and before Bronwyn could object, he added more, "just as women like you belong on the throne."

The princess smiled at the compliment. "Your plate is now full, Sir Greyson. I trust it won't be too much for you to handle?"

"Not at all, Majesty."

"I am not queen yet," she warned. "Highness will do perfectly well for now."

He bowed deeply. "Then I eagerly await the day I may call you thus."

Fitz paced back and forth, his temper flaring. "She did what?"

"She dismissed me," said Beverly, "as is her right."

"And who is to take your place? No, don't tell me, Sir Greyson?"

She nodded.

"Confound it," he roared. "The woman's a constant thorn in my side." He looked at his daughter, forcing himself to calm down. "I'm sorry, Beverly, it's not your fault, but the blasted princess has been nothing but trouble from the start."

"What would you have me do?"

He threw up his hands. "I'm afraid my troops all have their own commanders, but there's something else I think you might be able to help me with."

"Certainly. What is it?"

"I'm sending your cousin Aubrey to Hammersfield, to link up with the forces under Sir Heward's command. I was going to send an escort, but now that you're here, how would you like to accompany her instead? It would mean a two-day ride to Hammersfield, and then you'd need to get directions to wherever the army lies. I'm sure Heward can make use of your skills."

"Very well, Father."

"Good. You'd best go, and let Aubrey know you'll be accompanying her in the morning."

"I will."

"Oh," said Fitz, "and if you have any letters for Aldwin, let me know. We're sending dispatches back to Wickfield first thing."

"Anything else?"

"No, that's all for now," said Fitz. "I'm sorry you got caught up in all this, my dear. It's not your fault."

"I'll be fine, Father. I just feel guilty about leaving this in your lap."

He waved it away. "Give it no further thought. I'll take care of it. Now, off you go. I have things to do."

She left him, heading through the camp towards the Life Mage's tent. Fitz watched until he heard her call out to Aubrey, then turned around.

"Albreda?" he called out. "Are you there?"

Moments later, the Druid appeared. "Yes, Richard?"

"Did you have that chat with Bronwyn?"

"You know I did. I told you all about it."

"But you haven't seen her since?"

"No," replied Albreda. "Why? What's happened?"

"It sounds like our young princess saw fit to dismiss Beverly as her commander. She has appointed Sir Greyson in her stead."

"That's hardly surprising, is it?"

"I suppose not, but the timing couldn't be worse. We're beginning the march towards Galburn's Ridge in the morning."

"Shall I go and visit her again?"

"No, I think not," said Fitz. "It might make matters worse. She appears to have developed a bit of a spine."

"She's still young. Perhaps she'll see reason."

"One can only hope, but I must still take precautions."

"What types of precautions? You don't think she's going to attack, do you?"

"Bronwyn? No, but she might refuse to march, forcing us to commit our own Mercerian troops."

"Is she still under your command?"

"For the moment, but who knows when she might change her mind about that too?"

"I made it quite clear to her she must follow orders," said Albreda. "Give her a chance. She'll come around."

"We'll know by morning. Her troops are scheduled to follow the Dwarves."

"And if they don't?"

"Then I fear that stronger measures may be needed."

"Let's hope it doesn't come to that."

Morning found Aubrey and Beverly leaving the camp behind them. They rode down the road into the Deepwood, marvelling at the canopy of leaves that shaded the road.

"It's quite nice here," said Aubrey. "So peaceful."

"Yes," agreed Beverly. "Remarkable when you consider how close the army is."

"Why do you think they call this place the Deepwood?"

"I have no idea, nor do I really care if truth be told. The woods, I leave for people like Hayley to explore."

"Or Albreda," added Aubrey.

"Yes, she'd probably enjoy it here. Like you said, it's peaceful."

As if on cue, Lightning let out a rather pronounced snort.

Beverly noticed the behaviour and halted. "What is it, boy?"

Aubrey, seeing her cousin halt, did likewise. "Is something wrong?"

"I don't know."

A rancid smell drifted towards her, causing her to wrinkle her nose. "Do you smell that?"

Moments later, Aubrey made a similar face. "I do. It's rather strong."

"What is it?"

"I've smelled something like this before. It's the smell of rotting flesh."

"Here, in the woods?"

"It's common when treating wounded," said Aubrey, "but seems a little out of place here."

"We'd best investigate," said Beverly. "With all this talk of a Spirit Army on the loose, we can't afford to take any chances."

Aubrey wet her finger, then held it up to gauge the wind direction. "The wind is coming from the north."

They dismounted, leading their horses by the reins. The undergrowth here proved easy to navigate as they made their way deeper into the forest, the smell growing stronger with every step.

They soon found a small clearing, emerging into an overpowering stench. Beverly tasted bile in the back of her throat, and even Aubrey, accustomed as she was to healing the sick and wounded, found herself almost gagging.

"Look there," the Life Mage said, pointing. A small pile of flesh sat on the forest floor, but bits of blood and gore were splattered all over the surrounding area.

"What in Saxnor's name is that?" said Beverly.

"I'm not sure, but whatever it is, it's not Human."

"How do you know?"

"I see coarse hair mixed in with the flesh."

"It certainly made a mess."

"Yes," agreed Aubrey, "almost as if whatever it was exploded from the inside out."

"What in the name of the Gods could have done such a thing?"

"Only one thing I can think of—Blood Magic."

Beverly looked at her cousin, her senses suddenly alert. "But that would mean..."

"Yes. There's a Necromancer about, or at least there was. Whoever did this is likely long gone by now."

"What exactly is Blood Magic?"

"Most mages pull their power from an internal source of energy. Necromancers, however, have learned to harness the power of the creatures around them."

"Do they all use that technique?"

"I can't say for certain, but I doubt it. Think of Blood Magic like a specialization, the same way that Spirit Magic is a type of Life Magic."

Beverly stared at what was left of the grotesque body. "And you're sure of this?"

"As sure as I can be."

"We'd best return to the camp and report this."

"No," said Aubrey. "I'll relay the information to Kraloch. He, in turn, can contact Andurak."

"Can't you contact Andurak yourself?"

"I can, but it would use more energy, as I don't know him very well."

"But isn't Kraloch farther away?"

"He is, but the spell doesn't work that way. You see—"

Beverly held up her hand. "It's fine. You don't have to explain your magic to me. Will you contact him here, or should we move somewhere with less of a stench?"

"Here will do fine. Kraloch might have questions about the body."

"Very well. I'll take a quick look around the immediate area, just to make sure we're safe." The knight dropped the reins of Lightning and started making her way around the perimeter of the clearing.

Aubrey, meanwhile, began chanting her spell. The air buzzed, and then she was talking to an unseen person, presumably the Orc shaman, Kraloch.

By the time the knight had returned, her cousin had completed her task.

"Did you tell him?" asked Beverly.

"I did."

"And?"

"He agrees with my assessment and will contact Andurak. I'm sure your father will soon have soldiers out here looking for it."

"Good," said Beverly. "I'll mark the path from the road by notching trees. That should get their attention." She pulled out her dagger and began scratching on the bark.

They took their time getting back to the road, making sure the trail was easy to follow. Content their work was done, they turned eastward once more, trotting off at a fast gait to be rid of the smell.

TWENTY-NINE

Ravensguard

Summer 965 MC

The city of Ravensguard lay nestled between the two arms of a mountain, giving the place a majestic feel. Small watchtowers occupied the tips of each arm, allowing sentries there to hurl great rocks from their catapults at any approaching enemy.

Past the outstretched arms stood the city's main gatehouse, flanked by two large, round towers. The gate was an immense structure, with thick, iron-bound doors that rose past the height of two men. The entire city appeared impregnable.

Gerald gazed at the place in wonder. "How high would you say those walls are?" he asked.

Urgon thought carefully before answering. "Too high to climb with a ladder," he said. "And the ground here is too rough to use a siege tower. What do you make of the catapults?"

"They're poorly placed," the marshal replied. "Any army worth its salt would be brought up close for an assault. Those siege engines are only going to work against opponents at a distance."

"Nevertheless, it is still an imposing sight."

"Tell me, how is it you are so well-versed in siege techniques?"

The Orc grinned, showing his ivory teeth. "I had Kraloch consult the Ancestors some time ago. They are full of such knowledge. I first took an interest in such things during the civil war after we took Wincaster. Never did I think it would come in useful in the future."

"You likely know more than me, then," said Gerald.

"I might know more about fortifications, but you know Humans better than I, and the knowledge of our Ancestors is limited to our war with the Elves."

"Still, I doubt walls have changed much."

Urgon nodded. "I daresay you are right. But tell me, if you were defending this place, what would you do?"

Gerald turned his gaze to one of the towers. "I'd put men up there to report on the movements of the enemy. Behind us, we have our army, but they're camped in plain sight of those things." He waved his hands at the towers. "As soon as we begin moving, they'll know what we're up to."

"Then how do we neutralize that threat?"

"That's an excellent question." He stared for a moment, looking for any detail that might provide an answer. "I suspect there's a trail that runs from those towers up the arms of the mountain and into the city itself."

"Why would you say that?"

"Easy," said Gerald. "What's the point of having sentries if they can't send reports?"

"How does that help us?"

The marshal smiled. "I have an idea, but it will only work once."

"Care to share?" asked the Orc chieftain.

"How good are your people at climbing?"

"We live in the Artisan Hills; we climb all the time. Why?"

"Here's what I think we should do…"

Hayley crouched, peering into the darkness. Ahead of her, Orc rangers scaled the cliff while the Humans remained below waiting for ropes to drop.

"This is taking forever," she cursed.

"You must be patient," said Gorath. "Climbing in the dark is difficult, even for someone with night vision."

"I'd feel better if we knew what to expect."

The Orc grinned. "We can expect to fight, but darkness is no place for bows." He scratched his head, a sure sign he was thinking.

"Out with it," urged Hayley.

"It occurs to me I am wrong. Although it is more difficult, we are quite capable of using our bows by moonlight."

"That doesn't really help us, does it? The enemy is inside of a tower."

"True, but at least we can force them to keep their heads down."

"You have a valid point, but—" A sound off to her right interrupted her. "What was that?"

"I believe the first rope has been dropped."

"Good, let's get going, shall we? I want to be amongst the first up that cliff."

The climbing was awkward, to say the least. The Orcs managed well enough, but the Humans, unaccustomed as they were to their newly acquired armour, found the entire situation quite uncomfortable.

Hayley, now at the top, took the green hand that offered help. She was hauled up onto the cliff face where she stood a moment, catching her breath.

"I still don't understand why you are wearing that strange armour?" said Gorath.

"It's simple," replied Hayley. "It's Norland armour. We brought this with us to use once we're smuggled inside of Ravensguard. Of course, I never thought I'd be wearing it halfway up a mountain, but I suppose I shouldn't be surprised."

"It is the ranger way," said Gorath, "to do the impossible. Is that not what you did at Riversend?"

"How do you know about that?"

"Come now," said Gorath. "You cannot keep such a story secret for long."

"I don't know what you're talking about."

"A ranger and a mage single-handedly defeat a tower? How could such a tale be more heroic?"

"Yes, well," admitted Hayley, "it seemed more foolhardy at the time."

"And this?"

She shrugged. "I suppose one might consider it just as ridiculous."

"Some would say audacious," said Gorath. "Such things are the talk of the Ancestors."

Hayley moved aside as another ranger made their way up onto the top of the cliff.

"Gerald was right," she said. "This path leads back to the city."

"Yes, and to the tower in the other direction. Shall we get into position?"

"Yes. Make sure your Orcs are well hidden. It wouldn't do to have an actual patrol stumble onto us while we were unprepared."

Sometime later, Hayley found herself crouched behind a ridge of rocks. The sky was turning lighter, clear evidence that the sun would soon be rising over the mountain. A distant bird call alerted her, and she turned her attention eastward, back towards the city.

"They are coming," whispered Gorath.

Hayley looked at her Human contingent. "Make ready," she warned. "We'll have to act quickly once this thing starts."

~

The Norland troops walked down the path in a relaxed manner, secure in the knowledge all was safe. The enemy had been spotted, of course, but they were still some distance off, camping upon the outer plains. With a dozen men, they had enough to replace the tower's complement until the enemy actually began their assault.

Their captain smiled. By all accounts, the Mercerian forces were few in number, hardly enough to threaten the great fortress city of Ravensguard.

"Come on, you lot," he growled. "We haven't got all morning."

Life was good, thought the captain. Now all he needed was a decent woman, and he could settle down. An arrow ended those thoughts forever, penetrating his helmet and plunging deep into his brain.

~

The Orcs let loose with a single volley, then dropped their bows, closing the distance with axes in hand. The Norlanders, caught completely off guard, could do little to repel the fierce hunters of the Black Arrow.

Hayley watched the struggle, the shadow of the mountain bathing the area in darkness. The sounds of conflict drifted her way, but before long, they tapered off. She waited until Gorath gave her a nod, then rose, moving onto the road. The other Humans followed her, completing their small group.

"Let's go," she called out as she started running westward towards the tower, her men falling in behind. This was no organized march but a haphazard run as fast as they could manage.

Gorath counted to twenty, then gave the command. The Orcs began giving chase, calling out in their own language as they rushed after their prey.

~

Sergeant Victor Harrelson had spent a lifetime in the service of Lord Thurlowe. As a member of the Ravensguard soldiery, most of that time had been spent as just another man in the garrison, but recent events had allowed him to take advantage of losses, raising him to a sergeant's rank. He took his duties seriously, much to the chagrin of his fellow soldiers, who thought him a quarrelsome, vulgar man.

The first sign of trouble was when one of his men rang the alarm bell. Harrelson, who was in the middle of eating, looked up from the table to see his watch command ignoring the summons. His eyes caught those of Hawkins, one of the older warriors.

"It's probably just Dobbs," the old man remarked. "Dropped his bow again, likely."

Harrelson sighed. Was there no end to this drudgery? The sergeant rose, making his way up the stairs to the top of the tower. He took his time, eager to show no alarm that might spook his troops. What greeted him at the top, however, immediately made him regret his slow ascent.

Three of his men were up here. Dobbs was still ringing the bell, but the other two, both seasoned warriors, were peering over the edge of the parapet, looking not west towards the enemy, but east.

"We're under attack!" called out Dobbs.

Harrelson ran to an embrasure, leaning out to get a clear view of the path. Off in the distance, a group of men rushed for the tower, pursued by some greenskins.

"Open the gate!" he bellowed, turning to descend the steps two at a time. "Archers to the parapets!"

Most of the men were milling around below, still unsure of what was happening.

"The Orcs have attacked the morning replacements," he shouted. "Get that door open, or it'll be the death of them all."

Hayley slowed, adjusting her helmet once again. The cursed thing was too large and kept bouncing down over her eyes as she ran. She risked a look behind her, only to see the Orcs closing in fast.

"Open the doors!" yelled a ranger.

A crossbow bolt flew over their heads, directed, no doubt, towards their green-skinned attackers. In response, three of the Orcs paused in their pursuit, letting loose with a small volley of arrows.

As the tower loomed closer, the door began to open. She spotted a man still holding the drop bar while his companion pushed the door. Two more moved outside, taking positions on either side, crossbows ready. Hayley led her men into the tower, halting just within the door.

"What's going on?" demanded a soldier.

Hayley turned to face the door and drew her weapon as did the rest of the rangers. Moments later, she shouted a challenge, and the Mercerians struck. The guards inside the tower stood little chance against the surprise attack. The High Ranger took down two in the space of an instant, then turned her attention to the door where outside the two crossbowmen were reloading. Ayles moved out, taking one in the back with his sword while Sam stabbed the second in the neck. Both fell like stones.

"Get to the roof," ordered Hayley while she directed her attention to those waiting at the door. "Hold your position until the Orcs arrive, then follow us up."

She ran up the stairs in Mathers' wake. The young man had joined the rangers only six months ago but had already shown promise as a leader. As he took the steps two at a time, he received a bolt to the forehead and fell backwards, almost knocking Hayley down the stairs. Steadying herself against the wall, she struggled to regain her balance as Sommersby ran past with a shout.

After he disappeared through the doorway above, the sound of steel on steel drifted back to Hayley. She pushed herself away from the wall and ran after him.

Out onto the rooftop she went, heedless of the danger. There, Sommersby was down, clutching his arm, his foe dead before him. Hayley had only a moment to assess the situation, then she struck, stabbing out with her sword, driving a Norlander back. From the corner of her eye, she spotted a man reloading his crossbow just as an arrow took him in the chest.

Now the immediate threat was the man in front of her. Parrying her blow, he counterattacked with a vicious slash that cut across the front of her armour. The High Ranger moved in closer, pushing with all her might and forcing him back against the embrasure to make room for her to manoeuvre. Again he struck, but this time she parried the blow, then went low, falling to the ground and kicking out with her feet to sweep her opponent's legs out from under him. Down he went with a crash, and then she was upon him, driving the hilt of her sword into his face. Twice more, she bashed him, causing blood to fly before he fell back unconscious.

Footsteps surrounded her as she realized the fight was done. Dropping the sword, she looked up into the green eyes of Gorath.

"It is done," said the Orc. "You have won a great victory this day."

"It is not MY victory," said Hayley, "but OURS."

. . .

Gerald smiled as the Mercerian flag was raised over the tower.

"It worked," said Urgon. "You are truly a master of such things."

"It was a gamble," admitted Gerald. "It could just as easily have resulted in disaster."

"But it did not. The story of this victory will grow with every telling."

"It's only one tower. I doubt it will work a second time."

"True, but it now gives us a way into the city that cannot be seen by our enemy."

"Won't they be even more alert now?" said Gerald.

The Orc smiled. "True, but Ghodrug can show us a hidden path."

"And where is Ghodrug?"

"Kraloch tells me she will soon be amongst us. Even as we speak, she is traversing the mountains, far from the gaze of the Norlanders."

"Then we should prepare to greet her. What's the tradition amongst your people for this type of thing?"

"I have no idea," said Urgon. "It is not something I have done before. You, on the other hand, would have a better feel for such things."

"Me? Why would you think that?"

"You have spent more time in the company of foreign diplomats, have you not?"

"I suppose," said Gerald, "but they were all Human."

"Not so, my friend. You came to the Black Arrows in your time of need, and now we are firm allies."

"Yes, I know, but this is different."

"How so?"

"You're a different tribe."

"You forget," said Urgon, "an alliance with the Orcs is with ALL the Orcs, not only a single tribe. In that sense, Ghodrug is already a friend to Merceria."

"I suppose I hadn't thought of it that way."

"Ah," said Urgon, "I see Kraloch approaches. Let us see if he has news of our new friends." He called out to his shaman, "Have you word?"

"I have, my chieftain. Ghodrug and Kharzug approach from the north."

"Kharzug?" said Gerald.

"Yes," replied Kraloch. "He is a master of earth."

"Meaning?"

"He is what you would term an Earth Mage, although his specialty runs more to rock and stone than animals."

"I look forward to meeting them both," said Gerald. "Lead on, Master Kraloch, and let us greet them with open arms."

"See?" said Urgon. "It is as I said. You are better equipped than I for such a meeting."

Kraloch led them through the camp past Orcs sharpening their axes and making arrows while Trolls collected stones for the inevitable assault. Gerald was pleased to see the activity, for it kept the warriors' minds too busy to worry about the inevitable battle.

Finally, they reached the northern sentries: a trio of Orcs who stood ready with bows. Here they waited, watching for signs of their visitors.

It didn't take long to spot them. Ghodrug was easy to recognize in her chainmail shirt, and Kharzug, as was typical of a master of earth, wore a sleeveless grey robe and carried a strange-looking staff. It was only as they drew closer that Gerald realized the shaman's staff was made of stone.

They halted at a distance of twenty paces.

"We come in peace," called out Ghodrug in the Orcish tongue.

"Welcome, Ghodrug of the Black Ravens. I am Urgon of the Black Arrows, and this is my shaman, Kraloch."

"Honour be to you," said Ghodrug. "This is my master of earth, Kharzug."

"The honour is ours," added Kraloch. He took a step to the side, indicating Gerald. "This," he continued, "is Gerald Matheson, Marshal of the Mercerian Army, of whom I have previously spoken at length."

"It is a pleasure to meet you," said Gerald, bowing slightly.

"You speak our language well," offered Ghodrug. "Much better than I was led to believe."

"I have had much practice."

"I can offer you no milk of life," said Urgon, "but if you would accompany us back to our camp, we can give you food."

"Then lead on, Urgon of the Black Arrows, and you can tell us of everything that has befallen your tribe these last few years."

Gerald let out a burp, a sound the Orcs found most amusing. "Pardon me," he said.

"There is nothing to pardon," said Ghodrug. "It is common enough amongst my people."

"Has your tribe lived here for long?"

"They have indeed," said the chieftain. "This land was once the site of Gar-Rugal, the city of our Ancestors."

"I have heard it was destroyed by the Elves?"

"I see you are familiar with our history. It is true. Our home was one of the seven great cities of our people, a beacon of prosperity, culture, and learning. That all came crashing down when the army of Queen Kythelia arrived. They say the *siege of Gar-Rugal lasted for two years, but ultimately the city fell, its walls reduced to nothing but pebbles and scraps of stone. The Orcs of the Black Raven were scattered to the mountains, there to beg from the Dwarves."*

"The Dwarves?" said Gerald. "Are they there still?"

"No," said Ghodrug. "Their home was destroyed many centuries later. It is said they delved too deep and extracted a rare ore that killed them all off."

"A story that is likely only a myth," added Kharzug. "One thing is for certain, however, the Dwarves all disappeared within a short period of time. To this day, we do not know the true fate of Nan-Dural."

"And yet, if I understand correctly, you still have access to the ruins of your own city?"

Ghodrug grinned. "We do, and that, I think, requires an even longer tale. After the Elves left Gar-Rugal, our people wandered, split into many smaller groups, fighting for our very existence. Generations later, we migrated back, living amongst the ruins for a time. During that period, however, the Humans you call Norlanders expanded into this area. Gar-Rugal was built here due to the nature of the terrain. The mountains make an ideal fortress, or so we thought, until the Elves destroyed it. The Humans apparently took a similar liking to the area, deciding to build a city of their own. Much of it was built of stone stolen from the ruins. We resisted, of course, but the Humans came in large numbers, and soon we were driven back into the mountains once more."

"Did you try to negotiate?"

"We did, but none of us spoke their language, nor they ours. Each attempt was rebuffed at the end of a sword, and so there has long been animosity between our two peoples."

"We do not consider the Norlanders our people," said Gerald, "despite our shared past. They have been a plague upon us, just as they have you."

"And if you should win this war? What then? What will you do with Ravensguard?"

"I have discussed this very thing with my queen," said Gerald. "Providing you allow all Humans to leave, the city would be yours to do with as you please. Destroy it, or occupy it, if you like. Of course, we have to capture it first. I understand you have some thoughts on that matter?"

"I do," said Ghodrug. "We have tunnels that allow us entry to the ruins of Gar-Rugal. From there, it is but a short distance to the Human city of Ravensguard."

"And the Norlanders have not discovered these tunnels?"

"On occasion," said Kharzug, "but we seal the rock behind us using the power of the earth."

"How close can you get us to the city?"

"To the very streets themselves should you so desire, but it must be a small group, or it will attract too much attention."

"How small?" asked Gerald.

"No more than a dozen, I should think."

"Enough to take a gate," suggested Urgon.

Gerald grimaced. *"But not enough to hold it. Even the queen's own guard couldn't hold off the entire city garrison."*

"Maybe they do not need to," suggested Ghodrug.

"Meaning?"

"Once they have taken the gate, the enemy will send all the troops it can to recover it."

"That proves my point, doesn't it?"

Ghodrug grinned. *"With the garrison otherwise occupied, my hunters can attack in great numbers, throwing everything into chaos. Would that help your plan?"*

"It would indeed. Might I ask how many hunters you have?"

Ghodrug looked at Urgon.

"I trust him with my life," declared the chieftain of the Black Arrows.

Ghodrug nodded, returning her attention to Gerald. *"They are spread throughout the mountains, but give me a ten-day, and I shall have more than five hundred at my disposal. Will that suffice?"*

"I should think so," replied Gerald.

"Then let us begin to sort out the details."

THIRTY

Riverhurst
_____

Summer 965 MC

K ing Leofric gazed at the distant city. "There it is, Edwin. The fabled city of Riverhurst."

"Fabled, Your Majesty?"

"Well, maybe that's pushing things. Still, it's the end of a long march. I don't know about you, but I'm looking forward to a nice bath."

Lord Edwin chuckled. "We have yet to speak to Lord Creighton, my king. He may have other plans."

"So he might. Ah well, we'll never know if we don't enter the city. Come, let's not waste any more time."

He galloped off, leaving Lord Edwin to play catch-up. They thundered across the field through a mist that clung to the grass with great tenacity. The gatehouse soon loomed before them, the doors wide open in greeting.

"Impressive place, isn't it?" mused the king as they rode through.

"It is indeed, Your Majesty, even more so than our own capital."

"You shall have to keep notes, Edwin. I can't have some Norland city outshining Summersgate."

"Very well, sire."

"Greetings, King Leofric," called out a voice.

They both looked over to see a youthful lord sitting on his horse in the finest of clothes.

"I take it you're Lord Creighton?" asked the king.

"I am, Your Majesty, and I have come to escort you to the great hall."

"Then allow me to name Lord Edwin Eldridge, the Earl of Farnham. He's my right-hand man."

The Earl of Riverhurst bowed his head. "Good day, Lord Edwin. I trust your journey was uneventful?"

"It was," replied Edwin, "but perhaps we might discuss things inside? I find the chill of the morning to be quite uncomfortable."

"Of course," said Creighton. "If it pleases the king?"

"By all means," said Leofric. "Show us the way."

Two of the earl's guards rode in front, the better to push their way through the crowd while the rest fell in behind the royal party.

"It's a busy city you have here," said Leofric. "Is it always like this?"

"People are coming into Riverhurst from the countryside," explained Creighton. "They fear the war, you see."

"Don't you have the troops to protect them?"

"Naturally, but Lord Marley has failed to arrive. His absence has worried the local populace."

"Still no word? Have you sent any more messengers?"

"We have indeed."

"And?"

"None of them have returned."

"That doesn't bode well," said Leofric. "Do you think a stronger presence is required?"

"I sent another dozen men over a week ago, and yet still, we have heard nothing. I cannot send more without depleting my reserves. I'm afraid this whole situation may disturb the plans of our Mercerian allies."

"I understand," said the king, "but we cannot let this threat go unchallenged. To do so could be calamitous."

"But we have no idea of what that threat might be!"

"Are you sure Lord Marley hasn't gone over to the other side?"

"Absolutely," said Creighton. "He and I have known each other for years. The man's like a brother to me."

"Marley is from Walthorne, isn't he? Where is that, precisely?"

"About a hundred and fifty miles as the crow flies, but the road is more like two hundred."

"That's quite the march. Is there anything that could delay him?"

"That would prevent him from sending word? Nothing I can think of. If he's not here, he's either dead or driven from the field of battle."

"So," said Leofric, "it looks like there's another army marching around, likely either Lord Calder or Lord Waverly. What can you tell me about them?"

"Calder's lands lie far to the east. If anyone's stirring up trouble for Marley, it's more likely to be Lord Waverly."

"Why is that?"

"Their lands border each other."

"Does Waverly have a large army?" asked Leofric.

"I would have said no, but if he's threatening Marley, he must have more troops than we thought."

"What would be your best estimate as to their numbers?"

"I would think eight or nine hundred at the most."

Leofric smiled. "That's good news."

"It is?"

"Yes, my troops could handle an army of that size without even breaking a sweat."

"You would be willing to march to his aid?"

"I don't see why not," said the king. "It's why we're here after all."

They rounded a corner revealing the great hall, a large wooden structure far too rustic for Leofric's taste. It consisted of little more than a single room, with a high-peaked roof and a courtyard out front. Guards stood outside, impressive in their chainmail shirts, but looking rather primitive compared to the men of Weldwyn.

"Here we are," said Lord Creighton, his voice betraying his pride. "Shall we go inside?"

"Very well," said the king, "and could you find me a map of the region? I'm afraid our own limited surveys are proving most inconvenient in that regard."

"Of course," said Creighton. He dismounted, letting a warrior take his horse. He waited for King Leofric and Lord Edwin to follow suit, then led them into the great hall.

"How many men did you bring?" asked the Norlander.

"We set out from Weldwyn with sixteen hundred," replied the king, "but were forced to leave some garrisoned behind as we made our way into Hollis's land. Don't worry, we have more than enough to handle anything Waverly might throw our way."

"You appear quite confident."

"And why not? A finer army has never been raised."

"Are they veterans?" asked Creighton.

"Some of them are. We faced an invasion back in '61."

"From whom? The Mercerians?"

"No, the Twelve Clans."

"I don't think I'm familiar with them," said Creighton. "Where do their lands lie?"

"To the west of Weldwyn. They are a rather barbaric race of men, using primitive weapons and tactics."

"And yet they managed to invade?"

"They used subterfuge," said Leofric, sounding a little petulant. "Hardly what I would call a fair fight. We drove them off in the end, thanks, in no small part, to the Mercerians."

"Interesting. I had wondered how the alliance came about. Weren't your realms traditional enemies?"

"I could say the same of Norland," said Leofric, "yet here we are, both on the same side."

"So we are. It's strange, isn't it? How things can change so quickly?"

"I'm not sure I follow."

"Well," said Creighton, "your own country has a history of conflict with our southern neighbour, much as we do, yet within months of our king's death, we find ourselves both allied to them in a relatively short period of time."

"I suppose, when you put it that way, it does sound rather strange. Still, we are much better off for it, don't you think?"

"I would," said Creighton, "were it not for this whole situation with Marley."

Their entrance to the great hall saw servants scurrying to get food and drinks. The earl led them to a large firepit, around which were arranged tables and chairs. "Come," he said. "You must be famished."

They took their seats, then waited as drinks were laid before them. Leofric tried a tentative sip, then broke into a grin. "A fine vintage. You surprise me. I had no idea your winemakers were so skilled."

Creighton smiled at the compliment. "It's one of the few pleasures we enjoy."

"Oh? And what other surprises have you for us?"

"I shall have to give you a tour of our stables. We take pride in our stock."

Leofric leaned forward, resting his elbows on the arm of his chair, his drink all but forgotten. "Horses, eh? Now you have me intrigued."

"They are small, by Mercerian standards," admitted Creighton, "but amongst the swiftest of foot."

"Now that, I'd like to see."

"Agreed," added Lord Edwin. "I imagine they might give Lord Marlowe a bit of a challenge."

"Lord Marlowe?" said Creighton.

"Yes, Linden Marlowe, the Viscount of Aynsbury."

"Viscount? We don't have those in Norland."

"So I've heard," said the king. "That brings to mind another thing I was curious about. How do you rule such a large area without other, lesser nobles?"

"Our rulership is organized along more military lines. We appoint governors to the larger cities and sheriffs to the villages."

"Sheriffs?"

"I believe they are more like the Mercerian rangers," offered Lord Edwin. "I take it they keep the peace and collect taxes?"

"They do," confirmed the earl. "Although now you mention it, I'm curious as to how these lesser nobles you mention would function. Do they not crave power of their own?"

"Some do," said the king, "but usually, they behave themselves. Our system has worked well for us."

"Yes," added Lord Eldridge. "It was even copied by the Mercerians."

"Was it?" said Creighton. "I had no idea."

"Oh, yes. They were simple mercenaries when they first came to this land. I'm surprised you're not familiar with the story."

"I had heard they were warriors, but I had no idea we had you to thank for our system of nobility."

"It's true," added Leofric. "It's well known amongst our own people."

Food was brought, and more wine was poured. Lord Edwin ate sparingly, but the king dug in with gusto.

"Try the pheasant, Your Majesty," offered Creighton. "It's a particular favourite of mine."

Leofric ripped off a drumstick, brandishing it like a trophy. "Is everything here dipped in sauce?"

"It is. In the early days of our kingdom, it was done to hide the taste of decidedly plain fare, but now it has become our custom."

"It's quite nice," said Lord Edwin, "though messy, to be sure."

"Might I ask when you intend to march?" said Lord Creighton.

"I'd like to give my soldiers a day or two to rest. Can you provision us?"

"I can."

"Then we'll set out in two days."

Lord Edwin looked shocked. "That's not much of a rest, Your Majesty."

"It's all we can spare. Every day we wait is another day our enemies gain ground on us. We must act decisively if we are to regain the advantage."

"I shall send some scouts with you," offered Creighton. "Men who are familiar with the territory."

"Do you need me to leave some men here?" asked Leofric.

"No, Lord King. The walls of Riverhurst are more than capable of holding off any attack with the warriors we have. I am, however, concerned about our future plans."

"In what way?"

"We were to march to Burnford and seize the western shore of the Windstorm Depths."

"Then you may continue with that," said Leofric, "secure in the knowledge the trouble has been dealt with."

"Shall we await your return there?"

"No, I rather suspect we'll be on the road to Walthorne for some time. Are you heading across the northern shore of the lake?"

"We are."

"Then we shall rendezvous with you there. Once reunited, we can march all the way to the eastern shore and come down towards Galburn's Ridge, cutting off the capital from the north. With such a large swathe of the countryside in our hands, there'll be little left to oppose us."

"I shall look forward to it, Your Majesty."

"So it's to be a long march, then," said Roxanne Fortuna.

"Very much so, I'm afraid," replied Aegryth Malthunen. "They reckon the trip to Walthorne is more than two hundred miles."

"And what awaits us there, I wonder?"

"I'm told Walthorne is a large city, much like Riverhurst, but it lacks walls."

"And why are we going there?"

"To find Lord Marley."

"How do they know he's there?"

"To be honest, they don't," replied Aegryth, "but they must start the search somewhere."

"That I can well understand, but why there?"

"It's his seat of power."

"Why don't they just send a small force? Isn't using the entire army overdoing things a little?"

"That's not our decision to make."

"What aren't you telling me?"

The Earth Mage blushed. "What makes you think I'm hiding something?"

"Come now, Aegryth," said Roxanne. "We've known each other for years. Do you think I can't tell when you're holding something back?"

"It's not that I'm hiding something…"

"Then tell me."

"Very well. As you know, I've been sending messages back and forth to the Mercerians."

"Have they run into trouble?"

"Nothing they haven't been able to handle, but they've received warning of a new threat."

"What type of threat?"

"An army of spirits."

Roxanne scoffed. "The very idea is ludicrous."

"What makes you say that?"

"Do you have any idea how many Necromancers you'd need to raise an army?"

"No doubt many, and yet the Orcs claim it is so."

"The Orcs? How could they possibly know such a thing?"

Aegryth paused, working the problem over in her mind. "You have a good point, Roxanne, but shouldn't we take precautions regardless?"

"And what precautions would you have us take? It's not as if we would have any specific defence against such a threat. We must rely on the strength of our warriors to overcome such an enemy."

"You think they can fight spirits?"

"Anything that can hurt us must take on a physical form to inflict wounds," explained Roxanne, "and therefore, while they're in that form, they're susceptible to our weapons."

"I wish I had your conviction."

"Personally, I put little faith in the story. The Orcs are a superstitious lot and, therefore, prone to excitement."

"How can you say that? Have you not met Kraloch?"

"I'm not saying they're all prone to such flights of fancy, but you must agree they're a primitive race."

"Albreda would disagree."

"Of course she would," said Roxanne. "She's a wild mage. I would expect nothing less."

"What has that to do with anything?"

"She's a powerful mage, of that we can have no doubt, but she has no training. The secrets of her power lie within the ancient stones of the Whitewood. Stones that were likely created by our ancient pagan Ancestors."

"How is that of any consequence?" said Aegryth.

"Don't you see? In those days, we feared death above all else. Ghosts, or spirits as you like to call them, are nothing more than a manifestation of our primeval fears."

"Meaning what?" insisted Aegryth. "That they don't exist?"

"I have never seen any evidence of it, and I'm a Life Mage."

"The Orcs have their own Life Mages," said Aegryth, "and they claim to be able to speak with the dead."

"And I'm sure that's what they believe, but how can that be true? The dead are either in the Afterlife or the Underworld. Are you now suggesting these are one and the same?"

"Your logic is flawed. Spirits are said to linger between worlds, not reside in the Afterlife."

"There's no proof of that," insisted Roxanne. "Those stories are meant to frighten children, nothing more. Quite honestly, the continued belief in such things astounds me, but I suppose such superstition carries over from our past."

"Then what has happened to Lord Marley?"

"He's likely been fighting one of the other earls. King Leofric has a large army, far larger, in fact, than anything we've seen in all our history. I doubt there's much that could stand against such a force."

"Even so," said Aegryth, "should we not be cautious?"

"Cautious, or afraid? An army can't do its job if it doesn't take chances. Our king is a seasoned warrior. He will see us through this."

"It was not so long ago that you were cursing him," Aegryth reminded her.

"While I do not agree with the choices he has made, I can still respect him as a skilled military leader. Who better to lead us?"

"Who better, indeed."

The morning mist still hung heavy on the ground as the Weldwyn troops left the city. As usual, the cavalry led their way, the cavaliers taking point. Leofric watched them go with pride, knowing none could withstand their fury.

"They are quite the sight," observed Lord Edwin. "It fills the heart with pride to see such valiant warriors."

The king chuckled. "I never knew you for a poet?"

"Nor do I profess to be one, Your Majesty, yet I find I am overwhelmed with emotion at the sight of our troops."

"It shall be many miles until we do battle," said the king. "A lot can happen before then."

"And yet I am filled with pride. Assuredly the enemy will wither before their might."

"I am inclined to agree, my friend. We shall march to Walthorne by way of Marston and brush aside any opposition."

"You think it will come to battle, then?"

"Can there be any other explanation?" said the king. "Lord Marley is either unable or unwilling to march to Riverhurst. The only thing that can account for that is the presence of another army. We will seek out this force even if it takes us till the fall."

"And if we don't find it?"

"That will depend on what we DO find."

"I'm not sure I follow, Majesty."

"If we find Marley has been defeated, then we shall seek his destroyer."

"And if we can't find them?"

"Don't be absurd," insisted Leofric. "You can't march an entire army around without leaving some sort of trace. If there are enemy soldiers out there, we'll find them. Once we've crushed them, there'll be nothing left to oppose us."

"Then the war will be over."

"It will, but it won't be the last time our armies march."

"It won't?" said Lord Edwin.

"No. Upon our return to Weldwyn, I mean to march west and destroy the Twelve Clans once and for all. Only then can we have true peace."

"Never before have we entered their territory in such numbers, Your Majesty."

"Then it's high time we did. For years they have plagued us. Now it's time to put an end to it, and we may never have another chance. Our army is large, Edwin, large enough to subdue the Clans and occupy their territory. We'll annex their lands and put our own people in place to govern them."

"Your Majesty," said Lord Edwin, "it's a bold plan, and we know so little of their terrain."

"It's no different here, and yet our soldiers have performed well. Who knows, we may even invite the Mercerians to help us."

"I doubt they would agree."

Leofric gave his friend a quizzical look. "Why is that? Have we not helped them here in their time of need? What better way to return the favour?"

"This is different," said Lord Edwin, "as well you know. Norland invaded Merceria, and we were bound by our alliance to help in its defence. The Clans are another problem entirely."

The king waved him off. "Don't be ridiculous. Don't you think they want peace as much as we do? They will come to our aid. Just you wait and see."

THIRTY-ONE

Gar-Rugal

Summer 965 MC
(In the tongue of the Orcs)

H ayley let out a curse as her shin hit an outcropping of rock.
"Be careful," warned Gorath. "The footing here is treacherous."
"And you couldn't have told me this BEFORE I hurt myself?"
She ducked quickly to avoid a low-hanging rock, and then the tunnel opened up into a large cave.

"This is it," announced Ghodrug. "Gar-Rugal, city of the Ravenstone."
Before them lay a strange sight: crumbled walls of stone littered the ground, yet there stood massive pillars of rock at regular intervals, supporting a ceiling of closely fitted blocks.

Gerald could make out the remains of a wall, and he moved towards it, holding his lantern on high. "This reminds me of the ruins near Queenston," he said.

"The queen would love this," mused Hayley.
"I'm sure she would. This one even has carvings on it."
"More battles?"
"No, something else."
Hayley moved closer, examining the mural up close. "It looks like they're making something."
Kraloch poked his head between them. "They are making leather," he said. "See them in the background, with the skins?"

"So they are," said Gerald.

"Wait," said Hayley. "Is that depicting a book?" She moved her lantern closer.

"I didn't know you had a written language?" said Gerald.

"We do not these days," explained Kraloch, "but in the time of our great cities, it was different."

"Perhaps you'll learn to understand the language of your Ancestors. You adapted well to the Mercerian tongue."

"We would need examples of such writing, and that, to my knowledge, no longer exists."

"A pity," mused Hayley. "Your people have such a rich history."

Kraloch looked around the cavernous complex. "It is humbling to be here. Think of how much knowledge was lost when this city fell."

"How many Orc cities were there?" asked Hayley.

"Seven," replied the Orc shaman. "Each a power unto itself. You would refer to them as city-states."

"And they were all destroyed?"

"So I have been told."

"But why?"

"You would have to ask the Elves."

"The queen has a theory," added Gerald, "but I'd rather leave it for her to explain."

Ghodrug grunted. "I would like to meet this queen of yours. I think we would have much to discuss."

"And I'm sure she would welcome your presence. History has always been a passion of hers."

"Then we might both benefit from the exchange."

"These pillars," said Hayley, "did your people make them?"

"No," said Ghodrug. "They were made by the Humans."

"So the city is above us?"

"Part of it. What you see is the floor of the temple of your god, Saxnor."

"All these tunnels have left me a little disoriented," said Gerald. "Where are we in relation to the main gate?"

"We are at the eastern end of the city, beneath the mountain. Were we to climb up through that floor, we would then have to travel due west to reach the gate."

"And COULD we climb up through the floor?"

"Kharzug could certainly make it possible, but we would risk discovery. It is an option best left to the day of the attack."

"Just how far back does this cave extend?" asked Hayley.

Ghodrug chuckled. "Gar-Rugal was a great city at its height."

"And the entire city is in this cave?"

"No, of course not. This is but a small portion. The rest is above ground, or at least it was. Most of the debris there was taken by the Humans and used to construct their own buildings."

They wandered through the ruins, taking their time. Even the Orcs had torches, for there was no moonlight with which to see.

Gerald watched as the torches spread out, filling the place with small, flickering columns of lights. His foot knocked a small pebble, and he heard it fall, causing him to halt. When he swung the lantern around, it illuminated something that looked like a large, sunken wash basin. "What's this?"

"It looks like a bath," said Hayley. "Bev tells me they're quite common in Shrewesdale."

"Who would have thought the Orcs would have a bathhouse?"

"Come," called out Ghodrug. "Let me show you the Hall of Tears." Gerald made his way towards the Black Ravens' chieftain, keeping a firm view of the ground to avoid tripping.

Ghodrug was standing before a half wall, its top broken and jagged. The structure looked to be of solid rock, something that triggered a thought in Gerald's head.

"This is Earth Magic," he said. "I remember seeing something similar near Tivilton. Do you remember, Hayley?"

"Yes, where we found the drake," she replied. "Is this melded rock, Kharzug?"

The master of earth nodded. "It is indeed. Magic that we still practice to this very day."

Hayley moved farther into the ruined structure. "Why is it called the Hall of Tears?"

"Come," said Ghodrug, "and I shall show you." She took up a position in what would have been the centre of the room, extending her arms to the sides. "All around you can be seen the history of our people. The carvings depict our greatest leaders, whose names are lost to us now. It is said that when the walls finally fell, its leader, Gozar, came here to make his final stand. Many Orcs fell defending this last patch of ground, but the Elves showed no mercy, nor was it expected."

"So they all died here," said Hayley. "A sobering thought."

"Gozar they kept alive long enough to witness the destruction of this very room. It was not enough for the Elves to simply defeat us. They wished to erase our past." She knelt, clearing away a spot of masonry. "See here? The patch of green amongst the ruins? This is where he finally fell. We call it the Tears of Gozar, and this place the Hall of Tears, although in truth, its original name is lost to the annals of time."

"If I may," said Gerald. "I have a question."

"By all means."

"You referred earlier to something called the Ravenstone. What is that, precisely?"

"It is an artifact," replied the chieftain. "Lost to us when the Humans invaded."

"An artifact?" said Hayley. "You mean it's magical?"

"It has no magical powers, if that's what you mean, but it is of significant spiritual value to my people. It is a large stone, resembling a raven. According to legend, its presence here convinced our Ancestors to found this city. It is also the thing from which we took our name, for you see the stone is black in colour."

"So you settled here because of a rock?"

Ghodrug smiled. "You must remember, in those days, our people worshipped the old Gods. It was seen as a sign from Hraka—the god of fire who was said to have created our race."

"How is a rock a sign?"

"When our founders came to this mountain, the sun rose behind the Ravenstone, bathing it in all its glory."

"And making it look like it was on fire," said Hayley. "A fitting sign for Hraka."

"Tell me," said Gerald. "What do you know of your ancient people?"

"What would you have me tell you?" asked Ghodrug.

"In the ruins near Queenston, we found a relief depicting your fight with the Elves. From it, we discovered your people were once great warriors, marching in formation and wearing armour. Have you any evidence of that here?"

"We have indeed, although I think Kharzug is more qualified to speak of such things."

"The master of earth?"

"Yes. He is more well versed in our distant past than I, when it comes to such things." She turned her attention to her companion. "Kharzug, would you care to show them?"

The Orc bowed. "As you wish, my chieftain." He turned to the others. "Come with me, and I will show you what we have thus far discovered." He led them past more ruins.

Gerald could see little other than damaged walls and ruined floors, but he rather suspected they were houses if size were any indication. They halted by a set of thick stone walls, easily twice as thick as those seen anywhere else.

"This," explained Kharzug, "was the Zaga, the place of spears. It was here that our Ancestors honed their skills with weapons." He moved past the walls to the dusty interior. There he knelt, using his hand to brush away accumulated dirt. "The floor here is of inlaid tiles, though the secret of their construction is long lost to us. It depicts images of our people, training in the use of weapons." He shuffled to the side. "There's more here, but the tiles are damaged."

Gerald moved closer, setting his lantern on the floor to see the design clearly. "Fascinating."

"As you can see," continued Kharzug, "they primarily used the spear and axe. Shields were not uncommon, as was some kind of armour."

"It's difficult to discern what type of armour they used," noted the marshal, "but judging from the colours, I'd say it's likely some sort of leather jacket."

"They also used bows," added the Orc, "though they appear smaller than those we use these days."

"Did they have any mounted troops?"

"Not that we are aware, but it has long been a tradition to use wolves on the hunt. We suspect they were used in a similar manner by our Ancestors."

"Not large enough to ride though," noted Gerald.

"No. And the wolves in these parts are smaller than those used by our brethren, the Black Arrows."

"As fascinating as this is," said Hayley, "shouldn't we be more concerned with finding a way into Ravensguard?"

"Yes, of course," said Ghodrug. "If you will follow me, I shall take you there."

She led them through more ruins, then into a side passage that sloped upward. "We must be quiet for the next little while," she warned, "for we are passing by the very walls of the temple itself."

On and on went the tunnel, twisting this way and that, but always going upward until it finally ended in a small cave.

"It is safe to talk now," said Ghodrug. "That tunnel we have just traversed runs along the southern wall of the Temple of Saxnor. There are several spots where the bricks can be seen. It would be easy enough to break through when desired, though I fear our egress would not remain hidden for long."

"Where are we now?" asked Gerald.

"Above it," she replied, moving to one end of the cave. "Come here, and I will show you, but leave your lantern where you are."

He placed his light on the floor and moved closer.

Ghodrug knelt, pointing at a small hole. "This," she whispered, "leads to the main hall of the temple. We use it to observe our enemies. Similar spots can be found all over the ruins, carefully hidden from the sight of men."

Gerald lay down, placing his eye to the hole. It took a moment for his eyes to adjust, then he recognized the temple's distinctive layout. "It's laid out the same as the Grand Cathedral in Wincaster, but smaller in scale."

"If you listen carefully, you will find that sound carries well. It would have been of inestimable value had we the ability to understand your language."

Gerald rose, groaning as his knees complained. "You said you had access to a point that overlooks the city? Can you take us there?"

"I can," replied Ghodrug, "but we will have to retrace our steps to do so. Come, take up your light, and I will show you."

It took them some time to make their way back to the Hall of Tears, and then came a tiring climb up a set of steep, uneven stairs. By the time they reached the heights, Gerald's legs were burning from the effort. They exited the tunnel onto a narrow ledge, where the air was brisk despite the summer season.

"Below us, you see the city in all its glory," announced Ghodrug.

Gerald took a quick glance, then backed up. "I've never been one for heights," he announced.

"Really?" said Hayley. "I thought you spent a lot of time at the top of Bodden Keep?"

"I did, but that had nice thick walls to lean on. You take a look. You'll be the one assaulting the gate from the inside."

Hayley moved up, kneeling, and then lay down to peer over the ledge at the city below.

"What can you make out?" asked Gerald.

"I can see everything quite clearly. There's a nice wide road that heads straight from the gates to the Temple of Saxnor."

"Any signs of barracks?"

"Hard to say," replied Hayley. "The other buildings all look so similar."

"Do you see the structure with the domed roof?" asked Ghodrug. "Beside it is the barracks. The dark-coloured stone should be easy to identify."

"I see it, but I'm afraid that makes it that much easier for them to retake the gate." She stared some more. "Well, that's a bad design."

"What is?" asked Gerald.

"The two towers open onto the roof of the gatehouse."

"They do? That's rather strange. I would have thought they'd open to the city instead."

"I don't understand," said Ghodrug.

"The towers are meant to protect the gatehouse," explained Gerald, "and usually, that means their doors are separate. Otherwise, someone seizing the gatehouse could take control of the towers."

"Could they not also be used to counterattack the gatehouse, were it seized?"

"That's an excellent point," said Hayley.

Lowering himself to the ground, Gerald forced himself forward on his hands and knees. "I'm getting too old for this." He finally reached the edge of the cliff, looking down on the city. "That's quite the view."

"Look over there," said Hayley, pointing. "Do you see what I see?"

"Yes, it looks like stables."

"It is," said Ghodrug. "They house their cavalry there."

"Not much good if we take the gatehouse," said Gerald, "but it makes it more difficult to take the city streets afterwards."

"I'm not so sure of that," said Hayley. "See the road from the stables? There's a choke point there, by that large building with the orange roof tiles."

"Easy enough to block up," noted Ghodrug, "but I doubt it would hold them for long. There are other ways to the gate."

"True, but it buys us some time." She turned to look at the Orc chieftain. "What can you tell us of their garrison?"

"We estimate it to number close to a thousand warriors. You have already noted where they keep their horsemen. They only number about a hundred individuals. The rest of their army is roughly half bows, half footmen."

"Makes sense," mused Hayley. "Archers are better suited to manning walls during a siege."

Ghodrug looked at Gerald. "Do you still think this plan of yours possible?"

"Difficult, but I think we're up to it, don't you?" He looked at Hayley.

"I'd feel a little more confident if we had more men."

"I'm afraid there's not much we can do about that, but remember, as soon as you get that gate open, we'll have lots of our troops pouring through the gap."

"Still, some cavalry of our own wouldn't go amiss."

Gerald smiled. "Ask, and you shall receive."

She looked at him in surprise. "We have cavalry?"

"We do, at least a small number of them, anyway."

"And where did they come from?"

"Commander Lanaka."

"I thought he was tracking down Hollis?"

"He was," replied Gerald. "Still is, actually, but I'm sure he can spare us a company if we really need it."

"Why do you need cavalry?" asked Ghodrug. "Wouldn't footmen be better?"

"Under normal circumstances, I might agree, but that tower on the southern outcropping of rock is still in enemy hands. Any advance by our soldiers will come under attack from their catapult. Have you ever tried to use a catapult against cavalry?"

"I have never even fired a catapult," admitted the Orc.

"Well, let me assure you, galloping horsemen are a difficult target to hit, and Lanaka's men are the finest light cavalry in the land."

"What is light cavalry? Do they weigh less than normal horsemen?"

Gerald chuckled. "No, but they spread out when they ride, and their horses are fast. Both of those factors make them even harder to hit." He rose, stepping back from the lip. "I think we've seen everything here we need to. What about you, Hayley?"

She nodded, climbing to her feet. Gerald instinctively grabbed her arm, pulling her back from the edge.

"I'm fine," she protested.

He blushed. "Sorry, I was worried you might fall, and then where would we be? We can't very well assault the gatehouse without our High Ranger."

Hayley chuckled, looking out over the city one final time. "Well, I can't get much higher than I am right now."

Gorath burst out laughing. "You are so humorous, Ranger Hayley."

"Glad to see someone appreciates my sense of humour."

By the time they returned to their camp, night was upon them. Gerald met with Urgon and Hayley, making final preparations for the coming assault.

Urgon stared down at the map. "You have a good memory, Dame Hayley."

"Thank you," the ranger replied, "though I can't for the life of me remember what this building here was." She stabbed out with a finger.

"That is a smithy," said Urgon.

"A smithy? There? I find that surprising."

"It shouldn't be," said Gerald. "It's close to the barracks here."

She frowned. "I suppose." She looked up to her marshal. "Any word from Lanaka?"

"Yes, he's promised a company of horsemen. They should be here by first light."

"That's cutting it a might close, isn't it?"

"It can't be helped. He's already stretched to the limit."

Urgon shuffled his feet, a sure sign of impatience. "Can we go over the plan one more time?"

"Of course," said Gerald. "Hayley and her rangers will make their way into the tunnels well before daybreak. Kharzug will take them to the temple where he'll open a doorway for them by reforming a wall using his Earth Magic."

"Won't that be seen?"

"No, the Holy Fathers don't carry out their first service until almost noon. It's the same everywhere amongst the worshippers of Saxnor. The Orcs within their group will seize the temple and remain there while the Human rangers make their way to the gatehouse wearing captured armour."

"And how many suits of it do we have?" asked Urgon.

"Two dozen," said Hayley, "but we only have to hold on long enough for the Orcs to arrive."

"And if they can't seize the door?"

"Then," admitted Hayley, "the whole attack has failed."

"You must remember," Gerald said, "your Orcs will be advancing on the gate by then. The city will be calling out its garrison to man the walls. Hayley's rangers will merely be more men mixed in with their own."

"And if the gates are closed from the inside?" pressed Urgon.

"Don't worry," Gerald assured him, "they won't be. They need them open to reinforce the towers. If you remember, they're only accessible from the gatehouse."

"Ah, yes," said Urgon. "You mentioned as much earlier today. Where do the Kurathians fit in?"

"They'll be right behind your Orcs. If the gates should show any signs of opening, they'll gallop past you. That means your hunters must be in skirmish order."

"I understand."

"The Orcs of the Black Raven will wait till they've finished assembling their troops in the temple, then they will begin their attack from within the city. Their target will be to get behind the defenders and take the pressure off the gatehouse."

"It is a good plan," said Urgon. "And one which has a good chance of success."

"It relies on all of us doing our parts," said Gerald. "Should any one of us fail, it could well mean disaster."

The Orc grinned. "Then we shall strive to succeed."

THIRTY-TWO

Lord Hollis

Summer 965 MC

G arth Meldoch peered out from behind a rock.

"What can you see?" asked his companion, a short, stocky man.

"Not much, Telker. The place is crawling with greenskins."

"How many?"

"Several hundred, at least."

"Any signs of Humans?"

"A few, but by and large, this is an Orc outing."

Telker spat on the ground. "Filthy Mercerians, hiring such brutes."

"It will work to our advantage," said Meldoch.

"How so?"

"The Orcs might be savages, but they're not trained for battle. And, in any event, we outnumber them." He smiled, showing his yellowed teeth. "Looks like His Lordship has finally got them trapped."

"Where have I heard that one before?" complained Telker.

"Lord Hollis hasn't been running all over the place for nothing. I bet he hatched this plan months ago."

"You give him too much credit."

"Do I?" said Meldoch. "Others might disagree. Look, the fact is we've finally got that marshal of theirs caught between a rock and a hard place."

"Then why aren't we attacking?"

"It's quite simple," said Meldoch, relishing the opportunity to show his superior knowledge. "His Lordship's going to wait until they've committed to the attack."

"And then?"

"Then we come up from the rear. Simple, isn't it?"

"Yes, but will it work?" said Telker. "That's what I want to know."

"Why wouldn't it?"

"Orcs can be fierce fighters when cornered," argued Telker.

"Who told you that?"

"It's common knowledge."

Meldoch was about to retort but changed his mind. "You know what? It doesn't matter what either of us thinks. Our job is to get this information to the earl, that's it. Once that's done, we can sit by the fire and argue about this all you want."

"Then we'd best get going before daylight reveals our position." Telker moved back from their place of concealment, gathering the reins of his horse. "Don't let them see you," he warned.

"What do you think I am? Stupid?" Meldoch said as he moved towards his horse.

Telker waited until his comrade was mounted, then flicked the reins, sending his horse into a slow trot. Once they were out of sight of the enemy camp, they dug in, increasing to a gallop.

Lord Hollis stared down at the table. Someone had gone to all the trouble of making a model of the nearby terrain, using wooden blocks to represent the forces involved. Picking up a green one, he held it before his eyes. "Interesting, isn't it?"

"What is, my lord?" replied his champion Marik.

"This block represents the lives of dozens of individuals. Just think, by this time tomorrow, they shall be swept from the field."

"It's all due to your superior tactics, my lord," added a hooded individual.

The earl turned to face his newest advisor. "You always know exactly what to say, Jendrick."

Marik watched with a foreboding sense of danger. This fellow had wormed his way into the earl's confidence in only two months, but little was known about his past. Did he have his own agenda? Marik wanted to say something but knew the earl would not take kindly to such interruptions.

"Should we not be marching?" he asked instead.

"We have been patient thus far," said Lord Hollis. "Would you have us rush now and spoil the attack?"

"And when shall that attack commence?" pressed Jendrick.

"I'm waiting. I have people scouting out their forces. Once we have confirmation of their numbers, we shall proceed."

"A wise precaution, my lord."

"Is it?" challenged Marik. "There was a time, my lord, when you said fortune favours those who take bold action. You know we have the numbers in our favour. Everything you've done over the last few weeks has ensured it. The time to strike is now while we still have the element of surprise!"

"We cannot," argued Jendrick, his voice betraying his alarm if only for a moment. He took a breath, calming himself before continuing. "You have played a patient game, my lord. Do not spoil it now by acting rashly."

"Rashly?" said Marik. "How dare you speak thus to His Lordship!"

Jendrick turned on the champion, his face a mask of composure. "Do not speak of things you do not understand. I serve the earl's interest with every fibre of my being. Can you say the same?"

"Are you questioning my loyalty?"

"As they say, if the helm fits…"

"That's enough!" bellowed Hollis. "This is not the time for bickering. Rather, it is the time when we must come together to achieve victory."

"Of course," said Jendrick, returning his attention to his master.

"Come now, Marik," said the earl. "You have been my champion for years. Do not force me to reprimand you now, at the onset of our greatest victory."

The warrior nodded his head, too overcome to speak.

"Then it's settled," the earl continued. "We have only to await word from our scouts." Hollis returned his attention to the scale model, rearranging his own forces several times, looking for the best deployment. His ministrations were interrupted when the tent flap parted, revealing a rather worn-out warrior covered in dust and dirt.

"Ah," said the earl. "Finally."

The man straightened his back. "I bring word, my lord." He dug into his satchel, retrieving a note and passing it over.

Hollis unfolded it, reading its contents and then broke into a smile. "This looks promising." He turned to the messenger. "You may go."

Marik's ears pricked up. "News, my lord?"

"Yes. It appears our subterfuge has borne fruit."

"Meaning?"

"Meaning we now have confirmation that only a small portion of their army has marched to Ravensguard. The rest has been drawn north, to Anvil."

Marik smiled. "That's why you brought us here, isn't it?"

"It is," said Hollis, "though we laboured long to do so. It looks like we finally have the Mercerians where we want them, outnumbered and caught between two armies, Thurlowe's and my own."

Jendrick cleared his throat. "Might I ask the composition of the forces we will be facing, my lord?"

"It appears they have decided to send their greenskins to do their dirty work."

"The Orcs? How fitting. We shall destroy them much as we did last time."

Jendrick appeared to regret his choice of words, something Marik was quick to capitalize on. "Last time?" said the champion.

"Yes," added the earl. "What do you mean by that?"

The hooded man seemed uncharacteristically ill at ease but recovered quickly. "I merely refer to the founding of the great city of Ravensguard, my lord. It was taken from the Orcs, was it not?"

"More or less, but it was already in ruins."

"Still," said Jendrick, "the Orcs cling to their past like a rat clings to a sinking ship."

"A strange turn of phrase for a Norlander," added Marik. "How is it you come to use such a term?"

"I have travelled widely," the man explained, "as I have indicated in the past. It is this very experience that allows me to serve you so well, my lord."

"Get to the point, Marik," said the earl, "or cease this endless prattling."

"This man is no Norlander, Lord. How can he possibly represent our interests?"

"Are you accusing me of having an agenda?" demanded Jendrick.

Marik struggled to understand the words, his ignorance on full display. "You claim to be a sorcerer," he finally continued, "yet we have seen no sign of your power."

"Don't be ridiculous," said the earl, "of course we have. How else would he have communicated with Lord Thurlowe?"

"We only have his word for that," pressed Marik.

Lord Hollis waved his hand. "I've had enough of your insolence, Marik. You are dismissed."

"But, Lord—"

"Enough, I say! Now, begone from this place. I would suffer your presence no more."

Marik's gaze shifted to Jendrick, revealing his hatred.

"You and I will have words later," threatened the warrior.

"I shall look forward to it," said Jendrick.

Marik stormed from the tent.

"You must excuse my champion," said Hollis. "He means well but is perhaps a little over-enthusiastic in the performance of his duties."

"He undermines your authority, my lord."

"Granted, he does, but he has served me faithfully for years. I shall send word that he is to return to Galburn's Ridge. That should keep you two from clashing."

Jendrick bowed, a smile creasing his lips. "Very well, my lord. You know what's best."

"Have you any news from Thurlowe?"

"He reports they lost control of one of their outlying towers, but it's of little consequence. With your permission, I shall contact him again this evening to firm up our plans."

"Good. We'll begin moving our troops into position tomorrow at first light. In the meantime, I have much to do."

Jendrick bowed. "Of course, my lord. I should not like to overstay my welcome."

He bowed a second time, then left the tent, grabbing a lantern along the way. It was quite late, but the soldiers in camp were still awake, sharpening their weapons and checking armour, a sure sign they were expecting battle.

The sorcerer paused, listening to the camp, the sounds carrying him back to his early years so long ago. In those days, the words had been a different language, but their meaning was the same. Soldiers had not changed much in the two thousand years since he first trod this ground, but the meddling of their Human leaders was an entirely different matter. He shook his head, clearing such thoughts from his mind. He must do his duty, and that meant he could afford little time for this sentimentality.

At the edge of the camp, he found his own dwelling, a wagon with a wooden covering. Entering, he closed the door behind him and dismissed his spell of concealment, once more returning to his natural, Elvish state. Playing the role of a Human was a tiring activity, but he knew it was necessary if their plans were to succeed. He wondered, briefly, how Kalaxial was, but then put such thoughts from his mind. The Dark Council had known precisely what they were doing when they had sent the pair of them to Norland.

Sitting down, Jendrick withdrew a small key that hung around his neck and then unlocked a chest, extracting several items. First came a small silver plate, only a hand's length in size. Onto this, he poured some powder, adding a touch of water and mixing the contents with a small silver rod until it formed a paste. Once this was complete, he dabbed it with his finger, tasting the result, then held it up to his nose, sampling the aroma.

Convinced all was in order, he withdrew a taper from the chest, lighting it from the lantern.

Calming his mind, he then stared at the bowl, muttering words of power. The air grew foul, and then he touched the taper to the strange mixture. A dark flame leaped upward, producing a thick, greasy smoke that lingered in the air. More words poured forth, and the smoke began to twist and turn, forming into a ring before his face. Moments later, it hung before him, a writhing mass of darkness, its surface absorbing light. A final command caused the middle to ripple, then a woman's face appeared before him.

"You have something to report?" she asked.

"I have, my queen. The battle is about to commence. We have led Hollis to Ravensguard as you commanded, and tomorrow he will do battle with the Mercerians, convinced he will destroy them."

The woman's face smiled. "You have done well, Ilarian."

The Elf bowed, showing his respect, but his eyes betrayed him.

"Is something wrong?" the woman asked.

A moment of fear crossed his face. "It is a small matter, my queen, not worthy of your notice."

"Speak," she commanded. "I would know every detail."

"There is one here who works against us, a man called Marik."

"The earl's champion?"

"The very same," Ilarian said.

"We have waited far too long for our plans to be thrown askew. You must take action to ensure the threat is eliminated."

"Am I to kill him?"

"You may do whatever you deem fit," she replied, "but make sure it's done soon—tonight, if possible. We cannot risk exposure when we are so close."

"I shall do as you command, my queen."

"Good. Contact me after the battle. I would know the details."

"The Norlanders and Mercerians are bitter enemies. I expect the losses will be high on both sides."

"So much the better," the woman added. "After all, it is the very reason for your presence. It will weaken both their armies and provide us with more souls ripe for the harvest."

"Then I shall contact you when next I have news, my queen."

The woman nodded, then waved her hand, returning her image to the inky blackness of the smoke. Ilarian dismissed the spell, letting the effect dissipate. Marik was a problem, but one he was more than capable of dealing with.

The Elf rose from his seat, moving towards the door, only pausing long enough to cast his spell of concealment. Now, once more wearing the guise of the Human, Jendrick, he exited his wagon, intent on finding the earl's champion.

Marik stared into the fire as he ran the stone over the blade of his axe. With each push, he imagined it cutting deep into the sorcerer's flesh, the blood pouring forth to pool on the ground, staining the grass red. Halting his actions, he tested the edge with his thumb.

"Is it sharp enough, do you think?" came the annoying voice of Jendrick.

The champion leaped to his feet, caught by surprise.

"Come now," said the sorcerer, a look of mirth on his face. "If I wanted you dead, do you really think you'd see me coming?"

"What do you want?" demanded a scowling Marik.

"It's clear you and I do not get along. I thought it best we come to an understanding."

"Meaning?"

"Meaning Lord Hollis is sending you back to Galburn's Ridge, so I shall be rid of you."

"You shall never be rid of me," declared Marik.

Jendrick sighed. "I feared you might say that. I suppose this means we'll have to settle things the old-fashioned way."

Marik hefted his axe, tossing the sharpening stone to the ground. "I'm ready whenever you are."

The sorcerer looked around, taking note of the sounds of the camp. "Not here," he said. "The earl would not appreciate us airing our grievances in public."

"Then name a place."

Jendrick looked around, his eyes settling on the western end of the camp. "Over there," he suggested, "away from prying eyes."

"It's dark."

"Then bring a torch. We'll plant it in the ground and then have our duel."

"Duel? With what weapons are you proficient, little man?"

"I shall use my sword." Jendrick turned, showing the weapon scabbarded on his belt. "Will that suffice?"

Marik grunted. "Come along, then, let's get this over and done with." He took a nearby torch, lighting it in the fire. The dried pitch sputtered to life, throwing shadows that danced across his face.

Jendrick held out his hand, palm upward. "By all means, after you." He watched the fool lead the way. Words of power quietly began to issue from his mouth as he followed, and then a thin tendril of blue snaked out, ghost-like, and sank into Marik's back. The earl's champion gave no indication that anything was felt, but Jendrick appeared pleased with the result.

Some hundred paces later, Marik turned. "This is good enough," he declared, jamming the end of the torch into the dirt. It took several more tries before it would stand on its own, but the sorcerer merely watched patiently.

His task complete, Marik turned to face his foe. "Draw your weapon, and prepare to die."

Jendrick chuckled, leaving his opponent with a puzzled look. "Do you honestly think I came out here to match steel with you, fool?"

Marik turned crimson, knowing he was being mocked. "You'll pay for your insolence," he threatened.

"I doubt it," replied Jendrick. He held out his hand and made a fist, grabbing the air as if a rope hung there, invisible to the eye.

The champion felt his arms pull against his body, unbidden.

"What sorcery is this?" he demanded.

"It's not sorcery," said Jendrick, "it's Necromancy. Now, shut up and watch as I give you a demonstration." He pulled back his hand, and with an invisible tugging motion, Marik stepped forward.

The disgraced champion's muscles tensed as if held in a vice, and then it felt as though the very flesh was being torn from his bones. He watched his arms as the skin rippled and then began to wither even as he looked on in horror. Marik sank to his knees, unable to support himself as his muscles shrank and his body screamed out in agony.

Jendrick pulled his hand back some more, laughing as he did so. "You fool," he taunted. "Did you seriously think you could so easily defeat me? I have the magic of my Ancestors, magic I have practiced for thousands of years. Your cold steel is nothing compared to the raw power I control."

Reaching out with his other hand, the Elf made another fist, and then Marik's legs gave out. Lying on the ground, his limbs grew old and frail before his very eyes. He could even feel his hair falling out, and then the axe finally fell from his grasp. Jendrick moved closer, staring down at the help-less champion.

"What are you doing to me?" Marik grunted out, his voice now devoid of youth and vigour.

"I am draining you of your essence," replied the sorcerer. "Don't worry, I shan't kill you. That would be much too merciful for my liking. Instead, I shall leave you a broken man, old and decrepit." Jendrick knelt, peering into Marik's eyes. "I can see your eyesight beginning to fade," he remarked in a calm voice. "Your pupils are turning cloudy. How interesting."

"I shall kill you!" Marik said, his voice but a sliver of its former self.

"Kill me? I think not." Jendrick uncurled his fingers. "There, it is done. I have stolen your energy, the very substance of your life."

Marik stared back, even now unable to comprehend the magnitude of the attack upon him.

Jendrick sighed again. "Oh, very well, I will explain it to you. I have stolen a portion of your essence, years of your life, if you wish. Your weakness has only let me grow stronger." He leaned in until they were almost touching noses. "Tell me, my friend, do I look any younger? Stronger perhaps? More Human-like?"

Marik spoke, his voice raspy, now that of an old man, "What are you?"

"I told you. I'm a Necromancer. A Death Mage in the language of your people."

"You're not Human!"

"No, thank the spirits, I'm not. I am an Elf." He saw the look of surprise on the old man's face. "Yes, that's right, one of the elder folk. I must say it's been quite intriguing spending all this time with your race, but I fear it's soon coming to an end, your race, that is, not my time." He regained his feet, brushing off some imaginary dirt. "Now, I shall leave you to spend what days you have left in peace." He began walking back towards the camp but halted, turning one final time to gaze down at his adversary. "If you show your face anywhere around here, I shall have you killed, is that clear?" He laughed, the sound echoing into the still night.

With his fogged vision, Marik watched him disappear into the darkness. Struggling to stand, his limbs felt weak, his flesh frail, yet part of him screamed out to die in combat. His battle axe lay nearby, and he bent, wrapping his fingers around the handle, but he lacked the strength to even lift it as he had mere moments ago. With both hands now gripping the handle, he mustered his remaining reserves to lift the weapon to his shoulder. He stood, panting with the effort, then turned his attention westward, to the wilderness that awaited him.

THIRTY-THREE

Siege

Summer 965 MC

Hayley stretched her arms, trying to work out her nervousness. It was still dark outside, but the rangers were all here, leaning against the wall of a rock tunnel, waiting for the right moment to act. She had no idea of the time, for the darkness was illuminated not by moonlight but by a collection of torches.

She looked over at Sam, who was going through her quiver, examining each arrow. The young woman, noting her gaze, shrugged. "You can never go wrong if you make sure your arrows are in good shape."

"Spoken like a true ranger," said Hayley. "Nervous?"

Sam nodded. "I've never done anything like this before."

"That's not true. You were there when we took the tower."

"Yes, but that was all over in a moment. This... this is something else entirely."

"Don't worry," said Hayley. "You'll do fine."

"You've been in a siege," said the young ranger. "What's it like?"

"I'm afraid you're asking the wrong question. During the siege of Riversend, I was tasked with taking out a tower, not the main assault."

"I was actually thinking of Wincaster."

"Oh," said Hayley. "Sorry."

"You were there, weren't you?"

"I was. I was part of the assault on the wall."

"What was it like?"

"To be honest, it was all over rather quickly." Hayley glanced across at the other rangers, noting their nervous faces. "Just remember to keep your wits about you. Stay close to the others, and you'll be fine."

A commotion down the line drew their attention, and then Kharzug came into view. The master of earth took up a position by the exposed stone wall, then looked at Hayley.

"Are you ready?" he asked, using the Orcish tongue.

Hayley nodded, then turned to the rest of her rangers. "This is it," she called out softly. "Send word down the line."

The Orc turned to face the wall, placing his hands against the stone. He closed his eyes and let the magic flow through him, released by his words of power. When his hands began to glow, it reminded Hayley of Aubrey's healing, but here the light was a dull brown colour. She watched in fascination as Kharzug shoved his fingers into the stone and began spreading it apart as if it were made of clay. On and on he worked until a small hole appeared, letting light filter in from the room beyond.

The Orc paused a moment, leaning close to peer through. Once assured his ministrations had gone unnoticed, he continued, scraping stone to either side and widening the gap. Hayley gripped her sword, ready to enter the temple and secure it. At a nod from Kharzug, she moved forward, turning sideways to fit through.

The first thing she noticed was the smooth stone floor and the way her boots echoed on it. Moving aside, she made room for the next ranger, then advanced, her eyes locked on the distant door. The room was large, consisting of the nave and, to her right, the altar. Sam followed, her knuckles white as she gripped her own sword.

"Take a breath and relax," whispered Hayley, "or you'll have no strength left for later when you need it." She waved the young woman forward, letting her take up a position to the left of the door while she, as the leader, took the right.

Once the twelve Humans were through, Kharzug cast his spell again, widening the gap to allow the Orcs entrance. They soon began filing in, one at a time, their chance of success growing with every hunter.

Hayley waited until all of her rangers were through, then called up Gorath. "You remember the plan?"

"Of course," replied her aide. "Don't you?"

"I do. Sorry, I'm just nervous."

"You have every right to be. You are attempting the impossible."

Hayley grinned. "That's what we rangers do, isn't it?"

"Go," said Gorath, "and let the Ancestors go with you. We'll secure this area and wait for Ghodrug to bring her hunters through."

The High Ranger moved to the centre of the double doors and pulled one of them open a crack. The great oaken structure let out a groan, swinging back so easily she feared it might open too quickly and hit the wall.

Grabbing it, she slowed its progress and took a moment to catch her breath. Poking her head around the corner revealed an empty corridor heading to what she assumed was some offices. But the real prize lay directly ahead—the main outer doors that led into the city of Ravensguard itself.

Hayley slipped through, pausing only long enough to make sure the way was clear. Her task complete, she waved the rest forward, and the Human rangers began exiting the prayer room. They massed by the outer door as the Orcs followed, moving left and right to root out any opposition they might find.

Just as she was about to open the outer door, she heard footsteps and froze. When the door began to open, she quickly moved to stand to one side.

Someone, maybe a Holy Father, had decided to pay their respects to Saxnor early. A most unfortunate circumstance for the poor fellow, as the moment his foot crossed the threshold, a hand reached out, pulling him off balance. Before he could react, his mouth was covered, and then he was bound and passed off to the most massive Orc he had ever seen.

Hayley scabbarded her sword and adjusted her helmet. Taking one more look at her companions, she then boldly stepped out into the early morning sun. Expecting the worst, she was pleasantly surprised to see no sign of panic. People were going about their business, wandering up and down the street, seemingly without a care in the world.

She waited for Sam and Ayles, then began walking down the street with them. When planning the assault, they had decided a dozen men in a large group would garner too much attention. Instead, they went in threes, each making a slight change to their path. Some walked along the opposite side of the street while others wandered back and forth, pretending to examine shop windows, all the while making progress towards their ultimate target —the gate.

Shopkeepers and workers went about their day unaware of the Mercerian presence. Hayley halted her group some twenty paces from the gatehouse. The main gate was impressive, being two stories high and wide enough to allow ten men to walk abreast, but within this greater door was a smaller one more suitable for a single person to enter. It was this door that beckoned them.

"Let's go," she said, leading the others directly towards it. Closer they drew until her hand reached out and knocked soundly. She stood aside as it opened, revealing a disinterested guard.

"Replacements," said Ayles, putting on his best impression of a Norlander.

If the guard had any reservations, he certainly didn't reveal them, merely opened the door to admit the archer. Sam was next, followed by Hayley, both of them keeping their eyes low and letting their helmets mask their feminine features.

As the guard moved to close the door, Hayley struck, plunging her dagger into the man's neck. He slumped silently to the ground, dead, and Sam quickly dragged his body out of the way. Ayles waited a moment, then opened the door, searching for the other rangers. He soon made eye contact.

"They're coming," he announced.

Hayley strung her bow. "We'll wait till the others are here, then spread out." She glanced around the entrance. The door they had used to enter lay on the eastern side, while to the west sat its counterpart, hiding their Mercerian allies beyond. Ayles stood aside as three more rangers entered.

"The priority," announced Hayley, "is the gatehouse, directly above. Only from there can we control these gates. Once that's secure, we move on to the flanking towers. Any questions?"

She looked at her people, meeting each one's gaze, but they all appeared ready to act.

The door opened again, admitting the next group, bringing their count to nine. "Ayles, you stay here. Secure the door when the last group arrives. The rest of you follow me."

To one side stood a door that could only lead farther into the gatehouse. She pushed it open, only to see three men sitting at a table playing cards. Ignoring them, she passed by the game to reach the stairs beyond.

"Hang on," called out one of the players. "What are you doing?"

By now, she had reached the bottom stair. She turned, the bow still in her hands. "Hello, boys," she said. "I'm here to take your gatehouse."

The men all laughed, but then the sight of the other rangers entering with nocked arrows soon sobered them.

"Tie them up," ordered Hayley, "and if they give you any trouble, kill them." She started up the stairs, taking them two at a time.

∼

Urgon watched as the sun stretched its long arms out from behind the mountain. *"It is time,"* he said to himself. Turning, he faced his hunters. *"The day is upon us,"* he called out in his native tongue. *"A day the Ancestors will talk of for generations to come. Let us take back Ravensguard!"*

The Orcs roared back in exultation. Urgon drew his sword and held it high, marvelling at the blue glow of the magic blade. The Orcs of the Black Arrow began their advance. Behind them, Kurathian Light Horsemen waited, Gerald at their head, ready to spring into action at the first sign of trouble.

The march began at a sedate pace, allowing them to stretch out into an open formation. Archers moved to the southern end, lest the enemy tower there give them any trouble. To the north stood the captured tower, inside of which Urgon had placed a small group of hunters. Their target, the gate in the distance, loomed out of the early morning mist like some imaginary palace.

Urgon kept them spread out, well aware that a catapult watched them from on high. They had advanced no more than a hundred yards when the first stone flung towards them fell short, digging up dirt in great clods as it struck. The Orcs kept their formation, reassured that such a siege engine was slow to load.

They passed by the imaginary line that joined the two towers, and Urgon picked up the pace. It would leave the Trolls in their wake but meant the gate would soon be within their grasp. The mighty chieftain spotted archers forming up on the gate towers in the distance, their crossbows waiting to release a rain of death.

Gerald noted the increase in tempo but kept the cavalry steady. Glancing over his shoulder, he spotted Tog leading his troops right behind him. The great Trolls were lumbering along nicely as the sun rolled out from behind the mountain throwing light across the field before Ravensguard. And then the marshal saw it—a distant glint, a warning something else was behind them. He stopped and turned in the saddle, keeping his eyes westward, letting his riders continue the advance without him.

Tog, noting his position, broke off from his Trolls, coming to stand beside him. It created quite a scene, for he was so tall that, even on foot, his head was well above that of the marshal.

"Saxnor's balls," cursed Gerald. "I wish my eyes were better. I can't make out a thing. Something has caught the morning sun over there. Do you see it?"

Tog turned his attention to the west. "There are Norland troops behind us," he warned.

"So it would seem."

They watched in silence as the rest of their small army continued their advance towards the gate. Soon the enemy came closer, allowing Gerald to finally make out some details.

"It must be Hollis," said Gerald, "and it looks like he's got cavalry. Can you make out their numbers?"

Tog stared for a bit, then looked at his marshal. "I estimate one hundred fifty horsemen and double that in foot."

"And archers?"

"A similar number, and they look like they have crossbows."

"That doesn't bode well," said Gerald. "They're more than capable of penetrating your hide, my friend."

"Then we must take measures to deal with them."

"My thoughts exactly. Halt your troops, Tog, and I'll have Urgon lend us some hunters."

"And the assault?"

"We have no choice," said Gerald. "We can't call it off now. Our best hope is to take the gate. Make your stand here. I'll form the rest up on your flanks."

"Agreed," said Tog, his voice booming out in the early morning air.

Hayley let fly, her arrow sailing across the room to dig deep into her target's chest. The Norlander clutched the shaft, sinking back against the wall to then collapse to the floor, unmoving.

Rangers rushed past, striking down all opposition. The room was the full length of the gatehouse, with winches at either end to raise and lower portcullises. In addition, there were two giant gears designed to operate the great doors themselves. Rangers started examining the mechanism, trying to determine how it worked, but most of them were country folk, not used to such things.

"It's similar to the gatehouse in Bodden," said Sam, "only bigger."

"How do we open the gate?" asked Hayley.

"This winch raises and lowers the portcullis, while that over there"—she pointed—"controls the gate, but they'll have to go down and remove the drop bar first."

Hayley dispatched two rangers to see to it, then turned her attention to the two extra doors. Each led to a side tower that watched over the entrance, a dangerous place to allow the enemy to mass if the attacking Orcs were to be successful.

"Get that winch working, Sam," she ordered, "and you two come with me."

"Where are you going?"

"We need to secure one of the towers." Hayley slung her bow, drawing her sword. "This will be close-in work until we get to the top."

The sounds of fighting drifted up to her ears.

"They're below us," warned Sam.

Hayley swore. "Block off those two doors. We'll have to secure the entrance first and then take the towers afterwards.

∾

Gorath looked over the assembled Orcs. *"You have many hunters, Ghodrug. Are they ready to fight?"*

"They are," replied the chieftain. *"Is it time?"*

The Orc ranger peered back outside. *"Soon. The alarm has been raised, and the enemy rushes to the gates. We wait only to come upon them from the rear."*

Ghodrug turned to her people. *"The time is nigh,"* she said. *"The Ancestors have seen fit to place us here this day. Let us be worthy of such attention."*

She nodded to Gorath. The Orc ranger grasped the door, readying himself to take action. Outside, a troop of men rushed past, intent on the fracas at the gate.

"Now!" he yelled, pulling back on the great oaken door.

The Orcs of the Black Raven surged forward, their axes ready to bring death to their enemies. Out the door they went, spreading out in all directions, screaming out their defiance, terrifying all those who witnessed their descent upon the city.

Gorath watched them rush by, keeping his rangers in reserve. The Orcs of the Black Raven would spread throughout the city, but his job this day was to keep his head and ensure success at the gate.

More and more Orcs disappeared out the door. He waited until the flow slackened, then led his rangers into the streets of Ravensguard, their bows at the ready.

∾

Lord Hollis smiled as he surveyed the scene before him. "We have them at last."

"Just as you predicted," said Jendrick. "And we easily outnumber them, even without the aid of Lord Thurlowe's men. Your orders, my lord?"

"Begin the advance," the earl said. "Cavalry to the front so they can carry out a charge before those heathens organize any type of defence."

"It's too late, my lord. They already turn to face us."

Hollis stood in his stirrups, trying to get a better view. "It is a feeble defence, only a smattering of Orcs and those Trolls. Our cavalry will make quick work of them."

Arrows began to fly from the Mercerian line.

"They have archers, my lord," warned Jendrick.

"Move up the crossbowmen," shouted the earl, frustration evident in his voice. "Let them trade arrows for bolts."

He watched as his own archers ran forward. They halted in line, then started cranking their bulky weapons.

"We'll soon put them in their place." Hollis pulled his horse to the side, letting his footmen past. Three hundred of them marched, more than enough to deal with the pitiful Mercerians. "Where's your mighty general now?" he demanded.

"My lord?"

"Not you," said the earl. "I am merely thinking of our enemy."

"He shall not stand long, Lord. Our cavalry will cut him to pieces."

"Yes, and then our footmen will push past and force the rest of them into the walls of Ravensguard. Thurlowe will have a field day!"

The crossbowmen discharged their first volley. It fell short, but it wouldn't take long for them to find their range.

"Move them closer," ordered Hollis. "I want this done quickly."

An aide rode off, yelling orders as he went.

Hollis rode forward to get a better view. The enemy was in a fearful state; there was no denying it. The entire Mercerian force numbered little more than five hundred Orcs, with a smattering of Trolls and a handful of Human riders thrown into the mix. Now they were split, half attacking the city while the rest tried to form a desperately thin line to hold off Hollis's efforts.

The earl smiled. "This day will go down in history as my greatest victory," he said. "You mark my words."

Jendrick bowed dutifully. "As you wish, my lord."

THIRTY-FOUR

Battle

Summer 965 MC

Gerald turned to Kraloch. The shaman had remained with the rear guard even as Chief Urgon pressed the attack against the gate, and now he stood waiting, an archer at his side.

"Now?" asked the Orc.

"Yes," replied Gerald.

Kraloch turned to the archer, but words were not needed. The hunter pulled back on the string, sending an arrow skyward, a thin red ribbon trailing it.

Gerald looked north to where the captured tower stood sentinel over the battle. Moments later, a similar arrow flew forth, this time with a blue ribbon.

"It is done," said Kraloch.

"Yes," agreed Gerald, "but the real question is whether or not it will work."

"You must have faith."

"I trust my life with these people," he replied. "Quite literally, in this case, but one still can't help but worry."

A crossbow bolt sailed past.

"They have the range," he noted absently.

"Their horsemen are still approaching. We are in danger of being on the receiving end of a charge."

"Hold off on the volleys. We'll deliver a crippling blow once they've committed to engaging us."

~

Commander Lanaka saw the arrow with the tail of cloth, off in the distance.

"It is time," he said in his native Kurathian. He turned to Captain Caluman. *"Ready the men. We ride to glory."*

The captain raised a horn to his lips, blowing three clear notes that echoed off the mountainside. It was repeated down the line, and then the Kurathian horse, the finest horsemen in all the known lands, started their advance.

Conserving their strength for the final push, they began at a trot. All along the line, the harnesses jingled, while swords slapped against saddles as the pride of Kurathia rode south.

Off in the distance, Lanaka spotted the Norlanders advancing on the Orcs. The horns sounded again as he gave the command, calling out to their enemy, warning them death was approaching.

The enemy line was perpendicular to their approach, focused on the army before them, not the horsemen coming up on their flank. As Lanaka led his troops nearer, the enemy cavalry began a slow turn to face this new threat. The Norland horsemen were heavier troops, armoured in chainmail, making their mounts slow. That was something he aimed to take advantage of.

Closer the Kurathians drew until their commander could make out individual faces hidden beneath their nasal guards. With one final scream of challenge, they charged the enemy horsemen.

Lanaka slashed out with his sword, carving a thick red gash across a rider's arm. Had the Norland horsemen had sufficient warning, they could have closed up their ranks, but with the suddenness of the onslaught, they were ill-prepared for the tactics of their enemy. The Kurathians rode into their numbers, passing by riders with little more than a quick swing of their swords. Once in amongst the Norlanders, they spread out, doing frightful damage as their more heavily encumbered opponents struggled to manoeuvre.

Commander Lanaka lashed out, sinking the point of his sword into a rider's armpit. Withdrawing it quickly, he slashed to his left, deftly deflecting a blow as his mount surged forward. Feeling the press of horse-flesh as a rider bumped into him, he struck again, this time with the hilt of his sword, onto his foe's helmet.

Grunts and groans surrounded him as his countrymen struggled to deal out death and destruction. A blade sliced across his stomach, damaging his armour. Slipping his foot from the stirrup, he kicked out in a mad gamble, his boot striking a rider's shin and scraping across their armour until his spur got caught up in their stirrup. The Norlander's horse stumbled, pulling Lanaka from his saddle, and then he was dragged along the ground as the creature tore across the field.

~

Gerald saw the horsemen collide, and then the melee, from this range, quickly devolved into a swirling mass of riders. The marshal turned to his few horsemen. "Go," he commanded.

One word was all it took. The remaining Kurathians burst into a gallop, riding north to assist their countrymen.

To his front, Gerald watched as the Norland footmen formed a solid wall, several hundred strong. Hollis was there, beneath his standard, sitting on his horse like a pompous fool, his plumed helmet and colourful garb easy to distinguish amongst the more muted tones of his troops.

The marshal looked at his own lines where a small group of Trolls was backed up by a smattering of Orc archers and smiled. The warbows of these gallant hunters would play havoc with the enemy, while the Trolls would prove all but impervious to the swords of the Norlanders. His thoughts were interrupted by another passing crossbow bolt, and he swore, for they were the one thing that could throw their plans into disarray.

His eyes sought out Kraloch. The Orc shaman was concentrating on the enemy footmen, watching as they started banging their shields.

"Master Kraloch," called out Gerald. "I think it's time you contacted Aubrey."

The shaman nodded, closing his eyes, and ignoring all that was around him. Words of power drifted from his lips, lending an eerie feel to the battle. The Orc archers, knowing full well what he was doing, began stamping the ground with their feet to show their support.

Kraloch put aside all thoughts of battle, concentrating instead on the power that began to flow through him. On and on he intoned, spilling forth the words that would release the power from within. As he finished the incantation, he felt a surge rush through him and then opened his eyes to see the ghostly image of Aubrey Brandon floating before him.

"Lady Aubrey," he said. "We are under attack."

"Is it Lord Hollis?" she asked.

"It is," he confirmed.

Her image looked towards the side, speaking to someone out of his field of view. Moments later, she turned to face him once more. "Hold on, we'll be there as quickly as we can."

Kraloch dismissed his spell, then turned back to Gerald, who stood in his stirrups, peering at the enemy line, heedless of the incoming crossbow bolts.

"It is done," called out the Orc.

"And not a moment too soon."

Kraloch switched to his native tongue. *"Draw bows!"* he commanded. The Orc hunters pulled back on the massive warbows, ready to unleash a deadly volley.

"Hold," said Kraloch, counting the enemy steps. *"Hold,"* he repeated. The enemy moved ever closer, and then the Orc spotted what he was looking for—a small stone on the ground. It was much like the myriad of other small rocks that spread across the field, but this one had been painted white, dropped in their advance to mark the range. *"Loose!"* he commanded.

As one, the arrows flew, creating a dark cloud that rose into the air. The Norlanders, content the range was too extreme, took little notice of the barrage to their own detriment. The mighty warbows of the Orcs were far more powerful than those of their Human foes and easily sailed across the field to descend from the sky onto the Humans' heads. The footmen cried out in alarm as the Orcs let loose with another volley.

The crossbowmen on the south end of the Norland line, moved up, intent on taking revenge. Their weapons sang out, sending death and destruction into the lightly armoured Orcs.

Hayley cursed. Foot soldiers had swarmed the gatehouse, and now the rangers were struggling to close the access door. Ayles gave a grunt, then fell, a crossbow bolt taking him in the chest. Two more rangers tried to force the door closed, and even Hayley had her shoulder to it, pushing with all her might.

An arm stabbed out with a sword, taking a blind thrust through the gap. Slashing down with her own weapon, the High Ranger took the hand off at the wrist. The arm jerked back, and then the door slammed shut, allowing the drop bar to finally be pushed into place.

Hayley took a moment to catch her breath, then saw to Ayles. A bolt protruded from his chest on the left side, and he was wheezing badly. He tried to speak, but it was clear his lung had been punctured.

"Do what you can for him," she said, looking at the other rangers, "but we have to take those towers."

～

Urgon approached the gate. The walls were towering over him now, and bolts began to descend on his Orcs from the Norland crossbowmen. He cursed his luck, for he had sent his archers to help Gerald. Now he was stuck at the gatehouse, unable to enter, yet sitting prey for the archers above.

"*Axes!*" he yelled, desperate to gain entry.

A dozen Orcs ran forward, brandishing large, two-handed axes. They took up a position to the front of the door and began hacking away at it with all the strength they possessed.

Above them, he spotted the murder holes, diabolical channels through which boiling pitch or water could be poured. A movement above drew his attention, and then someone was waving at him. Moments later, the end of a rope was thrown down.

Urgon didn't hesitate. Scabbarding his sword, he rushed forward, seizing the rope and hauled himself upward. As he came to the top, a hand reached out for him, and he grasped it tightly. Through the hole he went, thankful it was large enough for him to fit. He sat, panting with the effort, and looked up at the young woman who had offered him aid.

"Thank you," he said.

"You're welcome," said the woman. "I'm Samantha, from Bodden, but you can call me Sam."

"Greetings, Sam," said Urgon. "Was it your idea to use the rope?"

"It was," she confessed, "though I wasn't sure anyone could fit through that murder hole."

"Where is the High Ranger?"

"Down below," she replied. "Fighting to keep the enemy at bay."

He pointed at another ranger. "You there, get more ropes down those holes." He returned his gaze to Sam. "How do the doors open?"

"This mechanism here," she said, "but we lack the strength to open it."

Urgon laughed. "Then it is good you have found a way for the Orcs to help. Show me how this works, and we'll see what can be done."

～

Gorath pushed his way through the mass of Orcs. The Black Ravens, having forced their way into the streets, were now pressing the defenders back towards the main gate. Townsfolk screamed in fear at the sight of the Orcs, but the great green hunters ignored them, for it was only Norland warriors they sought this day.

The Orc ranger heard a clamour, and then a group of horsemen burst onto the street, their swords dripping with black blood. Instinctively, he nocked an arrow, pulling the fletchings back to his ear, and then loosed it, striking the lead rider in the face, puncturing through one cheek to protrude out from the other, giving the man a macabre scarlet grin. The injured man gave a yell, now unintelligible, and turned in the saddle, but the Orc had not been idle. His second arrow took the rider in the chest, punching clean through the armour to emerge from the middle of his back. He toppled from the saddle, and Gorath turned, sprinting across the road.

A barrel sat by a house, likely there to catch rainwater. As he drew closer, Gorath tossed his bow onto the roof, then vaulted, using the edge of the barrel to propel himself upward. Reaching out, he grasped the thatched roof, and then his muscular arms pulled him up on top of it. Spotting his bow, he grabbed it right as it was about to slide to the ground.

The soldiers were still below him, cutting down Orcs in large numbers. Gorath took careful aim, sending his first arrow into one's head.

A second shot quickly flew from his bow, hitting another warrior in the arm. Taking their cue from him, other Orc rangers began climbing to the rooftops and loosing carefully aimed arrows. The riders were soon cut down, their horses running in fear at the sudden onslaught.

Jendrick turned to the earl. "The Kurathians are tying down our horsemen, my lord."

"It matters not," said Hollis. "We still have them between a rock and a hard place." He turned to an aide. "Send the footmen forward."

"How many, my lord?" the man replied.

"All of them!" he shouted in reply.

"Is that wise?" asked Jendrick.

"For Gods' sake," said Hollis. "One more push, and we'll be rid of them forever!"

The footmen began moving, closing with the enemy. Arrows flew from the Mercerians, tearing into their lines, but the sergeants had the men filling in the gaps as they went. Closer and closer they marched until Hollis could almost smell the sweat of the Orcs.

Jendrick saw the crossbows slacken their pace and then their cry of dismay as the archers began to panic. The earl's advisor cast his glance to the west to see a strange mist drifting towards them. "My lord?" he called out.

Hollis swivelled his gaze. "What sorcery is this?"

Closer came the mist, filling the earl with a sense of dread. He watched, unable to take his eyes from the scene. Figures began to take shape, huge, monstrous beings that dwarfed the largest of horses. Atop these behemoths were strange lizard creatures, brandishing exotic spears and javelins. Then out of the mist flew a hail of darts, small bone fragments that struck the bowmen with such force, many fell beneath the violent assault.

The crossbowmen, not used to such things, began to waver. Sergeants were running around, yelling at the men to return fire, but the sight of the massive beasts had stolen their courage. Men began dropping their cross-bows, then fleeing south in a desperate bid to be free of the area.

"NO!" screamed Hollis, but it was too late. The damage had been done.

～

Dame Beverly Fitzwilliam sat upon Lightning, her eyes glued on her queen. Her Majesty was riding on the back of a three-horn, enjoying the view the added height afforded her.

The queen turned to look at her, then called out, "Take them forward, Beverly, and drive all before you."

The knight pulled forth Nature's Fury. For a moment, the mist swirled around her, driving her allies from her view, until a fresh breeze cleared the air, and then the mist began to dissipate. All around her marched the Saurians, their spears held ready. They walked leaning slightly forward, their tails acting to counterbalance them, the strange gait carrying them towards the enemy at a rapid clip.

Beverly held the hammer above her head, calling out at the top of her lungs, "For the queen!" then urged her great Mercerian Charger forward. Lightning exploded into action, carrying his mistress to the forefront.

Amongst the fleeing crossbowmen, Beverly spotted a group gathered around an officer and angled her mount directly at them.

Lightning crashed into the group, knocking several to the ground like loose logs. At the same time, down came Nature's Fury, smashing into a man's head and collapsing his helm. Lifting the hammer, she swung again, this time twirling the weapon in the air to build up speed. She felt the magic pulse, then smashed out, taking a man in the chest. His armour collapsed, and he slumped forward, the life knocked from him.

In her wake came the Saurians, swarming over the defenders like an ocean wave, spears thrust out, taking men down left, right, and centre. A few Norlanders fought back but quickly succumbed to the superior numbers of the lizard folk.

"Now!" shouted Gerald.

Tog repeated the order, and then the Trolls lumbered forward. On their flanks, the Orcs shouldered their bows, drawing their axes instead. A primal scream erupted from their numbers, then they, too, launched themselves towards what remained of the earl's army.

Gerald, stunned by the ferocity of the attack, had little time to react and suddenly found himself rushing to catch up. Ahead, the Norlanders had increased their pace, and the two lines came together in a thunderous crash. The marshal had just enough time to draw his weapon before he was amongst the enemy, desperately fighting for his life.

The edge of a sword smashed into his chainmail shirt, forcing the air from his lungs. He counterattacked with a thrust, driving the point of his Mercerian longsword deep into his opponent's arm. His horse bucked forward, and he struck again, bringing his blade down onto a rider's leg.

A sense of calm enveloped Gerald as years of experiences took over even as he parried a blow, then quickly slashed his sword across a nearby arm. His horse slipped, but his legs automatically gripped tighter, compensating for the turmoil of battle. An Orc went down beside him, and a Norlander reached out with a sword to finish the job. Gerald twisted in the saddle, slicing down into the man's neck and putting an end to such foolishness.

Blood sprayed him even as he pulled the blade free, and for a moment, he was blinded. He automatically parried and heard the familiar ring of steel on steel as swords clashed.

He caught a brief glimpse of Tog through the red mist, and the mighty Troll had lifted a warrior high into the air and was about to toss him. The hapless fool flew into his companions, taking down three men in one go.

Gerald wiped his eyes and took in his surroundings. The Orcs had pushed back the Norland foot, but now the enemy was counterattacking, bringing up the second line to reinforce the first. He spurred his horse forward, seeking another foe, only to spot Lord Hollis, right behind this second wave, accompanied by half a dozen guards and a man in a dark robe.

"Tog!" he called out.

When the great Troll looked his way, the marshal pointed, singling out their common enemy. Tog nodded, then called out in his native tongue. The melee raged all around him, but in amongst the carnage, the Trolls suddenly started making their way towards the Norland leader.

Gerald pushed forward, heedless of the danger. The robed man began gesticulating, the air around him growing thick with vapours. The marshal instinctively ducked as the mage's arms extended, and a streak of darkness flew across the battlefield, narrowly missing him. He felt the hair on the back of his neck rise, but his horse didn't falter, carrying him through the fray.

Tog grabbed a man by the neck and lifted him from the ground. His foe went limp and then was tossed aside without a second thought. The Trolls were nearly there, leaving a gap behind them through which the Orcs poured.

Finding himself slowed due to the press of warriors and Orcs before him, Gerald did not see the second dark streak emanating from the robed individual before it exploded onto his chest with a crushing weight. Then he felt a burning sensation as if he were on fire, and he leaped from the saddle, rolling as he hit the ground. Screams erupted from his mouth as he tried to put out the fire, but it was no use; nothing could extinguish the searing agony.

A face loomed over him, and then he realized it was Kraloch.

"Hold still," said the Orc, calling forth his Life Magic. Gerald grimaced with pain, then a soothing coldness flowed into his chest, extinguishing the fire.

"What was that?" he gasped out.

"Acid," said Kraloch. "You are lucky I was here." The shaman extended his arm, helping the marshal to his feet.

"Where's Hollis?" asked Gerald.

Kraloch motioned towards the back of the Orcs. "Over there some-where, beyond our field of view."

"He's getting away!"

"Not if Tog has anything to do with it."

THIRTY-FIVE

The Gate

Summer 965 MC

Urgon looked at the door. "Is this it?" he asked.

Hayley nodded. "Yes. Beyond that door is the north tower, overlooking the entrance."

"Then ready your bows. We must begin the assault now!"

The Orcs began removing the furniture that had been piled to block the entrance while Hayley nocked her arrow, absently noting the playing cards strewn about the floor. The obstacles were soon cleared, but before the Orc could grasp the handle, the door flew open, and a group of Norland warriors rushed through.

Hayley's first arrow took their leader in the chest, and he fell to the floor, tripping the man behind. More arrows flew, and then the Orcs were reaching out with their axes, cutting down foes with quick, efficient blows.

Urgon didn't hesitate. As soon as the door was cleared of the enemy, he rushed forward, calling out to the Ancestors even as he crossed the threshold. Others raced after him, and then Hayley gathered her rangers and followed, taking the stairs two at a time.

The area opened onto the roof. Here, crossbowmen were leaning over the parapets, picking their targets from the Orcs who swarmed the great doors below.

Urgon kicked one of the Norlanders in the small of the back, sending him tumbling from his perch, then struck out with his magic sword, driving the blade through another's stomach. So strong was the blow that the tip protruded from the man's belly. A small gasp of air escaped his foe, then Urgon was moving past, letting the body fall where it may.

Hayley loosed another arrow, and it sank into a crossbowman's thigh, but she was already concentrating on the next target when someone moved up beside her, and out of the corner of her eye, she noticed it was Sam, who then let loose with an arrow. It struck a crossbowman in the arm, causing him to spin and randomly release the bolt he had been aiming. Hayley felt the shot graze her temple, and then blood was pouring down the side of her face.

An Orc pushed his way past her, then went down, a bolt to the neck while another tossed his axe through the air, spinning it end over end to embed itself into a crossbowman's forehead.

The room was suddenly spinning before her eyes, and Hayley struggled to make sense of it. As her vision blurred, she loosed off another arrow only to hear it clatter across the stone. No longer able to stand, she sank to her knees, and before she knew it, the cold floor was pressing against her cheek. A boot appeared before her eyes just before she passed out.

~

Lanaka was dragged northward, across the field. All feeling in his leg was lost, but in its place, his hip was now in excruciating agony. His body hit a rut, slamming his head painfully back into the ground, and then, at last, his spur finally broke free, and he skidded to a stop. He tried to catch his breath, but the agony of his injuries was too intense, allowing him only short gasps of air. Lying on his back, his legs splayed out before him, he lifted his neck, craning to see where he was.

The fighting was off in the distance, and he wondered, for a moment, how far he'd been dragged. Throughout his ordeal, his leg had been numb, but now that he was motionless, the blood began to flow once more, and with it, spasms began, sending shards of pain lancing through him.

Lanaka lay back down, staring up into the nearly cloudless morning sky. Had he been back in Kousa, he would have thought it a cold day, but here, in this Saints forsaken place, it was considered warm.

Closing his eyes as another spasm overtook him, he held his breath, waiting for it to pass. Something approached, its faint footfalls could be heard above the distant sounds of battle. Lanaka strained his neck but could see no sign of who, or what, was coming. His sword had been lost as he was pulled from the saddle, but he still had his knife. Drawing it from his belt, he held it up to his eyes to make sure it was intact, but all he could focus on was his shaking hand.

Nearer drew the sounds, and then a familiar snort caused him to let out a breath of air. He held out his hand, raising it over his head, and moments later, his horse nuzzled up to it. Lanaka sought out the reins, twisting to see them hanging loose. They were only an arm's length away, yet it felt like a mile in his present condition.

The Kurathian commander rolled over and felt his stomach constrict. An overpowering thirst gripped him, and then his pulse quickened. He could feel chills breaking out all over, despite the heat of the day, and vowed if he were to die, it would be on the back of his horse. He motioned his hand, drawing his mount closer. The lead now lay half the distance away, so he rolled, a desperate act to try and save himself. Pain shot up his leg once more, hitting him with another wave of nausea, but finally, he was able to grip the reins.

With the leather straps in hand, he began pulling the horse closer until the stirrups dangled before him. Now he had only to haul himself into the saddle, and he could die in peace.

~

Voices drifted up to where Gorath lay on the roof, his arrows expended. Crawling forward, he peered over the top of the building to discover who was talking. Much to his surprise, he saw a group of finely dressed Norlanders.

"My lord," said a thin man, "we must get you to safety. The Orcs have taken the streets, and the gate will assuredly fall. You cannot remain."

An older gentleman appeared to consider the words. "Very well, take me to the tunnels."

"North or south, my lord?"

"South, you fool. Would you have me captured?"

Gorath crawled over the roof's peak, then pulled his axe from his belt. Below, the Humans continued their discussions, unaware he lurked above.

He lined himself up with Thurlowe, and with a silent prayer to the Ancestors, he jumped, landing on the back of the earl's horse. Gorath grabbed His Lordship, desperate to maintain his seat.

The Norlanders, too surprised to react, could do little but gape in shock as Gorath struck out, smashing the edge of his axe into the top of the thin man's head. His foe slumped in the saddle, leaning to the right until he fell with a splat to the ground.

One of Thurlowe's other companions, a warrior by the look of him, countered with a sword thrust, but the Orc twisted, leaning back in the saddle, and the blade scraped across the earl's back instead, eliciting a cry of pain.

Gorath thought fast, grasping the offending warrior's wrist as his attacker tried to pull back. Clamping down with all his might, he then gave a tug, pulling the unfortunate man from his mount.

The horse beneath Gorath bucked, then raced off, desperate to throw the extra weight off its back. The Orc wrapped his arms around Lord Thurlowe's waist and hung on for dear life. As the horse raced through the city streets, Gorath was suddenly struck by the thought that Orcs were ill-suited to such pursuits.

Thurlowe, however, attempted to dislodge him, tearing at his hands, trying to pry the Orc's fingers apart. In his panic, the earl dropped the reins, losing what little control he had over his mount. Given his head, the beast exploded into a full gallop, thundering down the street, its horseshoes sparking as it ran across the stone roadway.

Gorath felt a sharp prick and pulled back his hand to see black blood dripping from his fingers. Thurlowe then stabbed him in the thigh, using a backhanded motion to drive the dagger into flesh.

Roaring in pain, the Orc struck the earl on the side of the head, but at that same precise moment, the horse turned, selecting a side street at random. Gorath, feeling himself slip to the side, grabbed Thurlowe by the upper arms, trying desperately to steady himself.

As luck would have it, he was now leaning to his left, allowing him to see the building they were fast approaching. A sign hung from the tavern, proclaiming it as The Raven, but more remarkable still was the low level at which it hung. Gorath threw himself from the saddle right as Thurlowe struck the wood, knocking the earl off his mount.

Gorath rolled as he hit the ground, then came up, ready for action. Thurlowe, however, was laying there, staring at the sky, his face a mask of peace. The Orc moved closer, prodding the earl with the toe of his boot. Lord Thurlowe stirred, a groan escaping his lips as the ranger stood over him.

～

Lord Hollis saw the approaching Trolls. "Do something, Jendrick! Use your magic."

The sorcerer looked at the man in disgust. "You fool, you've managed to doom us all!" He cast his hands in the air, mumbling archaic words as the air grew thick and foul while dark tendrils swirled around him.

"What are you doing?" called out the earl.

Jendrick ignored his pleas, concentrating instead on the steady build-up of magic. Part of his mind detached, watching the events unfolding around him even as he channelled all the dark power he could summon. He felt the final surge of power and then the familiar snap.

Lord Hollis stared in shock as Jendrick's horse exploded, sending blood and flesh flying in all directions. One moment, the sorcerer was there, the next, nothing but mayhem. The battle paused for a moment as combatants tried to make sense of the sudden turn of events, then a great Troll let out a tremendous bellow that turned the earl's skin even paler.

Hollis pulled on his reins, desperately trying to get his horse to back up, but then the enormous stone creature began to run. His warriors turned, fleeing in fear for their very lives as greenskins tore into them with bloodied axes.

Hollis drew his sword, determined to see an end to this, one way or another, but his mount was nervous, now refusing to stand still.

The advancing Troll stooped, picking up the carcass of a dead horse and lifted it over its head. The earl watched, unable to tear his eyes from the scene playing out before him. The great brute then threw it at Hollis, knocking him from the saddle and causing his mount to collapse from the sheer force of the blow. The earl crashed to the ground, and then his horse fell upon him, crushing his legs and sending a terrible pain up the side of his body.

Hollis struggled to extricate himself from his predicament, but his horse was dead, its life force fled, and he lacked the strength to force it off of him.

The sounds of fighting were dying down, and Hollis, unable to find his sword, pulled a dagger, determined to fight to his very last breath. The massive, grey Troll loomed over him, looking down with merciless black eyes.

The earl's own eyes went wild as the creature raised its foot and brought it crashing down.

~

Gerald cast his gaze around. The fighting was sporadic now, limited to small pockets of resistance. To the south, the Saurians were swiftly approaching, their great three-horns following in their wake.

He leaned on Kraloch. "Where's Tog?" he asked.

"This way," said the Orc. "Come, I will lead you."

They picked their way across the battlefield, the sounds of dying and injured men drifting to their ears.

They soon came upon Tog. The great Troll chieftain was staring down at a body, its head no more than a red smear in sharp contrast to the lush green grass.

Gerald stared down at the horror, feeling bile rise in the back of this throat. He looked away, seeking the face of Tog. "Hollis?" he asked.

The Troll nodded.

"And the mage?"

"Whoever it was, managed to escape."

"How?"

Tog pointed to a mass of pulpy flesh and bone scattered over an area of about ten paces. The smell was putrid, and already flies were beginning to gather, drawn, no doubt, by its Necromantic nature.

Kraloch knelt, examining the remains. "This flesh is rotting," he said, "as if it had been sitting here for weeks. Clearly, this is the result of Blood Magic."

"So whoever that was, is a Necromancer?" asked Gerald.

Kraloch nodded. "I am afraid there can be little doubt, though how he came to be in the service of the earl confounds me. What type of Human would deal with such a person?"

"A desperate one, perhaps. In any case, we may never know, now that Hollis is dead."

He stared eastward towards the Ravensguard gate, but his poor eyesight revealed little at this range. A movement to the south caught his attention as a large three-horn rumbled towards them at a sedate pace, Anna mounted upon its neck. Beside her rode the familiar sight of Dame Beverly upon Lightning.

"Gerald," called out the queen. "So glad to see you're all right."

He straightened his back. "Of course I'm all right. Why wouldn't I be?"

The great beast halted, and two Saurians ran forward, tapping the creature's leg with a padded stick. In response, the thing lifted its leg, allowing Anna to climb down. She ran forward, hugging Gerald, then turned to face the others. "Master Kraloch, Tog, you have served the realm well today. Your service is greatly appreciated."

They both bowed, an odd expression in a Troll, although the Orc shaman managed to make it look quite natural. Anna's eyes swept the battlefield while Beverly dismounted.

"You've been quite busy here," remarked the knight. "Didn't feel like leaving anything for us?"

"Don't look at me," said Gerald. "Tog was having all the fun."

"Where's Hollis?" asked the queen.

Gerald took a step. "Over here. Mind the mess."

Anna stared down, her fascination overcoming her distaste. "His whole head has been crushed!"

"That's what happens when a Troll steps on you."

Anna pinched her nose. "What's that smell? Is it Hollis?"

"No," offered Kraloch. "Something far worse."

"Worse?"

The Orc moved towards the carnage, crouching and opening his arms to encompass the immediate area. "All of this," he began, "is the result of Death Magic."

"I've seen it before," offered Beverly. "Aubrey and I found something similar in the Deepwood."

"That doesn't bode well," said Gerald. "Does Fitz know?"

"We sent word to Andurak, and he passed it on."

"I don't like it," said Gerald. "People like this don't just show up for no reason. What are they up to?"

"I don't know," said Beverly. "Perhaps they seek to turn Bronwyn?"

"That would certainly explain her behaviour of late."

Anna knelt, looking closely at the rotting flesh. "What does this tell us?"

They all looked at Kraloch for an answer.

"I cannot say for sure," the Orc replied, "but we know Blood Magic harnesses the life force of others to unleash power. Since there is no sign of a Necromancer amongst the dead or wounded, I can only assume he used his mastery over the dark arts to escape."

"Like a spell of recall?"

"Yes, though where it took him, I cannot say."

"How much energy would be released by a horse?" asked Beverly. "I only ask because the remains Aubrey and I found was of a much smaller beast."

"An interesting observation," said Kraloch. "I would suspect it indicates he or she travelled a great distance. The real question is where they went?"

"I'm afraid we may never know," said the queen, "but I think we can safely assume whoever it was is far from here."

Tog's voice boomed out. "Something is happening at the gate."

They all turned, staring off to the east. Even from this range, they could see the gates opening, and then someone exited.

"What is it?" said Gerald, his eyes straining to make out details.

"A rider?" suggested Kraloch.

"No," corrected Beverly, "someone on foot. An Orc, by the look of it, and he's leading a horse."

"Are you sure?" said Gerald. "I find that hard to believe. They don't like horses."

"Not true," said Kraloch. "We merely do not prefer to ride them." He stared eastward, watching the distant figure draw closer, and then smiled. "It is the ranger, Gorath."

They stood still, waiting patiently as the Orc came nearer. It was soon evident something was slung across the back of the horse. Closer he came until he was within hailing distance.

"Master Gorath," called out the queen. "What have you there?"

"A present for you, Your Majesty," called back the ranger. He slowed, leading the horse to turn, revealing its passenger. "May I present Lord Thurlowe?"

They all rushed forward, eager to see if the Norland earl was still alive.

"Do not worry," said Gorath, "he still lives."

"What did you do to him?" asked Gerald.

The Orc laughed. "I did nothing. He hit his head while trying to flee."

A groan escaped the lips of the earl. "What happened?" he finally muttered.

The queen looked quite pleased with herself. "This is what you get for invading our land," she proclaimed.

Beverly looked at Gorath. "Where's Hayley?"

"At the gatehouse," replied the Orc. "She took a nasty head wound during the fighting. She'll recover, though she may have a headache for a few days."

"And the city?"

"In the hands of Ghodrug and her hunters."

Anna turned to Gerald, displaying a large grin. "See?" she said. "I told you our plan would work."

"Plan?" said Gorath. "I thought the attack was designed to take the gate?"

"It was," explained Gerald, "but we also had to draw out Hollis. I just didn't expect things to develop so quickly." He looked around the field. "Where's Aubrey?"

"Tending to the wounded," said Anna. "It was fortuitous she and Beverly came to Hammersfield when they did. One more day and they would have missed us."

"I don't understand," said Gorath.

"We needed communications to coordinate our efforts," explained Gerald. "Aubrey and Kraloch made that possible. We couldn't have done this without them."

"All this carnage," said Kraloch. "What has it gotten the Norlanders?"

"They're the ones who started this," insisted Anna. "They brought it upon themselves."

"Yes," agreed Gerald. "This is what happens when you invoke the fury of the crown."

Epilogue

Summer 965 MC

Lord Creighton, Earl of Riverhurst, stared out across the uncharacteristically still waters of the Windstorm Depths. "Incredible, isn't it?"

His aide, Camden, strained to see what had captivated his master. "My lord?"

"This lake," explained the earl.

Camden scratched his head. The earl could be fickle at times, and the aide had to wonder if the young noble wasn't touched in some way by the Gods. "If you say so, my lord."

Creighton sighed, turning to face his companion. "You are my aide, not a servant. As such, I expect you to have opinions."

"Certainly, sir. What opinion would you like me to have?"

"Never mind." The earl turned from the lake and began walking back towards the camp. The army of Riverhurst had marched, and now, almost a month later, they waited on the shores of the Windstorm Depths for the arrival of King Leofric.

"Where can they be?" he wondered aloud.

"Surely they must be on the way by now, my lord."

"One would certainly think so. Have we no word at all?"

"None, my lord."

Creighton winced. Young Camden was forever using the proper

etiquette of court, but his constant use of the phrase 'my lord' drove the earl to distraction. "Send more horsemen north," he commanded. "Let's see if they can find any sign of him."

"Yes, my lord." The young man ran off, eager to be of service.

The earl wandered through the camp. Most of his soldiers were young, untested in battle, yet he possessed a small cadre of older, experienced veterans. His father had always instilled in him a desire for peace, yet at the same time had insisted on a sizable army. 'Peace comes at the end of a spear,' he would say, something Creighton had taken to heart.

Pausing by a fire, he warmed his hands against the early morning chill. It was often cold in the windswept area of the northern reaches, something he had no desire to become accustomed to. No doubt his wife would be snuggled up in her furs back in Riverhurst. The thought brought a smile to his lips, then he was suddenly struck by a sense of dread as if he might never see her again. His hands went to the symbol of Saxnor that hung from his neck. He knew it was nothing but superstition, and yet he couldn't quite shake it.

"Sir?"

He turned to see a rider coming towards him. The man halted, then bowed his head. "Message from the scouts, my lord. They've spotted movement to the northwest."

"The Weldwyn army?"

"It looks like it. We'll know more once they draw nearer."

"Fetch my horse. I would see them for myself."

The man bowed once more. "Aye, my lord." He turned, galloping off to do his master's bidding.

Creighton clapped his hands, then rubbed them together, desperate to warm them up. "At last!" he said. "Now we can get on with the business of ending this war."

Camden soon appeared, trailing the earl's horse behind his own. "Your mount, my lord."

The earl pulled himself into the saddle.

"Do you wish an escort, my lord? I can rouse a complement of cavalry if you wish?"

"I hardly think that necessary, do you? King Leofric is not one to stand on ceremony." He urged his horse forward at a trot, keeping his aide to his left.

"How shall we welcome him, my lord? A feast, perhaps?"

"That will largely depend on the condition of his army."

"I'm not sure I understand what you mean, my lord."

"The army of Weldwyn has likely been marching for many days. I expect they'll be tired, and Leofric will likely wish to rest a day or two before continuing on, in which case a feast would be appropriate. Of course, he may also wish to march immediately, in which case we cannot brook further delay."

Camden still looked confused.

"It means," added the earl, "we must ask the king his wishes in this regard."

"Ah, I see, my lord."

They passed the northernmost sentries, then turned west, following a natural trail.

"Over there, my lord," said Camden, pointing. "Our scouts."

Creighton shifted his gaze. Three horsemen stood upon a promontory, staring north. He and his aide rode up to them, acknowledging their presence as they reached the spot. "Sergeant Egbert, isn't it?"

The lead scout smiled, pleased to be recognized by his master. "It is, my lord."

"Where are they?"

Egbert pointed. "There, Lord. You can see their banners."

Off in the distance was a large mass of men and horses, kicking up dust as they made their way across the plain. Above them flew the flags of Weldwyn in all their glory.

"Magnificent, isn't it," said Creighton.

"They are moving quickly, my lord," said the scout, "but they are still in formation."

"A testament to their discipline. It bodes well."

"How so?"

"Had they suffered a defeat, they would not be so well organized."

The sergeant frowned. His Lordship liked to think of himself as a skilled tactician, but he lacked his father's experience. Did the man seriously believe the way an army marched revealed such details?

"Come," said the earl, "let us ride out and greet them." He spurred on his horse, not waiting for a reply as he left the rest to play catch-up.

They rode down from the promontory, then trotted across the plain, the distant flags drawing nearer. A low sound began drifting their way, and Creighton halted, trying to ascertain from whence it came.

"What is that?" he asked.

"I have no idea," said Egbert.

"It sounds like someone wailing, my lord," offered Camden. "As one does when they've lost a loved one."

"No," said the earl, "it's more than that. It's as if an entire village was in mourning."

The noise intensified.

"It's coming from them." Egbert pointed at Leofric's army.

"Don't be ridiculous," said the earl. "Why in Saxnor's name would they be wailing?"

Camden's face paled. "Those horses, my lord, they're..." His voice trailed off.

Lord Creighton shifted his gaze, his eyes falling upon the mounts of the cavalry. His eyes widened as he beheld the sight, for the horses were covered in flayed flesh, revealing the bones below. Worse yet, the riders were naught but ghostly shadows of their former selves. Above them flew the battered and burned flags of Weldwyn.

"Saxnor, save us!" shouted Creighton. He tried to turn his horse around, eager to be on his way, but the cursed beast was fearful and refused his commands. All he could do was watch in horror as the unholy army drew nearer.

At its head rode King Leofric, his image twisted by the dark magic holding him in bondage. Half his face was missing, revealing the skull beneath, and yet superimposed over this terrifying sight was the ghostly image of the man he was in life.

The spirit king came closer, drawing his sword as he approached Lord Creighton. Behind him, the wailing increased until it was all the earl could hear. Try as he might, the Norland lord could not find the courage to draw his sword.

The spirit of the Weldwyn king, however, had no such trouble. Raising his sword on high, its blue blade caught the early morning sun as he brought it down upon Creighton's head.

Robed figures moved amongst the dead, examining the bodies. Every so often, one would stop, arms would extend, and words of power would be spoken, drawing the spirits forth to be bound for all eternity to their new masters. Penelope watched as her minions wandered the field.

"It's a rich harvest," observed Margaret, "and our numbers swell."

"Indeed. Our Shadow Army grows with every victory."

"Queen Kythelia?"

Penelope turned to greet the new visitor. "Ilarian? What is it?"

The sorcerer bowed. "With the greatest respect, my queen, we have reached our limit. Our agents can bind no more souls this day."

She looked over the field once more, a smile creeping to her lips. "A situation easily remedied." She turned to Margaret. "Come, I shall show you."

Off they went, trotting through the dead to where the Spirit Army stood ready. All eyes were on her as she passed through the army that never slept. She rode up to the spirit of Leofric, halting right before him. "This, as you know, is King Leofric. At present, he is but a spirit, bent to my will by the spell of binding, but I shall now make him more powerful, a creature of darkness able to control followers of his own."

"How is that possible?" asked Margaret.

"Blood Magic," said Penelope. "Nothing is impossible with such power." Her eyes wandered, picking out one of her lesser Necromancers. "Sildan," she called out, "come here. Your queen would have use of you."

The Elf came nearer, throwing back his hood and bowing respectfully. "I am here, Your Greatness. How may I serve?"

In answer, Penelope began mouthing words of power, manifesting dark, wispy shapes that circling around her at an ever-increasing speed. Her eyes pulsed with a dull purple light, and then she pointed at Sildan with her left hand. Almost immediately, the Elf crumpled as if a great force had pulled all the fat and muscles from his bones. The air turned foul as she pointed her other hand at King Leofric. A dark shadow rose from the dead Elf to fly through the air, sinking into the former King of Weldwyn. A terrible screeching sound burst from his mouth, and then his entire image changed.

Where once stood the spirit of King Leofric, there now was the fearsome sight of an undead overlord, a creature of such malevolence that Penelope backed up. Leofric's features were still evident, but now the eyes were pitch black, swallowing up light like some foul creature born of nightmares. It shifted its gaze to Margaret, but she stood her ground.

"What is that?" the former princess of Merceria asked.

"It is a dark spirit," explained her mentor. "Summoned to us from the Underworld. Do not worry, it's bound to me as surely as any here. As it possesses the spirit of Leofric, it can draw on all his vast knowledge and experience. Think of it as a spiritual leech, but instead of living off blood, it feeds on spiritual energy."

"And this overlord can control spirits?"

"Oh, it can do far more than that. It is intelligent. Say hello to the general of my Shadow Army."

<<<<>>>>

CONTINUE THE ADVENTURE IN:
WAR OF THE CROWN: BOOK NINE

Share your thoughts!

If you enjoyed this book, I encourage you to take a moment and share what you liked most about the story.

These positive reviews encourage other potential readers to give my books a try when they are searching for a new fantasy series.

But the best part is, each review that you post inspires me to write more!

Thank you!

If you're enjoying the Heir to the Crown Series, then I have another series I think you would like. The new Power Ascending series starts with Temple Knight, and there is a great prequel as well!

Cast of Characters for Fury of the Crown

Mercerian Nobility:
Queen - Anna
Duke of Wincaster - Lord Gerald Matheson
Duke of Colbridge - Lord Markham Anglesley
Duke of Kingsford - Lord Avery Somerset
Earl of Shrewesdale - Vacant (formally Lord George Montrose)
Earl of Tewsbury - Lord Alexander Stanton
Earl of Eastwood - Lord Horace Spencer
Viscount of Stilldale - Lord Emery Chesterton
Viscount of Haverston - Lord Arnim Caster
Baron of Bodden - Lord Richard Fitzwilliam
Baroness of Hawksburg - Lady Aubrey Brandon
Baron of Redridge - Vacant
Baronet of Wickfield - Sir Anthony MacMillan
Baronet of Mattingly - Sir Raymond Crawly
Baronet of Uxley - Sir Geoffrey Hammond,
Baronet of Burrstoke - Vacant

Mercerians Characters (and friends)
Albreda - Mistress of the Whitewood, Earth Mage, Druid
Aldus Hearn - Earth Mage, Druid
Aldwin Fitzwilliam - Master Smith, husband to Beverly Fitzwilliam
Alric - Prince of Weldwyn, husband to Queen Anna
Anna - Queen of Merceria, wife to Alric
Arnim Caster - Knight of the Hound, Viscount of Haverston, husband to Lady Nicole
Aubrey Brandon - Baroness of Hawksburg, Life Mage
Bertram Ayles - Ranger recruited from Stilldale
Beverly Fitzwilliam - Knight of the Hound, daughter of Richard Fitzwilliam
Caluman - Kurathian Captain of Light Horse
Captain Carlson - Commander of the Wincaster Light Horse
Captain Harold Wainwright - Captain of the Wincaster Bowmen, the Greens
Captain Jaran - Leader of the Kurathian archers
Fang - Albreda's first wolf friend - deceased

Gerald Matheson - Duke of Wincaster, Marshal of the Mercerian Army, Anna's best friend

Gryph - Hayley's wolf pup

Hayley Chambers - Baroness of Queenston, High Ranger

Hill - Gerald's aide

Jack Marlowe - Weldwyn noble, cavalier, protector of Prince Alric

Kiren-Jool - Kurathian Enchanter

Lanaka - Kurathian Commander of Light Horse

Lightning - Beverly's Mercerian Charger

Lily - Saurian, Anna's friend

Linette - Servant from kitchens at Wincaster Palace

Lucas - Baron Fitzwilliam's head servant in Wincaster

Mathers - Ranger

Nicole Caster (Arendale) - AKA Nikki the Knife, wife to Arnim Caster

Richard Fitzwilliam - 'Fitz', Baron of Bodden - Father of Beverly, mentor to Gerald

Revi Bloom - Royal Life Mage and Enchanter

Samantha (Sam) - Former archer of Bodden recruited into the rangers

Sergeant Blackwood - a mounted warrior of Bodden and Sergeant-at-Arms to Fitz

Sergeant Hampton - a heavy cavalryman under Sir Preston's command

Sergeant Hugh Gardner - Sergeant, Wincaster Light Horse

Sir Preston - Knight of the Hound, likes Sophie, maid to Queen Anna

Sir Gareth - Knight of the Sword and Bodden Knight

Sir Greyson - Knight of the Sword from Shrewesdale, guard to Princess Bronwyn

Sir Hector - Knight of the Sword from Kingsford, guard to Princess Bronwyn

Sir Heward - 'The Axe', Knight of the Hound, Northern Commander

Snarl - Albreda's present wolf friend

Sommersby - Ranger

Sophie - Queen's personal maid

Tempus - Kurathian Mastiff, queen's pet

Turnbull - Mercerian cavalryman, member of the Guard Cavalry

Wilkins - Member of the Wincaster Light Horse

Mercerian Allies

Andurak - Shaman of the Orcs of the Netherwood, also known as the Wolf Clan

Ardith of Brooksholde - Spokesman of the rebel Norlanders

Ghodrug - Chieftain of the Orcs of the Black Raven

Gorath - Orc of the Black Arrow, aide to the High Ranger
Granag Hornbow - Ancient Orc, Grand Chieftain of the Crimson Hawks
Hassus - Saurian, High Priest of the Flame
Herdwin Steelarm - Dwarven smith, leader of Dwarven detachment
King Khazad - The Lord of the Stone, King of the Dwarven Realm of Stonecastle
Kraloch - Orc Shaman of the Black Arrow Clan
Kharzug - Orc of the Black Ravens, Master of Earth
Lord Arandil Greycloak - Elven ruler of the Darkwood, Fire Mage/Enchanter
Mazog - Chieftain of the Orcs of the Netherwood, also known as the Wolf Clan
Orcs of the Black Axe - Located in the Artisan Hills
Shular - Orc shamaness who trained Kraloch
Skulnug - Orc ranger
Sliss - Saurian from Erssa Saka'am, caretaker of watergrass
Tarluk - An Orc warrior under Chief Urgon
Telethial - An elf maiden of the Darkwood, daughter to Lord Arandil Greycloak. Killed by Norlanders at the Battle of Uxley
Tog - Leader of the Trolls
Urgon - Chieftain of the Orcs of the Black Arrow from the Artisan Hills
Urzat - Female Orc ranger
Wolf Clan - Orcs of the Netherwood

Weldwyn
King Leofric - King of Weldwyn
Queen Igraine - Wife of King Leofric
Lord Edwin Eldridge - Earl of Farnham, Noble of Weldwyn
Alstan - Eldest Prince
Aegryth Malthunen - Earth Mage
Roxanne Fortuna - Life Mage
Tyrel Caracticus - Grand Arcanus of the Dome, Water Mage
Osbourne Megantis - Fire Mage - Pyromancer

Norland Nobility:
Earl of Beaconsgate - Lord Hollis
Earl of Hammersfield - Lord Rutherford
Earl of Ravensguard - Lord Thurlowe
Earl of Greendale - Lord Calder
Earl of Riverhurst - Lord Creighton
Earl of Marston - Lord Waverly

Earl of Walthorne - Lord Marley

Norland Characters
Camden - Aide to Lord Creighton
Captain Dirk Kendall - Norland cavalry Captain based in Brookesholde
Dobbs - Soldier of Ravensguard
Finlad - Military aide to Lord Hollis, Earl of Beaconsgate
Garth Meldoch - Norland warrior under the command of Lord Hollis
Jendrick - Adviser to Lord Hollis, Sorcerer
King Halfan of Norland - Deceased Norland Monarch - Grandfather of Bronwyn
Lord Rupert of Chilmsford - Member of the Norland delegation
Marik - Champion of Lord Hollis
Sergeant Egbert - Soldier in the service of Lord Creighton
Sergeant Victor Harrelson - Sergeant in the garrison of Ravensguard
Telker - Norland Warrior under the command of Lord Hollis
Wilfred of Hansley - Lord of Norland,Representative of King Halfan

Others
Princess Bronwyn - Granddaughter to King Halfan
Queen Kythelia - Lady Penelope, the Dark Queen
Kalaxial - Elf masquerading as Lord Hollis
Gozar - Ancient Orc ruler of Gar-Rugal
Ilarian - Elf masquerading as a human sorcerer
Sildan - Elf in the service of Penelope
Saxnor - God of strength, revered by the Mercerians
Malin - God of wisdom, revered by the Weldwyns
The Saints - Worshipped by the Kurathians

Places (not on a map)
Erssa-Saka'am - City in the Great Swamp and home to the Saurians
Gar-Rugal - Ancient Orc city, Ravenstone, the ruins of which lie beneath RavensguardNan-**Dural** - Ancient Dwarven city, located somewhere near
Netherwood - The Great Wood in Weldwyn
The Twelve Clans - 'The Clans' - land to the east of Weldwyn
The Dome - Grand Edifice of the Arcane Wizards Council of Weldwyn
Toknar-Ghul - One of the seven Orc cities destroyed over 2,000 years ago
Zaga - Place of spears in ruins of Ravensguard
Hall of Tears - Where Gozar made his final stand in Gar-Rugal
Tears of Gozar - Where Gozar died in Gar-Rugal

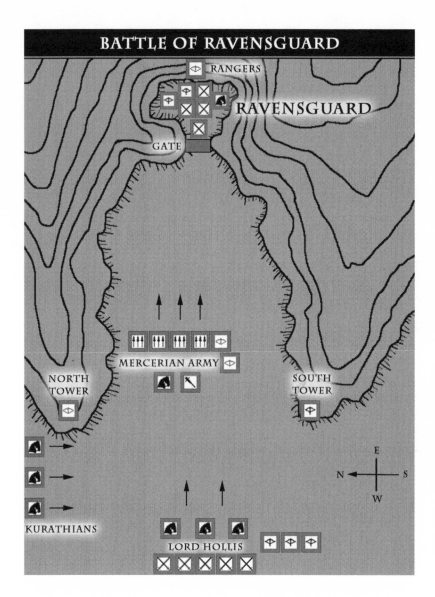

BATTLE OF RAVENSGUARD

RANGERS

RAVENSGUARD

GATE

MERCERIAN ARMY

NORTH
TOWER

SOUTH
TOWER

KURATHIANS

LORD HOLLIS

E

N — S

W

A Few Words from Paul

Fury of the Crown was always envisioned as a 'middle' book, bridging the storyline from books six and seven to nine and ten. As such, it introduces a number of plot lines, some of which carry over to the next installment. The character roster is slowly growing, but the main storyline concentrates on only a few individuals. If you didn't see your favourite, don't worry, they will likely show up in the next book, War of the Crown.

The original outline for this book was quite different from what I ended up with. Part of the reason is I didn't want the storyline to get bogged down by all the details of a military campaign. Instead, I have focused on the characters and the effect they have on the way events unfold. Yes, there are numerous battles, but at its heart, Fury of the Crown is all about these personalities and the difference they make.

One character that bears watching is Bronwyn. When I first introduced her, she was too easily manipulated, and the story suffered for it. After a discussion with my wife, I realized that she had to have a more assertive personality. It required reworking of the storyline, but I think it was worth it in the end. Of course, Bronwyn's story isn't done and will continue in the next book, where she plays a vital role.

My wife, Carol, has been of inestimable value throughout this journey, and I thank her for her contributions. Without her editing and promotion, my books would still be languishing deep in the bowels of online retailers. I should also like to thank Stephanie Bennett, Amanda Bennett, and Christie Kramburger for their support and encouragement, as well as give a shout-out to Brad Aitken, Jeffrey Parker, and Stephen Brown for their inspirational characters.

As ever, my BETA team had done a wonderful job, helping this book in its quest to be reader-ready. Your feedback is greatly appreciated, so thanks to Rachel Deibler, Michael Rhew, Phyllis Simpson, Don Hinckley, James McGinnis, Charles Mohapel, and Debra Reeves.

Last but certainly not least, I must thank you, my loyal readers, who have travelled the world of Merceria with me as I tell these tales. Your feedback on my books has proven to be a great source of inspiration for me.

About the Author

Paul J Bennett (b. 1961) emigrated from England to Canada in 1967. His father served in the British Royal Navy, and his mother worked for the BBC in London. As a young man, Paul followed in his father's footsteps, joining the Canadian Armed Forces in 1983. He is married to Carol Bennett and has three daughters who are all creative in their own right.

Paul's interest in writing started in his teen years when he discovered the roleplaying game, Dungeons & Dragons (D & D). What attracted him to this new hobby was the creativity it required; the need to create realms, worlds and adventures that pulled the gamers into his stories.

In his 30's, Paul started to dabble in designing his own roleplaying system, using the Peninsular War in Portugal as his backdrop. His regular gaming group were willing victims, er, participants in helping to playtest this new system. A few years later, he added additional settings to his game, including Science Fiction, Post-Apocalyptic, World War II, and the all-important Fantasy Realm where his stories take place.

The beginnings of his first book 'Servant to the Crown' originated over five years ago when he began a new fantasy campaign. For the world that the Kingdom of Merceria is in, he ran his adventures like a TV show, with seasons that each had twelve episodes, and an overarching plot. When the campaign ended, he knew all the characters, what they had to accomplish, what needed to happen to move the plot along, and it was this that inspired to sit down to write his first novel.

Paul now has four series based in Eiddenwerthe, his fantasy realm and is looking forward to sharing many more books with his readers over the coming years.

Manufactured by Amazon.ca
Bolton, ON

28003665R00206